BETRAYING SECRETS

FBI Agent Frank Zander opened his file on the Baker family to the photographs. He studied the girl's face. Sun in her eyes. Hugging her beagle. Smiling in the majestic Rockies against a blue sky. A pretty California kid. Her name was Paige Baker. She had her mother's eyes.

Emily Baker was thirty-five. Attractive. A photographer. Looked energetic. Zander gently covered her smile with his finger, concentrating on her eyes. They betrayed something unsettled about her. Something sad.

Whatever it is, Emily, you are going to tell me.

Zander's eyes then met those of Doug Baker. The former U.S. Marine sergeant. The high school teacher. Football coach. Positions of authority. Positions of control.

Did you lose control, Doug? How did you hurt your hand? What was going on in the time before your daughter had vanished?

Zander checked the file, then his watch. Thirty-one hours since Paige Baker disappeared into the Rocky Mountains. They had to move fast on this one. He was going to have to push it. He closed his file. Soon he would learn the truth about Doug and Emily: every fear, every heartbreak, every secret. If the Bakers were hiding something, he would find out.

He always did.

Also by Rick Mofina

IF ANGELS FALL

Published by Kensington Publishing Corporation

COLD FEAR

RICK MOFINA

PINNACLE BOOKS
Kensington Publishing Corp.

www.pinnaclebooks.com

PINNACLE BOOKS are published by

Kensington Publishing Corp.
850 Third Avenue
New York, NY 10022

All Kensington Titles, Imprints, and Distributed Lines are available at special quantity discounts for bulk purchases for sales promotions, premiums, fund-raising, and educational or institutional use. Special book excerpts or customized printings can also be created to fit specific needs. For details, write or phone the office of the Kensington special sales manager: Kensington Publishing Corp., 850 Third Avenue, New York, NY 10022, attn: Special Sales Department, Phone: 1-800-221-2647.

Pinnacle and the P logo Reg. U.S. Pat. & TM Off.

First Printing: July 2001
10 9 8 7 6 5 4 3 2 1

Printed in the United States of America

To the memory of my mother

For we wrestle not against flesh and blood, but against principalities, against powers, against the rulers of the darkness of this world. . . .

—Ephesians 6:12

Suspicion always haunts the guilty mind. . . .
—Third Part of *King Henry VI,* Act V,
Scene vi, William Shakespeare

BLOOD RAGE

PROLOGUE

The last thing Paige Baker saw before fleeing her family's campsite was the blood dripping from her father's ax.

Her parents had just had an argument, ending with her mom stomping off and Paige scrambling with her dog for the shelter of her tent while her father savagely chopped wood.

Inside the tent, Paige wept at the *thud-thud-thud* of his wrath, logs cleaving, splintering. She tried to calm herself, think of ways to make it better for her parents. But what was a ten-year-old kid supposed to do?

Find her mom, talk to her? Paige began jamming things in her backpack. Her family was falling apart. She was helpless. Maybe she should try talking to her dad.

Somehow she summoned the courage to approach her father, emerging from her tent, inching toward him with Kobee, her beagle, in her arms.

"Daddy?"

No answer. His muscles contracted as he chopped. Sweat

dropped from his face, darkly blotching the neck and underarms of his gray U.S. Marines T-shirt.

Thud-thud-thud.

"Daddy. Please. I need to talk to you."

"Get the hell away from me and go find your damned mother!"

His fury terrified her. Kobee yelped. She hugged him tighter, standing before her father.

"Please . . . I need to talk. . . ."

He steadied a log upright with his left hand, swinging the ax with his right hand.

"Daddy!"

Her pleading distracted him, the ax slipped, the blade struck his hand, blood spurted. He cursed, then without warning charged at her still gripping the ax, blood webbing down the handle.

"I told you to get the hell out of my face now, goddamn it! Go see your mother!"

Paige squealed, bolting with Kobee on his leash, items spilling from her backpack as she ran down the dark wooded trail, her heart breaking. She had never seen her dad like this before.

Later, Paige slowed down on the trail, halfway to where she figured her mother was. Her tears ceased when she was startled by a chipmunk. She gasped. It pinballed from a rock, to a log to a rock, disappearing into the woods. Kobee spotted it. Before Paige could react, his leash slipped through her fingers, jingling a fading good-bye as he chased it, vanishing into the dark, eternal forest.

"Kobee! Come back here!" Paige took a few steps into the bush to follow him, but it was so dense she returned to the trail. "Kobee! Get back here this instant!"

Paige sat down, slapping her knees. *Do something quick!* But she was uneasy about leaving the serpentine trail that threaded along some of the most breathtaking terrain of Montana's backcountry, a remote region known as the Devil's Grasp, where the Rocky Mountains grace the northern reaches of Glacier National Park.

Minutes passed and still no sign of Kobee.

Taking a deep breath, Paige started into the woods after her dog. She found a branch for a walking stick. The skylight dimmed and the temperature dipped as she entered the dense stands of sweet-scented spruce and lodgepole pine. Tree limbs scraped at her face and arms, snagged and pulled at her jeans and backpack. Thick wild growth, practically impossible to walk through. But Paige kept moving, banging her walking stick against the trees and brush, feeling herself moving in a downward slope.

"Kobee! Here, boy!"

Suddenly, Paige's feet slipped. She hit the ground, sliding on pine needles, knocking against trees, brush slicing into her hands. Her body rattling, bumping down, down, down, stopping in a shaded glade of soft moss. Paige held her breath. The distant tinkling of Kobee's leash. *That way.* Confident, she brushed dirt from her jeans, heading deeper into the forest.

"Kobee!"

Paige came to a small river. *Now what? Wait! Kobee's leash jingling? Faintly?* Yes, she heard it. From the other side of the river. Butterflies. Kobee would chase them. *Wait. To get back, just go through the forest up the slope.* She blinked. OK. She pushed on, finding a natural bridge of fallen trees, using it to carefully cross over the rushing water to the other side.

"Kobee!"

No sign of him. She was getting mad, worried. Which way?

Why did her parents take this stupid trip? Why didn't they just stay at home in San Francisco? Why come here? How was a ten-year-old kid supposed to figure out what was wrecking her family, or understand the terrible thing that made her mother so sad that sometimes she would not talk to anybody, just go off by herself for hours?

Was her mother a little crazy?

She heard the leash again, from deep inside the next dark forest.

"Kobee! Get back here, you stupid dog!" Paige considered returning to their camp to get her dad. No way. He was way too angry.

She decided to go a short distance into this next forest.

"This is it, Kobee! Do you hear me? You are in huge trouble!"

She came to another little river. The fourth one? Not a trace of Kobee. Paige rested on a rock staring at the snow-topped mountains. It was getting late. Tired. Hungry. She should start back soon. Kobee would know the way back. Paige had stupidly counted on returning with him. Stupid. Sniffling, she searched her backpack. Some stuff in there. Nothing good, though. She found an Oreo cookie and tapped it on her walking stick. This always worked. Why didn't she think of this sooner?

"Kobee . . . I've got a cookie for you. . . ." *Tap-tap-tap.*

Nothing. Paige kept tapping. For nearly half an hour. Still nothing but a high country wind fingering its way through the mountains, carrying the echo of a crow's caw. Soon, Paige ate the cookie. Gazed skyward. Only a few days ago, she was peering down from her window seat of the jet, marveling at the Rockies rising up to her from the earth below. About nine million snowcapped peaks stretching to the horizon, like the top of a big cream pie. It was pretty but scary, too. No cities, no buildings, no roads. Nothing down there but mountains, rivers, lakes and never-ending forests.

If you ever got lost down there, how could they ever find you?

Paige did not have a clue about the woods. She had never been camping before. She was from San Francisco. Her world was malls, clothes, music, cell phones, soccer and e-mail. She could click her way around the Net, no problem. But the woods? *It's like going back in time or something,* she had thought from the plane, watching one range blend into another.

Now she was down here. Fear gnawing at her.

She did not know the way back.

How did this happen?

It hit her like an avalanche.

She was lost.

On the brink of tears. Unaware she had been gone for hours, had wandered from the new Grizzly Tooth Trail, in the Devil's Grasp, one of the most remote regions in the nation. Parts of it curled into Canada.

Anxious, Paige began hiking in different directions, hoping, praying to spot something familiar. Other hikers? Maybe her mom decided to come this way. Maybe her dad lit the campfire and she could see it. It was getting colder by the minute. Her cuts, her bug bites, her scrapes, began hurting. Her legs ached. Her feet were sore. She was exhausted. Afraid.

She stood at the edge of a ridge, overlooking a forest so vast it seemed to encompass the entire planet.

"Dad!—*Dad!—Dad!—Dad!—Dad!—Dad!*"

Her voice echoed in vain.

"Mom!—*Mom!—Mom!—Mom!—Mom!—Mom!*"

Paige collapsed to the ground, gripping her walking stick.

Why was this happening to her? The sun sank lower. These mountains got so dark and cold at night. She did not know how to build a fire. Far off, she heard the rumble of thunder.

"Mommy!"

This is the place where Mommy said her monster dwelled! Shut up, Paige!

The sun dropped behind the mountains, turning part of the horizon a heavenly pink, orange and blue.

A twig snapped crisply in the darkened woods behind her.

She stood. Held her breath.

Nothing.

A bird, maybe? A chipmunk?

Then another twig; no, a branch broke. Something larger out there. Rustling. Closer. Something approaching her. Something coming from the darkness. Something bigger than Paige.

"Mommy?"

Nothing.

Her heart pounding faster.

"D-Dad? Is that you?"

Silence.

DAY 1

DAY 1

CHAPTER ONE

An eagle flew so near to Emily Baker she heard the swishing of its wings from the cliffside where she had sought sanctuary after her blowout with Doug. Maybe this trip was a mistake. Was returning to Montana the only way to end her torment? She searched the peaks for answers.

Her monster was out there.

Emily had to confront it. Had to tell Doug and Paige everything. *Everything.* She was so sorry for the arguments. For all she had put them through. And what she was *going* to put them through. She would never blame them for not understanding. Emily was bracing herself, after so many painful years, to reveal the terrible secret to her family.

I am responsible for the death of a child.

"Guess what I'm going to do."

The monster.

That's what Emily and her counselor had agreed to call Emily's issue, because they knew it was the key that got Emily talking, to the point that she was able to set foot in Montana for the first time since her childhood.

Your monster dwells back at the ranch, kid. Come on, Em, we talked about this. You must go back for that cliché called closure. You've let the monster call the shots in your life for too long. If you fail to do this, the monster wins. Everything. Are you willing to let it win everything?

No.

Emily had returned to battle her past.

To endure one more death.

Her monster had exacted such a toll—on her, on Doug, on Paige. It was gaining momentum. Emily had to stop it. The arguing, erecting walls, fracturing trusts, withdrawing from the people who needed her: it had to end. As horrible as it was going to be, it had to be done. This was the right place. The right time. Her counselor was correct. A few more days was all Emily needed.

Then the whole world would know.

The sun slipped closer to the western horizon. Mountain shadows pulled over the valleys like a blanket. Hours had passed since her argument with Doug. Emily hoped he had cooled off.

Returning along the twisting trail, Emily felt a pang of worry. *Something's wrong.* She stopped. Nothing looked awry. But something felt wrong. Emily shrugged, continuing to the camp.

Her heart warmed when she saw a calmer version of her husband reading near their blue tent. The ex-marine sergeant who taught English Lit to high school students when not coaching the football team. Doug Baker was a looker. An inch over six feet with a muscular frame beneath the faded Levis and blue U.S. Marines T-shirt, which set off his tan, gray-flecked hair and gray eyes.

"Where's Paige?" she asked.

"She went to join you." He was still cool to her.

"Very funny."

Doug immediately analzyed the circumstances, concern washing over him. Tossing his book, he rushed down the trail.

"Doug!" Emily's heart raced. "You're scaring me! Doug!"

"Stay at the camp, Em!" he yelled, then began calling for Paige, his deep voice booming as he disappeared. Emily's stomach tightened. She tore back the flaps of the tents.

"Paige?"

She circled the camp, calling her, calling Kobee.

Doug returned. Breathless. Doubled over. Gasping. Emily noticed his left hand was wrapped in cloth, as if he had hurt himself.

"Doug, where is she? What happened? I left her with you!"

"I sent her to you. She went with Kobee, not more than ten minutes after you left! I thought all this time she was with you!"

"No." Emily fought her tears. "I never heard her! I never saw her!"

"You never saw her?"

"No."

"What about Kobee?"

"No." Her eyes were drawn to Doug's injury. "What happened to your hand?"

"I hurt it chopping wood."

"Hurt it how? Doug, what happened?"

"I was chopping wood. I was distracted, hurt my hand. I sent her to be with you!"

Emily stared at him.

"Doug, you were supposed to watch her! My God! It's been hours! Why weren't you watching her?"

"Me? Well, where the hell were you? Huh? You go off for hours! What the hell are you doing out there all alone?"

Emily began sobbing.

Doug shook off his rage. They had no time to waste.

"Emily!" He grabbed her shoulders. "Emily! Listen to me!"

"Doug, she was so upset yesterday, remember—"

"Stop this, Emily!"

"And those people, yesterday, seeing us argue. Standing there watching us. That family, they said they saw a bear—"

"Stop this and listen to me! That thread of trail you were on is no more than a few hundred yards. It crests a ridge, right?"

"What, I—I, OK—"

"You and I will each take a side of that ridge and descend in a zigzag pattern, calling at one-minute intervals out to her and each other, making sure we can hear each other! We've got some time before dark. You got that!"

Emily did not move.

"Emily!"

She flinched. "Y-yes. I've got it!"

"Let's go!"

They had scoured the ridge; the sky had darkened faster than Doug had ever seen night fall in his life. Why had he behaved so brutally to Paige? Scaring her off when she needed him. What was wrong with him? Maybe she fell asleep somewhere. Maybe she fell. Or worse.

"Paige! Kobee!" His voice boomed, followed by the echo of Emily's calling, deepening his anxiety.

Doug pushed on, worrying about his daughter, his wife, grappling over their reason for coming to Montana. To deal with Emily's—what? Tortured past? Were they right to come? What the hell was happening to them? He probed a small hillside cave with a branch.

Nothing.

Doug knew little of his wife's childhood in Montana. She grew up just outside of Buckhorn Creek, a small mountain town. Her mother and father died when she was young. That was about all he knew, really. In the time he had known her, Emily would not talk about it.

Her only relative was her aunt Willa, who still called her "Lee," which was Emily's childhood nickname. Willa knew Emily's past but was just as reluctant to discuss it. Several months ago at a San Francisco art gallery's showing of Emily's photography, Doug had pulled Willa aside and pressed her unsuccessfully.

"Doug, she has to tell you when she's ready. It has to be Lee's decision." Willa bit her lip. "I just pray that it is soon. Very soon."

Emily was seeing a psychologist, but was guarded on her counseling until a few weeks ago, telling Doug the resolution for her was in Montana. She had to go back but was afraid to go alone. OK, he said, they would go to the mountains together. The three of them. They would meet head-on with whatever it was that was pulling her away from him, from Paige, from herself.

Then last night, after all these years, Emily seemed ready to open up to him. Paige was asleep in her little tent. They sat by the fire for some time, the flames painting her face as constellations wheeled by. Emily began talking about her life here, then retreated into silence, frustrating him.

It ignited another argument that erupted this morning.

And now this.

"Paige! Kobee!"

Doug hacked fiercely at some brush until suddenly he was overcome with futility. He reached a clearing, looked down the giant slopes through a treetop window, and his knees nearly buckled. At that moment, the size of the area was no longer breathtaking. It was horrifying.

God help us.

"Paige!" Doug's voice carried for miles. Forever. *My little girl.*

He ran his hands over his face. Exhausted. Emily's calling began to stutter. Doug knew she was sobbing at the fact they were searching in vain. Night had come without a trace of Paige or Kobee.

Maybe they found their way back. That shred of hope was enough for Doug to get Emily back safely to their campsite.

The temperature had dropped. The dark sky was starless. Doug built up the fire, flames reflecting the anguish of their glistening eyes.

"She'll be cold." Emily sniffed.

Doug nodded.

He was numb with fear, trying to remember the last tender words he had said to Paige, the last time he hugged her. He refused to accept that his last words to his daughter were spat at her in anger.

"We've got to get help, Em. At first light, I'll double-time it back to the shuttle bus drop. We'll alert the rangers."

"But it took us two days to hike to this spot."

"We have no choice. You stay here in case she returns. Do not look anymore. Stay here!"

Emily sniffed and nodded. "And hungry. She'll be hungry, Doug."

"She's a smart girl. She'll build a shelter or something."

"She's from the city. She has never set foot in the woods in her life. Not until I dragged everyone here! Why is this happening? She was so heartbroken yesterday at our arguing. She said she would run off a mountain because of me. Doug, it's me, it's ... Damn it, Doug. Why weren't you watching her? I don't understand how you could let her walk off. Why?"

"Stop it! This does not help! We cannot sit here blaming ourselves. This does not help, Paige. Do you hear me? Don't give up on her!"

Emily nodded, stifling her sobbing.

"Doug, *exactly how* did you hurt your hand?"

"I told you, chopping wood," he said, almost ready to confess. "I—I was distracted and sent Emily to be with you."

Emily said nothing. Minutes passed.

"You were gone a long time, Emily. What were you doing out there?"

Emily sniffed, whispering, "Dealing with my past."

Thunder rolled in the distant darkness. An hour later, the fire began hissing as the raindrops fell. Doug and Emily moved to their tent.

The rain intensified. Doug hoped with every fiber that Paige had built a shelter. He knew the rain would reduce the chances of picking up her trail.

Neither he nor Emily slept more than five minutes.

They stared at the flames, struggling to survive the rain.

But the fire died.

"Guess what I'm going to do."

Emily's monster had returned.

CHAPTER TWO

Fear seized Paige.

She stood absolutely still in the dusk, afraid to move, to swallow, to blink. Her heartbeat was deafening.

She heard the noise again. Very near. Coming from the dark stand of trees.

Huffing, then clicking.

She saw nothing. A branch snapped loudly under the weight of something colossal.

Gooseflesh rose on her arms.

Something is out there in the darkness. Something large is watching me.

Trembling, Paige moved slowly away. Every instinct screaming at her.

Run!

More branches breaking.

It's moving closer!

Run! Run! Run!

Groaning, panting, running, scrambling. Her andrenaline

surged, propelling her up a cliffside, then another, down a scree. Not feeling the rocks scraping and tearing at her hands and arms, she crossed a stream, slipping, driving hard, not stopping, scaling another small cliffside, racing. Her knees banged and slipped until she collapsed beneath an overhang with a concave rock roof, not much larger than the rear window dash of a midsize car.

Her gasping was deafening. Ears ringing.

Oh, please! Stop this! Please!

Several minutes later, her breathing decreased.

Safe. Please let me be safe.

From her shelter, she watched night fall over the mountains, listening to the loudest thunder she had ever heard blasting over the Rockies from one corner of the world to another. Lightning flashing in the angry sky, then a downpour.

In the dark, she extracted a T-shirt and sweatshirt from her pack, putting them both on. It helped. One may have been inside out. She did not care. She felt around for food; she knew she had stuff in there. Her fingers fishing, finding an apple, then a nearly full bottle of water.

Be smart. Take a small sip.

She lay in the darkness, shivering in rain-cooled air, flinching with every thunderclap.

Does it hurt to die?

Paige began to cry.

She cried until she fell asleep, only to be awakened several times out of fear that the huffing sound had returned.

DAY 2

CHAPTER THREE

In the frigid predawn light, Doug studied his wounded hand.

It was wrapped in a strip he'd torn from the T-shirt that fell from Paige's pack when she fled, a favorite from the Gap. It was pink, now browned with his dried blood. The flag of his guilt.

Shame would not allow him to admit to Emily what he had done. Chased Paige away, cursing, bleeding. An ax in his hand.

I am so sorry.

The rain had stopped. Patches of cool dawn mist quilted the forest slopes. Crows echoed in the valleys. Doug got busy restarting the fire, using wood he had placed in the tent. To warm Paige in case she returned.

While the kindling smoked and crackled to life, Doug gently nudged Emily, who awoke weeping softly. It was time for him to get help.

"Everything will be OK," he promised her, preparing his knapsack. She nodded tearfully, unable to utter words. "She'll probably show up a minute after I leave. We'll get through this together, Em.''

She hugged Doug tightly, as if her entire weight were pulling her down into an abyss. Tenderly, he pried her arms loose, then left.

Jogging, trotting, pushing himself to resurrect his Marine Corps training, Doug moved swiftly. He hoped to encounter someone in the remote region with a cell phone or radio. No luck. The area was isolated. To get here, they had left their car parked half a day away at their motel near Columbia Falls outside the west entrance to the park. They took a tour bus drop to the main gate. From there, they took a park shuttle along Going-to-the-Sun Road, the spectacular mountain highway that traversed the park. At a northern junction, they caught another shuttle that took them due north along the new Icefields Highway, a serpentine roadway hugging steep rocky slopes and cliff edges. It was dotted with hiker drop-off points at trail heads leading into the Devil's Grasp.

Doug covered miles of primitive harsh terrain quickly, praying Paige had survived the night. *If anything happened to her. Don't think about that. She is just lost, huddled somewhere with Kobee.*

By midafternoon, Doug made it to the backcountry road and the shuttle bus pick-up point. He was spotted by a park shuttle bus frantically waving. Its diesel roared after the driver picked Doug up, then radioed to the new Devil's Grasp ranger station.

Ranger Mac McCormick met Doug outside the small log cabin station.

"My daughter is lost in the backcountry! We have to get a search team! She wandered off yesterday afternoon. It rained up there. Please!''

The ranger got Doug into the office where a seasonal ranger was already talking on the radio about a lost little girl.

Mac was one of Glacier's brightest rangers. Fresh from training at the Federal Law Enforcement Academy in Georgia, he was awaiting the paperwork confirming him as a level 1 law enforcement ranger.

"Yessir, we're going to get help out there as quick as we can."

Helping Doug to a padded chair behind the counter, Mac mentally noted his haggard, unshaven, frenzied appearance and his wounded left hand. He likely fell on the trail getting here.

"Sir, we're going to need some information. Sally," Mac instructed the female ranger, "confirm to Park Dispatch to let the district ranger know we have a lost person report. Find out what is available right now from the air tours at West Glacier. Stand by to send out a hasty team."

Mac quickly began completing a lost person questionnaire, detailing Paige Baker's case: full name, her parents, health, physical description, time she was last seen, who talked to her last, what area, clothing, outdoors experience, fear of animals, the dark, adults, her personality. All the while, he punctuated his questions with assurances that help was on the way.

Doug told Mac about Kobee, Paige's beagle.

"Pets are not permitted. How did you—"

"We know. We sneaked him in for Paige. They're inseparable."

Mac noted Kobee. Then, in keeping with procedure, he had the seasonal ranger fax the information to the park's law enforcement rangers, who would pass it to other police authorities. Then Mac took Doug to the station's huge park map, which covered one of the varnished pine walls. He tried pinpointing the spot where the Bakers were camping.

It was a star in the universe of Glacier National Park, which contained over seven hundred miles of trails and elevated climbs that webbed through one million acres of glaciers, lakes, forests, mountains some sixty million years old that joined Canada's Waterton Lakes National Park forming the International Peace Park.

The Bakers were camping in the Devil's Grasp section of

northern Montana, deep along the new Grizzly Tooth Trail. Mac knew this was bad. Grizzly Tooth was the most isolated region of Glacier. It just opened this season. Few people knew of it. According to backcountry permits, less than a dozen visitors were in there.

Like most of the mountain country, it is subject to radical weather because of the elevation climbs, some nine thousand feet. Many areas had loose rock and were active bear-feeding zones. This is where they trained park staff. But all members were not yet familiar with every part of Grizzly. Nineteen miles of rugged, inspiring terrain curling into Canada.

Mac swallowed. Twenty-four hours gone already. This was bad. Why would this family go in there? It's such a challenge. Grizzly was not the place for a ten-year-old city girl with no wilderness experience. Especially now. It did not help that it had rained steadily in that area last night. The long-range weather forecast was not good. And with her dog. Pets attracted bears. Not good. Mac forced himself to maintain his professional calm.

"Better tell Dispatch to alert Waterton on the Canadian side about a lost girl deep along Grizzly. We'll send them more details when we have them."

Mac got Doug a coffee and a ham sandwich, insisting he rest during the short time they had.

"Got a chopper coming! ETA twenty minutes," Sally said, then answered a call. "Mac, it's Brady Brook and he's with Pike Thornton, who wants to talk to you." Thornton was the most senior level 1 law enforcement ranger. Not long after the call, the station began vibrating as a helicopter approached.

"Doug, we're flying out now." Mac raised his voice. "Our search and rescue people urge us to start setting up for a search now."

* * *

The earth dropped slowly under Doug's feet, adrenaline coursing through his body as the Bell helicopter ascended from the Devil's Grasp ranger station, its blades whooshing.

In seconds, the cabin shrunk and then vanished as the chopper banked and climbed over an eternity of mountain ranges, forests, rivers, lakes and glaciers. Doug's stomach fluttered as they glided over foothills, dipped into basins. Staring at his blood-scabbed hand, he felt exhaustion and fear work on his mind. The marine warrior. Gulf War and Somalia veteran. The hard-ass high school football coach who enjoyed the challenge of teaching Hemingway and Faulkner to wired teens.

The luckiest man in the world to be married to a dream named Emily: eyes the color of deep mountain lakes, with hair the shade of honey, which she often wore in a soft bun. He loved how strands escaped when she was engrossed in her photography. Loved those white painter pants and cotton tops she wore. Loved how fast she could slip out of them.

Emily was a smart, big-hearted woman whose smile put the sun in his sky. He could still picture her glowing the day Paige was born. God's gift to them. Daddy's girl. Happy again, popping the champagne cork in the living room of the small three-story Edwardian they had snagged for a bargain in outer Richmond. Adopting Kobee from a neighbor's litter. Building a good life together. And it seemed they were so close to putting Emily's troubles to rest. Doug took in the snowcapped Rockies, the dark green ocean of forest blurring below as if it were all passing before him. All slipping away.

Paige could be anywhere down there.

The helicopter slowed and started rattling. "Hang on!" the pilot said over the intercom. "Updrafts! From the valleys!"

Rapid deployment from the tail end of a Herc was smoother. They hugged a mountainside, arriving at a massive ledge.

"That's got to be it," the pilot said. "Here we go."

As they made their approach, Mac and the others spotted the tiny blue tents long before Doug. "We'll try for that flat

ridge there, about five o'clock.'' What flat ridge? Doug could
not see it. The pilot began bringing the helicopter down on a
clearing about as big as a basketball court. Suddenly, the tents;
then Emily came into clear view. Doug's heart skipped, scanning the camp, hoping to spot Paige or Kobee.

He found Emily, cutting a solitary figure, turning her back
as the Bell's rotors flapped her jacket, her hair.

The pilot landed, then lifted off the instant Doug and the
two rangers were safely on the ground. ''He's going back to
ferry more bodies and gear out here,'' Mac said, grabbing the
two large nylon bags they had brought.

The chopper disappeared.

Doug crushed Emily in his arms; she answered the question
in his eyes.

''Not a trace. Nothing. Doug. Oh God.''

CHAPTER FOUR

Mac approached Doug and Emily.

"Every second counts," he said. "Search and Rescue people, that's SAR, are on their way. More are coming. We'll need more specific information so that they can start searching effectively."

Together, they estimated the time Paige vanished, the area or possible direction.

This is not real.

Emily was numb to reality. It was not happening. She was not standing here with strangers on a ledge in the Rocky Mountains talking about the disappearance of Paige. Her only baby. Gone. Swallowed.

Her monster was out there.

The other ranger tested his radio saying how elevation, proximity of other radios and weather, made communication here erratic. Mac scanned the forests with huge binoculars.

"There's an old mining trail through the valleys and basins that was abandoned in the 1800s," he said. "We've got some searchers on horseback coming from the Blackfeet Reservation. They know this area well.''

A cool wind rushed over them bringing a *thump-thump-thump*. The helicopter had returned with three more park rangers and more gear. Then departed. More grim-faced people said their names, changing into jumpsuits, setting up big tents, tables, a canopy, generators, lanterns, stoves. A practiced ritual.

A different helicopter arrived. More people. Two official-looking men in that group. The first, well built, about six foot two, solid. Silver hair. Looked to be in his fifties. Leathery tanned skin. Poker-faced.

"Pike Thornton," he introduced himself, his voice deep and strong. "Law enforcement officer with National Park Service." Soft blue eyes, just like Emily's dad. "Folks, we've alerted the FBI. They're on their way—"

"FBI?" Doug said.

"We both have jurisdiction over a national park, but this is an official missing persons case involving a child. We take it very seriously. So we alerted them. They'll be helping."

Doug understood.

"Brady Brook." The second man, slightly younger and wearing blue overalls, introduced himself as the district ranger who was Incident Commander. "I'll be in charge of the SAR operation here in the field to find Paige." He removed his hat, revealing short-cropped brown hair. Neat and clean-shaven, he wore frameless glasses and the serious air of a soft-spoken, capable man. "I've been with the park for six years. In that time, we've done about forty major searches for lost people. Located them in every case."

"And in how many cases were they alive?" Doug asked.

Thornton and Brook exchanged glances.

"Most every one," Brook said.

"Except accidents," Thornton said, "falls and such."

Emily's hands went to her mouth. Doug put his arm around her.

"Each case has its own circumstances." Brook looked Emily and Doug in the eye. "Locating Paige is the park's priority. It's been over twenty-four hours. We'll need very specific information fast. Let's get started, please."

Brook took them to the table where a woman was typing on a laptop computer. Helicopters continued arriving with more people as Brook and the woman took information from Doug and Emily. Shouting over the noise, they entered Paige's vital statistics, her medical, physical, mental condition.

"Did she have any items with her?"

"She had Kobee, her dog, a beagle," Emily said.

The woman's eyes went to Brook, who looked at Mac.

Brook pursed his lips, refraining from telling the Bakers that a dog can attract bears, enrage them, lead them right to the owner. Emily and Doug had known the risk but ignored it. Brook caught their self-reproach.

"The dog can be an asset," he said. "It can keep her warm, force her to think of it, keep her spirits up. Be a psychological blanket."

"Really?" Emily sniffled.

"It's been the case in other wilderness searches for children," Brook said.

They inventoried Paige's tent. Thornton looked around on his own. It was deduced that Paige had a sweatshirt, T-shirts, hat, water or juice boxes, fruit, granola bars, candy and a penknife.

The searchers asked if Paige had any wilderness or survival experience. What was the family situation before she got lost? Doug and Emily exchanged glances.

"She was not having fun," Doug said. This was, *is*, her first time backpacking. She misses the city and the comforts of home."

Thornton ventured a theory. "Any chance she was angry and went off in a preteen tantrum?"

Doug looked at the ground. Emily looked at the horizon; the

sun was nearing it. Another helicopter was approaching, its increasing *thump* pressing for an answer. "Yes," Doug said, "there's a chance of that."

Using Paige's vital stats—four feet seven inches tall, seventy pounds—they estimated her step, measured it against the terrain and time, to determine a search perimeter, sectors, boundaries; then they dispatched teams, equipped with radios, water, food, warm clothing and gear.

"They will search in shifts until dark, when it becomes too dangerous. They'll camp, resume searching at daybreak," Brook said. "More volunteers, dog teams, fixed wing aircraft, all are on the way. We'll search until we find her, using every resource we can."

Emily thanked Brook. Doug took him off to talk alone with him.

"You've done your calculations." Doug's voice wavered. "Tell me now. How much time before it's critical, given what you know?"

"Doug, each case is—"

"Don't bullshit me now. I am her father. I am an ex-marine. I know about ratios of survivability. Now give it to me."

Brook looked at him. Man to man. Father to father.

"Three to five days."

Three to five days. His little girl could be dead in three to five days and they had already lost twenty-four hours.

"Doug, we've got lots of experienced people helping. Lots of hope." Brook put his hand on his shoulder, then excused himself.

Doug watched a helicopter conducting aerial searches. In minutes, the group of some forty people, which had gathered within an hour on the ridge, had virtually vanished into the forests. Brook requested Emily and Doug stay put with the base team at Incident Command.

Incident Command—that is what their family campsite had become. Their trip was a federal incident involving the FBI.

Doug was overwhelmed, exhausted. He wanted to go off to sit alone when Thornton approached him and Emily, producing a small notebook.

"Folks, I hate to trouble you. I've got to take down a few more particulars for the first report. I am sorry." Thornton recorded addresses and office numbers; then he asked for a picture of Paige.

"A picture?" Emily said.

"Yes, a recent one, to put out everywhere—at the park gates, police agencies. The press."

"We took some on this trip, but I—I don't understand. She's out there—"

"Well, ma'am, we have to be prepared for all scenarios." Thornton let that sit. Doug got it. So did Emily when Thornton asked his next question.

"Did you happen to see many strangers, or anything odd out here or on the way?"

They had not.

"Well, I am sorry. We won't get into this now, but the FBI might." Thornton grew concerned. "You want to get that hand looked at, Doug?"

Doug glanced at the bloodied gash on his left palm. "Looks worse than it is actually."

"Really? Looks bad. What happened?"

"Hurt it chopping wood. It's just a small cut."

Thornton's eyes went from the wound to Doug, measuring him for a few seconds. "With an ax?" he said.

Doug nodded.

"Well, you might want to get it taken care of."

"It's fine."

Thornton left it, then reminded Emily of the need for a picture.

"I'll get my camera," Emily said. "It's digital, is that OK?"

"Even better. Brook's people can transmit it to headquarters. We'll have it out far and wide in no time."

Emily went for her camera, leaving Doug with Thornton, who from the moment he had set foot on the ridge had studied Doug and Emily. Listening. Watching. Absorbing everything through soft blue eyes that seldom missed a thing.

Like that nasty wound on Doug's left hand.

Doug would be asked about that when the FBI got its people here. Thornton had been updating them on the radio-phone link to their field office in Billings, which in turn alerted the FBI's division office in Salt Lake City.

In keeping with procedure, Thornton had been assuming criminal intent from the instant he received Mac's report and the notation about Doug Baker's hand.

Checks through the National Crime Information Center, the FBI-operated crime computer, showed Doug served three days in Cook County Jail several years ago for a dustup in a Chicago bar. Beat up two guys pretty bad. Suggested a violent history.

Doug's recent history was more serious. The San Francisco Police Department's local computers showed that a few days before the Bakers left for Montana, a neighbor called 911 to report a violent domestic argument at the Baker home. The caller complained of Doug shouting, threatening to assault Emily.

A unit responded. No injuries. No charges. Emily said it was just a misunderstanding. A loud discussion.

Then there was the recent edict from the National Park Service Washington Office after the Yellowstone case. Just over a month ago, a father hiked out of a remote trail to report that his five-year-old daughter was lost. A search was launched. Turned out in the confusion no one checked out the dad. He had a laceration on his neck and a criminal history of abusing his ex-wife over custody of the child. A week later, when the girl's body was found, an autopsy determined she had been stabbed to death. By this time, the father had vanished and was thought to be in South America. That led Washington to demand immediate assumption of criminal intent in major missing person reports in national parks with a multi-agency response. This one fell into that category, and the FBI and SFPD were already on it.

Being an old mountain cop, Thornton had a few concerns. Like how Doug hurt that hand. Said he did it chopping wood. Funny, Thornton had already poked around some. No sign of an ax. Something was going on here. Something Doug and Emily had not told them.

Well, not yet anyway, he thought, tucking his notebook in his pocket.

CHAPTER FIVE

Walt Sydowski's eighty-eight-year-old father, John, played his last card, the queen of diamonds.

"Victory."

"You are a crafty old fox," Sydowski said in Polish, losing a round of crazy eights, their favorite game.

"Not too old to teach you a trick or two, eh?" John's eyes twinkled as he claimed his five bucks, folding it triumphantly.

"That's right, Pop." Sydowski patted his old man's wrinkled hands. "I've got to check on the birds, Dad. Want to help me?"

"Sure, let's go."

Sydowski was enjoying having his father stay with him during these few days he was off. Sydowski lived alone in Parkside in the house where he and his wife, Basha, had raised two daughters. It got a little lonely. His old man, a retired barber, still preferred to live at Sea Breeze Villas, a seniors' complex in Pacifica. He had his friends, his vegetable garden, and followed baseball. Sydowski liked his visits. Before their game, they had homemade cream of potato soup, the way Basha used to make it. With real cream.

They went to the aviary Sydowski had built in his backyard under the oak tree, a lifetime ago it seemed. Inside, they were met by the cooing of some five dozen caged songbirds. Photographs and ribbons won at bird fairs covered the paneled walls. Sydowski liked coming here to listen to the tiny birds and review cases. Like the doubleheader they cleared a few months ago. That beast almost brought him to his knees.

Sydowski was concerned about his new bred budgerigars. They offered appealing cinnamon and opaline wing markings, but he noticed their droppings seemed off color and lacked consistency. Maybe if he fortified their seed mix with some calcium.

"You know, Dad, I met a nice lady a few months ago at the Seattle show."

"Louise from San Jose. You got the budgies from her. You told me."

"I was thinking of asking her over for dinner."

"You need a woman? At your age?"

"Watch it."

Sydowski smiled at last week's conversation on the phone, Louise asking him for coffee.

"I could come to San Francisco, Walt. Or you could come here?"

"Well, I got some cases to work on," he said. "Can I get back to you?"

"I'm not going anywhere."

They'd hit it off in Seattle. Louise was a budgie breeder, also widowed. Her husband, a judge, had died three years ago. Stroke. Her daughter owned a small computer-graphics company in Sacramento. Her son was a medical lawyer in Pittsburgh. Aside from her birds, she taught drama classes and

was a working actor. She had done some national commercials
and had been an extra in a few movies. Louise was vibrant—
sixty-one going on forty-one. Gorgeous and, for some strange
reason, smitten with him the moment she came up behind him
on the floor of the Seattle show.

"Well, where did you come from, Mr. Walt Sydowski?"

He turned to meet mischief and flirtation in the green eyes
peering up at him over a coffee mug.

Sydowski had a pleasing, solid six-foot-three, two-hundred-
pound build, wavy salt-and-pepper hair touching off his dark
complexion and rugged smile, which glinted because of his
two gold-crowned teeth. Most people were intrigued by his
smile. Unless, of course, they were a suspected killer.

Louise had cast some sort of spell on him that day in Seattle.
She had done some investigating, learning from other exhibitors
all about Inspector Wladyslaw Sydowski of the San Francisco
Homicide Detail.

They talked over lunch, about raising a family, about losing
a spouse, about acting, about memories, about birds. He liked
her and told her of the anguish of cases involving children.

Being with her was like being with an old friend, and in the
weeks after Seattle, when they talked on the phone, Sydowski
felt something warm flowing into an area of his life that had
been cold and empty for so long. But why was he afraid?

"You think you are cheating on Basha after six years? Or
that the girls might not approve? You want my permission to
have a date?"

Sydowski stroked a fledgling with his pinkie knuckle and
shrugged.

"I guess, something like that. I don't know."

"Your problem is you maybe want to leave the job, or need
something new in your life. Those cases with the baby and the
kidnapped kids still shake you pretty good. I see it in your
face."

Sydowski would always be haunted by the case of two-year-old Tanita Marie Donner. Her little corpse hidden in Golden Gate Park. For over a year, he went nuts trying to clear it. Then two other kids were abducted, creating hysteria for the Bay Area, pressure from the brass. The fear that all three files were connected when another child was grabbed—the son of Tom Reed, a reporter for the *San Francisco Star,* who was covering the story. The kidnapper, a psycho twitcher named Keller, had planned to kill the kids.

"Yes, they were hard cases. You could be on the right track there, Pop."

After Keller, it took a few weeks for Sydowski to wind down. In all his years with the SFPD, in handling nearly six hundred homicides, he'd never seen anything like it. He hoped to hell he would never see anything like it again. During the darkest moments of the investigation, he would sit in the aviary with his birds and miss his wife deeply. That was his problem. The last big cases were not his career enders. He did not want to hang up his shield because of them. On the upside, they brought him together with his new young partner, Inspector Linda Turgeon.

Working with her was like having a third daughter. They got along well. Even when they argued. No, he was not ready to hang it up. He loved the job. It kept his brain functioning. He was a homicide cop. But when files got rough, they underscored the void of Basha's absence. He would never stop loving her, yet he did not want to be handcuffed to her death. This was his dilemma. Now Louise had come into his life, maybe not to fill a void, but to help him live past it. And she wanted to see him again. So what should he do?

"I think I am going to ask Louise out. What do you think, Pop?"

"You keep asking *me*. She is not my girlfriend." John inched his hand into a cage and let a Fife canary perch on his forefinger.

"You think it is appropriate after six years?"

"You're the cop. Is it against the law?"

The phone in the aviary rang. Sydowski got it on the second ring. It was his boss, Lieutenant Leo Gonzales.

"Walt, I'm sending Linda over to take you to the airport."

Sydowski was taken aback. It was his day off. Was this a joke?

"No, Leo. You say, 'Hello, Walt, how are you?' Then I say, 'I'm fine, Leo, and how are you?' "

Sydowski could hear Leo placing his hand over his mouthpiece, talking to people at the Homicide Detail. Tension leaking through.

". . . you tell them"—Leo was talking to someone else at his end—"that we are cooperating fully and quickly. Tell them that. Walt? You still there?"

"What is it?"

"I got to send you to Montana right now."

"Montana? What the—"

"You've been requested to assist the FBI on a breaking case."

"Requested by whom?"

"The feebees. Asked for our best guy and you got to be there now."

"Now?" Sydowski looked at his dad.

"Linda will take you to the airport and give you a file. Someone with the Bureau will pick you up in Kalispell."

"What the hell is going on in Montana, Leo?"

"Missing girl. Ten years old. From San Francisco. In a national park."

Sydowski's stomach clenched and his heartburn from the potato soup flared. The price for not holding the onions.

A missing kid.

"Why do they need me in Montana? This is unusual. It's an FBI case in Montana. They just don't do this. What's going on?"

"Kid's hiking in Glacier National Park, with Mommy and

Daddy. Wanders off. Lost. Dad hikes back to report her missing.''

"Find a body? Any evidence of a crime?"

"No, but Dad's got a hurt hand."

"Pretty weak, Leo. Come on. What's the family history?"

"The feebees asked us to run the old man through our system and we got a hit. A few days before they left for their trip, we were called to their house by a neighbor."

"Charges?"

"None."

"What are the details of the call?"

"Domestic assault complaint. Neighbor says the dad was shouting, threatening violence. Don't know all the details yet. Linda's going through the old report, making calls, putting it together with stuff the FBI sent us in a file for you. Seems the father got in a bar fight quite a few years back in Chicago. Did three days for that. The guy's got a temper."

"This requires me to rush to Montana? The FBI has people there and here. What, they lose the numbers?"

"It is out of our hands."

"Sounds like somebody's pumped to build a case, where maybe none exists. I'm going to pass, Leo. I've got plans and—"

"You are going to the mountains, Inspector."

"How's that?"

"Walt, you have no say. Unless you are retiring today?"

"What is the deal on this, Leo? What's going on here?"

"Rangers and feebees got a very bad smell on this thing the instant it broke." Walt heard Leo shuffling papers. "The strategy is to *quietly* pull out all the stops now in the event it turns into a homicide. Remember that case not too long ago in Yellowstone, it prompted the rangers and FBI to go hard at the outset. Then there was that old mess in Colorado, a missing turns into kidnapping turns into homicide?"

"So?"

"And the South Carolina case. Mom screams on the networks that a stranger took her two kids, when it turns out she killed them?"

"So? The rangers and FBI can handle their own cases. When we catch one, we don't wet our pants, call for help to come hold our hand."

"I suspect big political buttons were pushed here. The park is federal jurisdiction. It is the state's tourist jewel. The Montana governor has pull. He calls Washington, who calls Sacramento, who calls our employer, who calls us, and now I'm calling you. They want this settled fast. No mistakes. Whatever the hell happened in the mountains they want it cleared fast, solid and by the book. Preferably with a happy ending. No weekly TV panel discussions with experts pointing out the screwups."

Sydowski cursed under his breath and shook his head.

"Anybody think it may be a matter of a child missing in the woods?"

"It is your sworn duty as an officer assisting in this file to help the team determine if that is the case. Accomplish that, Inspector Sydowski, and your duty will have been done. Then you can go fishing."

"You know, Leo, you are a sycophantic boot-licking toady."

"You will be assisting Special Agent Frank Zander. I think he's coming in from D.C. A brass-balled mother who could build a case against the pope for Jimmy Hoffa. You are supposed to challenge him to make the case solid."

"If I see a bear, I'll cuff it, then bring it back and feed him your asshole."

"I knew you would see things my way, dear. Pack flannel."

"Up yours." Sydowski slammed down the phone.

His father said, "I take it that was not Louise?"

The call meant Sydowski's old man had to go home to Pacifica. So he called a cab for him, then phoned a friend in his bird club who lived a few doors down the street. The friend had a key to Sydowski's aviary and agreed to tend to his birds while he was away. Within twenty minutes, both men had finished packing when Linda arrived in an unmarked Chevy Caprice. Sydowski was upstairs. His old man let her in.

"Hi there. I'm Linda Turgeon, Walt's partner." She removed her sunglasses. Her brown hair had been recently cut in a jaw-length bob. She was wearing a tailored lavender suit and looked very nice.

"I am his wise father, John." He was wearing his Giants ballcap and a frayed navy sweater over a plaid shirt. "You look cute—like my granddaughters."

Linda blushed. "Thank you, John. Walt told me you were not shy." She was a little puzzled, noticing the old man's hat, his bag by his feet. "Are you accompanying him on this trip?"

"No, he is going home, Linda." Sydowski came down the stairs. "Grab your bag, Pop. Cab's here."

"My son is grumpy. He called his boss a toad because this new case is interfering with his new romance."

Linda's surprised eyes widened and she shot a pretty smile at Sydowski, who began shuffling him to the street. "Let's go, old man."

Sydowski got his father into the cab and on his way to Pacifica. He locked the house and dropped with an angry sigh into the front passenger seat of the Caprice. Turgeon had them on 101 in good time.

Walt stared at San Francisco's skyline rolling by the Golden Gate in the distance, the majestic spires of the Bay Bridge.

"Do you believe this case, Linda?"

"Given what we went through recently, are you kidding?"

"What could they possibly have that warrants this kind of reaction?"

"You had something better to do? You got a life now?"

"You got a file for me?"

"You're sitting on it. So who's your new honey?"

Sydowski grunted, fishing for the file.

"Never mind. How did your reunion date go with your ex-fiancé architect?" He glanced superficially at papers on Doug Baker.

"Had animal monkey sex on his dining room table."

"Never invite me for dinner." Sydowski could not find his glasses. He'd read Baker's file on the plane.

"We just talked, Walt. We're going to take it one step at a time."

"Still thinking about making babies?"

"Thinking about a lot of things, Dad."

"Let's talk about work now, please?"

"Your plane tickets are waiting at the counter. We're on this together. I am working local checks here with the FBI. It's their show, Walt. They're rushing, putting things together. Moving really fast."

"What is your sense of it at this stage?"

"They told me zero. We do not know all of their holdback. It's either a straight-up missing kid case . . .or a mystery."

"Well, we have this." Sydowski held up the file.

Linda nodded. Dead serious. "I'll be interested in your opinion on everything. Got a few pages there, including theories from Montana already."

"Based on the information we know, she's been lost in the woods, what, about twenty-four, thirty hours?"

"Yup."

"And this is a remote region of Glacier National Park?"

"One of the most remote areas of the U.S."

"Find out if the family is the avid, outdoors type. Or if this was an impulse trip. Like why there and why now. What was going on in their lives."

"There's the old cop I know. Welcome back."

* * *

Once his jet leveled off, Sydowski slipped on his bifocals and read every word in the file. Twice. The faxed copy of Pike Thornton's fresh notes had currency with Sydowski. He had met him several weeks ago at a detectives' conference in Kansas City. They led a panel discussion on "The Intangibles of Investigation," the virtue of heeding gut instincts.

Thornton believed Doug was hiding something about how he injured his hand, that the Bakers were not forthcoming, that there seemed to be much more beneath the surface. Doug's hand wound was disturbing. Said he did it with an ax, which seemed to be missing along with the kid. Sydowski went over the recent complaint San Francisco police had on the family. A neighbor reported that Doug Baker had threatened to assault his wife and daughter in their backyard. Dispatch sent a car to the house. There was tension but no assault. Mother said it was a misunderstanding. That was it.

Sydowski closed the file folder. There were lots of troubling points about this case. His heartburn flared; he chewed on a Tums as his jet banked north toward the Rocky Mountains.

CHAPTER SIX

"They found her head near Dallas," the cop on the phone was telling Tom Reed, a crime reporter with the *San Francisco Star*.

Reed drew a small circle in his notebook, placing it in Texas on his rough map of the country. Other, tiny pieces of a stick person were scattered throughout the southern United States.

"The head near Dallas." Reed looked at the newsroom clock. His vacation started in a few hours. He was flying to Chicago in a few days. His wife's sister was getting married.

"Hey, Reed, you with me, all-star?" Inspector Harry Lance from the SFPD Homicide Detail resumed his discourse on dismemberment cases.

"Yeah, Harry. Head near Dallas, a leg near Tulsa, a leg near Nashville, an arm near Wheeling, an arm near Savannah and the rest in Louisville."

"So who gets jurisdiction, Mr. Celebrity?"

Would it ever end? Reed shook his head. For some inexplicable reason, ever since the Keller case, just about every detective, reporter or armchair critic Reed met seemed obligated to mess with him.

You were an asshole getting so close to that story. Ever think of that?

After the Keller case, the national press portrayed Reed as some sort of hero whose "relentless investigation" helped find Keller. But Reed knew the truth. He had lived it. He had told everyone how stupid he was. How *unheroic* he was, how lucky he was, extending his concern to the other families involved. That is what Reed told every interviewer. But that was not what they wanted to hear: *Tell us about your "relentless investigation."*

That was several months ago. Interest was trailing off. Reed was thankful. Looking at Zach and Ann's snapshots taped to his computer made him smile. The ordeal had changed him. He found peace and focus with Zach and Ann. Zach was doing well in school. Ann's children's clothing stores in the Bay Area were successful. Their marriage was better. They were a family back in their house in the Sunset. He was working on his book, declined job offers with the *Los Angeles Times* and the *Washington Post* and returned to the *San Francisco Star* with restored self-confidence, minus the ego and obsession. He was a solid crime reporter, just working his beat today, fishing for news at the Homicide Detail.

"Come on, Reed, in dismemberment cases, who's got jurisdiction?"

"Louisville catches it. It's where they find the heart."

"You're a smart-ass, you know that, Reed?"

"So you going to give me my prize now?"

"Got my hand on it right now. Know where my hand is?"

"Keep it up and I'm going to come down there."

"I got to go, Reed."

"Hey, wait a sec. I'm looking for news. What's going on?"

"Nothing. Some addict in the 'Loin. Guys are in court, working on stuff."

"What's Sydowksi doing?"

"Not sure. Linda's out. Something to do with the feebees in Montana."

"What's going on there that's connected to here?"

"Remember when the Forty-niners had Montana?"

"You had more hair then."

"Missing kid."

"Missing how?"

"Like in not there."

"Harry, come on, I'm going on vacation in a few hours."

"Just a friggin' minute. You are a burr in my boxers, you know that, Reed?" Lance put Reed on hold. Then came back. "Ten-year-old San Francisco girl lost in the Rockies in Montana."

"Why call you guys?"

Lance was silent.

"What's the real connection to here?" Reed said. "The physical evidence doesn't match the story. Some link to San Francisco?"

"I don't know."

Reed had reported on so many homicides he thought like a detective.

"Something awry in the family's history?"

"I don't know."

"A conviction?"

"I don't know."

"That it?"

"Daddy's got a hurt hand."

"How did he do that?"

"I don't know anything, but your questions are interesting."

"Is there a mommy? What's Mommy's story?"

"I don't know."

"But they've got no body? Just a missing kid, right?"

"I suppose. I am not up on the details. I am sure the very capable FBI has it under control."

"Who's the family? Got names?"

"Don't know. All I heard is the feds are going hard on it. Walt might be going out to Montana to help. I got to go now." Lance hung up.

This was intriguing, Reed thought, checking the newsroom clock again. He was meeting Ann and Zach to pick up some things for Chicago. Going full out on a kid lost in the Rockies, as if it were a homicide. Secret suspicions about Dad. Flying Sydowski to Montana. He'd better alert the desk soon so they could pass it to somebody.

Maybe there was something out on this. The keys clicked on Reed's computer keyboard as he called up the newswires, entering terms like "Montana," "girl" and "missing" in the search mode. In seconds, one story appeared on his screen. A short one slugged LOST GIRL. It just moved out of Kalispell, Montana.

KALISPELL, MT—Searchers began combing the Rocky Mountain foothills of Glacier National Park for a 10-year-old girl whose parents reported her missing to park authorities earlier today.

The girl's family told park rangers that she had wandered from their backcountry campsite along the Grizzly Tooth Trail several miles deep into the park's rugged northern sector, near the Canadian border.

She was last seen some 24 hours prior to the time her father alerted authorities after hiking alone out of the trail. The isolated area where she is lost is known as the Devil's Grasp.

The girl, whose name has not yet been released, is believed to be from California.

Reed's investigative juices stirred. The wire item was the first take on the case so far. No mention of San Francisco or suspicions. Maybe he had a bit of a scoop. The story moved minutes ago. She'd been lost for at least twenty-four hours, which meant she'd spent a night in the high country. Reed thought of Zach, nearly the same age. Not much time before it got critical for her. Reed grew up in Great Falls. He was no backcountry hiker but he'd visited the Rockies enough to know that getting lost up there could be fatal.

Reed rubbed his chin. Aside from the elements, police had suspicions. Routine police procedure to check out the nearest and dearest in such cases. But all this other stuff about going full. Flying San Francisco cops to the mountains? Was that all just Inspector Harry Lance, or was there something to this? Why should Reed care? His vacation started in a few hours.

What if she was already dead?

Reed remembered one late night long ago sitting with some of the old Homicide bulls in Room 450 at the Hall of Justice. They were in an unusually friendly mood giving him their thoughts on the perfect murder. Some suggested "a wilderness accident." You push the victim off a cliff, and *whoops!* A fall. No witnesses. Not likely any physical or trace evidence. Just the killer's conscience. Maybe motive, but you cannot be convicted on that. And we don't have a body for a while. Decomposition and animals make an autopsy useless. Killer wins; justice loses. The deceased is not avenged.

A wilderness accident. Reed chewed on that.

"Tom, you've got that look in your eye." Molly Wilson, the reporter who sat next to him, returned from interviewing a fingerprint expert for a feature. Her bracelets clinked as she typed. "What gives?"

Wilson was Reed's partner at the paper. Surviving the Keller case together and Reed's marital strain had strengthened their relationship. They had become better friends. She was an astounding writer, a superb reporter. With a brilliant sunrise smile and auburn hair, she boasted a figure that turned heads, especially in copland.

"Pal, she is so easy on the eyes," a recently divorced FBI

agent told Reed. The reporter had to burst his bubble, telling him Molly was sorta-kinda dating Manny Lewis, a heavy hitter with *GQ* looks at the DA's office.

"You home? Care to tell me what's on your mind, usher boy?"

Reed told her everything and Wilson immediately logged into the *Star*'s computerized data files. "Suspicious wilderness accident. That sort of thing has happened. There was that case not long ago in Wyoming." Molly's keyboard was clicking.

"Here it is, a story we ran from the *Casper Star-Tribune*— a dad was hiking with his five-year-old daughter. He reports she fell or was lost near a gorge in Yellowstone. Rangers search for days. Dad slips away. When they find her body, an autopsy shows she had been stabbed. There was trouble in the family, a vendetta between the parents over custody of the girl. Meanwhile, Dad's fled to Brazil or Bolivia."

"Well," Reed sighed, "we know zip on this one. In a short time, I am outta here. Maybe you should brace yourself for a trip to Montana, kid."

Reed's line rang. It was Zeke Canter, the new metro editor. "Tom, come to my office, please."

Reed got along with Canter. In his mid forties, dressed in L.L. Bean shirts and Dockers, Canter was trim and fit, about an inch under six feet. Kind, thoughtful, razor-sharp and quick, stemming from fifteen years in New York with the *Daily News* and *Newsday*. National Editor Violet Stewart was on the phone in Canter's office and making notes.

"So the next one to Salt Lake leaves in ninety minutes, just in time to connect to Kalispell."

That was all Reed needed to hear.

"No. I am on vacation in—like almost now."

Stewart hung up, removed her bifocals, letting them hang from her fine chain necklace. "Tom, we really would like you to get there tonight."

"No."

"This is shaping into something. She's from San Francisco. Ten years old," Canter said, dropping a printout of an updated wire story.

"Look." Stewart had a color photo of Paige Baker. "This just moved."

A beautiful child whose face could melt your heart. Reed's stomach tensed. This was moving fast in the direction of a potentially huge story. "What about Molly?" he said.

"You will be a team. She'll work every angle from here, but we want you there. Tom, you are from Montana. It's tailor-made for you," Canter said.

"We guarantee you will not miss the Chicago wedding," Violet said.

"Let me make one call. Excuse me."

Back at his desk, Reed punched his wife's cell phone number. He never knew which store Ann was at. This was going to be sweet. Wilson blinked up at him with a grand smile. *"Who's going to Montana, cowboy?"*

Reed scratched his nose with his middle finger for Wilson as Ann answered her phone. Reed explained. She was not pleased.

"Tom, you're on vacation! We're visiting family and we have a wedding. We're both in the wedding party. Usher. Bridesmaid. Remember! And there's something else. Or did you forget?"

He had forgotten until that very moment, suddenly recalling how Ann had talked about privately requesting the minister to renew their vows because of all they had been through.

"You want to risk missing this?"

"No. Absolutely not," Reed said. "You go on ahead with Zach and I'll fly out from Montana, take all my stuff. The *Star* will have to swallow any costs. They have guaranteed that I'll be in Chicago for the wedding."

"Tom, you better not be falling into your old habits."

Reed sat down, explaining more to Ann about the story of

Paige Baker, the girl lost in the wilderness, while simultaneously glancing at the newsroom clock, estimating flight time, driving to Glacier, time zone difference. Filing a story. Finally, Ann said, "I did not sign on to be a single parent, *mister.*"

"Mister," that was the word. Anne's code for *I'm pissed off but here's my loving approval, you jerk.*

"Ann, I love you."

Reed was bent over, struggling to retrieve his emergency travel bag from under his desk. "I am nothing without you, Ann. Hug Zach for me."

Wilson rolled her eyes.

Reed returned to Canter's office, where the editors discussed what the *Star* wanted from Reed in Montana and Wilson in San Francisco.

"If the little Baker girl story fizzles," Violet said, "would you consider, stress *consider,* a full-page feature on the case of Isaiah Hood, the guy scheduled for execution in a few days? He is expected to lose his final appeal to the U.S. Supreme Court. You will be there, after all."

"Violet, please. Just staple the name of a divorce lawyer to that request."

"Tom, you're going to be right there, and again, we *are* going to have you in Chicago in time for the wedding. Promise. And we're going to make it up to you."

"But why the Hood case? It's nothing. No San Francisco connection. Nobody knows or cares about that thing. It barely makes the Montana papers. I don't even follow it. I think he killed somebody like fifteen, twenty years ago. Bump on the head or something, I don't know. He's a small-town loser. Nothing remarkable. He's sentenced to die. End of story. Why waste the ink? We all know not every execution is covered in this country."

"Tom"—Violet was legendary for her coverage of executions—"there is something in every tragedy that we can learn from. It's the human condition. And given this case is so old and forgotten means the story's value has just been fermenting. A man is going to be put to death. Tell me why; tell me what happened; tell me a story.''

During his cab ride to San Francisco International, Reed checked his two phones. One was a new compact sat phone; because of the expense, it should only be used if the cell did not work. He reviewed hard copy of the updated wire stories on the lost girl. Not much new. Ten minutes after leaving the *Star* building, he called Molly on his cell.

"You in Montana, cowboy?" she joked.

"You got anything for me?"

"No. Call me from Salt Lake."

"Don't tell anybody what we know about police suspicions just yet. I'm going to try to hook up with Sydowski if I can find him."

"OK. Watch out for bears."

When the jet leveled off, Reed opened up his laptop computer and went to all the background stories about Isaiah Hood he'd requested from the news librarian. Reed's jaw dropped. Expecting at least two dozen, he found three with apologies from the library. "We have little on this case, Tom."

Hood had killed a kid some twenty years ago. Convicted after a two-day trial. Sentenced to death. Usual years of appeals. Unremarkable for a murder, except for the last sentence in the most recent story. Hood's last appeal to the U.S. Supreme Court was made on a claim that Hood was not guilty.

CHAPTER SEVEN

Emily could not stop shivering.

Night had come. The second without Paige.

Since Paige's disappearance, Emily had not slept or eaten.

"You must be freezing, ma'am." A young ranger tried to drape a sleeping bag on Emily. She shrugged it off.

"My daughter has no blanket. I will go through this with her."

Doug was working with the searchers at the map table lit by lanterns. Their radios muted. Emily stood alone in the darkness at the edge of the camp, the distant lights of the searchers' campsites dotting the black valleys and mountainsides, blinking eerily as if a starlit sky had fallen to earth.

Paige.

Her child was out there; the clock was ticking away on her life. Every second, every minute, every hour, buying another piece of it. Oh, Paige, forgive me. It was all her fault. Her fault. Like before.

"Guess what I'm going to do."

Emily's monster was brushing against her, reaching for her, trying to pull her into the darkness. *No. Please. No.* It had taken hold. She struggled, hearing her counselor's voice. *When you feel it coming up on you, reach for the good things, Emily. The good things are your lifelines. They are real. They are unconditional. The good things will save you. Reach for them and hold on.* She reached into a good memory. . . .

Push, Emily! The hospital. The nurses. Doug squeezing her hand. The doctor urging her. A couple of deep breaths, Emily. Push for me. This is so hard. Here we go. Almost there. The sounds of the baby's first cry. Emily's heart swelling with joy. Congratulations, Mom and Dad, you have a daughter. Her scrimped little face, her bright eyes. The love washing over her. Doug kissing her. I love you. Holding their new baby. Tender, warm heart. Love. The pain subsiding. Have you chosen a name? Paige. We'll call her Paige. Emily would never let go. Paige was her new life. Doug was her new life. Her new life was complete now.

Emily's chain to the monster of her past was broken with Paige's birth. Or so Emily thought. But as the years rolled by and Paige got older, the monster beckoned her to return to Montana for a final confrontation. It must be done, her counselor said, or you will never find peace, never resolve your conscience. Go to Montana. Put things to rest.

Emily had forgotten how much she loved it here. How her girlhood on her family's small ranch near the slopes of the Rockies had been like a storybook. Her great-grandfather had built the house with its classic rafter roof in the 1930s. Her mother taught her to cook and sew. She took her to church in town on Sundays: "Emily, you must never forget that believing in yourself is as important as believing in God. Above all, never underestimate the healing qualities of forgiveness."

Her dad taught her how to camp in the backcountry and how

to drive a stick-shift pickup. He conveyed the value of honesty and the wisdom of never approaching a high-spirited horse when you're in a bad mood, " 'cause they can smell it on you." Emily remembered how the pine and cedar filled the house when he sat by the fire on winter nights looking at his dog-eared collection of *Life* magazines. How excited he was helping her learn to use her first camera, telling her that history was something to cherish, especially with a camera. "It's the only way you can hang on to the people in your life."

That's how it was for her, near Buckhorn Creek, where stars were near enough to be jewelry, where the mountains were so close she swore she could hear music as the wind danced through them. Emily embraced the belief that a place can be as important to a person's life as the people in it.

Emily studied the purple sky over the mountains, longing to hear their music again. She was struggling to tell Doug what had happened here. She needed him to know. He was her Sergeant Rock, her Gibraltar, trying so hard to be patient with her.

His life had been a lonely one and he didn't mind talking about it.

"What's to tell, Em? Grew up an only child in Houston. Dad was better at gambling and drinking than he was as a father and a mechanic. Walked out when I was thirteen. Left Mom with two kids, a mortgage and a shattered heart. She got over it by marrying a truck driver. We moved to Buffalo. I hated the snow. Left home before my seventeenth birthday, wandered the world alone, searching for someone like you."

Doug could always make her smile. Like when they first met and she told him her name. "Emily. Now that makes me think of a bouquet of mountain flowers." And here he was, this gorgeous hunk of manhood with his firm, lean body, broad shoulders, his chiseled rugged smile, the USMC warrior who was privately reading *Paddle-to-the-Sea*. How could she not love this man? When she showed him her favorite photos—not the weddings, portraits, freelance news, postcards and calendar work, which paid the bills, but her artsy slice-of-life pictures—Doug actually *got* it. Understood the story she was trying to tell in a single moment stolen from time. They connected. . . .

Ah, Doug and Paige.

She was Daddy's girl. He was so good to her, using just the right mixture of tenderness and U.S. Marine Corps discipline. Paige was bright and perceptive, like her dad. At times, Emily realized Paige and Doug had a bond so strong, it was as if *he* had given birth to her.

As Paige got older, it became clear to Emily her monster would not rest. She thought it was dead, that she had constructed a new life, become a new person. But the monster was only sleeping. As Paige got older, the monster had awakened and had begun coiling around Emily, tightening itself, pulling her back.

"Guess what I'm going to do."

Suddenly, an icy wind slithered from a glacier valley, gripping her in a flurry of images. Dragging her back.

Emily was thirteen. The day it happened, the county sheriff brought her home in that big Ford. Emily could not step far from the car. Her knees would not stiffen. She was drowning in fear. Her ears still ringing. *Oh God. Oh God. Oh God. This was not real. It was not . . . Oh God.* Her mother on the porch, her face, her eyes. A couple of deputies had arrived earlier to break the news. Her father coming to the sheriff's car, his tear-streaked eyes searching it in vain. The sheriff removing his hat out of respect. *"I'm so sorry, Winston. So goddamn sorry,"* he says, and her father, suddenly aged, looking so weak, moaning an awful animal squeaking-groan as if something buried deep inside of him was breaking with such agony that it forced him to his knees, his large fists pounding the earth. Her mother collapsed on the porch, one of the deputies catching her. Her mother's screams rolling from the home into the mountains.

That night, women and men from the church came to their house to be with them, talking softly. Her father staring at the floor. Defeated. Mrs. Nelson, the organ player, rubbing his shoulders, whispering psalms. Her mother had gone to her room to lie down. The reverend and his wife were with her, talking, comforting her. The reverend's wife, stroking her mother's hair, soothing her. In the kitchen, some of the men sat at the table, talking in low tones about what the hell happened. How could it happen? The house filled as word got around town. Emily in shock, walking from room to room. Embraced by a grieving adult, pulled tight to clothes smelling of perfume, cigarettes, alcohol and despair.

Oh, child. Poor Emily. You will get through this. God will protect. Be strong. Be strong for your mother and father. Her mother and father? What about her? She was there. She was part of it.

"Guess what I'm going to do."

It was her fault.

Emily running alone from the woods back to girls' camp. Heart pounding so loud, pulse ringing in her ears. The voices of the camp counselors were faint and distant, faces awash in concern.

"Lee, where's your sister? What happened to Rachel, Lee?"

Emily standing there. Just standing there, her mouth not moving. Eyes seeing nothing. The club camp going silent except for the counselors asking over and over about Rachel, her little sister.

It was all her fault.

"Guess what I'm going to do."

"No. Don't, please! No."

The monster was out there doing what monsters do.

Emily! Her sister screaming.

"No, don't. Oh, please! You can't have her!"

Rachel screaming. *"Lee, help me."* Squealing horribly. *"Save me!"*

"No, you can't have her! Stop!"

"Emily, shh-shh . . . Emily. . ."

Emily screaming at the darkness, her voice echoing from the sleeping peaks down into the valleys.

". . . you can't have her . . . oh God, it is all my fault. . . ."

Emily collapsing to the ground in tears. Rangers rushing to her. Pike Thornton watching in the lantern light as Doug took her into his arms.

"It's all right, Emily. We'll find Paige. We'll get through this."

His strong arms solid around her. Safe. The good things.

But the monster was right there. Breathing on her with the cold night winds from mountains. She could not stop shivering.

"What happened to your sister?"

It's all my fault.

"Guess what I'm going to do."

CHAPTER EIGHT

Emily slipped into a fitful sleep in Doug's arms as the eastern horizon awoke with predawn light. The rangers had draped blankets over them as they sat on the ridge silhouetted against the peaks.

Portrait of an anguished vigil.

How long had Paige been out there now? Two nights. Nearly forty-eight hours. It had rained. The rangers said the temps had ranged from the seventies to the mid-forties at night. Emily was certain Paige had a sweater. She also had Kobee and some food. Most importantly, her wits. Could their daughter save her own life? Stay put, Paige. Doug whispered advice. Do not travel; build a shelter. Stay put. Stay warm and dry. She had Kobee. They were bringing in dogs. They should be able to pick up Kobee. But there were bears out there.

Oh Jesus.

Doug rubbed a hand across his whiskers. How could he just let her go off? He should have known better. He was a teacher. He just lost control. Lost it. Over this trip. Over Emily. Over everything. He wanted it to end. His hand hurt, throbbed. He had the ax. He just . . . how did it come to this? How? Despite Emily's troubles, they had been happy. She owned his heart. She was so right for him. He always thought so, ever since he first set eyes on her.

He was a sergeant in the U.S. Marine Corps, among the first forces about to be deployed from Pendleton to trouble in the Eastern Hemisphere. Emily was a photographer, stringing for *Newsweek,* sent down from San Francisco to join the news hordes profiling "a day in the life" of his unit. Doug did not even notice her when she first arrived. Just another member of the press to be baby-sat, to be briefed on the mission, to be introduced to the members and afforded access. Even to personal quarters. Doug punctuated every part of the tour with his gruffest, hard-ass "Any questions?" Translated, it meant if you voiced one, you were going to be made to look stupid. So none were asked, until halfway through the day.

"I have one, Sergeant?" Emily said.

"Yes, ma'am."

"Why would a guts-and-glory warrior like yourself have a copy of *Paddle-to-the-Sea* in his locker?"

Doug was at a loss and Emily's camera caught it. After snapping the picture, she lowered her camera, revealing the most engaging, charming smile he had ever seen. He knew then that this woman had captured his heart.

The next evening, she agreed to go for a walk with him along the beach. While looking out at the Pacific, he told Emily he was preparing to leave the Corps and finish his college degree in English Literature so he could teach. The picture book *Paddle-to-the-Sea* was on the study list of one of his correspondence courses, along with classics like *Crime and Punishment* and Homer's *The Odyssey.* As luck would have it, he told her, he was accepted at Golden State in San Francisco.

"Well, I'll have to show you my studio." Emily grinned,

bouncing her eyebrows. "Look me up when you get there, soldier."

He did.

They were married a few years later. They had chemistry, but Emily always had an opaque air about her, a sadness that she would not talk about. She would close herself off. Doug could handle that. Theirs was a good life. He got a teaching job at a high school. Her photography work was steady. They had Paige, beautiful and with an eye for details, like her mother. They had a good life. Emily only began withdrawing recently.

Doug watched the morning sun paint the Rockies.

He had figured Emily's problems were related to her childhood here and the deaths of her parents. She would not, or could not, open up to him. She guarded her past, and despite his delicate probing, Doug was unsuccessful in learning more about that dark period of her life. At least she was getting counseling. It seemed to be working. Doug was counting on this trip to help resolve things. They were in this together.

If only the thing tormenting Emily were something alive, he would kill it for her. But how do you kill ghosts? He was powerless. It ate him up. Once they arrived, Emily infuriated him with her unwillingness or inability to tell him exactly what was the source of her anguish. They had come here to resolve things and still she held back. Until the other night. Dropping the mother of all loads on him: *She has a sister.* Then she clammed up. Instead of understanding, supporting her first major step to talk to him, he began an argument the next day. Emily walked off, headed up the trail to be alone to contemplate. It pissed him off further. So what did he do? Grabbed his ax, chopped wood like a madman, and took it out on Paige. He was furious with Emily. All Paige wanted to do was talk to him, but he screamed in her face until he wounded himself, then terrified her and chased her into the woods. *Chased her with an ax in my hand!* Ordering her away until she vanished into the Rocky Mountains. *How could I be so stupid? So cruel?*

Oh Christ. Paige, I am so sorry.

Doug ran his hand over his face. His heart felt as if it were about to shatter into a million pieces. He could hear the distant thumping of an approaching helicopter. Then he smelled fresh coffee and noticed a cup was being offered to him. By Pike Thornton.

"Thanks." Doug took a needed sip.

Thornton studied him from the brim of his cup.

"This chopper could be the FBI."

Doug's eyes met Thornton's and he did not like the way the old ranger was assessing him. So poker-faced.

"Doug, if there's anything you want to talk about, anything that's been troubling your mind"—the chopper grew louder—"now would be a good time to do it."

CHAPTER NINE

U.S. Marshal Rooster Cogburn squinted through his good eye and shouted across the plain at the outlaw Ned Pepper and his gang.

"I aim to kill you in one minute, Ned. Or see you hanged in Fort Smith at Judge Parker's convenience. Which'll it be?"

Pepper surveyed the odds of three against one, smiling. "I call that bold talk for a one-eyed fat man!" Pepper shouted back.

Special Agent Tracy Bowman pointed her remote at the TV, freezing the videotape. She turned to Mark, her nine-year-old son, slouched beside her on the couch, his hand resting in a nearly empty bowl of popcorn.

John Wayne's *True Grit* was their favorite movie; Rooster's standoff with Ned Pepper's gang their favorite part, the next line, their favorite line. It was a ritual with Mark's dad to stop the movie at this point to say the words together. Since his death a few years ago, Bowman kept the tradition.

Mark's bright eyes widened to respond to Pepper's taunting of Rooster as she chimed with her son:

"Fill your hands, you sonofabitch!"

Then Rooster said the line, commencing the shoot-out with Pepper's gang. Bowman smiled. It was another quiet night at home—just the two of them, with the lights dimmed, watching the movie in the living room of their modest home on a few acres outside of Lolo, Montana. Seeing the movie light flicker on Mark's face warmed her heart. She saw so much of Carl in him. How anguished those first months had been for her after Carl's death. Dreaming of him, reaching for him. Waking alone in their bed. She went through the motions of living without him. As months passed, her clothes gradually got pushed to the empty side of the closet. God, she missed him. Some days at home, she wore his old shirts that she had saved, loving how they still held his cologne, feeling him wrapped around her.

True Grit was Carl's movie.

He had operated a towing business based in Missoula. They were two solitary, shy people who met a lifetime ago it seemed, finding each other at a car wreck north of Milltown when she was a rookie Montana Highway Patrol officer. Got married in a little chapel in the valley south of town, built their own home near the Bitterroot River. Then she had Mark.

A few years later, when she learned the FBI was looking to hire more agents in Montana, Carl urged her to apply. "You're as sharp as the rest of them, Trace." She was accepted. Scored high during training and luckily landed a job at the Bureau's Missoula office downtown on West Front Street. Sometimes, Carl would meet her for lunch and they'd walk by the river.

Initially, she worked on government fraud cases, investigating corruption involving federal contracts, then on environmental crimes as part of multi-agency task forces.

She was among the dozens of agents who played a minor part in some of Montana's big cases—the arrest of the Unabomber near Lincoln, the Freemen standoff near Jordan. Those high-profile files involved agents from across the United States, and it was in Jordan during the militia operation she overheard two out-of-state female agents chuckling behind her back about her size.

After Mark's birth, Bowman had become some thirty pounds heavier than she should be for five feet seven inches. Her weight had been a lifelong struggle for her. She pretended she did not hear their remarks, but it hurt. She tried to shake it off; she knew she was fit, strong, a good, dedicated agent.

But somebody must have said something up the chain of command. For not long after the Freemen case ended peacefully with arrests, she was reminded constantly of fitness requirements and confined to computer work at her desk, assisting with NHQ on Internet crime.

The Bureau envisioned her post as holding potential to gather criminal intelligence, but that never really happened. Bowman became a vehicle for clerical requests made by other agents in the region needing data from the Internet. She soon tired of it. Many days, when she had little to do, she sat at her desk, chewing carrot and celery sticks, gazing out her office window, longing to be freed from her office job to do criminal investigative field work.

Then came the winter night Carl answered a radio call in a snowstorm. A bus carrying a girls' basketball team from Wyoming broke down on Interstate 90, west of Garrison. They had trouble getting someone to come out. Carl was on the road returning from business in Drummond. But he never made it home that night. He turned around to help the girls. Not long after he arrived, a Freightliner hauling Christmas toys for malls in Spokane jackknifed, crashing into the bus. Carl and one of the girls were killed.

Bowman's life changed forever that night. She thought she would never survive, but she hung on. For Mark. They helped each other.

It's okay if you feel like crying a little today, Mom, he would tell her in the months after it happened.

They endured.

After Carl's death, Bowman's attempts to escape her desk job seemed futile, but she did not give up. A few years later, she had shed some pounds but was still a little overweight. The hell with it, she thought, she was fit and strong and could perform her duties.

Her hope for a change came recently after she took more training at the Academy. Bowman had an analytical mind that took her to the top percentile when she completed specialized courses at Quantico in the Violent Crimes and Major Offenders Program. It covered everything from fugitives to sexual exploitation of children, kidnappings to assaults against the president. Bowman was hopeful her course work would make her a candidate for assignment to Violent Crimes, which had current openings in the Los Angeles, Chicago and Dallas divisions.

Just before Carl's death, Mark was diagnosed with a rare lung ailment. Those three cities had medical centers specializing in groundbreaking research on Mark's condition. It would give Bowman peace of mind to be close to one of them.

Medication helped Mark's lungs function properly, allowing him to live the normal life of a nine-year-old. He loved school, computers and dinosaurs. They had visited key sites in Montana, Colorado and Alberta. Mark designed his own dinosaur Web site and posted it on the Internet, which Bowman monitored. You never know what's lurking out there.

She was expecting to hear word on her applications for the out-of-town jobs any day now. She was originally from Miles City and was feeling bittersweet about the possibility of leaving Montana. The insurance claims had long been settled. She had sold Carl's business. They had a little money to start a new life. She and Mark both needed a fresh page, she thought, reaching into the popcorn bowl, watching Duke in all his glory, reins in his teeth, guns blazing.

Bowman's telephone rang. She grabbed it.

"Tracy, Roger Cole in Billings."

She sat up. Cole was the resident agent for Montana. "We've got a situation and you're going to be involved. In fact, your name came up from Washington for this."

Her mind raced. What could it be?

"It's a major investigative case out of Glacier National Park. A California girl missing in the wilderness. Ten years old. But there may be much more to it. A lot of political buttons have been pushed. There will be a multi-agency task force. We'll be working with the National Park Rangers, County; San Francisco PD is sending a body. We have the lead. Everything is being marshaled out of Salt Lake. Bowman, your file shows that before you were an agent and with Montana Highway Patrol, you were a seasonal ranger at Glacier, correct?"

"Yes, but, sir, I don't quite understand. I am the Internet GFP person out here."

"No, as of now, you've tentatively got the job at the Los Angeles Division. But I am sorry, Bowman, I have to hold my congratulations."

"I don't understand?"

"Look, I'm not very good at complicated political bull so I am going to tell you something so far off the record that they will take my testicles if they knew. Got it?"

"Yes, sir."

"Quantico was very impressed with your recent course results and so was Los Angeles. The supervisor at Quantico said you were, I'm reading notes here, 'blessed with incredible instinct and a natural talent for dissection.' You wowed them in the classroom. What I am saying is you have got the post in California; but unbeknownst to you, NHQ wants to see how you perform on this one. They picked you for this assignment because you are at the top of the curve. Our offices in Kalispell and Browning are down right now. Vacation, illness and assignments. At the moment you are the closest available FBI agent to the scene. Now, do you understand?''

''I don't believe this. I mean, I want Los Angeles for Mark, but I just can't—and I am not supposed to know this?''

''Know what?''

''Right.''

''Welcome to politics and policing. Bowman, this case is likely to attract attention. It is going to be investigated thoroughly from the outset. The brass does not want to risk having a legendary embarrassment, not only for us, but for several other agencies. The clock is ticking on this one.''

John Wayne was pinned under his horse. She watched him reaching for his gun as Ned Pepper neared to finish him off.

''But, sir, a little girl lost in the woods? With all due respect, aren't we overreacting? I'm sure the rangers can handle this.''

''I am sure you remember the Yellowstone case not too long ago.''

''Right.''

''No one wants a replay of that fiasco. The rangers at Glacier alerted us. There is suspicion that this could be a parental homicide. There are extenuating circumstances.''

''What sort of circumstances?''

''More details and bodies are coming in. You will be updated.''

Kim Darby had fallen into a pit and was eye to eye with an angry rattlesnake.

''Bowman, you will be partnered with Agent Frank Zander from Violent Crimes at NHQ.''

''I've heard that name before.''

''I have to warn you. Zander has a reputation for building a case against anybody on anything fast. His work has been critical to some of the big wins in organized crime, terrorism, kidnappings and serials.''

''Is that the warning about him?''

"He's a lone wolf, not a team player. A first-class prick void of personality. His wife recently left him."

Bowman tensed, muttering to herself, "Because of the prick part, or the personality part?"

"Anything else I should know about him?"

"He is already in the air. He'll run the show with Salt Lake and the rangers. You will work with him. Pack for the mountains. Have you been to Glacier recently?"

Bowman swallowed. "A couple of years ago." She and Carl used to go there with Mark.

"Zander's flying into Kalispell. You pick him up there, drive to West Glacier, grab some shut-eye. A chopper will be standing by to deliver you to the command site at daybreak. We expect the small joint task force to be assembled, formalize the game plan, and then begin immediately. Understand? We're pulling people from Great Falls, Helena, Billings, Coeur d'Alene, an army will come up from Seattle and Salt Lake. Lloyd Turner will supervise. We have to move fast; so much is at stake for everyone involved."

"Yes, sir."

"Good luck, Tracy."

Bowman hung up and put her face in her hands.

What had just happened?

Her mind was swirling. She had been given the new job she needed for Mark's health, for her peace of mind. But it was conditional she not drop the ball here on an NHQ file that was also a potential career ender. And she was to work with a man who comes with his own warning label. She had wanted to be sprung from her office prison, had wanted Violent Crimes, hadn't she?

Bowman peeked through her fingers to see Kim Darby bidding farewell to Rooster, whose horse reared as he removed his hat and waved good-bye.

"Well, come see a fat old man sometime," Rooster said

before his horse jumped a fence and galloped in the snow toward the mountains.

Mark had fallen asleep.

Bowman called her friend Roberta Cara, who had taken Mark in for several weeks when she went to Quantico. Roberta lived with her lawyer husband, J.T., and their seven children in a large ranch house south of Missoula. J.T. had handled Carl's will and business affairs.

"No problem, Tracy, I'll send a couple of the girls over to spend the night with him, then bring him here in the morning."

Gently, she woke Mark and told him that Roberta's daughters were coming to take care of him because she had an emergency assignment and she would be gone for a few days.

"Don't forget to call me, Mom, like when you went to Washington?" Mark threw his arms around her.

"Every day. I promise, Marshal." That was her nickname for him.

Smiling, Mark drifted back to sleep. She carried him to his bedroom, wrote him an *I love you and I will miss you* note, then began packing. First for him, then for herself, finishing just as the girls arrived. She briefed them on Mark's medication and schedule, then wrote it down for Roberta, leaving her cell phone and Salt Lake Division numbers. She lugged her bag to her Chevy Blazer SUV and headed for Interstate 93.

The drive to Kalispell would take well over an hour. For some strange reason, as she started out, she suddenly thought about Isaiah Hood, the killer who was going to be executed in a few days in Deer Lodge. Why did he come to mind? His case had been in the *Missoulian* recently. Hood was awaiting his appeal to the U.S. Supreme Court, which was based on the new claim that he was innocent. Why was she suddenly thinking of him? She shrugged it off, concentrating on the case at hand. Was her cell phone plugged in? When she looked to check, it began trilling, startling her for a second before she answered.

"Bowman."

"Who is this? Who have I got?" A gruff male voice.

"Agent Tracy Bowman, FBI. Who is this, please?"

"Frank Zander. You are the local assigned to this case with me?"

Sounded to her like he said "yokel," but the line hissed with static.

"That's correct."

"Where are you?"

"En route to Kalispell to meet you at the airport. Where are you?"

"I'm calling from the plane on an air phone. I stop in Salt Lake for a quick connect to Montana. I'll be there in a couple of hours. Can you get to a secure fax? I have a priority report I want you to have right away."

Bowman's brain raced as she drove. "Yes."

"Well, give me the number." His tone was condescending. She recited the fax number.

"I do not know that number as secure for your region."

"It is secure."

"All right, it will be on its way once our conversation ends."

"Fine."

"Bowman, do you know Pike Thornton, a ranger at Glacier?"

"Not really. I know of him."

"Do you know Inspector Sydowski with the SFPD?"

"No."

"Do you know anything about this file, about suspected criminal intent?"

"I have been briefed."

"You're with—what is it?—Internet liaison? GFP?" It sounded like he was reading something alien. "I never heard—and this is your first investigation?"

"Yes."

"You sure *you* are on this case? Did they call the right person out there?"

"Yes."

"Then that fax number you gave me better be secure. There will be no breaches of security. Understood?"

Two minutes and Bowman could not stand Zander. She was nervous and green, but she was not an idiot.

"Agent Zander, is the plane you are on Bureau or commercial?"

"Commercial."

"You alone on it?"

"No."

"I am alone in a Chevy Blazer on a Montana highway. The only threat to security is roadkill. You are discussing an active case in a public place. Look around at the other passengers pretending not to hear any of the words you just shouted at me. Is that procedure with you big guns in Washington?"

His line hissed with silence.

Just shot myself in the foot, Bowman thought, her mind reeling with the names of all the major cases Zander had likely worked and how for the last few months her major investigation was how to get a new mouse for her computer. Suddenly, she was painfully self-conscious of her inexperience, her weight, her self-esteem. *That does it. I am toast.*

"The fax is on its way. I will call you within the hour," Zander said, ending their conversation.

Bowman immediately punched a number on her phone, glancing at the Chevy's dash clock. She had twenty minutes before they closed.

"Turly's Gas, Don speaking."

"Don, it's Tracy. Sweetie, do me a favor, please. Put paper in your fax machine and turn it on. I got something coming in right now. Boring stuff about Mark's medical condition from an FBI friend whose family is going through the same thing. I'll be there in five minutes to get it and fill up, too."

"Sure, Trace, no problem."

Bowman scanned the nine-page fax while Don filled her

Blazer's tank and checked her oil. Her stomach knotted. The rangers were right; this one had a very bad aura given what she saw in the notes and the summary of the old SFPD complaint. The father's wound, the family's demeanor and evasiveness would warrant serious concern after their daughter vanished. How long had she been missing now? Bowman checked her watch.

Pulling out of Turly's, driving deeper into the night and the Rocky Mountains, she realized that she was heading into a significant case. One that was going to draw plenty of attention: a mother and father grappling with their fears for their lost daughter while the FBI investigates the suspicion that one, or both of them, killed her.

CHAPTER TEN

FBI Special Agent Frank Zander watched the icon on his laptop computer indicate his fax had gone through. He disconnected the computer line from the plane's air phone. Repositioning himself in his seat, he subtly inventoried his immediate area. The jet was sprinkled with passengers. Zander was alone in his section, the row of seats to himself to stretch out. Still, that Montana agent was right. He was guilty of risking security.

Who was she anyway? This Tracy Bowman from, what the hell was it, Internet GFP in Missoula? So she scored high on course work and was near the scene. That was justification for inflicting her on him? He had no time for training a junior agent. Maybe she was good. Maybe she was somebody's favor. Zander shook his head. Nobody talked to him that way. He did not need her . . .or any women in his life, for that matter.

He shut down his computer, set it aside, switched off the overhead reading lights and peered out the window at the night. He had digested everything they had so far on this case and formulated a plan on how he would go at it. Before he landed in Montana, he would go over everything once more and fine-tune his strategy. For now, he should try to get some sleep. Thirty-five thousand feet below, he saw the lights of cities and towns flowing by. He sometimes felt he lived in jet planes. With this Montana case, he would have investigated in all fifty states. What an achievement to go with his broken marriages. Some people get gold watches, a nice pen. What did he have? A collection of court papers calling him the defendant.

His first wife was Denise, the nurse at George Washington. They were young, sexually addicted to each other but incompatible as spouses. After three years, it ended as passionately as it began, with dishes smashed, screaming, tears, door-slamming and a call from her lawyer. Last he had heard, Denise had moved to London, married a doctor, had a baby girl.

Meredith, his second wife, ended things quietly six months ago with an e-mail. Error-free, grammatically correct, as surgically effective as a scalpel to the heart. That was her style. Zander could just imagine her calendar that day, certain it went something like: *White House Counsel meet, book spa, New York trip, Ritz for one hour of illicit sex with DA lawyer in Manhattan, alert husband it is over, pick up gown for Lincoln Center gala.* They lasted six years until she typed the words, "As of this date, I am seeking a divorce." Typical of Washington's cover-your-ass bureaucracy. "As of this date." *Nice one, Meredith.* Near the end, when she booked the sessions with the counselor for them, she never made the appointments. Twice, he had sat alone in the waiting room of the counselor's office in Alexandria, leafing through the same outdated copy of *People* magazine. Looking out at the Potomac and the capital, realized her no-shows were intended to humiliate him. A metaphor for her middle finger.

He remembered that day he received her marriage-ending e-mail, he typed back five words.

"I know you're fucking Pearson."

She responded, "Good."

She loved what he loathed: the power, the politics, the parties, the sycophants, the networking. It actually turned her on. He was a federal cop who dreamed about escaping his life inside the Beltway to a place with real people, who looked you in the eye and meant what they said. A place like Montana or Idaho. Lots of antigovernment sentiment there. *I'd fit right in,* he laughed to himself. But for now, he'd settle for his small rented bungalow on a dead-end street shaded by a forest in College Park, near the university. Thank God, no kids. Zander then realized he was forty-three, and it saddened him.

For the past twenty years of his life, the only marriage that had worked for him was the one between him and his job. Zander had always been a front-line agent. He had developed a reputation for being a stubborn, thorough, SOB investigator, one of the Bureau's best. He missed nothing. It was common for him to be assigned to the FBI's top teams on major files, like Oklahoma City, Lockerbie, the World Trade Center. He joined Bureau teams assisting other police agencies, or helping salvage a messed-up case. His expertise grew out of his early successes in crimes against children: parental kidnappings, exploitation, stranger abductions. Zander took those cases personally. He was the champion of the victim, and virtually everyone else, living or dead, was a suspect in his eyes until he seized the truth by the throat and presented the file for prosecution.

Whenever his name came up—and it always did—whenever agents sat around over a beer, the younger ones would inevitably ask: *Anybody work with Frank Zander? What's his story? I hear that guy is a cold machine, a guilt detector. He does not miss. Was he born that way or constructed in a secret basement lab in the Hoover Building?* Case-hardened agents, those who knew, would usually recount a variation of the legend that circulated among the tribal camps of the FBI across the country.

Francis Miller Zander was a rookie working a junior role for the Bureau assisting locals in Georgia. A young mother of two small boys, who lived in a rural trailer park, supporting her family as a hairdresser, reported her older son missing. She told police she suspected that her abusive ex-husband, with the help of one of his ex-con friends, took the boy with him to Florida, violating a custody order. The mother's story held up because the abusive ex had done time and had been seen in the area arguing with her. The locals and supporting lead agent went with it, letting their guard down, concentrating on the information she provided. Soon the locals and the Bureau and Florida police were all over the ex.

But Zander had a bad feeling about the mother from the start. He noticed empty whiskey bottles in her trash, saw a variety of medication in her medicine cabinet. He also noticed, under the seat of the mother's car, a crumpled toll receipt for the Florida Turnpike dated the day she said her boy vanished. Zander was a rookie; the local old boys knew the ex, a cop hater who gave off the vibe that he would have done anything "to hurt that bitch who put him in jail."

They found the little boy's body in a Florida swamp near the apartment complex where the ex-con lived. Days later, while the full force of the investigation remained focused on the ex, the mother in Georgia vanished with the younger boy, who was four.

They found the mother and the four-year-old in their van at an I-75 rest stop between Lexington and Cincinnati. She had tied a plastic bag over her son's head and had overdosed herself on pills from six different prescriptions.

Within fourteen months of that case, every cop connected to it had resigned from police work, unable to deal with the fact a child was murdered right under their noses. The lead FBI agent took his own life. He died in a single-vehicle traffic fatality. Cops knew how guys did it so their families still got the insurance. Zander nearly resigned. He could not forgive himself for also buying the mother's story, for not speaking up, for not insisting they go harder on the mother.

He vowed from that point on never to fear getting in some-one's face, to never hold back. He would never apologize, and would follow every gut instinct no matter whose feelings he hurt. He vowed to assume that everyone was hiding something, that no one told the truth at first, and to never, ever lose sight of the reason why he had to be that way. To remind himself, Zander would go to a little cemetery outside a small Georgia town every year or so, and he would look at the headstone under a peach tree.

Two very good reasons were buried there.

The jet began its descent to Salt Lake City. Zander fired up his laptop and opened his file on the Baker family. This time, he reviewed the photographs of them, the recent ones Emily Baker had given to the rangers.

He studied the girl's face. Sun in her eyes. Hugging her beagle. Smiling in the majestic Rockies against a blue sky. A pretty California kid. Her name was Paige Baker. She had her mother's eyes.

Emily Baker was thirty-five. Attractive. A photographer. Looked energetic. Zander gently covered her smile with his finger, concentrating on her eyes. They betrayed something unsettled about her. Something sad.

Whatever it is, Emily, you are going to tell me.

Zander's eyes then met those of Doug Baker. The former U.S. Marine sergeant. The high school teacher. Football coach. Positions of authority. Positions of control.

Did you lose control, Doug? How did you hurt your hand? What was going on in the time before your daughter had vanished?

How long had she been gone now? Zander checked the file. Made his best estimate. Thirty-one hours. Zander set a special timer on his Swiss watch, adjusting it to tell him at a glance how many hours had passed since Paige Baker disappeared into the Rocky Mountains. They had to move fast on this one. He was going to have to push it. Smart and hard. He closed his laptop. Soon he would learn the truth about Doug and Emily: every fear, every heartbreak, every secret. If the Bakers were hiding something, he would find out.

He always did.

CHAPTER ELEVEN

The sun was setting when Reed stopped his rented Taurus as instructed by the Montana Highway Patrol officer at the West Gate of Glacier National Park.

"Who you with?"

"The *San Francisco Star.*"

The officer directed him to where the rangers had set up the command center. It was busy with people and vehicles coming and going. Reed saw TV-news satellite trucks from Spokane, another from Great Falls. A ranger was explaining something to news crews, while handing out sheets of paper. It was an updated press release on the search for Paige Baker and an advisory explaining how federal authorities had designated the airspace over Grizzly Tooth restricted. No TV or still news cameras could fly over the area. It was dangerous to aerial search operations. This angered the networks who were arguing about establishing elevation levels for the press, or at least pool access.

"We'll sort it out in the morning. We'll discuss reviewing

the restriction with the park superintendent and the incident commander,'' the ranger told the TV people. For that evening, no press could access the area, period. They could drive to the trailhead, which was nearly ninety minutes away by way of Going-to-the-Sun Road, then the Icefields Highway. But all information would be coordinated from the community center.

"Where are the parents?" a TV crew member asked. "Can you bring them here now?"

"They're deep in the trail at the command post. At this point, the only way in and out is by chopper, really. We'll look into the request."

Aware his deadline was ticking, Reed needed to find better data. He strolled around the area of small and large buildings. At the rear of one, he found a young ranger talking on his radio. Reed kept a respectful distance until he was finished, then approached him.

The ranger was in his early twenties, built like a college defensive tackle. A blond brush cut, ruddy tanned face. From what Reed overheard, he was one of the first searchers to the family's campsite. He had just returned to gather more maps and radios before heading back to resume searching at dawn. Sensing the guy was pumped from the search, Reed took advantage, drawing him into a quick conversation.

"Sorry, they sent me to wait for somebody over here."

"Who you looking for, I can—"

Reed cut him off. "They say the parents are having a rough time?"

"Yeah." The ranger nodded. "They're pretty shook up. She ran off yesterday afternoon. Looks like she was chasing her dog. Rained last night, washing away her trail. It's been well over twenty-four hours. I don't get it. Why did her parents take her there? That region is for advanced hikers, experienced hikers."

"I guess it doesn't look good."

"Not good at all. Elevations are high. The temperature drops drastically. We could get snow. There are bears up that way who feed in that sector. Between you and me, if we don't find a trace of her soon, some kind of sign, we're not looking for a lost kid, we're looking for a dead one."

"Who else we got helping?"

"The FBI's got jurisdiction. Nobody really knows what they're doing—" The young ranger stopped himself. "Who did you say you're with? You're with SAR, right? I'm a seasonal. Was at Yellowstone last year. I just finished some rescue training on Grizzly Tooth a few weeks back—"

"Ronnie!" Somebody from inside called the ranger, who pointed a finger down at Reed. "You better not be a reporter, pal." Then he shouted: "Coming!" Then back to Reed as they parted. "You're with SAR, right?"

Reed waved but did not answer.

Back near the satellite news trucks, one of the rangers was standing in a halo of white light, a small microphone clipped to his shirt, an earphone inserted in his left ear as he talked to a camera, summarizing the search for Paige Baker. He said nothing about what Reed had learned from the young searcher. As the ranger wrapped up, Reed overheard a crew member saying that the feed had gone smoothly to CNN. When the TV interview ended, Reed, along with several arriving reporters, talked to the ranger.

The story was skyrocketing, Reed thought later, making notes from the on-the-record interview with the ranger who was on TV, mixing in details from his conversation with the searcher and the press release.

He tried his cell phone, getting through to the *Star*'s night desk, coming up on first-edition deadline. Alyce Buchanan, a senior copy editor, took his material. He could hear her keyboard clicking rapidly as he read to her from his notebook.

"Things look pretty dire for our little San Francisco girl, don't they, Tom?" Buchanan said when Reed finished.

"Yeah. Very grave."

"Your stuff will likely top Molly's for front. She's on the phone and asked me to tell you to check your e-mail in the morning. She has stuff for you. Says it will all be there."

"Got it. Thanks, Alyce."

Reed drove to the Sunshine Motel outside Kalispell, where he had reserved a room. He had a late supper of nachos and a ginger ale at the sports bar while watching the Mariners game on the big-screen TV. He reflected on Ann and how lucky he was to have her and Zach. Wondering, for an intense moment, where things could have gone had he taken Molly up on her offer. He pushed the empty nachos plate aside, pulled out his cell phone and made a short call home to say good night to Ann and Zach. Then he called the rangers while watching the game.

"Command center, Wilcox."

"Tom Reed, *San Francisco Star*. Any developments in the search?"

"None. Things have tapered off for the night. Operations will resume at first light with more personnel."

Reed went to his room, settling into his comfortable bed, thinking of what it must be like for a ten-year-old girl lost in the Rockies with nothing but the night, the cold, the dog. Nothing for her hunger to feed on but her fear. Jesus. Reed shuddered under his blankets.

Only one thing could be worse.

Daddy's got a hurt hand.

Reed tried to imagine the terror Paige Baker would have felt in the final seconds, knowing her father was going to . . . Reed drew on the images of his son, Zach, the horror in his boy's little eyes when he exploded on him during the dark days, his drinking days. Back when he had lost himself in an investigative series on the murder of a two-year-old girl who was abducted and whose body was found in a garbage bag in Golden Gate Park . . . Christ.

The picture of Paige Baker smiling in the mountains. Would it haunt him like the others he had written about? Was she alive? What the hell happened out there? Maybe Sydowski would tell him? He had to find him.

DAY 3

DAY 3

CHAPTER TWELVE

The pilot of the idling FBI helicopter at West Glacier signaled to Zander and Bowman that it was clear to board.

They emptied the remainder of their coffees on the ground, tossed their paper cups in the trash, and trotted to the pad, crouching against the noise and pulsating air currents that whip-snapped their jackets. They buckled in with Zander next to the pilot. He lifted off without wasting a second as morning broke.

It had now been some thirty-eight hours since Paige Baker vanished in the backcountry.

"The command post's at Grizzly Tooth," the pilot said. "Should have you there in twenty-five minutes. A lot of up-drafts with that range. Ride could get rough."

Zander nodded.

Behind those classic FBI aviator sunglasses, with the early light in his face, Zander cut an attractive but icy all-American profile, Bowman thought as they swept over the Rockies. He was stone-cold, all business.

It was evident when she picked him up a few hours ago at

Kalispell and they made their way to her Blazer and the motel.
He was wearing a sport coat, no tie. About six foot one, 180,
with a solid, firm build. Deep-set blue eyes, square-jawed, dark
hair. No smile. The instant she saw him she felt self-conscious
about the way she had bitched at him over the phone. Zander
stared into the night, checking the luminescent face of his
watch, saying nothing as they came to the motel. Bowman
saw three TV-news satellite trucks parked there and felt the
magnitude, the immensity of this case building. Was she ready
for this? She wanted to call Mark. It was too late. She took a
few deep breaths and forced herself to calm down and relax.

She thought of Paige out there in the night.

Alone. Lost. Dead?

That morning, during their predawn drive from the motel to
the chopper, Zander told Bowman of their objectives, talking
almost in point form. Confident. Authoritative. Cold. He knew
what he was doing.

"Everything is confidential. This is the FBI's file and I am
the case agent. Publicly, we are assisting the National Park
Service in a missing person's case. Operationally, we are conducting an investigation on the assumption foul play is involved.
Only the primary investigators will know this, those from NPS
and the inspector from SFPD. It is a small JTF. Our job is
to eliminate foul play here, or establish the foundation for
prosecuting a case. We are not here to make friends with Mom
and Dad. With a situation like this, you only get one shot. It
is critical you start the process as quickly as possible. This is
going to require careful work, knowing when and how to push
and when to back off. Got it?"

"So what do you expect from me?"

"To do as I tell you."

"The parents are going to get suspicious right off."

"Drive home the point that we are here assisting, ruling out all possible scenarios, for the sake of their daughter. Insist they keep all discussions confidential, for the sake of their daughter."

Some twenty-two minutes after lifting off, the command post came into view as they made their approach to the ridge. Zander locked onto the small tents belonging to the Bakers and the dozen or so people on the ridge steadying themselves against the force of the descending helicopter. Pike Thornton, law enforcement ranger, and Brady Brook, the district ranger who was the incident commander, greeted Zander and Bowman, taking them aside privately, waiting for the helicopter's rotors to stop so they could speak. Everyone knew not to waste time after it was stressed the rangers were in charge of the search and rescue, and the FBI was in charge of everything else.

"Search is going full bore," Brook said. "We got two hasty teams out there within an hour or so of the father's report. They put in about six hours yesterday, covered a lot of territory."

"Find anything? Clothing, candy wrappers, human excrement. Anything?" Zander said.

Brook shook his head. "We're increasing the search. Got more people coming in as soon as possible. We're setting up a command center at park headquarters for you. Your Salt Lake people are coordinating your help in the operation. We're restricting all of Grizzly Tooth, keeping the press there at the center. This is snowballing, since the alert went out over the news wires. The networks are already demanding briefings and access."

Zander nodded. "We'll sort that out, but I expect your chief will designate a press person," he said. "I am sure you are informing park staff the FBI is merely assisting in the search of a missing child in a federal park and they should not under any circumstances discuss anything with the press."

"Absolutely," Brook said.

"More of our people will be arriving within a few hours with equipment. Everyone will be, or should be, directed to the center." Zander checked to ensure they were out of earshot from the rest of the team on the ridge, including the parents. Satisfied they were separated by nearly forty yards, he said, "Pike, we've read the information you provided. What's your read on the parents?"

"I don't think they've told us the whole story. Dad's evasive. Got that nasty wound on his left hand. Something just isn't sitting right."

"What about the moth . . . ," Bowman began, but Zander raised her hand as if she were a child speaking out of turn. He halted her question, then hijacked it.

"What's your read on the mother, Pike?" Zander said.

"Well, it's hard to put your finger on it. But it just doesn't add up with her, either. She said she was nowhere near this camp when her daughter disappeared. Had gone off down the wooded trail to the ridge about a hundred yards to sit alone and take in the view. That could very well be the case."

"But . . . ," Zander said.

Thornton exchanged a glance with Brook.

"A few hours ago in the middle of the night, the mother had a bit of an emotional outburst, screaming into the mountains. That would be in keeping with her daughter being lost. But the few words we could make out were disturbing."

"What were they?" Zander said.

Thornton took out his notebook and quoted Emily. " 'You can't have her. . . . Oh God, it is all my fault.' "

For a moment, the four of them grappled with the significance. Bowman felt a chill but repeated the words to herself and considered the circumstances. Zander remained poker-faced.

"The father also said they had encountered another family on the trail yesterday. A mom, a dad, and a boy about ten. He said they seemed strange to him."

"Strange how?"

"Didn't specify."

"You looking for any witnesses, people in this area at the time?"

"We're going through permits," Thornton said. "Can't hike in here overnight without one, which requires a name and address, vehicle plate, contact person. It's routine in case a hiker gets lost or hurt."

Zander nodded.

"What about Dad's history?" Thornton asked him. "You get much there?"

"We've got something but it requires more work. We'll need the SFPD to help us there. Their guy, what's his name, Sydowski? He arrive?"

"Got in last night and will meet you at the command center," Brook said.

"Good," Zander answered. "Time for us to say hello to Mom and Dad. Bowman and I will go alone, if you don't mind."

Zander and Bowman could not see Emily as they approached the tent area, where Doug waited to meet them, catching the FBI seal on Zander's jacket.

Zander extended his hand. "Doug Baker?"

"Yes."

"Frank Zander. FBI." Zander ignored Bowman. She introduced herself.

Doug regarded both. He was tired, unshaven, tense.

"The rangers said you were coming but we don't understand. Our daughter is lost out there. She could be hurt. How does the FBI help us with that? We need more searchers, more people looking for Paige. Not police. And why the FBI?"

"Doug," Zander said, "more searchers are on their way. A huge search and rescue operation is being coordinated. This area will soon be saturated with people determined to find your daughter."

"We need them here now. We can't waste any more time." Baker rubbed his reddened eyes. "She's just a little girl out there.'' Zander looked at Doug's injured left hand. "So why is the FBI here?"

"Federal parks are our jurisdiction. We get involved in all serious matters, especially those involving children. Your daughter's case is very serious. It is important. We're calling in a lot of people from a lot of agencies to make sure we do everything right."

"Like what?"

"Making sure we haven't missed any possibilities."

"She just wandered off, likely chasing Kobee, her dog. What other possibilities could there be?"

"That's where we need your help, Doug."

Zander was smooth, Bowman thought, seeing how a gentle, assuring conversation was evolving into something more.

"What do you mean?"

"Did you see anything or anybody that strikes you as strange or odd during your time here, or on the way?"

"I don't see how that has got anything to do with this. I'm telling you she just wandered off."

"Doug, please. Was there anything?"

Baker thought about it. "Just that other family we met. Might have been our first day in. We were tired and stopped for lunch and they just came upon us, spying on us. Just staring. I mentioned that to the rangers. But we left in separate directions. You're writing this down? You think that might be important?"

"Could be. We have to be thorough."

"You don't think that somehow they—that someone—"

"Doug, it's our job to eliminate all other scenarios here as quickly as possible. The search is a priority and it will be exhaustive, but we will also examine everything else."

The nylon of one of the family's blue tents swished and Emily emerged in jeans and a flannel shirt. Her hair was mussed and her eyes reddened. She was exhausted, stressed. Approaching Doug and the agents, she lost her balance and slipped. Bowman caught her. "Easy there," Bowman said.

Doug introduced Emily to the agents, explaining their presence as his wife struggled to grasp it. Shaking her head, a hand covering her mouth, she stood, with eyes glistening, as Zander asked her about anything or anybody that struck her as strange in the time before they entered the park and the time leading up to her daughter's disappearance.

"Nothing," she said.

Zander studied her, watching her reaction, reading her body language in relation to her husband's as he explained how Paige's photograph and details had been circulated widely to news and police agencies.

"You think that maybe she didn't just get lost?" Emily said. "You think someone in the park may have abducted her? Oh God!" Doug comforted her.

"Emily, we have nothing to suggest that," Zander said. "We just don't want to overlook anything. It's a big park. And we need your help to make sure we don't miss anything. Please understand that we will use every resource to ensure Paige is returned safely to you. I trust you would expect nothing less. But your help is critical."

Emily nodded and sniffled. "What can we do to help you?"

"We'd like to fly you with us to the ranger command center. To talk to you some more in a comfortable place. As I said, we've got a team of people there from different agencies. Everybody's got a different job but we just need a little time for more information from you to be effective as quickly as possible. It is easier than bringing everybody out here."

"But what if Paige comes back, or they find her while we're gone? She'll need us," Emily said. "We should be here."

"That's right," Zander said. "One of you should be here. So we'll take you in separately."

Emily nodded.

So did Doug, but secretly he was uneasy.

". . . take you in separately . . ."

Doug did not like this. Did not like sensing that something

more was happening. He could not see it in Zander's or Bowman's eyes but felt they were concealing knowledge about Paige's disappearance. He had no idea what it could be. Maybe he was wrong. Maybe it was nothing. He was exhausted. He had not slept. He was sick with worry. Not thinking clearly. He was glad for the FBI's presence. Yet something gnawed at him. Doug thought about that other family. How strange they seemed, spying on his family's argument.

". . . it's a big park . . ."

What if someone had been stalking them, had taken Paige? Is that it? The FBI suspected a crime?

Jesus.

Doug ran his hands over his face, not realizing that Emily was telling him something as the helicopter's rotors began slicing the air. "Doug, I'll go with Frank and Tracy now." Then kissing his cheek. Watching her turn to wave before crouching, boarding the idling chopper. The noise and wind as it lifted off, disappearing

. . . vanishing like Paige . . .

Doug sat down, thrusting his head into his hands. Overwhelmed, looking into the mountains, he begged them to return his daughter.

CHAPTER THIRTEEN

The phone jangled. Reed's 5:15 A.M. wake-up call. He lifted, then replaced the handset. His body was locked on 4:15 Pacific Time. He nestled into his warm bed. Disoriented. Automatically he reached for Ann, feeling nothing, forcing his drowsy brain to focus.

In Montana. Lost girl. Story. Deadlines. Coffee. Food. Work. Let's go.

Reed's body felt like lead as he started the room's coffee-maker, then went to the bathroom and began rubbing his electric razor over his face. *Montana. Come home to Big Sky Country.* He had not spent time here since the Freemen standoff in Jordan, during which the FBI arrested the Unabomber in Lincoln. The warm aroma of fresh coffee soon filled the motel room. Reed gulped some, then stepped into the shower. The hot water eased his early-morning pain. Maybe he was getting too old for this. He had just turned thirty-four. He chuckled at himself as the water soothed him. Sure. Too old. He was ancient. At times, it seemed like his life was nothing but airplanes, deadlines, lonely hotels and apologies to his wife.

Toweling off, Reed checked the local time on the coffee-maker's digital clock: 5:55 A.M. The motel's Mountaineer Restaurant began serving Sunriser Breakfasts at six. He drank more coffee while dressing. He switched on the local TV stations and the room's radio to catch any news updates on the story. For all he knew, the drama could have ended.

The search for Paige Baker was the lead item of the newscasts. Her face glowed from the TV screen under the graphic, LOST IN MOUNTAINS. A female reporter was gripping a mike and reporting live from the command center. There wasn't much new. The reporter listed agencies involved, which included the FBI because it was a federal park and the Royal Canadian Mounted Police and Waterton Park officials who were helping on the Canadian side. "Over forty hours after Paige Baker became lost in the mountains, the search continues," the reporter said. No mention of the San Francisco Police Department. Maybe Harry Lance was jerking his chain and Sydowski's not here, he thought, grabbing his computer, then heading to the restaurant.

Reed bought a few newspapers, the *Daily Interlake,* the *Great Falls Tribune, USA Today,* and found a booth. A dour-looking waitress took his order of a Denver omelette with hash browns, white toast and milk. A postage-stamp-size photo of Paige Baker stared from an inside page of *USA Today*. It was accompanied by a summary of the news release. The story was front-page news in the Montana papers, a larger picture of Paige, a photo of the rangers with gear boarding a helicopter, a map of Glacier National Park with a box and arrow near the Canadian border showing where she was lost. Not much new in the stories. But one thing in the *Interlake,* the local paper, caught Reed's attention. It was buried deep in the story: "A park official said they would check backcountry camping permits for possible witnesses in the girl's case." Witnesses? Why that phrase? Witness to what? Likely just routine, Reed thought, sipping some coffee, but it made him curious.

Reed pulled out his laptop computer and switched it on. While it fired up, he sipped coffee and scanned the *Interlake*'s story below the fold on Isaiah Hood, the killer on death row whose execution was coming up. Hood was now claiming innocence and awaiting word on a last-minute appeal to the U.S. Supreme Court. All these years on death row and now he claims he didn't do it. Reed shook his head. Many condemned killers do that as their death date nears.

And some have been proven innocent.

Hood had killed a little girl, Rachel Ross, in Glacier National Park over twenty years ago. Hood's appeal said he was convicted on shaky testimony and circumstantial evidence, arguments lower courts had not bought. Not really much out of the ordinary here, Reed concluded as his computer beeped it was ready.

He connected his cell phone to his computer and entered the commands to access the *Star*'s computers in San Francisco. His breakfast arrived and Reed ate as the phone and computer began a soft symphony of digital-cyber trilling and beeping before connecting him to the paper. He brought up the front page of that morning's edition. His story was below the fold under the headline S.F. GIRL MISSING IN ROCKIES. The bylines were Tom Reed and Molly Wilson with a Glacier National Park, Montana, placeline.

Paige Baker's pretty face, as she snuggled her beagle, Kobee, stared in color from the front page. The story was a thirty-inch hard-news piece. It encompassed the unofficial fear held by some rangers that given the rugged region and conditions, the prospect of the ten-year-old child not surviving the ordeal was terribly real. Reed forced away sudden images of Paige Baker freezing in the mountains.

The article turned to page 3, filling the top half with a wire photo of searchers, shots of Doug and Emily Baker, and a

graphic locating Montana, the park and the area being searched.
Doug Baker was a high school teacher and popular football
coach. Emily was a freelance photographer. Their San Francisco
friends were worried. Some wanted to fly to Montana to volunteer as searchers. Nothing negative in the piece about their
family history. Nothing about police suspicions.

Reed ate a few forkfuls of hash browns and omelette, then
opened his e-mail and found Molly's note. It was hurried,
almost in point form:

> *TOM: TALKED WITH TURGEON IN HOMICIDE.
> OFF THE RECORD, SFPD IS DEFINITELY "DOING
> ROUTINE CHECKS ON BAKER FAMILY." HAVE
> CONFIRMED THAT SYDOWSKI IS IN MONTANA TO
> HELP FBI AND RANGERS (THAT ANGLE IS ALL
> OURS, SO FAR). EMILY BAKER USED TO LIVE IN
> MONTANA, MAYBE THAT IS WHY FAMILY WENT
> THERE??? EMILY'S AUNT WILLA AND UNCLE HUCK
> MEYERS LIVE IN SF BUT ARE ON RV HOLIDAY IN
> THE EAST. AUNT KNOWS MORE ABOUT FAMILY. I
> HAVE GOT TO REACH THEM SOMEHOW. YOU
> WORK SYDOWSKI AT YOUR END AND I'LL WORK
> THINGS AT MINE. TALK LATER, COWBOY.—MOLLY.
> CELL 415-555-7199*

Reed finished off his breakfast quickly, convinced that
beneath the surface of this story something very dark was
lurking. The rangers were checking for "possible witnesses in
the girl's case." He pondered that, clicking back to the picture
of Paige Baker on his computer screen, glimpsing his cluttered
table and the ancient grainy photo in the Montana paper of
Rachel Ross, the little girl murdered years ago in Glacier. The
children resembled each other. Funny how that was, when kids
were about the same age. Reed overheard a reporter a few
tables over gesturing to no one and talking loudly on his cell

phone. The guy was pretty pissed at being punted to the story from his news organization's Chicago Bureau, when it was supposed to be covered by its Denver Bureau. Reed packed up, paid up, then left, estimating that Paige Baker had now been lost for forty-two hours.

On his way back to the park, Reed passed two slow-moving news trucks, one from Salt Lake City, the other from Seattle. Helicopters whomped by overhead before Reed reached the command center, which had blossomed over night with more satellite trucks, news vans and cars crammed into the area near the building.

After finding a parking spot, Reed learned a news conference was planned for some point in the day. He inventoried the vehicles and activity—a lot of state and federal cars and trucks, an increasing number of grim-faced officials coming and going, mixing with the press crowd, which was loud with cell phone chatter, idling diesels, hydraulic adjusting of satellite dishes, antennas, newspeople yelling to each other. Amid the bustle, Reed spotted someone familiar. All alone, leaning against a car, he was looking through his bifocals at pages on a clipboard. Reed approached him.

"Excuse me, Officer, can you point the way to San Francisco?"

Inspector Walt Sydowski's eyes widened slightly at seeing Reed.

"And it started out being a good morning."

"I am so happy to see you, too, Walter. It's been how long?"

"Not long enough, Reed. Go away."

Reed planted himself toe to toe with Sydowski, who looked around to ensure they were not drawing anyone's attention.

"Walt, I am not leaving until you help me with the obvious."

"*Boychick,* have I not taught you anything? You should be home with your family, counting your blessings." Sydowski went back to his clipboard.

"Walter." Reed dropped his voice. "What is the best homicide cop with the SFPD doing here?"

Sydowski looked up to the peaks, blinking, remembering what happened the last time Reed tried this dance with him.

"I got nothing to say to you, Reed."

"There's more going on here than a search for a child lost in the woods, right, Walt?"

A low, distant thunder rumbled. A helicopter, one returning from the command post, was approaching.

"I have to go, Reed."

CHAPTER FOURTEEN

The cutlery on the table rattled as a helicopter passed over the crowded Eagle's Nest Restaurant, a log cabin in central Glacier National Park. It was filled with the aroma of bacon and the murmur of customers hunched over coffee, talking about the activity out there.

"What do you think is going on, Dad?" Twelve-year-old Joey Ropa looked out the window.

"Guys at the counter said it was a search for somebody lost in the backcountry," Joey's mother, Lori, said.

Her husband Bobby's attention was outside in the parking lot, on the arrival of two park ranger trucks and a Montana Highway Patrol four-by-four. Their waitress arrived, taking their orders, chatting.

"So are you guys from Brooklyn? I love your accents."

"You know what's going on outside?" Bobby said.

"A mountain rescue, or something. I'll get a newspaper for you."

After collecting the menus, she left.

"Why you pumping her, Bobby? We're on vacation." Lori pulled postcards from her bag, spreading them out.

Bobby steepled his fingers, mulling something eating at him from the other day when they were coming out of Grizzly Tooth. Something unsettling. Ah, maybe it was nothing. Forget about it. Why get in a knot over it? He looked around the restaurant—a great place, log cabin motif. Cedar floors and tables. Rustic. The fragrance of the forest, the frying bacon. He loved it.

This trip was a celebration of sorts for his promotion and Lori getting a raise as a manager with the Port Authority. They were thinking of moving to Glen Ridge, or buying a cabin. He should be thinking in that direction, not on something from the other day on their trail. He said little when the food came. He watched the parking lot, the increasing activity with the rangers.

"What is it, Bobby?" Lori knew. "What's your quandary?"

"I should have said something."

"About what?"

"The other day."

"What? The other day? A few details would help here."

"With that family the other day on Grizzly Tooth."

"Would you drop that? You are not working."

"Something was not right with them."

Another helicopter passed overhead.

"I should have said something."

"Bobby, this is crazy. You're upset because you missed a chance to what, fight with the guy? Tell him off?"

"No, Lori, it's not like that at all."

"What then?"

"Look around. The helicopters. The search." He left their table and approached a ranger at the cash register.

"Excuse me," Bobby said. "I understand there's a search."

"Yes, sir." The young Ranger was all friendly. "A little ten-year-old girl wandered away from her campsite and is lost."

"What trail?"

"Grizzly Tooth. Real deep in there near the border."

"That so? We were there two days ago. When was this reported?"

"Yesterday afternoon. Seems that Dad double-timed it out of there to alert us. Sir, you have to excuse me. We've got a lot on the go."

Bobby returned to his table.

"What happened, Dad? Is it that girl we saw the other day?"

Bobby looked at his son. Tenderly. "Could be, Joe."

Another helicopter, or maybe the same one, pounded overhead.

"Dad?" Joey said. "Can't you do something? You're a cop."

Bobby had just made detective first grade with the NYPD. The guys in his detective squad respected Bobby Ropa for his superior eye for detail. Or so they said, following a shift and several beers at Popeye's Bar on Flatbush Avenue. Now, he sat here, hands covering his face. Eyes blinking. Thinking. Had he dropped the ball on something? He knew why he was so unsettled. It was not that they happened on a family having a blowout in public. You see that in stores, restaurants, supermarkets—stress spots—but that it was here, in such a serene setting.

And that it was so disturbingly intense.

"Maybe you will feel better if you talked to somebody."

"Here you go." The waitress set that day's *Daily Interlake* near Bobby's plate. "This is the cook's copy. More coffee?"

Paige Baker's pretty face stared at Bobby. When he finished reading the article, he looked for the Montana Highway Patrol vehicle in the parking lot.

It was gone.

"Bobby, what is it?" Lori asked.

"Hurry up and finish," he said. "I've got to find out who is in charge of this case." Then he flagged the waitress. "Excuse me, miss, is there a phone and park directory I could use?"

CHAPTER FIFTEEN

Community Building #215, originally a schoolhouse built in 1923, is a green frame hall found among the government compound buildings in the shade of lodgepole pine at Glacier National Park's headquarters.

Used primarily for fire-rescue exercises, staff meetings and social functions, it was now the command center in the search for Paige Baker.

The wooden walls of its large meeting room were papered with huge, detailed maps of the park, dotted with colored locator pins. Large tables were covered with radio chargers, new phone lines, fax machines, photocopiers, computers, TV monitors and VCRs, all for the operation.

Inspector Walt Sydowski arrived shortly after dawn, watching it fill with local, state and federal authorities. He was met by FBI agents and taken to the criminal investigative section, which was hidden within the massive operation. Known only to a few officials, the specially formed secret joint forces unit was headed by the FBI. It had one aim: to investigate the disappearance of Paige Baker as if she were the victim of a criminal act.

Its operations were set up, out of sight, in a storage room, where Sydowski had not yet seated himself at a table to await the unit's first meeting when the door opened.

"Inspector Sydowski," a young male FBI agent said softly. "You have a call, sir. You can take it in here. And I've been advised that Agent Zander will be here momentarily to convene a briefing with all team members. He and Agent Bowman are en route from the command post."

Sydowski nodded his thanks and picked up the land line phone, noticing a number of other senior ice-cold police-type men in jeans and casual shirts taking seats at the meeting table, studying files. Sydowski nodded a hello to them as he took his call.

"Hi, Walt, it's Linda. Been up all night. I've got some stuff."

Sydowski sat down to make notes on his clipboard.

"First off, Walt, you got a fax there?"

He saw a machine and got its number from the young agent. Turgeon took it down, continuing.

"Emily Baker is a professional photographer. Has her own studio. No charges, convictions or warrants. Not even a traffic violation. Nothing much on her family. She has an aunt in San Francisco who is on vacation in Eastern Canada with her husband. The feebees have a line to the RCMP, who put them on the tourist alert."

"Hope you reach them before the press does. What about the domestic call to SFPD?"

"Pulled tapes from dispatch, had them transcribed. I am faxing that to you along with the summary from the responding unit. Trying to hook up with the officers who took the call and the neighbor who made the complaint. No charges, convictions or warrants for Doug Baker, either. He's an ex-marine. Honorable discharge, a high school teacher, football coach at Beecher Lowe in the Richmond District. Very respected."

"That it for now?"

"Talked to one of Doug's teacher friends late last night. Seems Doug confided to him there was stress in the Baker family that he refused to elaborate on, only to say that his wife was receiving psychological counseling and that they *needed* to go to Montana."

"Why did they *need* to go?"

"He didn't know."

"Or wouldn't tell you. Know who the shrink is?"

The word "shrink" prompted one of the cop strangers to look from his file as though Walt had found a key to the case.

"Not yet," Turgeon said.

"Go back on that friend," Sydowski said. "Also find out if Paige talked about her family with any little friends; try to get some profile on her. What has she been telling other kids, that sort of thing. Time's working against us."

"I am working full throttle on all of that—damn, Walt, what is that?"

A helicopter hammered the morning air overhead, sounding as if it were about to crash through the roof.

"I think my briefing's about to begin here, Linda. I'll take your information to the meeting. Talk to you later."

The helicopter landing outside made conversation impossible. A gray-haired man stared at Sydowski and passed him his card:

LLOYD TURNER FBI SPECIAL AGENT IN CHARGE OF SALT LAKE CITY DIVISION

Turner was the boss here. Sydowski received other cards from other agents under Turner. Then Park Superintendent Elsie Temple arrived, accompanied by Nora Lam, legal counsel from the U.S. Justice Department, and several local officials.

The helicopter subsided and within minutes, more people entered, led by Special Agent Frank Zander, followed by Agent Tracy Bowman and Pike Thornton, law enforcement officer with the park.

Zander, who was carrying a file folder, acknowledged the FBI brass. He shut the door, taking his place at the head of the table and control.

"I am Agent Frank Zander, the case agent in this matter. Park rangers received a report approximately fifteen hundred hours yesterday by Doug Baker that his ten-year-old daughter, Paige Baker, got lost in Grizzly Tooth Trail, some twenty-four hours previous to his contacting help. The Baker family was on a camping trip in the Devil's Grasp region. By all estimates, the girl has been lost about forty-three hours. We will not waste time. Before we go further, I'll go around the table, make sure everyone present should be here."

Introductions went fast. Satisfied, Zander then stressed the critical need for confidentiality of the aim of the task force. "Our objective is to rule out foul play or lay the foundation for prosecution," Zander said.

"Why?" Park Superintendent Elsie Temple was upset. "Could it be we're moving too fast here? Can't we let the search run its course? I don't like this approach. It all seems pretty circumstantial to me."

"I believe we are proceeding responsibly, given the facts, Ms. Temple," Turner said.

"Which are?"

Zander supplied them.

"Doug Baker has a very bad wound on his left hand. He said he injured it chopping firewood with an ax, which appears to be missing. Both he and his wife, Emily, were evasive when asked about the emotional state and details of their daughter before she vanished with her dog. Both parents state they did not see her. A few days prior to departing for their trip here, the San Francisco Police Department was called to the Baker home after a neighbor reported a violent family argument. When that complaint was investigated by the SFPD, Emily Baker dismissed it as a misunderstanding. Last night, at the command post, Emily Baker screamed into the night, 'You can't have her. Oh God, it is all my fault.' We are just beginning to assemble résumés on the parents."

"I do not like this approach to build something against the family at this stage. I'll say it again, it still seems pretty circumstantial," Temple said.

"Excuse me, Superintendent Temple, there is more." Sydowski was looking at his fresh notes. "This is unconfirmed, but late last night, Inspector Linda Turgeon of the SFPD Homicide Detail learned that Doug Baker had recently told a friend there was stress in the Baker family. Emily Baker was receiving psychological counseling and apparently the family *had to come* to Montana, for reasons unknown to us."

Temple weighed the information while Turner reasoned.

"Ms. Temple, given these factors, it would be irresponsible if we did not act quickly to confidentially probe the background of the family and the circumstances under which the child disappeared, in the possible tragic event that criminal intent is confirmed."

Temple placed her face in her hands.

"This is just terrible. Horrible."

"It is possible there was an accident and they are trying to cover it up," Zander said.

"It is also possible Paige Baker wandered off and has become lost, like her parents have told us," Bowman said.

Zander dismissed her comment by looking at his watch.

"Time is working against us. Weather could destroy a crime scene or damage physical evidence that would either support what the parents say or contradict it. And we cannot rule out any possibility."

"The Evidence Response Team should be here shortly," Turner said.

Zander nodded.

"Bowman, you will escort Emily Baker here straight away. We'll conduct an interview, for more details from her, then we'll bring in the father. We'll likely request a polygraph very soon."

Zander noticed the concern in the eyes of Nora Lam, the Justice Department lawyer. "At some early point, you will have to Mirandize them," Lam said.

"Of course."

A message came from an agent at the door. It was passed to Zander. His face creased. A Mr. Ropa was holding on the phone with information on the case of Paige Baker.

"I'll take it here," Zander said. "You have information?"

"I do. My family encountered the Baker family on Grizzly Tooth the day before she disappeared."

"What's your name?"

"Ropa. Bobby Ropa, R-O-P-A."

"What sort of information do you have?"

"We saw her family having a terrible argument the day before she vanished. They looked like a family imploding. It was not good."

Zander immediately shuffled through the small stack of permits until he found one for Ropa. Address was Brooklyn. As if the accent didn't give it away. "Where you from, Mr. Ropa?"

"New York. We're here on vacation. Look, I'll come in and give you a statement. You're at the command center?"

"That's right."

"We're in the north, but we'll be there as soon as we can."

Calling in was the right thing to do, Bobby told Lori after hustling everybody into their rented Explorer, driving off to the center. In his experience as a New York cop, Bobby knew how an isolated tip, even a crumb of mundane information, could be the linchpin in a complex case.

"Joey, try to remember everything you saw, heard and felt about that girl's family we met in the backcountry the other day."

A C-130 roared overhead.

"I think it would be hard to forget, Dad."

Lori saw Bobby's jaw muscles bunching the way they did when he was working a case. She knew her husband was on the job now. Their vacation ended the instant they came upon that girl's family and saw what they saw. Then came the news story and the search for her. Lori wished with all her heart Bobby was wrong, but he was a good cop. She worried about Joey. What if this turned into something and he had to pick somebody out of a lineup, or testify, or hear details? She stopped herself. The places your brain takes you as a wife to the NYPD.

They left the Icefields Highway for the narrow fifty-mile ribbon of asphalt named Going-to-the-Sun Road. It slithered east to west, severing the huge park in two. It bordered mountain lakes, passed through clouds, necklaced sheer rock faces as it followed a breathtaking roller-coaster route, clinging to cliff edges that dropped so suddenly your stomach quivered.

The entire drive Bobby kept running his hand over his chin, his mouth. It dawned on Lori what he was really thinking.

"Bobby, tell me you are not thinking those parents—"

"I should have done something. I should have said something." Bobby slammed his fist on the steering wheel. "I should have jumped in his freaking face. If this goes bad, I'll never forgive my—"

"Bobby!"

He slammed the truck's brakes in time to avert a collision with the back end of a slow-moving car. Lori said nothing. Bobby took a deep breath.

CHAPTER SIXTEEN

Zander entered the investigation room, setting his clipboard on the table.

"Are we all set over there? Confirm with two knocks," he said aloud.

Two knocks sounded on the wall.

The FBI had equipped the room with a tiny powerful microphone in the overhead lighting system and a hidden camera lens near a wall poster of the park.

Only Zander, Bowman, Sydowski and Thornton would be present for interviews with the Bakers. The others would observe from the second adjoining room. Before she left, Nora Lam had taken Zander just outside of microphone range and cautioned him.

"You know you cannot use anything unless you Mirandize her?"

"And you know I won't get anything if I do."

"You drop the ball here, Agent Zander, and you have no case."

"Ms. Lam, if I do not talk to her, we have no way of knowing if we have a case."

"I'm just letting you know you're on thin ice here."

"All part of my job."

They saw Bowman approaching with Emily, who had emerged with her hair pulled back in a tight ponytail. She had scrubbed her face in an attempt to freshen up, but her reddened eyes and sniffles betrayed her anguish as she was directed to a chair at the table.

"Emily, you've met everyone here, except Walt Sydowski from the San Francisco Police."

"Hello, Mrs. Baker." Sydowski extended his big hand. Emily took it and nodded. Zander sat across from her, Bowman to her left, with Sydowski sitting a nonthreatening distance away at one end of the table and Thornton at the other. All had notebooks and file folders, the contents of which Emily could not see.

"We have juice, muffins, tea, coffee, fruit?" Bowman offered.

"No thanks."

All of them wore dead serious faces. Sydowksi looked very familiar to her, but she could not place him. Why was someone here from the San Francisco Police Department? She was so confused, so tired.

"Emily, as you know, everything is being done to find Paige," Zander said.

She nodded.

"And as we told you, we're part of a team whose job it is to make sure we've not only searched everywhere but looked at all the possibilities that could help us find her."

Emily nodded.

"We'd just like to get a clear picture of how she became lost, maybe we missed something. Will you help us with all you remember?"

"Of course." Her voice was weak.

"Tell us what happened that morning."

"We were going to stay at the campsite. I decided I would go off by myself to the ridge, ahead on the trail. Paige was picking flowers near the campsite. Doug was gathering firewood and was going to read, I think."

"What were you going to do on the ridge?"

"Just meditate, take pictures."

"So you went alone?"

"Yes."

"Down the ridge, about one hundred yards from your camp?" She nodded.

"Could you see or hear your campsite from there? See or hear Doug and Paige talking? Hear the dog if it barked?"

"No, it was too far and wooded."

"How long were you gone?"

"A couple of hours. Three, maybe four."

"In that time, did you see anyone, any other hikers, anyone?" Emily shook her head.

"What was Paige's state of mind when you left?"

Emily looked at her empty hands on the table in front of her. "She might have been scared." Emily sniffed. "Oh God."

Bowman put a hand on her shoulder. "It's OK."

"Doug and I quarreled along the trail the day before. Just stupid husband-and-wife stuff about how long we should hike in the park. We were all tired and stressed from the flight and rushing from San Francisco to get here. But Emily thought the quarrel was serious. She thought we were getting a divorce."

"Are you?"

"No." Emily sniffed; Bowman passed her a tissue.

Zander surveyed the others with glances.

"If Paige were upset, why would you leave her?"

Tears rolled down her face. "I was upset, too. I wanted to be alone. I was upset with Doug." Then she weakly added, "Myself."

"Was there stress in your family before and during the trip?"

Emily nodded.

"Tell us about it."

"Like I said, just normal suburban-living crap. Doug's job, my job. We could not decide where to go on vacation. Doug wanted Paris. I wanted the mountains, you know, get away from everything, take pictures, recharge. Paige wanted Paris, too. She had never hiked before. I thought it would be good for her to get away from all cities, know that there is more to life than the mall and the Internet. We decided on the mountains at the last minute. Sort of rushed out here. But the trip became a disaster with us arguing. Just stupid family arguing and we hurt Paige with it."

"What do you mean?"

Emily put her crumpled fists to her mouth and closed her eyes tight.

"I think she got mad at us. Ran off on purpose to be alone, too, not knowing the danger. Then got lost. Got really lost. Oh God. It's my fault. It's all my fault!" Emily covered her face with her hands.

"It's OK." Bowman comforted her as a helicopter rattled overhead.

Zander noticed Thornton and Sydowski touching up their notes. When the noise outside subsided, Zander continued.

"You work as a photographer?"

"Yes, I have my own studio. I freelance. I've been busy."

"And Doug, he's a teacher?"

"Beecher Lowe High School. He teaches English and coaches football."

"What was Doug's state of mind when you left alone to meditate?"

"He was upset, too, at me and everything."

"Just arguing and stuff?"

Emily nodded.

"And you think it forced Paige to run away?"

"Yes."

"Has she ever run away before?"

"No."

"Would you say there was additional stress in your family prior to the trip?"

Emily thought for a long time. Zander repeated the question. She shook her head.

"No career problems, money problems, marital problems?"

She shook her head.

"Are you or Doug under a doctor's care, taking any medication?"

"No." Emily's tone signaled that she was becoming offended by some of Zander's questions.

"No psychiatric care?"

"No, I usually talk to my friends about personal problems."

"Emily, did you meet anyone in the park who seemed unusually friendly to Paige, or your family?"

"No."

"Paige was familiar with the Internet?"

"Yes. She chatted with friends about clothes, movies, music."

"Is it conceivable Paige could have arranged a secret meeting here with a friend she met on the Internet?"

"I don't know, we monitor her fairly closely. We have filters."

"Since arriving, do you recall any incidents along the way, any altercations, or anyone that may have followed you here to settle a score?"

She shook her head.

"Is there anyone in San Francisco who might want to harm your family or hurt Paige, anyone who has upset her?"

"No. Nothing like that. Not that we know. I—you think it's possible she was abducted from us? Do you know something? Oh God—"

"We don't know anything like that. We have no evidence of anything, nothing to indicate that anyone has harmed Paige.

Emily, we're just trying to learn everything, every aspect of the circumstances before she got lost."

"I am so scared. I am so confused. It is all my fault, don't you see?"

Zander was silent.

"What kind of mother lets her child run off into the mountains?" Emily asked.

Zander let her self-recrimination sit in the air for a moment.

"Emily, what did Doug tell you about Paige's state of mind before she got lost?"

She stared at the table, collecting her thoughts.

"He thought she had gone down the trail to be with me, to join me."

"Why did he think that?"

"Because she was upset."

"Upset? How?"

"From our argument; then he hurt his hand chopping wood."

"Did you see him hurt his hand?"

"No. When I left, Paige was picking flowers or playing with Kobee in her tent. I am not sure. I was upset."

"Did Doug have a hurt hand while you were there? Did you see him injure himself?"

She shook her head. "I told you, no."

"Do you think other hikers could have come by your campsite after you left?"

"I did not hear or see anyone."

"Tell me what happened after you returned to the campsite, how you discovered she was gone, and what Doug told you and what you did?"

"I remember at the halfway point back getting this strange feeling that something was wrong."

"What kind of feeling?"

"Just a chill or shudder and I stopped. I did not see or hear anything. It was just a feeling. Mother's instinct." She sniffed. "When I returned, Doug was reading. I asked about Paige. He said he thought she was with me, then ran down the trail where I had come, looking for her."

"Did he say what happened?"

"Only what I just told you."

"Was his hand hurt then?"

"Yes, after I got back."

"Did he tell you how he hurt his hand?"

"He said from chopping wood, I keep telling you."

"Then, as far as you know, he was the last person to see Paige?"

It was as if all sound stopped and the room held its breath.

Her fists went to her mouth, her eyes glistening, staring down at nothing. She nodded.

"Emily, why did you rush to Montana? Why did you have to come here?"

She covered her face with her hands and wept.

"Guess what I am going to do."

Zander leaned forward.

"If there is something you think we should know," he said, "it might help if you shared it with us now."

Emily raised her eyes to Zander's.

He saw a woman drowning in something dark as the distant thundering of another helicopter grew louder. Emily sat there, a portrait of pain, a suspect in her daughter's disappearance. The helicopter grew more intense as the four investigators regarded her.

Zander checked his watch. Time was running out.

CHAPTER SEVENTEEN

Immediately after Emily Baker's first interview with the task force, Zander pulled Bowman aside in the few minutes they had alone.

"Emily's demeanor at this stage is absolutely critical. She could bond, open up. She may need a little nudge."

A female ranger had taken Emily to find an unoccupied rest room. Zander's attention darted between where she would emerge and Bowman.

"I want you to begin working on securing Emily's trust before you fly back with her to the command post. Work on her woman to woman." Zander's blue eyes bored into hers. "It is vital you not fail. You will not get a second chance at this."

The full weight of what was at stake began settling on Bowman. Through the command center windows, she saw the news trucks. Inside, the TV monitors in the operations room played the muted chatter of live network reports. Bowman swallowed. A few hours ago, she would have been at her desk, quietly dealing with forms, her keyboard and her little frustrations. This was huge. Moving so fast. She could not afford to screw up.

"You understand, Bowman? Can you handle that? Or should I request someone else?"

Zander was an ass. He might be a legendary detective, able to pick up her twinge of self-doubt, but he was still an ass.

"Tell me, Zander, with you being an expert on the 'woman-to-woman approach,' what advice can you provide so that I don't fail?"

"It's evident she likes you, Bowman. Get her talking to you. Beat us up if you like. Win her confidence. Whatever it takes." Zander checked his watch. "You'll have an hour, maybe less, with her. Then we bring the dad in."

"What do we want to know?"

"The truth."

Emily returned, nodding her thanks to the ranger, giving a half-smile to Bowman, who escorted her through the chaos of the command center.

Emily's face tightened, her eyes glistening as the impact of her daughter's drama hit her with the force of a sledgehammer.

Paige staring back at her from the TV monitors from the early-morning news reports, still pictures of her and Doug. The entire country was watching.

"This way, Emily."

Bowman took Emily outside through a back entrance to an empty FBI SUV with Utah plates, filled with manuals, maps, empty fast-food wrappers and newspapers. At least it would be private. They climbed in.

Emily was tearful, drained.

"How long before I can get back to the campsite? I want to be there in case they find her."

About an hour, Bowman explained. Because the search was

going full throttle it might take that long before a helicopter could ferry her back and fly Doug in. Emily stared at the mountains.

"Have they found anything?"

"I'm sorry. Nothing so far that we're aware of."

Emily was dabbing her eyes, sniffling. "Do you think I am a horrible mother?"

"Every mother thinks they are a horrible mother when something bad happens."

"I think Zander and the others think I am a terrible mother."

"Why?"

"For losing my child."

"I think they just want to know everything that happened so they can find Paige."

"I told Zander everything. I know he doesn't believe me. I saw it in his face, heard it in his tone."

Emily looked at Bowman, assessing her as a friend or an enemy.

"Do you have children, Tracy?"

"A son, Mark. He's nine."

"Have you ever had anything horrible happen in your life?"

Bowman rolled to Carl's empty side of the bed the night he took that call. Then the pounding began on the front door. Barry Tully, highway patrolman, stood there, his hat in hand. He couldn't get the words out. He didn't have to, because she knew. . . .

"Yes, I have," Tracy said. "My husband died a few years ago."

"I'm sorry. How, illness or . . ."

"Highway crash."

Emily looked at nothing in the treetops. "Then you know what it's like to get pulled into a surreal whirlwind where nothing makes sense, where it is so painful you would give anything to stop it, to go back to better days."

Bowman could feel Emily reaching out to her, subconsciously trying to bond. Woman to woman, mother to mother. Be careful, she told herself.

"Yes, Emily, I've known terrible things in my life, like most people."

"I know Zander and the others are trying to find out if I had anything to do with Paige's disappearance."

"It's more complicated than that."

"Is it?"

"We're"—Bowman caught herself—"they're just trying to learn the truth surrounding the time Paige got lost, I mean—"

"The truth? That implies you think I'm lying—"

"No, Emily, I mean, I mean the facts, the details—I am sorry—"

"What about you, then? Do you think I had something to do with Paige's vanishing? And I want *you* to tell me *the truth* and let me judge *you.*"

Bowman searched her heart. She found no evidence that convinced her Emily committed any crime other than having an argument that resulted in her ten-year-old daughter running off and getting lost in the Rocky Mountains. But somewhere in a dark corner, Bowman felt, Emily was hiding something, something disturbing.

"I do not think you committed any crime."

Emily brought her fists to her mouth. "Thank you."

Oh Jesus, was that a mistake, telling her that? Bowman thought quickly.

"But I do think you and Doug are, or were, in the midst of something very troubling that you fear is related to Paige running off."

Emily said nothing for a moment. Then, "Do you think we will find her?"

"I'm praying that we do."

Bowman's pulse was racing, not seeing the activity, the mountains. She was torn between her fear that Emily was so calculating and cunning she had just been played for a fool, or Emily was the innocent victim of tragic circumstances.

"I understand you used to live in Montana, grew up here?"

Emily nodded. "But it's been years."

"Why did you come back?"

"To bury something from the past."

Bowman felt gooseflesh surface on the back of her neck.

"Would you like to talk to me about it, Emily?"

Emily shook her head. "I can't." A curtain of sorrow fell over her. "I can't tell anyone. I—I." Emily began weeping softly, her voice dropping.

Bowman strained to listen, Emily was almost whispering to herself, making Bowman unsure of what she was hearing.

"I need my daughter back. I cannot go through this again. I will not survive this." Then Emily's voice rose, her face lifting to the mountaintops.

"God, please, where is she?"

CHAPTER EIGHTEEN

Paige awoke, shivering and hungry.

It was cold and damp in her shelter. She should get into the sun. Try to find her way back. Was it safe? She was afraid.

Was the thing that chased her last night still out there?

So afraid. She had to stop shivering.

Where's Kobee?

She inched her head out, began looking in every direction, her entire body aching, cuts and scrapes stinging. She was starving. Her throat was raw. She coughed. It hurt a little.

She threw small rocks in every direction, hoping to hear the thing stir if it was waiting for her.

Nothing. She continued tossing them, only farther.

She had to get back. Her parents were going to kill her. Maybe they would be so mad they would leave without her.

No. Don't let that happen! Please! Somebody help me!

But why were they fighting so much? They were getting a divorce. That had to be it. They brought her on this trip to tell her they did not love each other anymore, that she would have to decide which of her parents she wanted to live with, then tell a judge or something.

Some of the divorced kids at school said that's how it happens.

She prayed it would not happen to her.

Mom and Dad still love each other, don't they?

Paige had to get back. Had to help them stay together.

Carefully, she stepped out of her shelter, shielded her eyes from the morning sun, scanning the slope, then decided on a direction. Walking warmed her, made her feel a little better. But she had no idea where she was going. She walked into a forest that looked inviting, easy to travel through.

She was so hungry.

She started thinking about a cheeseburger, fries, a milkshake, tacos, the fridge at home, a ham and cheese sandwich, yogurt, fruit, orange juice with shaved ice, her mom's spaghetti with mushroom sauce and garlic bread, homemade apple pie.

She missed San Francisco, their house near Golden Gate Park, her room with her cool loft bed, her books, the computer, her poster of Leonardo DiCaprio. The big beautiful picture Mom took of her and Kobee at the beach.

Where was Kobee?

She called for him. "Kobeeee!" Stupid beagle.

Paige stopped to sit on a flat sun-warmed rock. She was so hungry.

The trees, the slopes and mountains that went on forever and ever. She hated this place. It was not beautiful; it was scary. Something had chased her last night. Something frightening that she did want to even think about.

Paige had overheard her mother telling someone on the phone once that her monster "dwelled in the mountains." Paige now knew monsters were real. One almost got her last night. Would she ever get back home? She had no idea where she was going. Her feet were sore.

She was so hungry.

She swallowed and searched her pack.

Two granola bars, an apple and a bottle of water.

She was starving. Licking her lips, she forced herself to eat only the apple, to eat it as slowly as possible. Savoring every bit, sucking the juice, actually tasting the skin, nibbling down to the core, leaving no meat on the seed pockets or the stem, contemplating eating them, too.

When she finished, she was still hungry. Gripping the two packaged granola bars. One blueberry. One strawberry. Sitting there craving, aching to eat them.

But then what?

What would she eat when they were gone?

She wept.

Mommy. Daddy. Come and get me. Please. Take me home. Please.

She sobbed, believing her parents, the entire world, had forgotten about her; fearing she would never see them or her friends again. At first, she didn't hear the distant sound as it drew closer, familiar, pricking her ears. A jingling, then panting.

Paige blinked.

Kobee?

Suddenly, out of nowhere, he was in her lap.

"Kobee!"

Licking her face.

Squeezing him, hugging him, kissing him.

"You bad, bad, wonderful mutt. I love you—don't you ever leave me again!"

Paige placed her hand on either side of his head, staring at him eye to eye.

"Now you have to show me the way back! You!"

What was wrong? His eyes were not right. They held something bad. Terror. Body trembling. Her fingers. Wet. Something gooey on them pulling them away, stained red. Blood. Kobee was bleeding. Paige's heart raced.

"What happened?"

She swallowed.

His side had been sliced, like it had been raked with sharp knives. Flesh torn.

What was that?

Huffing. Snorting.

Coming toward her, crashing through the forest. Branches snapping. Louder than the sound of the distant search helicopter.

"Oh God!"

Paige scooped Kobee in her arms and ran for her life.

CHAPTER NINETEEN

In the task force room, while the investigators awaited Doug Baker's arrival, Inspector Walt Sydowski reviewed Frank Zander's approach to go hard on Emily Baker, then have Tracy Bowman pick up the pieces.

"Frank, I think you are pushing the right buttons, but—"

"But what?"

"I think you need leverage before going any harder. We have nothing but disturbing circumstances. Things are not always what they seem. We need something physical, irrefutable. The father's wound might be a start, or finding the ax."

Zander hated being second-guessed. He glared at Sydowski, on the verge of snapping at him, but chose to hold his words.

"Well, I for one do not approve of this approach." Elsie Temple, the park's superintendent, peered at Zander over her glasses. "Why put the Bakers through this? It serves nothing. I think you should wait until you have evidence of a crime."

"And your opinion is based on how many criminal investigations, Ms. Temple?" Zander shot at her, causing her face to redden. "We've seen what happened in Yellowstone when people waited until they tripped over the evidence."

"Agent Zander, it just appears—"

"Ms. Temple, a liar tells a tale a thousand ways. The more distance you get from the crime, the more opportunity for the suspects to fortify themselves. It seems Emily has already lied about stress in her family before the trip and counseling, if the San Francisco information holds up. There is the domestic call, Doug Baker's wound, the absence of his ax. You rarely get the truth first time around. If you collect statements while aggressively searching for physical evidence that contradicts the family's account of things, then your case strengthens."

"And if you are wrong?" Temple challenged.

"Then it's a price I'll gladly pay, considering the alternative," Zander said. "If we are wrong, then hopefully the Bakers get their daughter back alive and well. But if Paige Baker has been harmed and we have bungled so badly that no one answers for it, consider the legacy. Not something you will feature with pictures on the lovely brochures for your pretty park, is it?"

Temple's jaw dropped. "How do you live with yourself?"

Zander did not answer her. Instead, he took a call advising the task force that Mr. Ropa had arrived.

Bobby Ropa was wearing a New York Giants T-shirt and faded Levis. Looked to be in his early thirties and in good shape. First thing he did after introducing himself to the investigators was produce his NYPD blue-crested shield.

Zander seated Ropa, professionally reminding him about confidentiality; then they got down to business.

"You looking at the dad?" Ropa said, eager to help.

"We're talking to everybody, looking at everything."

"You should look hard at the dad."

"Tell us about your information," Zander said.

Ropa recounted how his family was coming out of Grizzly

Tooth, along a twisting part of the trail, when they heard voices carrying loud and clear.

"This family, the Bakers from the news pictures, it was them. They had stopped for lunch in a clearing but were arguing."

Ropa explained how quiet it can get up there and how they heard much of the argument before they came up on the Bakers.

"First thing I picked up was the girl, Paige, upset, says she thinks she knows why her parents brought her to the mountains. Then her old man says, tell us. The girl figures her parents are divorcing because of her mother's problems, that she's got to choose a parent to live with.

"The mother denies it, and the kid is crying. The mother says it is complicated. We kind of round a bend and come up on them, in time to see the old man explode. Big time. It all goes down fast.

"He demands the mother tell them 'exactly what the hell is going on with you!' She starts wailing and he screams at her that he is sick and tired 'of this veneer. This pretense of a happy family.' He blames it all on the mother.

"We're just stunned, like we're watching a play. Street theater.

"She gets hysterical, accusing him of thinking she's 'wigged out,' dragging them all to the mountains for some inexplicable reason. The kid gets into it, threatens to run off a mountain because of the parents. The mother answers her with something like, 'Don't ever say that.'

"That's when I step in with, you know, 'Everything okay there?' The old man gets cool fast, switching it off as I eyeball him. He makes a joke, a little first-day stress or something. I see he's got an ax, a small hatchet, hanging from his pack. I ask them if they have bear spray, because we spotted a Grizzly sow with cubs in a meadow by a river a day or so earlier.

"Then I see they got a dog concealed in one of the packs, against park regs. Part of the family, the father says, could not leave home without him. About then I marshal my family out of there. It was a weird scene. We see nothing more until the news hits that the father reports the daughter lost.

"The way I figure it, we saw their fireworks display the day before she vanished. I don't know what to make of it. Don't know what else you got, but this thing—she smells to me."

None of the task force members spoke for the longest time as they ingested the new disturbing information from Robert L. Ropa, detective first grade with the NYPD 67th Precinct in Brooklyn.

CHAPTER TWENTY

Worry gnawed at the pit of Doug Baker's empty stomach as he scanned the forests from their campsite command post.

Radios broadcasted reports and instructions between the planes and helicopters overhead, the search teams scouring the high country and the scores of rangers and now FBI agents ferried in to help.

So far, they found no trace of Paige.

Doug's fear for her was like a leaden cloak enshrouding him, weighing him down, exhausting him. How long could she survive? Now, Emily was with the FBI. It all seemed out of control since police arrived. The way they never let them help search, the way they always watched them, kept them from being alone.

"... We'll take you in separately...."

The tone of that remark implied so much. The FBI knew something. Doug felt it in his gut. They suspected a crime. Something. There was that other family. Or maybe strangers on the trail. What did they know? He had to do something.

Anything. He was supposed to wait here until Emily returned and they sent for him. But Doug was tired of waiting. It was time to do something.

"Excuse me," he said to the nearest FBI agent. "Could you find out if my wife is still at the command center or on her way back?"

The agent made a radio inquiry.

"She's still there, sir, but they say we can take you there now." He indicated a helicopter whose pilot was climbing into the cockpit, engaging the ignition.

The helicopter rattled, making its landing approach over the command center. Like Emily had been, Doug was astonished by the scene below, the news crews, satellite trucks, the dizzying scale of the operation geared to finding Paige. Some fifty feet from the ground, Doug saw the banks of news cameras aimed on the landing pad from behind yellow police tape, just as the voice of the young FBI agent alerted him to it.

"Sir, we advise you not to talk to the press at this stage."

"Why not?" Doug was growing more resentful of being controlled.

"Better to first coordinate with all the agencies, when we know more. So we're all on the same page."

Doug swallowed hard. The *agencies* had failed to turn up anything or offer much hope. *It's time we took control.* He searched the scene for his wife as his chopper touched down.

Emily recognized Doug in the cockpit of the descending chopper.

"There's Doug," she said, leaving Bowman in the FBI SUV.

"No! Please wait!" Bowman said to the slamming door. *Damn.*

Emily hurried to the edge of the helipad, waiting for Doug as he crouched until clearing the rotors, taking her tenderly in his arms.

More than three dozen news cameras recorded the scene, pulling in tight to catch the fear and exhaustion in their faces:

Emily's anguished beauty, Doug, haggard but handsome. The image of the well-groomed middle-class couple trapped in torment would become a touchstone for the nation gripped by the drama of a ten-year-old child facing death in an American paradise.

"Doug! Emily! Please talk to us!" Reporters shouted over the chopper, which was lifting off. Bowman and the male agent were tugging at the Bakers.

Doug stopped in his tracks, considering the request.

"This way, Doug, please." Bowman had his arm. "They're waiting to talk to you inside."

Doug ignored Bowman and searched Emily's glistening eyes. "I think we should make a statement to the press, Emily."

"I don't know what I would say."

"We'll speak from the heart. Let's go."

"Sir, I would not advise—" The male FBI agent was cut off.

"Doug, it would be best if you spoke with all the officials first." Bowman did not want a scene in front of the cameras and realized it was futile. Doug put a protective arm around Emily and approached the press line. The chopper was gone, underscoring the quiet, and the pack began murmuring over cell phones to newsrooms across the USA.

"Grab the air! Go live! It's the parents. Right, first time they've spoken!"

Bowman rushed into the private joint forces room and alerted Zander and the others, who were wrapping up their interview with Bobby Ropa.

"You try to stop them, Bowman?" Zander fired.

"Yes, Doug refused."

Zander was scanning the networks, finding one with the BREAKING NEWS graphic, then cutting to Doug and Emily Baker, embracing, standing before a cluster of microphones less than one yard away.

"Why not stop it?" Ropa asked.

"Too late now," Zander said, picking up the nearest phone and ordering the event recorded. "I'm not sure we want to," he said, watching the TV as if contemplating a chess move.

Different questions were called out simultaneously. Doug took the ones he could pick up.

"Please share with us your thoughts at this point."

"We came here as a family. We'll leave here as a family. We will not go home without her," Doug said.

"Emily, has Paige ever run away?"

"No. Never."

"Does she have wilderness training or experience?"

"No," Emily replied, "this was her first outing."

"It rained after her first night. The temperatures are expected to plummet tonight, which will mark over forty, maybe close to forty-eight, hours for her alone in some of the most dangerous terrain in the nation. What are officials telling you her chances are, Doug?"

"It's serious. We are well aware this is a life and death situation for our daughter, but we are praying. We will not give up hope."

Emily joined in. "Paige is an intelligent child. She has her dog, Kobee, with her—"

"What breed, ma'am?"

"Beagle. We're told that will give her some psychological comfort and a source of warmth. She had a sweater, some food." Emily's voice began to break. "She has our hearts, our prayers. . . ."

"Mr. Baker, there've been reports that your daughter used the Internet. Has the FBI indicated any suspicions of an abduction scenario that may be a line of investigation here?"

"Yes, we're aware of that possibility also and we understand they are examining every potential aspect, but primarily the thinking is Paige wandered from us and became lost. Thank you, that is all we can . . ."

Is that what the thinking is, Doug? Why don't you wave that hand for the cameras? Zander thought coolly.

"Sir, sir, just what happened?" Tom Reed asked.

"As I said, we were camping along the remote Grizzly Tooth Trail and Paige wandered from our campsite—"

"Can't you please elaborate a little?" Reed persisted.

I like that guy, Zander mused. *Yes, Doug, please elaborate a little.*

"We have a meeting with officials, thank you—"

The Bakers turned but were stopped by one last reporter. It was an older woman from a local newspaper.

"Mr. and Mrs. Baker, do you have any other children?"

"No." Emily wept, her face crumpling. "She is all we have in this world."

Doug comforted her and they headed to the command center.

Nearly a fifth of the nation had witnessed the event.

Zander switched off the set.

"I'll tell you guys something right now," Ropa said to Zander and the others on his way out after watching the Bakers' press conference. "That guy on the tube was acting totally different when we came upon him the day before his daughter disappeared. To me, it's like they're two different guys."

Ropa left a motel card on the table.

"Call me if you need more. We're here for a few more days."

Zander thanked him, waiting until the door was closed, before polling the others. "Walt, what's your read on the press conference? What do you think Doug's up to?"

"Hard to say at this point. Could be totally innocent."

"Pike?"

"Curious that he went to the press before talking to us. Like maybe he felt he had to do something preemptive."

Zander nodded.

"Emily tell you anything, Bowman?"

She hesitated, reflecting on Emily's pretty, pain-filled face on the TV screen. Her heart breaking for her as she deliberated on how much of their conversation she should reveal.

"Bowman?" Zander reminded her she was an FBI agent assisting in an investigation. "Did Emily tell you anything when you were alone with her?"

"She said she came here to bury the past."

The others exchanged glances.

"What past?" Zander demanded. "She offer any more on that?"

"No," Bowman said.

"Well, what do we have on her background? Walt, the SFPD was chasing her aunt, right? We need to nail this quickly. What past?"

"I have a strong feeling she wants to tell me about it," Bowman said.

"Fly back with her, work on her." Zander told Bowman to make notes on everything that Emily told her.

The task force had a few minutes before they interviewed Doug Baker.

Zander studied his watch. How long did their daughter have? If she had any time left at all?

"Frank, what's your take on the news conference?" Sydowski said.

"I think it's a cunning, calculated move, if they committed a crime."

"How so?"

"If they're culpable, Doug knows where they are vulnerable, maybe with Emily talking to us. So he moves, preemptively as you say, to put his face and Emily's face out there through the press. Let America see the image he wants them to see, build up huge credit in the bank of public opinion. That is vital strategy because it puts us among the forces of evil, should we go after them. We all know that often cases are not won in courts based upon evidence but in the press based upon perception.''

''So what do you propose?''

''We'll keep overturning each stone and give the Bakers all the rope they want. If they're innocent, the rope is tied to nothing. But if they're guilty, that rope will tighten. Around their necks.''

CHAPTER TWENTY-ONE

Montana State Prison is located some three miles outside Deer Lodge, rising from the sweeping grassy prairie like the fortress of a dark kingdom that laid claim to the snow-capped Beaverhead and Bitterroot Ranges of the Rockies behind it.

The massive penitentiary stood as a gate between condemnation and the promise of heaven, or so David Cohen thought as he drove his rented Neon down windswept Lake Conley Road. Parking in a visitor's stall outside the prison's main entrance, he watched a perimeter surveillance patrol pass.

He was bracing for the U.S. Supreme Court to render its decision in the case of Isaiah Hood, his client. He was beyond the wire a few hundred yards away on death row, awaiting his execution, which would happen in some seventy-two hours if Cohen could not save him.

The young Chicago lawyer paused to gaze at the mountains, then the manned towers, the twin rows of twenty-foot chain-link fences topped and separated by coils of razor wire. It was futile for Isaiah. But this morning, Cohen would explain clemency options in the event of a negative ruling, which he knew was inevitable. Inside his briefcase, next to his court papers, Cohen had a file folder with a page detailing how his client wished his remains to be handled.

"Morning, Mr. Cohen."

The guards at the desk knew him, as they did most death row attorneys. All endured the same security ritual of having their belongings inspected, then having to pass through a metal detector. To the chime of keys and the hum and clang of half-ton steel doors opening and closing, they were escorted past the cold hard walls of a maximum security prison.

"Hello, David. I'll take you over," one of the older, more serene guards offered. He met Cohen after he had passed through the security labyrinth of the main gate and stepped into the prison's inner open-air courtyard, save for the high mast poles with cable strung between them to deter aircraft escapes.

The two men chatted about the weather while moving along the walkway. It paralleled the graveled interior sterilized of 'ground clutter' between the chain link fences with waist-high waves of more barbed wire and motion detectors. They came upon death row, a small cinder-block prison within the prison, set back from the buildings that housed the general population. It resembled a low-ceilinged bunker. Privately, some lawyers called it the mausoleum.

Inside, stern-faced guards received Cohen, bringing him through more steel doors, leading him to the small visitor's room, furnished with a wooden table and chairs, along with a TV that was muted. The guards left it on to calm inmates. Alone, waiting for his client, Cohen opened his briefcase, scanned his court papers, then studied the page for Hood's final arrangements: "After cremation, ashes will be distributed in the Livingston Range." This would be his task after he watched Hood die. He ran a hand over his face, wishing he had not become a lawyer. He glanced at the silent color TV showing news updates of the little girl lost in Glacier National Park. He wondered, for a moment, if she would be found.

Isaiah Hood sat at the edge of his bed, staring at the large color poster of the Rocky Mountains. Sometimes he believed he could step into it, feel the crisp purifying air, inhale the alpine, hear the murmur of the crystalline streams. As his death sentence neared, he would fall into long, statuelike trances that lasted entire days. He would slip into another existence as he raised his arms, reaching into the picture, preparing to receive the message he believed would save him.

It was an eerie scene for the guards who looked in on him, haunting some at home as their final conscious image before they fell asleep.

When Hood first arrived on death row, the doctors who saw him concluded that he had abnormally acute senses of smell, hearing and sight. Plus, he had a disturbingly high "apprehension of the mind." One doctor put it simply: "The patient has an almost animallike sense of intuition." But more important, the psychiatrists said, Hood was a psychopath with a destructive psychological neurological disorder with stress-activated seizures, which, if unchecked, risked cardiac arrest. They believed his problems had their genesis in the severe beatings he endured from his father, Brutus Hood.

Brutus was an angry, violent man whose hands were amputated cleanly at the wrists in a sawmill accident near Shelby. For years afterward, the coworkers who saved him talked about it at the town bar: "It was like someone splashed buckets of red paint everywhere." Hood's old man went through life embittered by the hooks at the ends of his arms, taking out his rage on his wife with daily beatings, until one day she "stepped off" a mountain.

"She was depressed because her slut of a daughter got herself pregnant again, by some brave over in Browning. And

she's gonna get rid of it. Like we should have done with you. You're a worthless piece of nothing."

The old man had screamed that at Hood on the day they found her. In a whiskey rage, he clubbed his son on his head, his jaw and his forearms as Isaiah tried in vain to defend himself from those terrifying metal hooks. Hood's pregnant sister tried to protect him.

"Stop beating him. It's not his fault."

"He's no good to anybody. Your mother killed herself because of you both. You know that's true."

Hood's bruises and welts stayed longer than his sister. A short time after the funeral, she took a bus to Seattle and never returned.

Keys clanked on Hood's steel cell door.

"Your lawyer's here, Isaiah. Let's go."

Hood stood and slipped his hands and wrists through the handcuff port so they could be snapped into cold steel handcuffs.

"Stand back, please."

The heavy cell door opened to two large guards, one holding a belly chain. He slipped it around the waist of Hood's orange prison jumpsuit, locking a link to the wrist cuffs so that Hood appeared to be holding his hands navel-high in prayer as they escorted him to the interview room where Cohen waited.

After Hood's sister ran off, it was just Isaiah and his old man living in their ramshackle frame house far away from anybody else near the edge of Glacier National Park. They existed on his old man's disability pension and self-pity. Hood essentially raised himself and came to spend most of his free time in the mountains, wandering off for days to camp in the park, explore lost trails, survive by hunting and fishing. After dropping out of high school, he became a backcountry guide, one of the best because he knew virtually every inch of the region as it evolved into his sanctuary, his home, the place where he healed, where he did not have to pay for the sins of his father.

Then came the day Hood encountered the two little girls and he committed a sin of his own.

It happened so long ago—the passing of time had reduced his contented years in the mountains to a fading boyhood memory, one that Hood had been trying desperately to recapture as a middle-aged man. *Did it even happen? Was there ever a time I was free?*

He had just turned nineteen when it happened. Twenty when convicted. For twenty-three hours of every day, for the last twenty-two years, he had been paying for his sin. Caged and forgotten in an eight-by-four-foot stone and steel tomb.

Over the past months, Hood felt his father's rage seething beneath his skin, bubbling in increasing degrees. All his life he had been paying. And in a few days, the state of Montana would demand payment in full.

They would take the shred of life he had left.

Well, it was not going to happen.

Hood knew from his visits into the picture.

A message was coming to him.

He was *not* going to die in this prison.

Cohen accepted that Hood's case stood a million-to-one chance of success with the Supreme Court. He and Lane Porter, Hood's other lawyer, had scrutinized the file relentlessly since taking it on. Lane was experienced with death row cases but was back in Chicago working from home because she was due next week to give birth to her second child. It had always troubled her that some early records were destroyed in a storeroom fire in Helena years ago. The state's staff assured the attorneys a complete file had subsequently been assembled from copies stored elsewhere, but they could never completely shake the fear that something was missing.

It made the case even more difficult. The chances for a successful appeal were not good, according to the other lawyers Cohen and Porter consulted at their high-powered law office in the Sears Tower. Most attorneys there opposed the death penalty, and the firm took on many hopeless cases pro bono. At the outset, Hood pleaded not guilty, assured by counsel he had a case of reasonable doubt. But he lost. Now, Hood's appeal argument was that not only was he convicted on circumstantial evidence and represented by ineffective counsel at trial, but he categorically claimed innocence. It was dramatic and raised Hood's constitutional rights, but there was no startling fresh evidence, nothing found in case law to form the foundation of a potentially successful challenge. Although Cohen and Porter had submitted a solid appeal citing Eighth Amendment violations and other facts to support their client's claim, Cohen knew Isaiah Hood would soon be dead.

The clinking of chains and keys signaled Hood's arrival, the guards delivering him to Cohen, who stood and positioned a chair for Hood. Once they were alone, Cohen said, "How are you doing, Isaiah?"

Hood's brown hair was flecked with white strands. His tiny black eyes pushed into a face creased, pitted and scarred, as if a glacier had passed over it. It held the pallor of skin deprived of natural sunlight.

Hood's eyes searched Cohen's.

"Any word from the court?"

"Nothing. I am sorry."

Hood's chains clinked and knocked as he flattened his hands on the table.

"Lane have her kid yet?"

"Not yet." Cohen opened a file folder. "Let's go over a few points. I've spoken today with the governor's office and the office of the attorney general in Helena about seeking relief. Their response is to wait for the outcome with the Supreme Court but they have not closed the door. . . ."

Hood gave part of his attention to the TV news as Cohen began summarizing the strengths of their appeal to the Supreme Court, most of which Hood knew by heart. The sound was off but it was clear from the pictures it was something significant about the big story the guards were talking about, that little girl lost in Glacier National Park.

". . . that the Petitioner's conviction was derived from a constitutionally invalid confession and from the testimony before the Court of a sole witness, being a thirteen-year-old child . . . counsel failed in effective cross-examination at trial . . . mitigating and circumstantial evidence . . ."

Hood could locate anyone lost in Glacier National Park. It is sunny and warm the last day he sets foot in it, twenty-two years ago. He can hear the girls and smell the fragrance of freshly laundered clothing before they near the spot where he is sitting. It is at a forest edge near a goat ledge deep in northern Glacier, not far from an abandoned turn-of-the-century trapper's trail. They are laughing, chasing butterflies.

He is just there.

They stop dead in their tracks and swallow. He has startled them and it makes them laugh nervously.

"Hello," he says.

The older one glances over her shoulder, as if knowing they should return. Sensing danger. They just stand there. Frozen.

"How about a game?" he says.

The little one giggles.

The older one recognizes him. He sees it in her face: You're one of the Hoods. Trash. Keep away from us. *That look broke*

*his heart. The others in town would never know how much they
had hurt him. He was nineteen and never had a friend in his
life.*

*"We're not supposed to play with you. We should go back,"
she says.*

*"Don't say that. It hurts. Don't go. Please. How about a
little game?"*

"Okay," the little one says.

"Guess what I'm going to do."

*"What are you going to do?" The little one wants to play.
Hood had no friends in his life.*

Suddenly, he has two.

It was CNN reporting the live news conference of the parents
of the lost girl. There was an inset picture of her, ten years
old. Paige Baker. The anguished mother was talking about her
disappearance in front of several dozen microphones.

Hood knew. *It's her.*

He stared so intensely at the TV news pictures his knuckles
whitened. His hands were gripping the table with such force
it creaked and his chains chinked.

"Petitioner's rights were violated under these articles of the
Constitution of the State of Montana and the following Amend-
ments to the Constitution of the United States because . . . What
is it? Isaiah, are you OK!"

Hood's body began trembling.

Cohen banged on the door.

"Guard!"

Yet Hood's brain had slipped into a tranquil trancelike state.
That face. The older one. The little one.

The message was coming through now.

Isaiah would not die in this prison.

CHAPTER
TWENTY-TWO

FBI agents encircled Doug and Emily Baker after their news conference near the command center. Bowman was among them.

"Everybody OK?" She placed her hand on Emily's shoulder. "Doug, these fellas will take you inside to talk to Agent Zander and the other guys. Emily and I will go back now on this flight to wait at the campsite." Bowman indicated an approaching helicopter.

Doug took Emily quickly into his arms. His worried eyes were searching hers for something—he didn't know what. They didn't have the chance to talk privately after Emily talked to the police. Was that coincidence? Doug felt something was happening, something deep beneath the surface compounding his anguish and his guilt for having screamed at Paige before she vanished.

Bowman gestured. It was time to go.

Emily pulled Doug's head to hers. "Be careful," she said into his ear, then kissed his cheek.

Doug turned from Emily's embrace and froze.

Less than ten feet away, at the entrance to the command center, Bobby Ropa had been watching them.

The contempt in Ropa's icy stare chilled Doug, making him uneasy—even more so than when this jerk came upon them arguing on the trail. The way this strange family just stood there spying on them for such a long time before declaring their presence. It was unusual. Now the guy's face was telegraphing scorn. Disturbing. What if he had something to do with Paige's disappearance? Doug's jaw clenched. *If this asshole harmed my daughter in any way.* Doug swore to God he would—he should just walk up to him and ask what he's doing here.

"Dad, I just counted the news trucks. Guess how many?" The man's son, who was about Paige's age, ran to his father's side. Noticing the standoff with Doug, the kid stared, then looked away, as if he possessed a secret too risky for him to conceal. Had this family just been questioned by police? What the hell was happening? The father took his kid and walked off.

"Right this way, Doug." Zander had witnessed the tense moment.

Inside the task force room, Doug finally exhaled, rubbing his face. He agreed to a cup of coffee.

"You know everybody here, Doug, except Inspector Walt Sydowski from San Francisco PD." Zander set a ceramic mug on the table before Doug.

"San Francisco? I don't understand why you're here."

Zander answered. "It's basic procedure, in assisting the physical search, that we investigate every link to Paige. That means working with the FBI and local law enforcement in San Francisco, in the remote case her disappearance was premeditated, or involves someone there who followed you here."

"But we told you she just ran off."

"That's right."

Doug ran a hand through his hair. *That other man.* "Oh God, you really don't think there is more to it?"

Zander regarded Doug. "We hope not. While the searchers are doing their job, we are working as fast as we can to eliminate all the terrible possibilities, or immediately act on anything concrete."

"Well, who was that man who just left? You know he was on the trail the day before Paige got lost. Did you talk to him?"

"Just finished. You know him? Ever see him before the trail?"

Doug shook his head. "Just the one time. What did he tell you?"

"That he and his family came upon your family having a discussion."

"What else?"

"Doug, can you tell us about everything before Paige got lost? It might help us if we overlooked anything. Take us back to the decision to come here for vacation. Would you do that for us? Then we'll fly you out to Emily."

Doug collected his thoughts.

"For the past few years, Emily was having trouble coming to terms with the deaths of her parents. She grew up here. She witnessed her father's death. He fell from his horse and was stomped to death. Her mother moved her to San Francisco, then abandoned her to relatives before she died in a homeless shelter. It began when Emily was around Paige's age, so it was coming up on her and she was having a hard time dealing with it. In fact, she refused to discuss it or reveal much of it to me."

"Was it a source of conflict within the family?"

"Yes, particularly in recent years as Paige reached the same age. We argued a lot. First in private, then openly in front of Paige." Doug stopped to grip his coffee mug with both hands, peering into it. "I am ashamed to admit that one argument a few days ago was so loud it forced a neighbor to report it to police. A patrol car came to our house. The officers calmed us down.''

Zander and Sydowski exchanged lightning-fast glances.

"So why come here?"

"Emily had never, ever returned to Montana since leaving with her mother. About a year ago, in San Francisco, at my insistence, she began getting counseling. We learned she was enduring a sort of post-bereavement crisis. Her counselor advised her that the most effective way for Emily to deal with her past was to return and confront it. Lay her ghosts to rest. So we took a vacation here, for her.''

"How did that go?''

"Not so well. Paige did not want to come. So I agreed to smuggle Kobee in as part of the deal. Dogs are forbidden in the backcountry, but that beagle is like a brother to her.'' Doug shook his head. His eyes glistened. "Emily was having a rough time with her ghosts and shut me out when I tried to talk to her. We argued. I figured it would be cathartic to get it all out, scream therapy in the mountains. We thought it was private until we discovered that guy's family was watching us for an abnormally long time. Paige had convinced herself that Emily and I were getting a divorce and it was breaking her heart.''

"That was the day before she got lost?''

"Yes. The fallout of our battle carried into the next day. We all needed some space. Emily went off to a cliff by herself. I was chopping firewood and was going to read. Paige and Kobee were alone in her tent; then she came out and tried to, to—''

Tears pooled in Doug's eyes, which were focused on the last images of his daughter. He rubbed his chin, as if summoning the strength to reveal what happened.

Noting that Doug used his right hand, Zander said, "Doug, it might be better if you tell us. It might help things.''

Doug swallowed.

"Uh, I was angry at Emily, at the whole damn thing, and I was chopping wood, working it off. Paige, she just wanted to talk to me. She came out and I'm just chopping away, angry at the world, and I screamed at her to get out of my face and join her mother up the trail on the ridge. Paige knew the way. We had all gone there the previous day a few times for Emily to take family pictures. It was no more than seventy yards or so.''

"Then what happened, Doug?"

"She wouldn't go. I was upset, chopping, and I hit my hand with my ax, bleeding all over. Looks worse than it is."

"How's your hand now?" Zander asked.

"It's OK. Like I said, looks worse than it is."

"You got a white strip around it?"

"Yes." Doug rotated his hand. "Tore my T-shirt to tend to it."

"Doug, would you mind showing us the cut?"

Doug looked at them.

"I said it's not that bad."

"Please."

He removed the strip to show a bloodied incision beginning at the knuckle of his right forefinger and flowing several inches into his palm.

Zander reached for Doug's hand, holding it palm out.

"Does it hurt? You want someone to look at it? You could have tendon damage, or need stitches."

"It's OK, really."

"Mind showing how you did it? Demonstrate."

Doug considered the request while wrapping his hand.

He raised his right hand in a chopping motion, holding his left hand extended. "I was holding the log with my left hand when I swung and cut it, like that."

Doug brought his ax hand down in one swift arching movement; that image burned, lingering like the intense flash of a crime scene photographer's camera at a homicide. The room fell silent . . . until Zander spoke.

"Then what did you do, Doug?"

"I screamed at Paige, worse than I ever have at any football player. I terrified her. I was bleeding and yelling. I chased her off with Kobee. I was so angry. Not at her. I chased her off. I am so sorry."

"Why didn't you go after her?"

"I was white hot, not thinking clearly. I tended to my wound and thought she would be better off with her mother. A couple of hours passed with me thinking Paige was with Emily, but then Emily returned alone. She thought Paige was with me. That's when we realized what had happened. We rushed to the trail, took opposite sides, searching for her, calling for her and Kobee until it got dark. The next day, just before dawn, I hiked out for help."

Doug cradled his temple in his right hand, staring down at the table.

No one in the room voiced a word.

Doug sighed, exhaustion and anguish overwhelming him. His tears splashed on the table; his left hand relaxed from the coffee mug and the strip slipped, revealing that horrible gash.

Zander, Sydowski and Thornton each evaluated what was just witnessed: a father consumed by the anguish of a faultless tragedy, or the calculated display of a cold-blooded killer.

FBI agents had secretly searched the Bakers' campsite.

They had not found Doug's ax.

CHAPTER TWENTY-THREE

Inspector Linda Turgeon waited at her desk in Room 450, the Homicide Detail of the San Francisco Police Department, in the Hall of Justice, checking her watch. *Where are they?*

Turgeon could almost hear the second hand ticking down on Paige Baker as she studied the *Chronicle*, then the *San Francisco Star*, whose headline blared: S.F. GIRL MISSING IN ROCKIES. *Is she still alive?* Wilson went to the faces of Paige's father and mother, which accompanied the front-page article. *A horrible tragedy, or something worse?*

Molly Wilson from the *Star*, like the other local reporters, was all over her, pumping for data. Wilson was one of the best diggers. She and Tom Reed produced a pretty good piece in the *Star*. Sooner or later, the lid was going to come off this thing. Turgeon and the press were tugging at threads, each one leading to another that would bring them closer to the truth.

Her own brass and the FBI were demanding more instant information, information they did not yet possess, to be sent to Montana. It was a whirlwind of bureaucratic hysteria.

Sitting here waiting on Jones and Pace, the two officers from the Richmond District who took the stale domestic call to the Bakers' home, she was getting a little ticked. They were late.

Flipping through her notebook, the scores of appointments, of people she needed to contact, Turgeon was relieved her boss, Lieutenant Leo Gonzales, had assigned more bodies to help with the overwhelming file. *Where are Jones and Pace?* For a moment, Turgeon found comfort in the fragrance of the dozen peaches-and-cream roses her boyfriend had sent to her. A thank-you for their reunion date. HERE'S TO POSSIBILITIES was printed on his card. Turgeon smiled.

Back to work, Inspector.

Turgeon reviewed all she had so far on the Baker call. Dispatch tape and CAD records. All she needed were the unit log notes and the recollections of the responding officers.

Turgeon could not dismiss the growing feeling something was not right in the lives of Doug and Emily Baker. She was anxious to hear from Willa Meyers, Emily's aunt. Hopefully, the aunt could elaborate on the information that had come from Kurt Sikes.

The athletic-looking history teacher at Beecher Lowe High, where Doug taught and coached the football team, was deeply concerned for the Bakers. After Turgeon sidestepped his pressing her to arrange for players and students to go to Montana to aid in the search in some sort of "go, team, go" demo of school pride, Sikes gave her something useful.

"Well, not long ago, Doug told me how Emily was driving him out of his mind."

"How so?"

"Well"—Sikes dropped his voice to a confidential tone—"Doug said she was under psychological counseling for some past problem she was having trouble dealing with, and it was creating tension at home because Emily would not discuss it with him."

"What was the past problem?"

"I never found out because Doug only mentioned it that one time. We were having a beer at my place, watching a ball game. He seemed lost, almost haunted by it. He never talked about it again and I never asked him. Now this happens with Paige. Man, we got to find her. Doug and Emily have got to be hurting bad."

Turgeon closed her notebook and bit her bottom lip. She should go back to Sikes.

"Inspector Turgeon?"

Two uniformed officers, Jones and Pace, introduced themselves. Turgeon collected her file.

"We'll go to an interview room. You guys want a coffee?"

Both shook their heads. Hard faces. She should not have been surprised by the attitude. Turgeon had done a quick check on them. Pace was six feet four inches, a ceiling-scraping bodybuilder, an eleven-year veteran you wanted to keep happy and on your side.

Jones had sixteen years on the street. Her cynicism manifested itself in the taut lines around her eyes, her gray-streaked hair and her black belt in karate.

They were hardened warriors behind the shield. Between them, they had four citizens' complaints, all unsupported. Fourteen citations: rescuing attempted suicides, thwarting an armored car heist in progress, saving a baby in a burning building, disarming a gun-toting hostage-taker. Like most street cops who had a nanosecond to make life-and-death decisions, and years to be judged on them, they resented being second-guessed. Being defensive was an auto-reflexive action.

Their leather utility belts squeaked and their Kevlar vests pushed against their uniformed shirts as they scraped chairs out from the table and occupied them.

Pace circled his index fingers in tandem, inquiring if Turgeon was taping them.

"This is not being recorded."

"We were late because we talked to our rep."

"Why?"

"In case you guys are coming after us, for missing something on that call with that family," Pace said.

"What the hell—"

"We see the news. Read the papers. We figure you got something on the family in Montana and are hauling us in here to CYA on the domestic."

"Dead wrong."

Jones and Pace let a cold moment pass.

"Convince us," Pace said.

"We have nothing," Turgeon said. "We are looking everywhere. I need your help with anything you remember about the call that I can throw to Montana. That is it, kids."

"You building a case against the parents?" Jones asked.

"No, I am working one. Eliminating possibilities."

"That call was from last week. I barely remember it." Pace folded his massive arms.

Turgeon slid the thin file to them.

"Refresh your memory and get out your notebooks, because I know you brought them. Can you hurry it along, please."

After a few minutes, Pace began shaking his head, sticking his bottom lip out. "It's all there. Nothing more."

"It is not 'all there.' You guys were booked out on that scene for thirty minutes. Get out your notes."

Pace summarized it, flipping through his notebook.

A neighbor, some angry old coot, called in shouting and suspected assaults to the address. Claims he saw Doug raise a baseball bat to somebody in the house. The unit responded. No signs of violence and they were welcomed in without resistance. First, they put Paige alone in her room, out of harm's way. Other than crying, she seemed fine. Then Pace took Doug aside and Jones took Emily. Each parent was rational; no weapons present but there was a bat in the garage. No drugs or alcohol. No assaults. A loud disagreement over the wife's mood and refusal to discuss her feelings with her husband. Shouting and a smashed plate. The daughter confirmed it. No bat used. No charges. No report. No big deal.

"It was a nonevent," Pace said, closing his notebook.

"OK, that's the straight-up solid police-work version," Turgeon said. "Do you remember any little thing from that call, something that bothers you, or that you can't put your finger on?"

Pace shook his head.

"Jones?"

She was reflecting, studying her notes.

"Who talked to the daughter?" Turgeon said.

"I did," Jones said.

"Well, something in there strike you?"

"It was nothing really, but I remember the kid telling me how scared she got when her parents had an argument."

"She say they argued often?"

"No, not often."

"But something about it scared her? Scared how?"

"Like they were going to get a divorce because of her mother's problems," Jones said. "I dismissed it at the time. The girl was sobbing at the sight of police officers in their home. It was not the kind of home we go to. It was an emotional time, so I didn't think then that the divorce talk was anything out of the ordinary."

"But . . . ?"

Jones and Pace exchanged a look. Whatever they were going to give up had to be significant; the reason they went to their rep.

"The girl said her dad got mad at her mom because she would not tell him more about her problems."

"What were her problems?"

"She said her mother heard voices."

"Voices?"

"Something to do with people who died a long time ago."

"That's it?"

COLD FEAR   165

"They died in Montana and her parents had to go back there if things were going to get better."

Turgeon did not ask another question. She was too busy writing.

CHAPTER
TWENTY-FOUR

By mid-morning, a Montana forestry helicopter had touched down on the makeshift helipad of the command post at the Bakers' campsite deep inside Grizzly Tooth Trail.

Emily Baker and Agent Tracy Bowman were met by Incident Commander Brady Brook. There was no encouraging news.

"Nothing so far, ma'am." He shook his head sadly. The other rangers attempted to look off, or got busy in a respectful attempt at giving Emily privacy to absorb the negative update.

Emily nodded, wiped her eyes with a crumpled tissue, then returned to her lonely vigil at the camp's edge overlooking the forest.

The search planes and radio chatter somehow comforted her, like the din of a choir practicing in a church.

"Emily, please, have some of this."

Bowman had brought her a tin cup of chicken noodle soup.

"It's mostly broth. Please, you need something."

She reached up with both hands to accept its warmth.

"Thank you, Tracy."

Emily sipped some of the broth. It was good. She gazed at the view.

Bowman sat next to her with a cup for herself.

"Tell me about your husband, Tracy. Please?"

Bowman remembered Zander's advice to befriend Emily. "All right," she said, conjuring up Carl's handsome, kind face. "He was a loner. Grew up near Butte. Joined the U.S. Army Corps of Engineers. Served in Desert Storm. Never talked much about it, except to say Kuwait was like Montana without the grass and the mountains. After that, he started his own towing business. We met in a godawful snowstorm outside of Missoula when I was working as a highway patrol officer before I was accepted into the FBI Academy. Just talked and joked the night away. He had a good heart. I fell in love with him that night. We were married about a year later, had Mark a year after that. Carl had dreams of expanding his business statewide. He just loved driving around out here looking for people to help. He had a big-sky soul. He belonged to Montana, and Montana belonged to him."

Emily's face was sympathetic. "Tell me about your son."

"Just like his dad. I see Carl's eyes and hear his voice in Mark. He's good-hearted like his father. They were good together. Buddies."

"That must give you some comfort."

"Mmm, it does."

"You ever think about what would happen if you lost him? I mean—having lost Carl—you—I'm sorry." Emily sniffed. "It's none of my business."

"Don't apologize. It's OK. Yes, I think about it. Mark's got a congenital lung condition. It makes breathing difficult for him at times. It's not terminal but he'll always have it."

"I guess you know how life is so fragile, so very . . . temporary."

"Yup."

"Do you think I will ever see my daughter again?"

Bowman scanned the forests and ranges of mountains that stretched to an eternity. "I don't know."

"Thanks for the honest answer."

Bowman reminded herself she was an FBI agent assisting in an investigation. Zander's words echoed with the choppers over the valley.

All she may need is a little nudge. You decide when to push.

"How was it for you growing up here, Emily?"

"Heavenly. We had a place my grandfather built near Buckhorn Creek."

"That's not far from here."

"No. It had a rafter roof. I had a horse. Dad worked on a feedlot. My parents got me my first camera and I started learning about photography here, studying Dad's old *Life* magazines."

"Why did you leave?"

Emily looked to the mountains for the answer.

"Guess what I'm going to do."

Bowman thought it best to wait her out. A full minute passed.

"I moved with my mother to San Francisco after my father was killed."

"What happened?"

"He fell from his horse while working on our ranch, got kicked. I saw it happen."

"Oh my God. I am so sorry."

"I was fifteen. It happened because he was distracted. He was upset with me."

"What on earth for?"

"A rumor was going around town that I lied about something. Something important."

"What was it?"

"I can't tell you."

"Did you lie about this important thing?"

"No, I did not. But now, things have gotten so crazy. It's like—"

"Guess what I'm going to do."

"Stop it!" She hurled her cup down the mountain, the tin tapping and tinking all the way down, underscoring the echo of her "Stop it! Stop it! Stop it!" Emily thrust her face into her hands and sobbed.

Bowman held her.

"Emily. Please. You have got to talk to me."

"It's happening again. It's happening again. I cannot let this happen again. Oh God, please! Paige!"

Bowman struggled to hold Emily. Her entire exhausted body was writhing in torment. Others rushed to her aid as her echoing screams were soon drowned out by the approaching thunder of an FBI helicopter, forcing the command post staff to struggle to hold down the flapping maps, as Emily rocked in Bowman's arms.

What the hell is this family hiding?

CHAPTER TWENTY-FIVE

In San Francisco, a few days before Paige Baker vanished in the Rocky Mountains, Sheila Walton was having trouble sleeping.

It arose from a call Walton had received from Henrietta Umara, principal of Beecher Lowe, requesting a meeting. A day or so before the school break, Walton's fourteen-year-old daughter, Cammi, confided something that had alarmed Umara.

"She told me one of her teachers had"—Umara searched for the precise word—"*allegedly* struck her."

"*Hit her?* Who was it? What happened?"

Walton's body numbed, her ears rang, as she sat there in Umara's office, absorbing the words. Not believing them.

"Ms. Walton, has Cammi told you anything of this?"

Walton shook her head, eyes stinging with tears. "Not a word. I can't believe she did not come to me. What did she say happened? When?"

Umara passed her a tissue.

"She was vague about it. She provided no details. Did not even identify the teacher, until this morning. She called me."

"She called you?"

"It could be a misunderstanding. A misinterpretation. Or, it could be serious. She alleged to me that something happened a few days ago. I had to attend a conference in Sacramento. I could not reach you. Cammi told me the incident took place five days prior to the start of the school break."

"What happened?"

"Her words: 'My teacher slapped me.' "

"Slapped her?" Walton blinked back tears. "Who is this teacher? Have they been suspended? I want to know more."

"I will deal with the teacher first."

"You mean before I press charges?"

"Ms. Walton, I know this is difficult, but we're moving a little fast here."

"You don't want me to press charges?"

"No."

"No?"

"Nothing like that yet."

"Well, what then? You call me down here and—"

"Please, I'd like you to try to learn more from Cammi about what is alleged to have happened. So far I only have her allegation."

Walton's gaze went beyond Umara to the office walls, the U.S. flag, the framed certificates, a photo of her with the first lady, and the plaques of the school's achievements. She now understood why Cammi had seemed so withdrawn, so sad, recently.

Why didn't you tell Mom first?

"What do we do now, Ms. Umara?"

"Proceed cautiously. I'll speak to the teacher. He does not know yet. No one else knows yet. This is extremely confidential. As I said, Cammi was vague. I am hoping you will be able to clarify what she believes took place. Although school is recessed, I have the safety of other students to consider. Please get back to me as soon as possible."

"I will. Thank you."

After walking Walton to her car, Umara returned to her office and the personnel file folder on her desk. She flipped through it again and sighed. Doug Baker's reputation, his accomplishments, were exemplary. Stellar.

What is it, Doug? Drinking? Drugs? Stress at home? You need some time off? If we could have talked first. I hope you check your machine at home for messages. Doug, I have to go by the book. No protection. She looked at his school ID photograph. Into his eyes. *It can't be. I thought I knew you. But if it is true. Cammi Walton!* The daughter of Sheila Walton, the junior partner in Pitman Rosser and Cook, specializing in criminal trials. Sheila Walton, the San Francisco police commissioner, pegged by some as the next mayor or U.S. senator.

For several days at their uphill home straddling the Richmond District and Presidio Heights, Walton struggled to get Cammi to discuss the incident.

"It was Doug Baker, my English teacher. I don't know why he hates me. He got mad at me and just slapped me. I don't want to talk about it anymore."

"Besides Ms. Umara and me, have you told anyone else?"

"No."

"No friends? Not even Lilly or Beth? Be straight."

"Nobody."

Cammi distanced herself from her mother at the far end of the sofa. Her knees pulled together under her chin as she gripped the remote and flipped between muted music-video channels. Tears rolled down her daughter's cheeks. Walton felt helpless.

She had met this guy once at some school function. They talked about football and city politics. Good-looking and virile. Beautiful wife. Daughter.

None of this made sense.

"Cammi, tell me exactly what happened. Everything."

Tears continued welling in her daughter's eyes.

"It was after class. I went up to ask him a question about *Lord of the Flies* and he pushed me against the wall. He got so angry with me. I was so scared. He called me stupid for not understanding the book. He said people who have problems should talk about them, not keep them to themselves. Then he slapped me, telling me not to be so stupid."

Walton was stunned.

It did not make sense. The image of that man hurting her child appeared in her mind like a scene from a nightmare. Such a violation. Walton reached for the phone to call this guy right now. *Stop. No, not yet.* It just did not make sense.

Could this be more complicated? Could it be fallout from her divorce with Greg? From three years ago? Lord, would she have to tell him? She anticipated his reaction from his cell phone in Santa Monica: *"Why aren't you taking care of her, Sheila? What is more important to you than Cammi?"*

The bastard was getting married next month. Cammi seemed to be handling it well.

Maybe Walton could resolve it without calling Greg. But Cammi had been on a path of defiance for the past year—over clothes, friends, curfews, phone time, make-up, the unicorn tattoo she threatened to get on her ankle. Her grades had slipped drastically.

Walton looked in on Cammi one night while she slept, marveling at how her child was changing before her eyes. From diapers to body piercing. Her baby was gone. A confused, headstrong young woman in a fourteen-year-old's body had replaced her. She stroked her hair and kissed her forehead.

She called Umara at home to tell her she needed a little more time to try to get her daughter to talk more about the incident.

A few mornings later, Walton reached the peak of her crisis. As usual, Lupe, Walton's housekeeper, placed that morning's

San Francisco Star next to the ceramic coffeepot on the table, in the nook, overlooking the huge shade trees of the backyard.

The article and pictures on the search for Doug Baker's daughter, Paige, awaited her. *What is this?* Walton devoured it before touching her coffee.

"Cammi!"

They went over the article several times with Cammi repeating, "Oh my God! That poor little girl!" Walton's fears increased while looking at Paige Baker's picture in the newspaper, then at Cammi. She looked hard at the picture of Doug Baker.

Walton sent Lupe out to buy all the newspapers. She and Cammi read every story on the case while flipping through the TV news. Cammi sat before the set, a hand covering her mouth. Watching the helicopters, the tense faces of the reporters in Glacier National Park, Walton struggled to think clearly. Her instincts as a criminal-trial lawyer, a seasoned police commissioner, a guilt-ridden single mother, all churned in her stomach as she watched her daughter's reaction to the story. Cammi turned to her, eyes filled with worry. "Mom, what do you think happened?"

Walton searched the TV news for her answer, concentrating the same way she did when she studied confidential police reports.

"I may want you to talk to somebody, honey."

"Talk to somebody?"

"Let me make a few calls first."

Walton went to her study and sat at her desk. She shuddered, placing her face in her hands to collect herself. A moment later, her hands were shaking as she dialed the first number. The cellular phone for the chief of the SFPD.

CHAPTER
TWENTY-SIX

Time was Brady Brook's enemy.

Second by second, minute by minute, hour by hour, it was defeating him.

Despite all that Brook, the searchers and the dog teams had tried, they could not locate a trace of Paige Baker or her beagle.

The hope of using a helicopter equipped with an infrared heat-sensing camera was abandoned because the region was too perilous to fly night searches. Paige had been in the wilderness for more than fifty hours. If they did not find her within the next two days, three at the most, it was not good. Dread grew for the awful moment he would have to look into the faces of Emily and Doug Baker to tell them their daughter was gone forever.

Or would he face something worse?

Brook glanced from the map table at the Bakers, huddled at the edge of the site, looking so small against the mountains, hanging on to each other under the eyes of the FBI agents.

Was he in the presence of a pair of cold-blooded murderers?

It hinged on what his people turned up. He went back to concentrating on the search, quietly talking on the radio, studying maps and the terrain data on the laptop computers.

He went over everything. Areas of probability according to Paige's weight, height, speed of travel, weather conditions, her clothing, her food supply, her experience. Outlining new sectors, searching others again. He had the very best people out there who knew every ledge and loose rock zone. They had out-of-state SAR people, volunteers from surrounding counties and the Blackfeet Indian Reservation, all experienced in the backcountry, searching outer sections; the Royal Canadian Mounted Police and Waterton Park wardens were scouring the Canadian side that borders Grizzly Tooth Trail. Several helicopters and fixed wing aircraft helped from the sky.

Yet, so much was working against them. The first night it rained, washing out a scent for the dogs. She was in bear territory. And having her dog was like ringing the dinner bell. Why had they not discovered a single shred of this kid? It was disturbing. The park superintendent, the planning and operation chiefs, all agreed when they flew out earlier for an on-site status briefing. It was puzzling. By this point, they usually found something, a footprint, a candy wrapper. *Something.*

Brook was a God-fearing, churchgoing father of two daughters aged seven and nine. It was as if he was searching for one of his own children. He never counted on it taking such a private emotional toll. As district ranger at Glacier for six years, he had been Incident Commander in scores of major searches. He knew each one had its own circumstances. In this one, Paige could be hiding. She could be surviving. She could have fallen. Injured. Slipped into a crevasse. Slipped into a river, drowned, her body carried downstream. She could have been taken by a bear. Abducted by a stranger. He glanced at the Bakers. *Or worse.*

He removed his wire-rimmed glasses and rubbed his face, remembering the Bakers' first reaction when certain questions about Paige's demeanor were raised. They were so obviously evasive, guarded, not forthcoming.

He also remembered the sobering section of the SAR Plan that advised in major cases to consider criminal intent no matter how remote the possibility. Brook's radio on the map table received a static-filled transmission. A distant one broken up badly, until the signal bounced off a repeater in a passing helicopter and came through clearly.

Ranger Tim Holloway was one of the park's best SAR people. He was in outstanding physical condition. He could move his lean, firm surfer's body over the roughest territory, faster than anyone else in the park. "Only an eagle could cover more ground faster than Holloway," other rangers joked.

Last year, when he turned twenty-five, Holloway climbed Mount Everest with friends from England and New Zealand. He reached the summit. It had been a dream since he was a kid growing up in Santa Ana, California. So Holloway was Brook's natural choice to backtrack on Grizzly Tooth to scour the treacherous shoulders of the trail.

But Holloway had found zero since he started, and it was upsetting him. Determined to find the missing girl, he pushed himself, moving swiftly, scanning thoroughly every inch of the trail's shoulder. If there was anything to be found, he would find it. He had passed along a hair-raisingly narrow ledge about twenty yards beneath the trail, a mile or so, south of the campsite, when he saw it. Holloway grunted as he made his way to a stand of spruce, on a steep incline below the trail.

"Bingo, dude."

A small pink T-shirt entangled in the branches. It looked so out of place, creepy, like a primitive offering. Did a griz do that? Holloway swallowed. It looked bloodstained. Holloway reached for his radio.

Within a half hour, the FBI had its evidence people at the

scene, sealing the area, photographing it from the ground, from the trail above, even from the helicopter pounding overhead and the airplane from a higher altitude. They were also videotaping the entire procedure.

"Like I keep telling you, nobody has touched it since I found it," Holloway told the FBI people.

They put on blue coveralls, pulled on surgical gloves, sifted the area, took more pictures and then up close video before plucking the shirt from the tree. One produced a kit with test strips, dipped one in a small bottle of distilled water and touched it against the stain. It turned dark green confirming the stain was blood. The T-shirt was placed in a bag and sealed; more pictures were taken.

One of the agents with a small suitcase told Holloway to sit down.

"Take off your boots and give them to me. Need an impression of them."

"Sure thing." Holloway began unlacing them. "You know, a bear or animal could have put the shirt up there."

"Also looks like it could have been tossed up there from the trail. Like someone was trying to get rid of it in a hurry."

Holloway turned to gauge the height and angle. FBI dude could have a solid theory there.

The T-shirt was choppered to the command center. Inside the FBI's large white evidence van, the T-shirt was subjected to a special reagent test; its stained fibers were examined under a microscope. Conclusion: the blood was human. Urgent calls and arrangements were made to fly the T-shirt immediately to the crime lab used by King County in Seattle, to undergo further analysis.

In keeping with chain of evidence procedure, an agent who helped recover the shirt was rushed to Kalispell Airport. The FBI and the Justice Department delayed departure of a Seattle-bound Northwest DC-9 in time for the agent to board it. The shirt was in his briefcase.

In the task force office of the command center, Agent Frank Zander and the other investigators watched the video recording of the scene where the shirt was discovered. They studied the images in silence. The T-shirt looked so small when one of the evidence team members displayed it for the camera. It was horribly stained with blood. Zander stared at it coldly.

After the video ended, Agents at the table had transferred the digital still color photo of the shirt into their computer, with the enlarged monitor. They selected an image of the shirt unfurled to its full size, emblazoned with the browned blood. They froze the image, split the screen, clicked on the mouse until the faces of Doug, Emily and Paige Baker and Kobee appeared. It was the pictures Emily had taken at the outset of their trip to Glacier.

Smiling. Happy. Breathtaking scenery. All-American bliss.

The agents stopped on one photo of Doug and Paige. His arm was around her; both were grinning. Paige was wearing a pink T-shirt. The agents sized the two photos, unifying their scale. Paige, happy and bright in her pink shirt; next to it, the shirt found in the trees. Bloodied.

Zander looked into Doug's eyes. Into Paige's eyes.

In most child homicides, a parent or guardian was the perpetrator. The nearest and dearest rule. Zander knew that. In crimes of passion, frenzied rage, involving the use of knives or bladed instruments, it was common for the attacker to cut or injure himself. Zander knew that. What he did not know—his eyes boring into those of Paige, Doug and Emily—was the truth about this family. Something happened and he was going to find out.

"I think I'd like to get Doug and Emily Baker back in here and put them on the box."

Lloyd Turner, FBI Special Agent in Charge of Salt Lake City Division, nodded. "It's already on its way, Frank."

The tapping of a pen on a yellow legal pad distracted Zander and the others to Nora Lam, legal counsel from the U.S. Justice Department.

"You're intending to polygraph the parents, which you know cannot be used as evidence."

"I am aware of that," Zander said.

"You're walking a fine legal line here. Depending on how you proceed and when, or if, you Mirandize these parents, you could cross it. You understand what is at stake?"

Zander turned back to the picture of Paige Baker.

Remembering the fragrance of magnolias and peaches, the red mud of a country road to a rural Georgia, and the graves of two little boys, one of whom he failed to save.

"I understand what is at stake. Believe me. I understand."

CHAPTER
TWENTY-SEVEN

Molly Wilson's bracelets tinkled as she typed at her computer terminal in the *San Francisco Star* newsroom.

She had been on the story for several hours today and had nothing fresh on the Bakers despite all of her legwork in their neighborhood. Huck and Willa Meyers, Emily's relatives, were definitely on the road. Seniors don't sit at home in their rockers anymore.

But Wilson was counting on a lead she got from a neighbor girl who baby-sat for Doug and Emily: the Meyers' home address in Lake Merced. Wilson drove down there, did some door-knocking and found out that Huck and Willa were members of the Wander the World RV club. At her terminal, she called up the club's Web site. It had message service linked to all affiliated RV parks. She fired off an urgent one, then worked on her story.

Wilson had a few interviews to deal with, some reader phone-in reaction to the story. Psychics wanted to help. Church groups were going to pray. The usual. Nothing grabbed her. Some of the students and football players from Beecher Lowe, the school where Doug Baker taught, were planning to fly to Montana to help with the search. That wasn't bad. Tugged at the heart. They could go with that and—

She caught the BREAKING NEWS caption of CNBC off one of the large newsroom TVs. The Bakers were live with a news conference at Glacier National Park in Montana. Wilson snatched her Sony cassette recorder and her notebook. She trotted to the set, increasing the volume. Other newsroom staff had collected around it.

"... We will not go home without her. ..." *Reed better have this.* Wilson was taking notes. Studying Doug and Emily, curious about the secret police work she knew was going on behind the scenes. "... It's serious. We are well aware this is a life and death situation for our daughter, but we are praying. ..." Doug was a good-looking guy. Emily was beautiful. Paige was a pretty child. If the FBI determined anything criminal, the story would rock the country.... "Yes, we're aware of that possibility also and we understand they are examining every potential aspect, but primarily the thinking is Paige wandered from us and became lost. ..."

Primarily.

Now that's the pivotal word. Someone shouted Wilson's name.

"Molly, phone call!"

"Take a message."

Emily weeping. In pain. "... She is all we have in this world. ..."

"It's Huck Meyers in Canada. You said it was urgent."

"Hold him!"

Wilson raced back to her desk, bracelets clinking. She connected her recorder to the phone and took the call.

"Hello. This is Huck Meyers. We received an urgent message to call Molly Wilson at the *San Francisco Star?*"

"Yes, that's me." Wilson was relieved her red recording

light was blinking. She cleared a fresh page in her notebook and began.

"You know Emily Baker, Mr. Meyers?"

"I beg your pardon?"

"Emily Baker? You know her?"

"Well, yes. She's my niece. Willa's sister's girl. How can we help you? I got Willa right here. You said it was urgent. Is anything wrong?"

He had a kind, soft voice that was filled with trust. But Wilson was a skilled miner of information.

"Well, I am not exactly sure, sir. We're trying to learn more." Wilson spoke fast to deflect Huck's defenses and ingratiate herself. "You know, Emily did some work for the *Star?*"

"Oh yes. She's a photographer. Very good."

"Well, I am trying to learn a little more about her, her family history."

"Well, did you call her? They live in the Richmond. They're in the phone book."

"They are out of town. I thought you knew they were out of town."

"No. We left California several weeks ago, been out of touch. . . ."

Huck was bewildered and hesitant. Wilson could not allow long silences. *They obviously do not know about Paige.*

"I am just trying to learn a little more about her family history. She did some work for us and I understand she grew up in Montana. My colleague is from there. Is that where she learned photography? Maybe I could talk to Willa?"

"Is everything all right?" Huck asked.

Wilson threw him a fast question. "Does Willa know how long Emily lived in Montana?"

"Just a moment, please."

The phone was muffled. Wilson strained to listen, picking up "Something for the newspaper . . . they're out of town." Then Willa came on.

"Hello, this is Willa Meyers."

Wilson apologized and immediately spun some quick lines, engaging Willa, drawing her into the innocuous beginnings of a conversation.

"Yes, she is a very good photographer, did some work for *Newsweek* and *People,* too," Willa boasted. "That's how she met Doug."

"At *People?*"

"Newsweek. He was a marine at Camp Pendleton. She did a story on his outfit or something. They fell in love. He's such a nice man."

Wilson nudged Willa along, practically portraying the *Star* as an extension of Emily's family because of some freelance work she did about the Golden Gate Bridge.

"Tell me about her time in Montana, her life there?"

"This is for the paper?"

"Yes, we're writing about her in relation to some other news events and need to learn about her background. Tell me about her childhood in Montana and how she became such a good photographer."

Wilson could hear Willa thinking.

"Just a little biographical stuff," Wilson said. "Then I have to get going myself."

Willa Meyers began telling Wilson about Emily's childhood, about how her father taught her photography, and then about his death. Willa said his death devastated her mother, Willa's sister, forcing her to take Emily and leave their Montana home and come to San Francisco. Emily's mom could not cope and began drinking. She left Emily with her, then died.

"Such tragedy, but she came through OK?" Wilson said.

Willa hesitated.

"There were also some other things related to her time in Montana but it was so long ago. Emily was a child."

"What sort of things?" Wilson was losing her in the silence. "I'm sorry, Willa, I don't understand. What sort of things?"

"It had something to do with the death of a child years ago. Very sad. She was getting counseling. I shouldn't be—"

Death of a child.

Wilson's pulse and breath stopped.

"What do you mean? What were the circumstances?"

Silence. Wilson could hear some talking in the background at Willa's end.

"Willa, what do you mean? A crib death? Willa?" Wilson said. "Did this happen years ago in Montana?"

A long silence passed.

"Willa . . . ?"

"Yes, it happened in Montana. But . . . I think I've told you enough."

The line went dead in Wilson's ear.

She clicked off her tape recorder.

CHAPTER TWENTY-EIGHT

Lieutenant Leo Gonzales, head of the SFPD Homicide Detail, craved another coffee. He set down a file from early this morning, reading as he unwrapped an imported cigar. That's as far as he got when his line rang.

"Homicide. Gonzales."

"It's Web, Leo. What's the latest on our missing girl?"

"The mom was getting some sort of counseling, 'heard voices' linked to people who died years ago. That's how the kid put it to two of our people who took the domestic call to the house a while back."

"Anything else?"

"We're still waiting to contact a relative."

"Sheila Walton called me. Wants us to talk to her daughter. Seems Doug Baker is her English teacher."

"That so?"

"Kid claims he had an angry outburst and slapped her a few days before taking off to the mountains."

COLD FEAR
187

"We're talking about the daughter of Sheila Walton, the police commissioner?"

"Camille Rebecca Walton. Age fourteen. So take care of it right away. Here's her number."

"Will do, Chief."

Gonzales contemplated his cigar, which he was forbidden from enjoying within the environs of a municipal government office. *Sheila Walton.* Life used to be so simple. He shook his head and grimaced, then punched the extension for Inspector Linda Turgeon.

In less than forty-five minutes, Turgeon and Inspector Melody Hicks from General Works stood on the porch of Walton's home in Presidio Heights.

Lupe led them to the living room and Walton joined them. She wore a dark skirt and cream silk blouse; small pearl earrings accented her raven hair. The lady was elegant and attractive, exuding authority and intelligence.

After quick introductions, Walton offered tea, but they asked for coffee.

"You may use my study. I'll get Cammi."

The large study was dark and soothing, lined with floor-to-ceiling bookcases, Boston ferns in the corners, an exquisite Chinese vase—looked like Ming Dynasty—on one shelf. Lupe left the tray of coffee and cookies on the desk. The two detectives helped themselves.

Cammi was about five feet two inches, with a slender figure, short dyed red hair, and a stud in her left ear. She wore Capri pants and a powder blue top. No make-up today, Turgeon figured. Her eyes were reddened.

"Sit over here, Cammi." Hicks indicated the large leather chair facing the matching sofa, where she and Turgeon sat down.

"I'm Melody Hicks and this is Linda Turgeon. We're with—"

"San Francisco Police, I know. Mom told me."

Hicks set her coffee on an end table and produced a tape recorder.

"Look, Cammi. We have to record our chat. Those are the rules."

"I guess I'm OK with that."

"Good."

Hicks set her recorder on the table next to Cammi. She stated the date, place and who was present.

"Any questions, Cammi, before we begin?"

"I don't know why Sheila called you here. She seems to think this is a big deal. I don't. Do you think this is a big deal?"

"That is what we're going to try to determine." Turgeon smiled at the girl.

"I don't think it is a police thing. I just think maybe my dad should know."

Turgeon exchanged a quick, puzzled glance with Hicks.

"Why don't you tell us what happened?"

"It was after class. The term was ending and I stayed behind to tell Mr. Baker how much I liked *Lord of the Flies*. I told him I thought it was a good book. He told me he thought so, too."

"Were you alone?"

"Yes. So we're talking about the book and how it showed how people can lose control when they're isolated, or something; then he starts mumbling."

"About what?"

"Well, something about his wife. I didn't really understand. So I ask him, like, what's wrong. And all of a sudden, he got angry, telling me I had no right to ask about his personal life. Then he just slapped me."

"Show me exactly how."

Cammi gestured a slapping motion to her face.

"Did it hurt?"

"It stung."

"How were you positioned during this conversation?"

"I was against the wall, looking up to him."

"So he was very close?"

"Yes. It scared me. He called me stupid; then he slapped me. I think he was sorry the minute he realized what he did. But I ran away. Just got out of there. I didn't know what to do about it. So I went to my principal. I don't think it's that big a deal, do you? I mean, are you going to tell my dad that my teacher slapped me?"

"Your parents are not together?"

Cammi shook her head.

"Divorced three years ago. My dad writes movies in L.A. He has a girlfriend and they're getting married in a few weeks."

"You all right with that?"

Cammi shrugged. "Sure. We never see him anyway."

"How do you get on with your mother?"

"Sheila and I get along fine." Cammi stood. "So are we all done?"

Turgeon had a thought.

"Cammi, what do you think of Doug Baker's daughter lost in the mountains now?"

"It's terrible. What do you think?"

"Yes, it's terrible."

"I guess I don't want to see him get into trouble over this thing with me. I think he was sorry for it. Maybe I shouldn't have said anything."

"Well, leave it with us for now, okay?" Turgeon smiled.

On their way out, the two detectives spoke privately with Walton about keeping her apprised of their investigation.

"Thank you. I'd like to get to the bottom of this as soon as possible," Walton said, passing them both cards with her cell phone number.

190 *Rick Mofina*

During the drive back to the Hall of Justice, both women shook their heads in the wake of Cammi Walton's strange account.

"Doug Baker's looking *real bad* in my book right now," Hicks said.

Turgeon could not figure it out. Doug Baker was either some kind of ticking time bomb, or Cammi's version of events was a little out of focus.

"None of this makes sense," Turgeon said.

CHAPTER TWENTY-NINE

After Molly Wilson's call, Tom Reed tossed his cell phone into the tangle of maps, newspapers and take-out wrappers covering his passenger seat.

Emily Baker was undergoing counseling for the death of a child.

Wilson had succeeded with some impressive digging. It was up to him to see what he could do with the data.

He resumed writing today's story on Doug and Emily. His laptop computer was balanced against his stomach and the steering wheel. In between composing paragraphs, he was keeping an eye on the command center.

Activity was picking up. Agents were trotting back and forth between the building and the FBI's rented SUVs. Choppers were landing and taking off with more frequency. Something thudded on the roof of his car.

"Hey, Reed, what do you figure it is?" A friend with the *Philadelphia Inquirer* bent down to the driver's window.

"Beats me."

"Rumor is they found something out there."

"Any idea what?"

"Nobody knows. Nobody's talking. But the FBI guys are jumping around as if they were going to make a full-court press."

"If they found the girl safe, we'd hear."

"Yeah. I'm going to poke around. See ya."

Moments later, Reed left his car to get a handle on whatever was happening. The area surrounding the command center had become a virtual media village with dozens of ensconced news crews largely corralled by the Montana Highway Patrol to one area. Lawn chairs, sunglasses, satellite dishes and cell phones—that scene blended with the scores of police, park, emergency, rescue vehicles and personnel at the other side of the center. This was an intense midway vigil that had overwhelmed the small lot and surrounding roads.

Reed noticed that the paramedics at the ground ambulances and medi-vac helicopter were stationary and calm. OK, if they had found the kid alive, those guys would be activated. And if they found her body? Reed walked on, coming to the roadway's checkpoint and its two Montana Highway Patrol officers. One had a clipboard tally of the vehicles.

"Excuse me," Reed said, "can you tell me where the county coroner is parked? I missed the vehicle's arrival."

"Coroner? The coroner is not here."

"I was told they just arrived."

The officer with the clipboard flipped through sheets. "No, sir. Just a minute." The officer made a radio inquiry about the coroner. His radio responded with some static the officer understood. "Negative, sir."

"Sorry," Reed apologized. "I was misinformed."

No coroner. No paramedics. What could it be? On his return walk, Reed noticed two agents with the FBI's Evidence Team nearly out of sight between two vans, talking on their radios. He strolled over to the far side of the paneled van, pricking up

his ears, catching fragments of their low-key transmissions:
"Soon as they're done photographing the scene, it will be
choppered to Kalispell. They're holding a Northwest commercial. Sorensen's delivering it to the lab in Seattle. . . ."

The information was like found money, a recovered fumble.
Reed scooped it and tucked it away.

This thing was going to bust open soon. He scanned the area
for either Sydowski or a familiar FBI agent, someone he could
pump. No one around.

Back at the car, he closed his eyes for three seconds. This
and Wilson's stuff could add up. He considered it along with
Wilson's angle.

Emily Baker was from Montana. She was undergoing counseling for the death of a child.

He called the Associated Press Bureau in Helena. He had
friends there.

"AP, Larry Dancy."

"Hey, Dance. Tom Reed."

"How you doing, you old beach bum?"

"Older but no wiser. Yourself?"

"Can't complain. We're expecting our third next month."

"Congratulations, Dad."

"Thanks. So what're you up to? Still the big gun in San
Francisco?"

"Sure, a really big gun. Say, Dance, I'm out here in Glacier
on this missing girl story and I thought I'd give old Chester a
call, say hi. You know how I can reach him quick?"

"406-555-3312. Got a beautiful little place in Wisdom. He
still does some anniversary pieces for us."

"Thanks."

Chester Murdon was a living legend who had put in forty-
two years as a reporter with the Associated Press in Montana.
He knew every inch of the state and its history because he had

reported on much of it. He was a walking encyclopedia on Montana. Librarians for the state and universities throughout the country often consulted him. Chester retired several years ago but continued his series of state history books. Reed recalled when he was a summer cub reporter at the *Great Falls Tribune*. People in the Montana press were talking about Chester researching a book on summarizing every murder in the state's history, *A History of Murder Under the Big Sky*.

If Emily Baker's counseling was for a child's death related to a murder in this state, Chester would know. Reed heard the line ringing clearly. Finally, it was answered.

"Hello?"

"Chester Murdon?"

"That's me. How can I help you?"

CHAPTER THIRTY

In his Deer Lodge motel room next to the Four Bs Restaurant on Sam Beck Road, David Cohen flipped through the nightstand Bible while contemplating the lonely diesel whine and rush of air brakes of rigs negotiating Interstate 90, a quarter mile away.

An hour earlier, the clerk of the United States Supreme Court had alerted him to stand by for a response to Isaiah Hood's petition to the appeal of his death sentence. Not a hint of the decision in the call.

Cohen accepted the insurmountable odds of a favorable decision, but he could not restrain his human nature to search for hope.

His room phone jangled. It was the clerk in Washington, DC, confirming Cohen's fax number. The response was coming now. His eyes went around the room, to the muted TV on CNN, the two double beds, one unmade, the other buried under legal briefs, files, records, newspapers. Then to his portable fax, connected to his cellular phone, which trilled and blinked dutifully as his machine came alive, clicking into receiving mode.

Paper curled out of the machine. Cohen read it before the transmission was completed.

The decision came like a blow, forcing Cohen to sit on the cluttered bed, clutching the pages. *It's over. I've lost him.*

There was no reason given for denying the appeal. They never give one. Cohen shut his eyes. *The ashes will be distributed in the Livingston Range.* He then opened his eyes to the room's closet, seeing his dark suit hanging there, the one he would wear to witness Hood's execution, evoking the Grim Reaper as another solitary rig growled into the mountains. He stared blankly at the news pictures. He would have to tell Isaiah it was over. He was going to die. He was sorry, so sorry. And when it was over, he would fly back to Chicago and struggle to put it all behind him. He would go to a ball game. Friends would console him over beers at bars and parties. Others would change the subject. He'd take a trip, maybe Bermuda, in a Pilate-like attempt to cleanse the blood from his hands.

Soon he would have to stare into a man's eyes and tell him he had failed to save his life. He would watch him die and then carry his ashes in his rented car to the Rocky Mountains.

His motel phone rang. He knew who it was.

"David, it's Lane. I just got it. We tried everything. We knew going into this how hard it would—"

"Lane. Please understand, I don't feel like talking right now."

Cohen hung up, then swatted his files across the room. They scattered as he thrust his face in his hands. He sat in silence, listening to the trucks for a few minutes. Come on now, get a grip. He collected himself and his papers.

Much of the spilled file was that of the sole witness, the thirteen-year-old girl whose testimony sealed Hood's death warrant. There were pictures of her in a yellowing portion of the folder that Cohen had almost forgotten. Black-and-white images. Almost like police mugs. Maybe taken by Goliath County Sheriff's Office when she was first questioned. Cohen was not sure of the source. Pretty kid. Looked familiar.

Cohen lowered the photograph just as his attention was pulled to the muted TV and the report of the search for Paige Baker. A still color photograph of the lost girl flashed as the report played excerpts from her mother's news conference. Cohen's concentration pinballed at the speed of light to her face, her daughter's picture, the picture in his hand.

His jaw dropped.

He scrambled, rummaging through the newspapers for the lost girl stories, studying the news photos there, comparing them to those in Hood's files.

It's her. How could I have missed this? Emily Baker is the witness. It was her testimony that convicted Hood.

Cohen snapped through the files. The names were different. The firm had hired private investigators to track her down. But they were unsuccessful. Her mother had taken her from Montana years ago. They could not locate her. The investigators reported no record of her death, convictions or military service. She may have changed her name, her date of birth, her Social Security Number, or lied on records about eye and hair color. All the usual identifiers. But why would she or her mother go to such lengths?

In the early part of the case, Isaiah had said little in his own defense. Cohen flipped through the old records. Now he maintained his innocence in the death of five-year-old Rachel Ross.

Emily Baker's eyes stared at Cohen from the *Missoulian* splayed on the bed and from the old black-and-white court photo of her taken at the time of Rachel's death. He pored over her statement and the transcripts of her testimony.

Three people were on that ledge in the backcountry that day twenty-two years ago.

Isaiah Hood was backwater trash, the product of pitiful circumstances. He had less standing and sympathy in the community than a stray dog. No one was interested in the truth of the tragedy. Guilt suited Hood like his worn clothes. His court-appointed attorney barely performed his fiduciary duty. He never really challenged the confession of the county attorney's sole witness, a thirteen-year-old child.

Cohen shuddered. Throughout his handling of the case, he had secretly doubted his client's innocence, choosing to believe Hood's conviction was based on elements that violated his constitutional rights. They were enough to mire his case in year after year of appeals, in what was the judicial equivalent of false hope for a dead man.

But now, staring at the old pictures and those in the news stories, knowing that Emily Baker's ten-year-old daughter was missing in the same region and under similar circumstances as the case with her sister all those years ago, with the clock ticking down, Cohen feared—for the first time—that the state of Montana was about to execute an innocent man.

His motel phone rang again, reminding him that the attorney general's office would be calling after receiving its copy of the U.S. Supreme Court decision.

"David, John Jackson in Helena," said the AG's senior counsel.

"You got it."

"As you know, the case can now go to the Board of Pardons and Parole for executive clemency."

"It's done, John. I've set the mechanism in motion."

"As expected. But as I've told you, nothing has surfaced to give the governor reason to intervene. You and Ms. Porter must brace yourself for the inevitable likelihood that your client's sentence will be carried out at the date and time indicated on his warrant. We'll send you paper on that. I have your fax. We're issuing a press statement immediately. I am sorry, David."

"Hold on there, John." Cohen's voice was wavering, his eyes going to the TV screen and Emily Baker's face.

Could she have killed her sister and now her daughter? *They cannot execute Hood.* Somehow he had to stop it.

CHAPTER THIRTY-ONE

She is holding her little sister Rachel's hand. It is smaller, softer with the trust and vulnerability of a younger child, feeling like it belongs in hers forever.

All is right in their world. They are walking down the lane from their house near Buckhorn Creek to wait for their dad's pickup. Sitting in the summer grass, Rachel looks up to her, blinking in the sunlight.

"I love you, Lee."

"I love you, too, Sun Ray."

"Sun Ray." That's what Emily called her. She loved how Rachel had trouble pronouncing her name. She loved everything about Rachel. Little blue eyes twinkling from an angel's face, snow-white teeth, a sprinkling of freckles, tawny hair, which Rachel let her braid on long winter nights. They shared stories and dolls. They cried when their mother read them *Charlotte's Web*.

Emily would never forget those terrifying summer storms, pounding the mountains with thunderclaps rattling the house; lightning illuminating the sky as if the Rockies were collapsing. On those nights, Emily's bedroom door would crack open. Rachel would be standing there in the doorway holding her teddy bear, the lightning streaking her face.

"I'm scared, Lee."

She would lift her blanket, inviting her into her bed. Put her arm around her protectively, inhale the sweet scent of her little sister's hair, feel her warmth as she snuggled against her. Together, they were safe.

"I don't feel scared anymore."

The storm would subside and the whispering rain would lull them to sleep. How Emily would listen to it, wishing they could stay that way. Freeze time. Then the monster came.

"Guess what I'm going to do."

She is in the church now. The scent of candles, the polished wood of the pews, the oak floors, the fragrant flowers. Rachel's white casket is open. She is walking toward it. Her sister is lying inside, looking smaller. She is wearing a cotton dress with lace trim, her church dress their mother has made. Hands clasped and fingers entwined. Her teddy is tucked under her arm. The sleeves cover the bruises.

"Back of her head was split. Much of the damage was internal." The sheriff's deputies and some local men were behind the church, passing a small bottle, and talking.

Rachel's face is clear. Her eyes closed. Lee reaches in and takes her hand. It is cold. So cold. My Sun Ray.

"I don't feel scared anymore."

Rachel's death had fractured Emily's family. Her father never smiled. Every ounce of happiness had left him. Her mother

would sit alone for hours in Rachel's room not allowing anything to be touched. In their grief, her parents were melting
away from her when Emily needed them.

The words were never spoken, but in their anguish, they held
her responsible for her sister's death. They branded her with
blame, searing it into her soul.

It was her fault.

She was there.

*It is the annual summer camping trip with the Buckhorn
Creek Girls Club. Four days and nights in the backcountry of
Glacier National Park. Mothers and fathers are dropping girls
off at the Town Hall. Lee and Rachel's folks give them hugs
and kisses.*

"Remember to watch over your little sister."

"I will."

*Hauling their sleeping bags and packs from the car, waving
good-byes from the bus. Her parents waving, smiling for the
last time.*

*The group hikes deep into the park. The mountains, the
fragrant trees and clear water streams sparkle in the sun. This
must be the way to heaven, Lee thinks. Everything about the
trip is perfect. Rachel loves it. They pick flowers, make crafts,
sing songs by the campfire, toast marshmallows, tell ghost
stories, count stars. It is perfect.*

*The third afternoon the group has a scavenger hunt. When
her turn comes, Rachel reaches into a leader's hat and pulls
out a folded slip of paper with instructions to catch two butterflies and place them in the empty glass jelly jar.*

"Will you help me, Lee?"

*Rachel holds the jar while her big sister takes her hand and
they go to the meadow nearby.*

"Not too far, girls," one of the leaders calls after them.

The meadow is abundant with flowers, glacier lilies. Butterflies flit about them, white, pink and yellow. Emily is taking pictures of Rachel, laughing in the sun, chasing butterflies.

"Look, a blue one."

Rachel trots up the meadow hill to a forest edge.

"Rachel, wait!"

Rachel vanishes into a stand of spruce.

She follows, catching up to her as they come to the cliff, gasping as they halt in their tracks.

He is standing there. Smiling.

The monster.

Emily fought with every fiber of her being to tell Agent Tracy Bowman the things she could never tell anyone, not even Doug.

Paige had disappeared into the same abyss as Rachel. How could this be happening? Emily could not bear it. Could not. *Please.* She wept.

Arms wrapped around her, holding her together. Someone was saying her name. "Emily, it's OK to cry."

Doug? It was not Doug. He was off talking to searchers.

"Emily, it's OK." Bowman comforted her. "Tell me what is tormenting you."

Emily could not stop sobbing. *Doug.* Could not get the words out.

How do you begin to say *my daughter is lost where my sister died, and I am the one responsible?* How do you say that and keep yourself alive?

She should tell Doug.

But before she realized it, Emily could no longer contain her pain.

"It's happening again," she cried.

"What is happening again, Emily?"

"I was there when she died."

"When who died?"

"My sister. Now it is happening again."

CHAPTER
THIRTY-TWO

Stay focused, Dolores. Focused. Fidelity Bravery Integrity. I cannot let the team down. Got to find the lost little girl. But right now, FBI Special Agent Dolores Harding had to sit down to catch her breath.

She and Orin Mills had been scouring their assigned patch of Grizzly Tooth ever since daybreak. Coming up on fourteen hours.

"Over here, Mills!"

Twenty yards off, he raised his walking stick, signaling he would join her on the rock ledge in the shade of a stand of pine.

The sun was high. Harding's calves and thighs ached as she reached for her water bottle, scanning the mountains' majesty from behind her sunglasses. She was a marathoner, a twenty-nine-year-old hard-driving agent assigned to the OCPD at the Salt Lake City Division. It seemed only yesterday she was surveilling two case targets who were to arrive at Salt Lake City International Airport from Mexico City via LAX. They were no-shows. Could have been bad information. Or they were tipped.

It was two days ago, wasn't it? She was exhausted out here. For after that job, Harding suddenly found herself partnered in Glacier National Park with Special Agent Orin Mills with White Collar at the Division. Cerebral guys. Harding and Mills were part of the horde of agents dispatched from Utah. Even for some case-hardened agents, it was a gut-wrenching assignment. Harding saw how some of the agents who were fathers were quite pensive about this one, while the young jerks were quietly tabulating availability pay.

Mills was a big, friendly, soft-spoken, fifty-two-year-old Mormon with three grandchildren. Took this emergency assignment personally. Harding, a blue-collar girl who left Pennsylvania's Rust Belt to study criminology at John Jay in New York, and Mills, a churchgoer who was raised in Provo, had scoured Sector 21 three times. Heartache written in Orin's face as he joined her on the ledge, inhaling the air as it cooled in the sunset.

"Not much time left for looking today, Dolores. Can you imagine the horror this child is enduring?"

Harding regarded the mountains, the glacier valleys, and felt bad for quietly complaining about her body aches and discomfort. She was an adult FBI agent in jeans and a T-shirt, equipped with heavy socks, boots, water, food, a semiautomatic .40-caliber Glock, bear repellent, bug spray, first-aid kit, radio, training, physical conditioning. If a few hours searching a mountain slope had exacted this much on her, what would it do to a lost, frightened child from the city? Harding became angry at the mountains, as if they were an informant refusing to disclose life-and-death information. Come on, give her up. You do not need her. Give her up. This has gone on long enough.

Harding reached for her well-thumbed sector map. Precision-folded and marked.

"We've got some time, Orin. Any areas you want to revisit—*darn!*"

Harding dropped her water bottle; it tumbled and swished for a few yards. She climbed from the ledge carefully to retrieve it. It had rolled into a small surface fissure. As she reached for it, a metallic glint seized her attention. Harding shone her penlight into the crack, which was about two feet. She removed her sunglasses, eyes adjusting to the light on a small ax.

"Mills! We got something here!" Concentrating, Harding was certain she saw a lace pattern of browned blood on the head reaching to the handle. Gooseflesh rose on her arms. "Mills! It's not good! Stay where you are and get ERT on the radio. We need them here now!"

The FBI's Evidence Response Team descended upon the scene. Yellow crime scene tape sealed the area. Radios crackled; helicopters landed nearby or hovered; photographs were taken. Harding was instructed to remain at the scene, to maintain the evidence chain.

Suddenly, she found Frank Zander next to her.

"You're Harding? You made the find?"

Even dreamier up close.

"Yes, I found it. Just dumb-ass luck."

"Good work."

It was a camping ax. A one-and-a-half-pound Titan Striker with a drop-forged steel head and a sixteen-inch curved handle with a rubberized cushion grip. It was placed in a plastic evidence bag and flown from the area on Harding's lap under the last vestiges of daylight.

It fit the description of Doug Baker's ax given earlier by the New York detective, thought Zander. They could check the serial number for distribution points, run credit cards. He was standing off by himself at the scene, staring at the Rockies. A bloodstained T-shirt, a bloodied hatchet, a public argument, a domestic dispute at home, a mother undergoing counseling.

The pieces were falling into place. A noose was being fashioned. Zander's jaw clenched.

It was time to talk to Doug Baker again.

Time to learn the truth.

CHAPTER THIRTY-THREE

Concern flowed through the phone line from John Jackson, the chief lawyer for Montana's attorney general in Helena.

"David, are you all right?"

Since David Cohen had taken on Isaiah Hood's case three years ago, the two lawyers had developed a strong professional kinship.

"John, there's been a development."

"*A development?* What sort of development?"

Standing alone in his disheveled motel room in Deer Lodge, Cohen ran a shaking hand through his hair.

"A grave, urgent development."

"David, the governor will not intervene. The sentence will be—"

"John, I believe he *is* innocent."

Jackson knew losing a death sentence appeal was a punishing blow for death penalty lawyers to absorb. Jackson had lawyer friends in Florida and Texas. Few people know of the horror they often endure. One committed suicide. Jackson gave the eulogy.

"I absolutely believe that the state will be executing an innocent man."

Cohen's eyes burned into the TV news.

"David, the Supreme Court has rejected you. There is no basis of law—"

"To hell with the law."

"David, have you been drinking?"

"No, John. Just hold off on your press release and give me some time—"

"I can't. I—"

"John, I swear, if you go ahead with this, Montana will never recover. You will have your place in history for having sealed its fate as the judicial pariah of the nation. I swear—"

"David, I know this is a difficult time—"

Cohen sniffed and checked his watch.

"Listen. Hear me out. All I am asking, John, is for two hours to talk to my client. Then let me talk to the governor. I guarantee he will want to hear this before you kill Hood."

"I don't know. . . ."

"Just hold off on anything for that long. Christ, John, we're still two days away. Please just hold off. No press releases yet. Not a word."

Jackson sighed. Cohen heard his chair squeak.

"John, please. You have a man's life in your hands."

Jackson's concern was for Cohen, not for Hood, the child killer. No one in the entire state was concerned for him, except the candle-holding protesters, but they were not abundant in Montana. Still, Jackson could not see what harm two hours would do. The state had all the power. He could stall the release for that long without much difficulty. Most people were distracted by the search for the little girl in Glacier. Seemed to have eclipsed Hood's case.

"I will see what I can do. You've got two hours."

* * *

Now with the sun setting, everything became clearer to Cohen as he sped his Neon along Lake Conley Road to the prison, going through the security ritual, the razor wire, the clanging doors, icy stares from the guards, to see Hood on death row.

Hood's reaction to the TV news reports on the search now made sense.

He had a seizure. He recovered shortly after, but his nervous system short-circuited, sending him into a trance when he saw her.

He knew right then it was her.

Cohen was admitted to death row and was taken into the visitor's room. The TV there was switched off.

"Could you please turn that on, to one of the twenty-four-hour news channels and leave the sound on low so we can hear it?"

"You want to watch TV?" the guard said.

"Yes."

"Suit yourself."

Above the TV's sound, he heard Hood's chains approaching. Suddenly, Cohen was drowning in anguish and doubt. What the hell was he doing? He could not pull this off. This was unethical. He had to face the truth. He lost.

". . . . *the ashes will be distributed . . .*"

The door handle turned. Oh God. Cohen swallowed.

Hood stood before him, shackled in his orange prison coveralls. He sat down, his eyes shooting up to the TV, then to Cohen.

"Supreme Court turned me down, right, David?"

Cohen peered into Hood's eyes, believing for the first time he was seeing into the soul of an innocent man. He could not find the words to tell him he was going to be lawfully executed.

"I—I am so sorry, Isaiah."

Hood flattened his hands on the table.

"Well, I guess that's all she wrote, huh?" Hood attempted a smile. Then Hood stood, shuffled over, extended his handcuffed hands to shake Cohen's, his chains chinking.

"David, you did your best. You're a fine man. Thank you."

Hood returned to his seat.

Cohen sniffed. "Um, we still have an option."

"You don't mean the Board? There's no chance there."

"No." Cohen sniffed again, unsnapping the locks of his briefcase to produce some files. "Your claim of innocence."

Hood unleashed a chilling con stare, his voice was damn near cold-blooded. "This some sort of fucking joke?"

"No joke." Cohen opened the file to the photograph of the girl whose testimony secured his death sentence. "Who is that in the old picture?"

Hood stared at it. All those years ago. He did not think he ever saw that particular picture of the older one.

"That's the sister of the dead girl. The one who testified."

"Uh-huh." Cohen turned, indicating the TV. "And who did you see up there earlier in the report of the missing child? It will come up again."

Hood looked at Cohen, unsure if he was nuts ... or his salvation.

"It was her. Same one, only older, and now her kid is lost in the mountains."

"That's right, but nobody knows it's her, Isaiah. Her name is different. She changed it. Which is curious."

"So what. David, I know almost as much about the law as you. So her daughter is missing. So what?"

"Look at it this way. Admittedly, we presented nothing new in your Supreme Court petition, which was an attempt to create reasonable doubt, which I believe should have been a factor."

"Your point?"

"You told me you did not kill Rachel Ross. Her death was

not murder and her sister is the only living person who knows the truth.''

"That is right."

Cohen cleared his throat, swallowed anxiously, then dropped his voice.

"Suppose it got out through the news in a story as big as the search story itself that your claim of innocence is directly linked to the disappearance of Paige Baker, daughter of the only witness in your case?"

Hood stared long and hard at his young Chicago lawyer.

CHAPTER THIRTY-FOUR

The sun was dropping as Tom Reed pushed the accelerator to the mat. The rental was gliding south on Interstate 93. He was gambling with time.

It was a calculated risk.

Chester Murdon in Wisdom was convinced of something familiar about Emily Baker. He was quite certain he could find something in his collection of personal archives that would help Reed. He promised to wait up for him, no matter the hour, if he decided to come. A professional courtesy from one newsman to another.

Before leaving the command center, Reed filed a news story encompassing the press conference given by Doug and Emily. He incorporated theories and probabilities and the fact "FBI sources had not ruled out the possibility of criminal intent." It was a standard line. Police seldom rule out anything until they have an investigation under control.

"The desk will advance your lead, Tom," Wilson said from the *San Francisco Star* newsroom over Reed's cell phone as his rental approached eighty miles an hour. "I'll work in my stuff. So you think we should hold back on the psychological counseling? It is very strong."

"I know it is risky, Molly, but Chester is confident he can help us with more information. We can fill in the blanks about the family. Then put it all together. Let's just hold it."

"Tom, I don't know. The *Chronicle* could get it. I mean, I am sure I am the only one who reached the aunt, but somebody could nail it from other sources. It is very risky."

Reed entered a river valley. Traffic was light. All the RVs and campers were in for the night.

"I trust what you have, Molly, but I just want to get more—"

"Tom, you're breaking up. Repeat that."

"I said I trust what you have. I just want to get the whole story. Look, we'll have virtually another twenty-four hours to work on this. And what if they find the kid safe and sound and we put the shrink story out and then learn it had nothing to do with the kid?"

Wilson knew Reed had a point, and that he had become more cautious in the wake of his son's abduction ordeal. It taught him some hard lessons about pushing so hard on a story that you fall into it.

"OK, Tom. It will be our little secret to develop tomorrow, unless someone kicks our asses on it."

Reed passed key ranger, FBI and other vital cell phone numbers to Wilson. If the story broke wide open in his absence from Glacier National Park, Wilson would have to cover it from San Francisco. They were so close to final deadline now, the window of risk was minimal.

Reed estimated he could be in Wisdom in just over three hours. For the latter portion of the 220-mile trip, Interstate 93 paralleled the Bitterroot River. It was spectacular scenery that

rolled by the Columbia Cascade region and he regretted that
much of it was enveloped in darkness. Recently, hundreds of
thousands of acres in the area were burned by forest fires, some
near Wisdom, close to Murdon's ranch.

Reed sailed through the Bitterroot Valley and Lost Trail
Pass, passing Big Hole National Battlefield. Depending on your
view of history, it was either the place where the U.S. Army
upheld the law in 1877 over the Nez Perce Indians, who did
not want to be forcibly squeezed onto a reservation, or it was
the scene of a genocidal massacre of men, women and children
by American forces. Reed shook his head. Any way you cut
it, there were a lot of ghosts out there.

Some from his own life.

His dream of being a reporter was nurtured here in Big Sky
Country. He grew up in Great Falls where his father was a
pressman at the *Great Falls Tribune*. He used to bring home
a newspaper for Reed every day. Just before he turned twelve,
Reed got his own paper route. From that point on, it seemed
his life became a blur: high school, summer reporting at the
Billings Gazette, graduation from J-School at the University of
Missouri, a job at AP in San Francisco, getting married to Ann,
his job at the *San Francisco Star,* having Zach. But during
most of those years, Reed seldom visited or called home, disap-
pointing his father who used to save his articles in a yellowing,
dog-eared scrapbook, especially proud of his son's wire stories
that ran in the *New York Times*.

Reed reached for his cell phone. He had to think, then pressed
his parents' number in Great Falls. It rang. He had no time to
visit but at least he should tell them he was in the state. It rang
six times. The machine clicked on. His father's voice.

"You've reached . . ."

Reed hung up without leaving a message. He rubbed his tired
eyes. Remembering his mother during their last conversation
saying something about their plans to go to Arizona to visit

her sister. He called San Francisco and talked with Ann and Zach until his connection was lost.

Wisdom was a few miles east of Big Hole. One or two folksy restaurants, a general store, little else. Chester's place was on ten acres of painted horse country, just a few miles north. Reed shook his head at the tragic irony of it all. Murdon, who cherished history, living on ten acres, and all those Nez Perce Indians dying because Washington had stolen their land and tried to imprison them on a reservation.

Reed yawned. He was exhausted.

Murdon never married. Lived in a pretty ranch house with an old golden Lab he called Sonny. A sprawling place. Murdon had two separate rooms for his records, which he loved to share.

They greeted Reed at the porch after he eased his rental up to the house.

Sonny yelped.

"Settle down, Sonny."

"Chester, you look good. It's been a long, long time."

"Good to see you, Tom. Can I get you something, a snack, a beer?"

Murdon had a ruddy face, a brush cut and a neatly trimmed goatee. He was wearing dark jeans, a denim shirt with pens peeking from his breast pocket. He looked and moved pretty good for a man his age. He led Reed into his spacious house, to the ranch-style dining table covered with boxes, binders, files and envelopes spilling papers of all descriptions. He had already put in several hours of work on Reed's request.

"Much of this material is from my book. Now I've got the *Montana Standard* and the *Missoulian* stories on the ongoing search for Paige Baker."

Reed was impressed.

"Your information was that Emily Baker was from Montana

and undergoing counseling relating to the death of a child. Possibly in Montana.''

"Right, Chester. I want to know if anything was written on that death. I know virtually nothing about it. I was hoping you might find something.''

Murdon slipped on his glasses and stooped over the papers on the table. He had used Emily Baker's age and had begun searching death cases statewide. "Well, Tom, I am sorry I found nothing with her name. . . .''

Reed's heart sank. Maybe Wilson was right, they should have gone with what they had.

"But as I told you on the phone, I could not help thinking that the poor mother, this Emily Baker, looked so familiar to me. And the answer was staring right at me from the newspapers reporting on this death row fellow, Isaiah Hood.''

"What?''

"Well, it is her sister that Hood murdered twenty-two years ago. It's in my book and staring from the papers.''

Reed grabbed the *Missoulian* and scanned the story on Hood. Again, his heart sank. The old guy must be senile.

"But, Chester, the names don't even match. The sister who died was Rachel Ross. We got Emily's maiden name. It's not even the same.''

Murdon smiled.

"Of course not, Tom. She changed her name years ago after she left Montana.''

"You got paper on that?''

"Sort of.'' Murdon passed Reed an old file folder with a letter he had written to Montana's archivist while researching his book. "See, I asked for their help to contact the sister for my book. Interesting response, don't you think?''

Reed read the one-page letter. It acknowledged records were damaged in a storage fire well over a decade ago, but that in reassembling the files in the homicide of Rachel Ross, there was an indication there were subsequent deaths in her family and members had moved out of state: "While this office is not offering confirmation, it did make inquiries on your behalf and as a result came to the understanding that the subject of your request underwent a name change making contact extremely difficult."

"Now, Tom"—Murdon produced a magnifying glass for Reed—"examine today's newspaper pictures of Paige Baker, the missing child, and her mother and the old file of Rachel Ross, the child Hood murdered."

Reed studied them. Yes, there was a mother-daughter resemblance between Emily and Paige, and a striking resemblance to Rachel, the dead girl. He recalled seeing a similarity between the girls at breakfast.

"Tom"—Murdon's finger tapped the photos—"Emily Baker is the sister of Rachel Ross, I am convinced of it."

Reed continued studying the pictures, assessing everything—Hood's claim of innocence, Emily Baker's counseling for the death of a child, her daughter, Paige, now missing in the same area where Rachel Ross was murdered, Doug's injured hand. Police suspicions. *They must know.*

Hood was going to be executed within forty-eight hours.

"Christ, Chester."

The old newsman nodded. He knew what Reed was thinking. "Does not look good for the Bakers, does it, Tom?"

CHAPTER
THIRTY-FIVE

Amid the helicopters constantly landing and lifting off, the roaring Hercules C-130 rescue planes scraping the sky, the urgent nonstop radio chatter, the scores of arriving searchers, Doug Baker was alone at the command post.

No one could reach him.

He was at the edge of the campsite, watching the shadows blanket the vast alpine forest as the sun dropped behind the jagged peaks. Isolated and imprisoned by exhaustion and guilt, he had nothing to hold on to, except memories.

One day several years ago, Emily had gone to Sacramento for a weekend job. Paige was just about three at the time. It was a beautiful, clear Sunday morning and he took Paige to the beach. They had each other to themselves all day. Paige played in the sand, searching for shells as the Pacific surged and rolled. Gulls cried in the salt air. He remembered squatting as Paige ran to him, full speed out of the sun, trotting, cheeks bouncing, eyes bright, into his open arms, crushing his neck.

"I love you, Daddy."

"I love you, sweetheart."

Would he ever be able to hold her again?

Doug studied his wounded hand and the mountains.

Forgive me, Paige.

Emily. He should be comforting Emily.

His attempts to have a private moment with her had been futile. All day long, since returning to the campsite from talking with the FBI at the command center, they had been separated. A couple of young FBI agents were near Doug. *"To help you through this ordeal, sir."* And Emily had been inseparable from Bowman, the friendly female agent.

Doug never had the chance to be alone with Emily, other than to hug and console her in the presence of others. He did not know what the FBI told her during her talk with them that morning, whether they had learned anything in their investigation about any strangers or *that other family*. The father gave Doug a bad feeling. The icy way he stared at him. But no one told them anything. They would show him maps of the sectors searched or being searched. But no one knew anything about the investigative aspects. *"We are not aware, or informed, of any new developments, sir."* Still, Doug sensed something was bubbling beneath the dark glasses and poker faces the agents wore in his presence.

It all made him feel sick to his stomach.

Maybe Emily did not want to be near him? He understood if she blamed him for this. He was the one who chased Paige away. It was his fault. This all happened at such a critical point for them, when Emily was beginning to confront her problems. Revealing to him that she had a sister was a breakthrough. And how did he handle it? He blew up at her. Emily was doing it right. It was Doug who had blown it. If they could only get through this, maybe they could find Emily's sister and learn how *she'd* coped with the deaths of their parents. Become a bigger, stronger family.

Emily was sobbing again. It was tearing him up watching Bowman comfort his wife. He went to Emily. Bowman waved him off.

"This isn't a good time, Doug."

His heart crumbled. His family, his life, his existence, were disintegrating and there was not a damn thing he could do. Hope was evaporating. He had to do something. He rubbed his hands over his stubbled face. *Just go find her. You're her father. You lost her. You find her.* But the region held an infinity of possibilities. The search helicopters disappeared like ticks over the vast glacier valleys. Where would he start?

He felt a strong hand on his shoulder.

"Doug, we need your help again," Agent Frank Zander said over an idling helicopter.

Tears and desperation pooled in Doug's eyes.

"You find something?" Doug raised his voice over the chopper.

"We're not sure."

"Well, can you tell me what it is? I mean—"

"Doug, would you come back to the command center with me so we can talk some more about it? It would be a big help."

Doug searched Zander's face for a positive or negative signal, finding neither.

"Okay. Sure. Anything. Emily too?"

Zander shook his head. "I think she's fine here right now with Agent Bowman. We should get going now. It's getting dark."

Before Zander joined Doug in the chopper, he waved to Bowman, pulling her aside for an update. She'd had a full day with the mother. They turned their backs to the helicopter, their jackets rippling in whipping air. The noise assured the security of the information.

"What do you have?" he said into her ear.

"She was somehow present when her sister died here years ago," Bowman shouted into Zander's ear.

"Her sister? Do you know any more details?"

"No. She's vague. Comes out in pieces because of her emotional state."

"This is more than what Doug told us. He said Emily was receiving counseling related to the deaths of her parents. He said nothing about her sister. She give you any other details?"

"No."

"She tell you anything more about Paige's disappearance?"

"No, just that she and Doug were arguing, going through a rough time."

"Keep pushing it, Bowman."

During the flight back to the command center, Zander found himself thinking of Tracy Bowman. How she had obtained key information. She was very good. He reflected on her switch-blade intelligence, the way she had given him his comeuppance for his arrogant security breach on the phone from the jet. He knew he would never admit it to anyone but she was right. She was a fine investigator. Seemed like an exceptional person. Looking over the mountains, he wondered if she was married.

Soon the chopper touched down. Zander returned with Doug to the command center and the cramped room used by the task force.

Doug took his place at the table, nodding to Pike Thornton and Walt Sydowski from San Francisco. Each man, including Zander, had a clipboard and file.

"Coffee, Doug?" Zander offered.

"No. Did you find Paige?"

"No."

"Kobee?"

"Nothing like that."

"What have you got? You said you might have found something."

"We're coming to that, Doug. First, we'd like to be clear on a few things. Can you tell us again exactly how you hurt your hand?"

Doug tried to comprehend the question. He was exhausted, slipping into near intoxication from not sleeping or eating for the last few days. He was worn out, unshaven, eyes reddened from his anguish.

"I'm sorry?"

"Your hand, Doug. Tell us again how you injured it, please?"

"I am sure I told you. I was chopping wood."

"And arguing with Paige?"

Doug swallowed. His face reddened with shame. "Yes."

"Before we go further, we can't fly you back until morning. Too dangerous to fly in the mountains at night."

Doug was silent.

"We have a room for you here."

Doug thought for a moment.

"Are you arresting me for something?"

"Why would you think that?"

Doug did not answer. He could not even think of an answer.

"You are not under arrest," Zander said. "It is just that we might be a while. We told Emily."

"All right. You said you wanted to be clear on something?"

"What was Paige wearing when you argued?"

"Jeans. T-shirt."

"Remember the color of her T-shirt?"

"Pink. Maybe."

Zander slid the picture Emily had taken of the Bakers in the mountains with Paige in her pink T-shirt. "That the one?"

"Maybe. Why?"

"Now, the ax you had at the time. Was it a one-and-a-half-

pound Titan Striker with a steel head and a sixteen-inch handle
with a rubber grip?"

"Sounds right." Doug shrugged.

"Serial number 349975. Purchased four days ago at Big Ice
Country Outfitters in Century, Montana."

"Sounds right. But I don't understand?"

"Charged to your credit card?"

"Yes."

Zander leaned forward, invading Doug's space.

"Where is it?"

Doug's pulse stopped.

The eyes of three veteran detectives from three different
agencies who shared sixty years of experience had locked onto
Doug's eyes in the worst way.

CHAPTER THIRTY-SIX

Montana's five-member Board of Pardons and Parole recommended against Isaiah Hood's receiving executive clemency, but Governor Grayson Nye was not bound to the decision. David Cohen was less than thirty minutes away from appealing to him face to face.

The governor was Hood's last legal chance to live.

Upon receiving the fax from the board after it convened an emergency night meeting to ultimately reject Hood's petition, Cohen called John Jackson, the attorney general's top lawyer, from his cell phone while exiting at Garrison and heading for the capital.

"David, the governor is aware of the board's not recommending executive clemency. He'll make his decision in the morning."

"I just need fifteen minutes, John. He's in town. I'll be there in an hour."

Static passed between the two cell phones.

"David, he's at a black-tie fundraiser. This is really not appropriate—"

"Damn it, John! He should be concerned about the man's life in his hands, not the wineglass! Please! Give me the address so your conscience will rest."

Jackson sighed and dictated the location.

"Leave your phone on, John. I'll call you when I arrive."

Cohen never expected the Board to recommend clemency. He would have to make his gamble with the governor, who would grasp the scope of the political ramifications of executing an innocent man.

The gala was in Helena's mansion district, an area of grand houses built in the late 1800s by the territory's mining millionaires. They were opulent structures in Victorian, Romanesque and Queen Anne styles.

Cohen parked his rented Neon on the street in front of the one where the governor's function was, then placed his call. Jackson was dressed in a black dinner jacket, which set off his silver hair and tan, when he came to the front steps. Cohen was wearing a Ralph Lauren polo shirt and khakis.

"Come this way," Jackson said, leading him upstairs to a large private study with a massive mahogany board table, floor-to-ceiling windows and bookshelves. "I'll be right back with him. You'll have ten minutes."

"Thanks, John."

Cohen sat alone at the board table drumming his fingers on his briefcase. He was well aware of the governor's connections to Washington, DC, and his plans to run for national office. He sat upright when he heard the state's most famous voice say his name.

"I've heard much about you." The governor's handshake was solid. Jackson and another man accompanied him. "Of course you know our attorney general and John."

The governor sat beside Cohen.

"Sir, have you made your decision to accept the Board's recommendation that Isaiah Hood not receive executive clemency?"

"Not yet. I'll do that in the morning. I understand you want me to consider a serious new development in the man's case?"

"Yes."

"Something outside of what the Board saw today?"

"Yes. I believe with all my heart Isaiah Hood is innocent."

"I understand you're an idealistic, young attorney. I admire that."

Cohen unsnapped the locks on his briefcase and produced a file.

"It's simple, sir." He handed the governor all the pertinent photographs of Emily Baker, Rachel and the unpublished archived photos.

The governor knitted his brows, studying all the pictures. "This is the woman whose child is missing in Glacier? And the others? I am not sure I understand the point you're attempting to illustrate here." He shot a glance to Jackson and the attorney general.

"Governor Nye," Cohen said. "Isaiah Hood, who maintains his innocence, was given the death penalty solely on the testimony of this child, the only other witness to the death of Rachel Ross. Her sister. Now the *same* woman's child is missing in the *same* area, under the *same* circumstances."

The governor studied the pictures intently.

How could his office not know this?

He was the one who had quietly pressured Washington to get the FBI involved to clear the case of the lost girl because of the suspicions surrounding her disappearance. Because he was determined not to sit on his hands the way some states did and let the thing fester into a cancer on the justice system of this country.

Why the hell didn't he know about Emily Baker's connection to Hood? He had just been blindsided by a Chicago lawyer with an earring.

"Governor, I think you appreciate the ramifications should you proceed in executing my client. Now knowing full well that this woman"—Cohen touched Emily Baker's news photo—"was most likely involved in the murder of her sister twenty-two years ago, and has possibly repeated the crime with her daughter, under your watch. I appreciate that the names do not match. I understand hers was changed when she left the state years ago, then changed again when she married Doug Baker. I am searching for documentation to confirm Emily Baker was originally Natalie Ross. As far as I know, no one in the press has *yet* made the connection, but it is only a matter of time before they do. This is not something your office has kept quiet, is it, sir?"

The governor's eyes narrowed slightly. He was seething inside but managed a political grin as he studied Cohen's evidence, sitting on the polished mahogany table, staring him in the face.

"Mr. Cohen, your client was convicted under the laws of this state. His conviction was upheld by the supreme court of this state. Your attempt to appeal it to the highest court in the nation failed. The Montana State Board of Pardons and Parole has not found merit in your petition to recommend executive clemency for your client. A lot of people have studied this file before it came to me. I cannot interfere and undermine the laws of this state and nation. As you know, I do not retry cases. I am limited in what I can do.

"The case of Paige Baker, the little girl from California, is tragic. She has been reported missing and every resource, every effort, is being utilized to locate her. For you, at this stage, to attempt to draw a hideous connection between the case of your client, convicted of the cold-blooded murder of a child, a case that is all but concluded, and the tragedy endured by a family in Glacier is at best, tenuous, and at its worst, morally abhorrent.''

"I'm sorry you see it that way, sir. I disagree.''

"That is your privilege. What I will do is take your concerns, as weak as they are, under advisement. I'll make my decision known to you tomorrow.''

The governor stood, signaling that Cohen's time with him had ended. The young lawyer took in the gazes of the other men. He shook the governor's extended hand and left. Jackson saw him out, through the house, to the front steps.

"I'll say one thing for you, David. You better have brass ones. After pulling a disgraceful stunt like that.''

Cohen stopped, turning on the step.

"Why's that, John?''

"Because you just squeezed the governor's balls. Now he's likely to squeeze yours"—Jackson winked—"so hard, they'll hear the scream in Chicago.''

Cohen took the comment, tapping his fingers on his briefcase, chuckling to himself. "You're forgetting something fundamental here, John.''

"I am?''

"My client and I are already fucked. Got nothing to lose. It is all on the line. Now Grayson Nye, on the other hand, well, let me put it this way, when's the last time your boss had his picture on the front page of the *New York Times?*''

A scowl emerged on Jackson's face.

"You wouldn't dare.''

Cohen stepped into Jackson's space.

"Watch me. And when your boss screams, they'll hear it in Washington.''

Jackson returned to the study, where the governor was on the phone. Upset. The attorney general raised a hand of caution to Jackson. The governor dialed a number but slammed the phone down, abandoning the call. "Why the hell did we not know about the mother's connection to Hood?"

The attorney general was on his cell phone demanding someone commence emergency research. "Sir," he said, snapping his phone shut. "I was just getting a status report from Glacier. They're no closer to finding the girl."

Grayson Nye shook his head. "This is a goddamn mess."

"You are clear on the execution on all legal grounds. Cohen presents nothing in the way of solid evidence that warrants clemency. The U.S. Supreme Court has green-lighted you here."

"And politically?"

The attorney general cleared his throat.

"If you delay this guy, you will be seen as being soft on crime. He is a convicted child killer. If you delay under the *suggestion* it is linked to the tragic ongoing case in Glacier, you risk offending the state of California in the perception you are convicting an anguished woman in a time of torment, based on what? A Chicago lawyer's strategy of smoke and mirrors?"

"I could delay for thirty days."

"Based on what?" the attorney general said. "You'll be pegged as soft and indecisive. Not assets to national aspirations, Grayson."

"What if she is guilty of harming her child in Glacier?"

"Then she will be prosecuted," Jackson said.

"And we'll have executed an innocent man."

"You cannot retry his case. She would have to confess and provide some sort of irrefutable evidence," the attorney general said.

The governor thought of his family.

He had an eighteen-year-old daughter heading off to Yale. The study's grandfather clock began chiming. Time was the factor. Hood's execution was scheduled in the next forty-eight hours. The FBI found a bloodied T-shirt, a bloodied ax. The mother was undergoing counseling. As far as he knew, the investigators knew nothing of Cohen's claim, were unaware of who the mother really was. Not yet. Jesus, please let them find that kid alive.

"I'll decide in the morning."

CHAPTER
THIRTY-SEVEN

FBI Special Agent Tracy Bowman watched the helicopter's blinking strobe lights shrinking, vanishing into the dusk after Zander and Doug Baker left the command post.

She would leave later on the last flight before nightfall.

Bowman scanned the mountains, feeling the temperature drop. She pulled her jacket tighter and bit her lip. She reviewed everything so far.

What had befallen this family?

Emily had tried to escape her torment by crawling into her daughter's tent. A tense calm descended upon operations. No sounds could be heard, except for the low crackle of radio traffic as searchers throughout Grizzly Tooth prepared to dig in for the night. Each of them privately tabulating the time and conditions surrounding Paige Baker's disappearance, then calculating her odds of survival. Coming up on sixty hours. Not good.

Snow and rain were forecast for part of the night.

Suddenly, Bowman felt alone. She had not talked with Mark

since rushing here. She took an FBI satellite phone, went to the edge of the campsite, called her home in Lolo. It had been, what? Two days? No, one. It felt like a lifetime. She just needed to hear his voice.

No answer at her home. She dialed the home number of her friend, Roberta Cara.

"Roberta, it's Tracy. I can't talk long. How is everything?"

"Fine, but you sound funny."

"It's a satellite phone, Wait a beat before answering. I'm on a mountain in Glacier. How's Mark?"

Roberta counted one Mississippi.

"He's fine. He's here. We tried to call you on your cell. He wanted to stay at our house with the boys. Lord, I pray they find that little girl. Wait, I'll put Mark on."

Static, beeping, commotion, overhearing Roberta, explaining how the phone worked, then Mark. "Hi, Mom. You're really on a mountain. Cool."

"Hey there, Marshal. Yes, I am. You having fun?"

"Yeah. I saw you on the TV news. In the background walking with some people. How long before you're done, Mom?"

"Hard to say. Are you taking your medicine?"

"Yup. And Logan is teaching me how to whittle with a penknife."

"You be careful with that knife. I'll be home as soon as I can, but I got to go. I love you."

"Love you, too, Mom. Hope you find the little girl."

Bowman felt a bittersweet rush of warmth and heartache pass through her. Sitting on the mountain miles from Mark, cradling the phone, she counted her blessings, gazing upon the tent where Emily wept as wind rustled its walls.

What happened to this family?

Bowman felt Emily was on the brink of opening up to her. She was learning more about her past, her childhood in Montana. If she could only get her to continue talking so she could pull the curtain back on the truth of what happened out here. The clock was ticking. It was critical.

Succeed here, and she could move Mark to Los Angeles and better treatment. Did she even know what she was doing? Was she handling Emily Baker the right way? Zander gave her no indication. He was icy. *"Keep pushing it, Bowman."* Why was he so cold?

She had overheard other agents gossiping about how Zander was haunted by a screwup in a Georgia child murder case years ago. Then a female agent from Seattle said Zander was in need of comforting, that he was going through a wildly ugly separation back in DC. That might have been why he behaved like a jerk, thought Bowman.

Stop it, Tracy. What are you doing? This is inappropriate. Not right.

Bowman admonished herself, studying Paige Baker's tent flapping in the cold wind. Like a burial shroud. Would they ever find Paige?

Bowman had a few hours before her flight. Exhausted, she checked with one of the agents assigned to keep the early-night watch on Emily, then crawled into the tent the rangers had set up for her. As the wind did its work, she fell asleep dreaming of Mark, California and Carl. They were there together walking in the sun, happy . . . until the screaming. . . .

Screaming?

Bowman scrambled from her tent.

Emily Baker's demon had returned.

CHAPTER THIRTY-EIGHT

A dark wind had taken Emily as the night neared.

Seized her at the command post and took her back . . . forced her back to the days of Buckhorn Creek . . . back to that day.

The day of the monster.

Butterflies. Darting. Fluttering. Leading her and her little sister, Rachel, through the forest to . . . *the monster.*

Suddenly standing there at the cliff, waiting for them.

"Hello," he says, "want to play a game?"

Sensing trouble, she squeezes Rachel's hand.

"No thanks, we can't. We have to go back."

Rachel giggles. She wants to play.

The monster is beckoning.

"Stand closer to me. Watch me." He laughs.

"No. We should go back."

"It's just a game."

Rachel pulls her hand away; the warmth of it vanishes. She goes to him.

"Rachel, no, don't."

He turns, takes two steps. "Guess what I'm going to do. Watch." He disappears off the cliff before them.

"He's dead!"

Rachel stands there, giggling. Peering over the cliffside. Giggling! It is all horribly wrong!

Now Rachel is Paige standing there.

Emily screams . . . and screams . . . until—

"Emily!" Hands on her shoulders. "Emily!"

The FBI agent. Bowman. In her tent, shaking her.

"It's OK, Emily. Wake up, Emily!"

Her heart is throbbing against her chest. Her hands are moist with sweat, fear. Bowman is rocking her as she weeps.

"I think I am losing my mind. It's happening again. I cannot—"

Others have come, murmuring concern outside the tent. Everything's fine. A bad dream, Bowman tells them.

"I cannot take it anymore. . . . If I lose Paige, I—"

"Shh-shh. You need rest. Talk it out. Tell me, whatever it is you're carrying inside. It's OK, Emily. It's time to tell someone. Shh, it's OK. It's time."

A game. That was how it began. A game with a monster.

Emily struggled to talk. It was so painful. It hurt so much. In the weeks, months and years after Rachel's death, she was gripped by a dark obsession to understand what her sister's final moments were like.

Did she suffer?

My Sun Ray.

Her sister's death destroyed everything. While she searched to understand why it had happened, her mother and father withdrew into prisons of pain, leaving her under a cloud of accusation.

"Why didn't you save her?"

The wound would not heal. About a year after the trial, her father confronted her with the rumor slithering through Buckhorn Creek.

"It's going around that you lied about what happened out there that day."

Lied? No.

He was working in the corral on his horse, a big bay that seemed uneasy.

"I told the truth, Daddy."

"That's not what I'm hearing. People are saying *you* pushed your sister."

"You pushed your sister."

His words had burned like a branding iron into her soul.

"It's a lie!"

"Is it?"

His horse was snorting and jerking. He yelled at it, "Settle down there!"

The blow of her father's words brought her to her knees.

"You're my father. Why are you saying such a horrible thing?"

"Because a man has been sentenced to die, *goddamn you!*"

Goddamn you. Was that directed at her? Or his horse?

It began bucking wildly, throwing her father from his saddle, the animal's hind legs kicking. Its hoof like a sledgehammer to his temple, killing him instantly in front of her, his accusation hanging in the air, rising up to the mountains with her terror.

"Daddy!"

Her mother rushing from the house, throwing herself on the soft earth. *"Winston! Winston! Oh sweet Jesus!"* Her eyes turning to Emily, filling with horror, hurt, *blame*.

It was as if her father had bequeathed his suspicions to her mother. He died, never knowing the truth; while her mother lived, refusing to hear it, taking her first drink the night after they buried him next to Rachel.

Not long after, her mother sold their ranch. Their perfect, happy home nestled against the Rocky Mountains. They moved to Kansas City, where she changed their names.

Natalie Ross no longer existed, except as a headstone for a beautiful life that died in Montana.

She was now Emily Smith.

"We'll start over. New people. New life. No past."

They moved into a stifling apartment above a shoe store. Her mother waitressed in a small diner six blocks from a school and they never spoke of Montana. Sometimes at night, when she heard the chink of glass, Emily would slip from her bed to see her mother, sitting in the dark, talking to her dead sister and father.

They stayed in Kansas City for a year or so, then moved to Toronto. Changing their names again; her mother drinking more. Next, it was Dallas, then Miami. They fell into a haze of moves, staying in one city long enough to get bus fare to take them to the next.

There was one night she heard her mother mumbling incoherently about the county attorney debating whether to reopen the case.

Finally, her mother took her to San Francisco where they stayed with her mother's sister, Willa. But that didn't last. One morning, her mother was gone. Vanished. A year or so later, Emily's aunt got a telephone call from Toronto. Emily's mother had died of a heart attack in a women's shelter, clutching pictures of her family taken when her daughters were little.

Her aunt claimed her mother's body. The service was in Buckhorn Creek, Montana, where they buried her next to her father and Rachel. Emily refused to attend the funeral. She stayed in San Francisco, staring at the Pacific Ocean, thinking her parents died suspecting she was responsible for Rachel's death.

She was sixteen years old. She was alone.

No one knew the truth about what happened that day.

Except the monster.

"You can tell me, Emily." Bowman was listening. "You have to tell somebody before it is too late."

Emily stared into the night, forcing herself to go back to the butterflies that led them to the cliff.

The monster.

He is just there. Waiting. Dirty jeans, boots, layers of shirts, frayed. In his teens. Tall, brown hair pasted to his head. Small, dark animal eyes hidden deep in a face lined and scarred so badly it looks like he is in pain. His smile reveals jagged brown teeth that have never known a toothbrush.

She knows his name.

Isaiah Hood.

The kids in town speak of him as if he were a myth, a spirit in the Rockies. Some sort of psycho. His father has hooks for hands. They live in a shack in the forest near the Blackfeet Reservation and the Canadian border. People rarely see him. But on this trip there are whispers around the campfire that he is out there.

And anyone with any sense knows, you do not ever go near him.

In fact, no one in Buckhorn Creek wants anything to do with the Hoods. They are regarded with scorn for what they are, pitiful.

But the butterflies lead her and Rachel to him that day, stopping them dead in their tracks.

"Hello. How about a game? Want to play a game?"

Tightening her hold on Rachel's hand.

"We should go back."

Rachel giggles. She wants to play.

"No," he says, "stand closer to me. Watch."

"No. We should go back."

Rachel pulls away, steps closer to him. Closer to the cliff.

"It's just a game. Guess what I'm going to do. Watch."

He turns and steps off the cliff before them.

"Oh no! He's dead!"

Rachel is peering over the cliffside. Giggling! Looking back at Natalie.

"It's just a game, Lee, see?" She's laughing.

He's sitting cross-legged on a large flat ledge, a few feet below, grinning at having fooled her into thinking he had jumped from the mountain.

"OK, very funny. We have to get back. Time to go, Rachel."

He stands. "No. The little one wants to play. Come on. You try it, Rachel. I'll catch you down here."

"OK." Rachel giggles nervously. Counting one-two-three. Jumping from the higher cliff. "No, Rachel!" She is reaching for Rachel's hand but she is not fast enough. Rachel is now on the lower ledge with him. Laughing.

"Don't worry," he says. "I've got her."

They are sitting on the sun-warmed ledge. It is as big as a large bed.

She extends her hand to her sister.

"Time to go, Rachel. We're not supposed to play with you, Isaiah Hood."

Hood's smile disappears and his face darkens, cold black eyes burning into hers.

"You think you're better than me and my dad, don't you?"

"No, that is not what I mean," she lies.

"All of you in town think you're better than us. We hear it. We know it."

"Rachel, come on. We have to go."

"Not yet," he says. "I say when you can go. One more game."

He stands with animal swiftness. Takes Rachel by the wrists, pulling her arms straight up—"Owww"—lifting her. He is so tall, strong, baring his dirt-brown teeth. Scarred face grimacing. She is a small doll in his grip, light and easy to play with.

"Lee!"

She jumps to the ledge. "Let her go! You can't have her!"

"Guess what I'm going to do."

Holding her, he inches to the ledge, letting her toes brush the rock.

He is laughing.

"God, please! Let Rachel go. Please!" She pounds on his arms. Futile. They are so strong.

"Think you're all better than us, like you just walk on air, my daddy says."

"Lee!" Her sister is terrified. "Please!"

He is at the ledge. A sheer drop of five hundred, maybe six hundred, feet.

"Guess what I'm going to do."

Slowly, he extends his arms

"No! Oh—Lee!"

Slowly, he holds Rachel over the cliff, chuckling as she tries in vain to reach it with her toes. Gasping, breathless, sobbing. "Please!"

Rocky Mountain winds are curling through the ranges, shooting up. The earth below is a dizzying drop.

She is stretching to reach Rachel's wrist, but his arms are longer.

"Lee! Oh, please! Oh, please!"

"Guess what I'm going to do. I'm going to see if she can walk on air!"

"Noooo!"

"But you help me, big sister."

Suddenly, Hood releases one of Rachel's wrists.

"You get her now, big sister. You save her now! Unless she can walk on air." He laughs.

She reaches for Rachel's free, flailing hand, brushing it, touching it in time to feel it slipping from hers as Hood releases his grip.

Rachel is suspended for an instant.

Their eyes meet. Rachel, horrified, terrified. Knowing. Face is contorted with fear. "No, Sun Ray." Hand brushing hers, a feathery touch so fast, Rachel's head lifting.

Falling. "NOOOOOOO!" Her screams rising to the heavens as she plummets.

"Oh God! Oh God! Oh God!"

She cannot breathe, cannot think. Horror is hammering her senses. Pounding.

Laughing. Hood is laughing.

"Guess she can't walk on air and she can't fly. No better than anybody."

His brown teeth turn to her.

"How about you, big sister?"

She scurries up the ledge, sobbing, gasping; his laughter chases her as she runs and runs and runs from the monster.

Running all of her life.

Running from her sister's falling eyes, the death brush of her little hand stained with mountain flowers and the powder of butterfly wings. The last touch, the last look of horror.
"Watch over your little sister."

"I'm not scared anymore, Lee."

Running all of her life.

Free-falling from the horror that destroyed her family; now feeling a measure of comfort from an FBI agent investigating the suspected homicide of her daughter.

CHAPTER THIRTY-NINE

Paige and Kobee ran for high country, scrambling along treacherous ridges, ledges. Dipping into forests only to gain elevation or traverse a difficult section.

It was the only way to stay ahead of the thing chasing them. The only tactic keeping her alive. She continued moving as fast as she could for much of the day. The grunting thing never emerged. She stopped to examine Kobee's wound. Did the thing do that? She tore a strip from a shirt in her pack, bandaging him with it. Far off, she heard the helicopters. At times, she waved but they always missed her. Paige forced herself to keep moving.

Oh God, I am so hungry.

So afraid.

Please help me! Somebody!

When Paige stopped to eat one of her granola bars, she began crying and could not stop.

Does it hurt to die?

Paige whispered weakly, "Mommy, please help me."

Kobee licked her salty tears. She shared some of her food with him.

"Don't worry. I'll look after you, puppy."

Paige moved on, but later as the sun began dropping, fatigue, exposure and fear continued taking their toll.

Got to keep moving. Climb higher and maybe they'll find me.

She believed it was safer at higher levels.

It gave her the advantage of distance to see what might be ahead, waiting for her, or behind, gaining on her.

As dusk approached, Paige sensed that it was going to rain again. It was clouding up, getting colder. She began thinking of searching or trying to build a shelter as she continued ascending a rocky region.

Earlier in the day, she frequently spotted deer and bighorn sheep. It gave her comfort seeing harmless forms of life keeping her company.

But as she worked her way up the harsh slopes of this region deep in the Devil's Grasp, the deer and sheep became scarce.

Wonder where they all went.

The few she did spot seemed to be moving downward in the opposite direction of her ascension.

Why?

Finally, with little light remaining, Paige chose a spot atop a jagged zone of high cliffs, which was dotted with forests. The ledges overlooked a sweeping valley from several hundred feet up.

Paige began building a lean-to shelter, using some spruce boughs against a large fallen tree. She used some as a floor, to soften the hard, rocky ground. She crawled in, hugging Kobee for comfort and warmth. Meanwhile, hunger and exhaustion battled within her.

Thoughts of a huge pizza with ham, tons of cheese, spicy sauce, pineapples, taunted her. As the night neared, she slipped into sleep.

A large branch cracked.

What is that?

Paige was fully alert. Pulse racing with fear.

A horrible, foul smell filled her nostrils.

It was back!

Kobee whimpered softly.

"Shhh."

Like her first night.

Ohgodpleasehelpme!

Snorting. She heard guttural snorting. Then a woofing, popping sound. More branches snapping.

It was so close. She heard paw pads, slapping on rock; claws, scraping near her. Panting. Growling.

It brushed by her in the twilight.

A massive wall of fur, stinking fur, matted with excrement.

A bear. A giant bear. So close she could touch it.

Paige went numb.

She was going to die.

She prayed. *Mommy. Daddy.*

A massive claw swept the branches away; fur brushed against her. Paige shut her eyes. The second swat sent her hurling across the ledge top, rolling like a rag doll toward a yawning crevasse.

Paige opened her mouth to scream, hearing the beast charging and snarling. Its claws scratched across the rock, driving an unstoppable, unconquerable, carnivorous force as old as time toward her.

Mommy, Daddy, please save me. . . . Please, oh please, don't let it hurt!

DAY 4

CHAPTER FORTY

In the predawn light deep in Search Sector 23, a vast slope of lodgepole forest blistered by rock cliffs and fissures, excitement wakened Lola.

The three-year-old Belgian shepherd's wagging tail was brushing the interior of the green nylon pup tent as she worked to rouse Todd Taylor, her nineteen-year-old handler. Nuzzling, panting and licking his ear to no avail. Taylor groaned, pulling his goose-down sleeping bag over his head. He was exhausted. Lola persisted.

"Just a few more minutes, girl."

Taylor pulled her into the warm sleeping bag with him and listened to her heartbeat. It was racing, stirring him to the sudden realization she had detected something.

"OK, OK. Take it easy."

He sat up, shivering, in the frigid morning air. He quickly pulled a sweatshirt over his T-shirt, then whipped on his fluorescent yellow windbreaker, which bore the words TALON COUNTY SEARCH AND RESCUE, COLORADO. The volunteer group was one of the first out-of-state agencies to arrive. Taylor, college freshman from Boulder, was studying to be a paramedic. Lola was regarded by SAR people across America as one of the best scent-trackers in the field.

"Coffee," Taylor moaned, pouring a cup from his thermos.

Sipping it cleared his drowsiness. He faced the dreadful fact it had rained again in the night. *Cripes.* Theirs was one of the most remote eastern search zones, and between sunrise and sundown yesterday, they grid-swept it twice. Taylor kneaded Lola's neck. He never ceased to marvel at the ability of tracking dogs to locate people, or traces of them.

Humans constantly give off streams of scents that flow into the air like vaporous clouds, emissions originating from the bacteria in the millions of cells in hair, skin, blood, urine, sweat, saliva, which the body replaces each second. The process produces a distinct human odor that trained scent dogs like Lola can detect. But Taylor knew the success of the so-called probability of detection all depended on scores of variables like the dog's health, wind conditions, time of day, air quality and density.

Taylor hustled pulling on his jeans and boots. Lola had picked up something and would bolt the instant he opened the tent. But he had to take care of business fast; afterward, they would go.

"You stay, girl! Sit!"

Lola yelped but sat. Her tail wagged her impatience as Taylor crawled out to relieve himself by a tree. Quickly, he slipped on his lighter pack, affixed a fresh battery to his radio, clamped a peanut butter and strawberry jam sandwich in his mouth, gave Lola a dog biscuit, opened the tent.

"Go find it, girl."

Lola yelped, leading Taylor at a trot deep through the forest they had gridded early yesterday. He knew they were skirting the edge of a grizzly's feeding zone. He double-checked his pack for his bear spray and bell.

During a search for a lost woman in the Rockies in Colorado, he had startled a sow. Miraculously, he backed away without a scratch, although he trembled uncontrollably for the rest of the day. The next morning, he and Lola found the woman, or what was left of her. The grizzly had disemboweled her. One of her arms was missing. The woman, a tourist from Germany, was the mother of a little boy and little girl. Taylor cried that night. Rangers tracked and killed the bear. Lola was now moving faster, leading him out of the forest to the rocky edge.

"Whoa!"

The ledge was a sheer drop of several hundred feet, a shocker to come upon without warning from the forest.

"Dead end, girl."

Lola yipped back. Panting, assuming her posture that said, *This is it, Todd. I've found it.* Then she sneezed. Taylor surveyed the rocky stretch of ledge, beautiful against the brilliant, rising sun.

"But there's nothing here."

Lola barked, giving an indication it was somewhere along the rugged clifftop.

"Hey, careful!"

The entire ledge was fissured with crevasses, some no wider than six inches, some a foot or two. But they were deep, plunging treacherously into darkness. Lola was panting, tail wagging at one. At the surface, it ran about twenty feet from the edge into the forest, a gash in the rock maybe twenty inches wide that descended into a dark eternity.

Lola stood steadfast at one point along the crevasse and yelped as Taylor realized its mouth was big enough to swallow a child. He dropped to his knees next to his dog.

"Hello!" Taylor called into the crevasse.

Silence.

For the next three minutes, he called, lying flat on the rock, listening for the faintest sound of life. Nothing. Suddenly, Taylor's blood turned cold. Nearly touching his nose were a few threads of fabric, like something torn from a shirt. Next to it quivering in the wind, a few strands of hair. Some blood droplets. Taylor reached for his radio.

The FBI evidence team had trouble finding a safe place to put down their helicopter. The winds at the altitude of Sector 23 were rocking the aircraft. Eventually, they found a spot some two hundred yards from Taylor's detect point and humped it in.

"Something's down there," Taylor said. "Lola's going nuts up here."

"You hear anything?" an agent asked Taylor.

"Nothing."

Powerful flashlights were aimed down the hole; long aluminum poles were extended, prodding the depths for any indication of life. Nothing.

More experts arrived within minutes.

SAR people worked one side of the opening with the aim of rescuing a victim, while FBI technicians meticulously studied the evidence at the surface. Using tweezers and a powerful magnifying glass, a technician was confident the strands of hair were similar to Paige Baker's. They began tapping at the rock to remove blood droplets. Preliminary on-scene testing indicated the trace was human. The fabric was cotton. White. Material and color were consistent with the socks Paige was wearing when she vanished. Everything was photographed and recorded. The area was regarded as a restricted federal crime scene.

Agent Frank Zander arrived. "What have we got here?"

Agent William Horn, one of the FBI's senior evidence people, explained the blood, hair and fabric at the mouth of the crevasse.

"It doesn't look good, Frank."

"She down there?"

"At this point, odds are she is."

"How soon before you can confirm?"

"Don't know. The opening is too narrow and tight for us

to drop a rescuer or tech down there. We're flying in some small fiber-optics cameras, listening devices. Looks like this thing stretches to the bottom, four hundred feet, maybe more. We need an exceptional length of fiber for the camera, we're waking up a high-tech firm in California. We'll need some time, Frank.''

Zander nodded.

"This is your scene, Bill, and my investigation. Nobody who is here now is permitted to leave. All radio contact goes through you to me. It's all need-to-know. Nobody talks to anybody until it is determined exactly what we have here. It is critical now that nothing leaks from here. Critical.''

Horn nodded.

Before Zander returned to the command center, he looked at the FBI evidence technicians in their hooded jumpsuits with gloves. They glowed in the dawn against the backdrop of the sky and mountains as they worked silently on what Zander believed was the grave of Paige Baker.

CHAPTER
FORTY-ONE

A nation away from the FBI's secret at the crevasse of Sector 23 in Montana, a constable with the Ontario Provincial Police was ending her night shift east of Toronto, patrolling RV campsites near the Sandbanks Provincial Park.

The waters of Lake Ontario lapped against the vast sand beaches as she cross-checked license plates with the tourist alert sheet on her clipboard. She locked onto a California tag for Meyers, knocked on the door of their thirty-foot motor home, informing Willa Meyers to call the San Francisco Police Department right away. "A family emergency."

An SFPD dispatcher took Willa's call at approximately 4:00 A.M. Pacific Time. She paged Inspector Linda Turgeon, who was sleeping but had the call patched to her home. Turgeon told Willa Meyers what had happened in Montana.

"My dear Lord, no!" Willa was horrified, explaining that she and Huck had no idea their niece was lost in the Rocky Mountains.

"We purposely avoided the news because of Isaiah Hood's impending execution," Willa said; then she told Turgeon about Lee's secret family history. "We wanted them to join us in Canada. It was a delicate family matter. Lee was receiving counseling. Doug didn't even know everything. We wanted to get Lee as far away from the Hood case as possible at the time of the execution. We didn't know they had returned there."

Willa told Turgeon that when a San Francisco reporter recently reached them asking questions about Emily's past, she figured it was somehow related to Hood's execution, not to Paige.

Turgeon consoled Willa, then called Sydowski, catching him on his way out of his room in the Sky Forest Vista Inn near Kalispell. He took extensive notes as Turgeon enlightened him.

Now, Sydowski was finishing his third coffee and watching the sun climb as Zander's chopper returned from Sector 23 to the helipad near the command center. The two men talked near a stand of spruce behind a fire crew dorm.

"I think we found her, Walter."

"Alive?"

"No. Blood, hair and clothing fragments at the mouth of a narrow and deep rock fissure, just under two miles from the campsite."

"You confirm her body is there?"

"No. It's going to take a few hours to get some equipment up there. No one, absolutely no one, knows what we've got there."

"I've got an update on Emily Baker," Sydowski said. "SFPD contacted Emily's aunt. Emily is the sister of Rachel Ross, the child murdered in Glacier twenty-two years ago by Isaiah Hood, the guy who is going to be executed."

Zander was dumbfounded.

"Why didn't we know this from the outset?" He shook his

head. "That happened in the same region. The Bureau, or Montana, should have known."

"Turns out Emily was *Natalie Ross* at the time. Natalie's mother changed her name shortly after the tragedy. As you know, Natalie Ross was the witness, the only witness, who saw Hood kill her sister. Her testimony helped seal his death warrant." He filled in Zander on the rest of the story. "Emily would never speak of her past. Began undergoing counseling for it as Hood's execution date loomed."

Zander stared into the sunlight piercing the spruce.

"Damn, Walt. What do you make of it?"

"In my time, I've seen them all. The devil told me to do it, the voices told me, my dog told me. I've had the most upstanding people, finest-looking people, look me straight in the eye and say they had to kill their infant child because God told them it was the Antichrist. But—"

Zander looked at Sydowski. "But what?"

"To me, the pieces here just don't quite fit."

"I think they do. It's just a matter of which category. Just a matter of time, Walt. Look at everything we've got so far. The ax, the T-shirt, his hand, her past, his temper, the girl's corpse. I think we've got them beyond a reasonable doubt."

"I don't. Not yet. It is still largely circumstantial."

"What about the mother's background, her history?"

"I see it as reason for their strange behavior."

"I see it as damning."

"Frank, you have no linchpin to bring it all together. Nothing physical, irrefutable."

"She's in the crevasse."

"What if she fell?"

Zander's eyes narrowed.

"I'm going to find out, Walt. Give me time. I am going to get them on the box as soon as possible."

"It's your case. How you handle it is up to you."

Within twenty minutes, everything was conveyed to Lloyd

Turner, FBI Special Agent In Charge, and Nora Lam of Justice, who immediately shook her head.

"What's your hurry? Why not see what your investigation at the crevasse yields? It might give you your trump card."

"We're holding a pretty winnable hand now, Nora," Zander said.

"I agree with Frank. A polygraph might help at this stage," Turner said.

"You know he has to agree, cooperate and be Mirandized?" Lam said. "You must advise him of his right to a lawyer."

Doug was escorted once again to the task force room and seated before the investigators. He listened as Zander explained the situation.

"Doug, we've got a problem and we need your help."

He emphasized how the search was expanding, "more people, more resources," but the job of ruling out all other possibilities in Paige's disappearance required a lot of work. "We're going through permits trying to locate and talk to every other party in the area at the time."

"How can I help?"

"Well, Doug," Zander said, "an investigation is largely a process of elimination. We want to eliminate all potential options quickly so we can concentrate on valid ones."

"I see."

"The most disturbing one we have to deal with is that something has happened to Paige—an animal or a stranger in the park. Do you follow me?"

Doug looked at his hands. That other family made him uneasy.

"I—I, yes."

"We have to look at everyone. It is critical."

"Yes."

"We want to eliminate you."

Doug said nothing He had known for a long while that was coming.

"Doug, your wound, the ax, her T-shirt . . ."

Doug sniffed; tears welled . . . he knew.

"Can you appreciate where I am going here?"

His pulse galloped. "Yes," he said, his heart breaking.

"Would you agree to take a polygraph?"

Doug swallowed.

"It's just a tool, but it might help us, help everyone."

Before Doug realized his head was nodding, Zander asked him to voice his answer.

"Yes, I will take a polygraph."

"Then I have to tell you certain things first because the law requires it."

"What things?"

"You have the right to remain silent. . . ."

Jesus, Doug could not believe . . .

"Anything you say can and will be used against you in a court of law."

How does a life come to this . . . ?

"You have the right to consult with an attorney and have them present with you while you are being questioned."

Screaming at Paige. Shouting at my daughter with the bloody ax in my hand. The terror in her eyes . . .

"If you cannot afford to hire an attorney, one will be appointed to represent you before any questioning, if you wish one."

For God's sake, I'm just a teacher, a husband, a father. Days before, we were like any other American family, struggling through an airport, embarking on a vacation.

"Do you understand each of these rights I have explained to you?"

No, I do not understand any of this. Lord, help me . . . help Paige. . . .

"Having these rights in mind, do you wish to talk to us now?"

Doug looked into Zander's eyes.

"I want a lawyer before I take the test."

CHAPTER FORTY-TWO

The phone rang in David Cohen's Deer Lodge motel room at 5:14 A.M.

"I'd like to speak to David Cohen, the lawyer for Isaiah Hood?"

"That's me. Who's this?"

"Nick Sorder, Capitol News Radio in Helena. I'm calling for your reaction to the development in the case. Governor Nye's office issued a statement this morning. Actually, late last night, from the time on our fax."

A statement? He knew nothing about this.

"Tell me what it says."

"Summarizing quickly, it says with respect to the U.S. Supreme Court's denial of Hood's petition for appeal and the Board of Pardons not recommending executive clemency, the governor will not grant your request for a delay. The AG's office adds that the sentence will be carried out tomorrow as scheduled."

Oh, goddamn it.

"Your reaction, sir?"

John Jackson in his dinner jacket, winking his warning about the governor squeezing his balls so hard they'll hear the scream in Chicago.

"Your reaction, sir?"

"I'm very disappointed. But I have no further comment until I speak with my client."

Cohen hung up and hurled the phone to the floor.

"I will take your concerns under advisement and make my decision known to you tomorrow." His black suit waiting. Ashes to be scattered. He did not do it. Whatever happened out there, it was not murder. Emily Baker, or whatever her name is, knows the truth. She knows the goddamned truth. Somehow, it has to be squeezed out of her.

Cohen sat at the edge of his bed in his boxers and Chicago Bulls T-shirt, elbows on his knees, head in his hands, tears stinging his tired eyes. His stomach quaked.

Think clearly. It is not over. Cohen attempted to console himself with a hot shower, then flipped on the TV news and pulled on jeans and a fresh shirt. He downed some hot coffee, bit into a muffin he picked up the night before at a truck stop on the return drive from Helena.

"The long-awaited execution of Isaiah Hood, who murdered a five-year-old Buckhorn Creek girl twenty-two years ago, will go ahead as scheduled tomorrow. In a statement released this morning from Helena, the governor said he will not intervene...."

Local news mocked him as he worked, sifting through his files.

"...the search for Paige Baker enters another day in Glacier National ..."

A blue file, a pink file. Case law, that wasn't it. The green file. Nope. Here, the yellow file. It contained e-mails, faxes, business cards and scribbled contact numbers from reporters with the most recent requests to interview Isaiah Hood. He went through the file. Cohen had rejected all requests. Hood had never, ever been interviewed. Now most news attention had been drawn to the lost girl story. Here it was. Cohen had a priority list of cell numbers for about half a dozen big outlets. All print because it was easier and quicker to get a print reporter inside the prison. Most of the people on the list had called recently saying they were in Montana on the lost girl story in Glacier.

The *New York Times*, Denver Bureau, Dianna K. Strauss. Cohen dialed the number. Busy signal. But a strange one. Maybe a bad connection? He tried the *Washington Post*. Phillip Braddock. It just rang and rang, unanswered. Cohen dialed the *Los Angeles Times*. Francis Lord. Out of service range. Damn. *USA Today*. Lawrence Dow. Voice mail. Cohen wanted to talk to somebody now. Right now. The *San Francisco Star*. Tom Reed. He'd heard of him. A hotshot on some big story in California. Saw him on CNN talking about it. Emily Baker was from San Francisco. This could work. Cohen punched Reed's cell phone number. *Come on*. The clock was ticking. Ticking. The number rang.

Not long after the morning sun lit the eastern sky, Tom Reed was waving good-bye to Chester Murdon, standing with his Lab, Sonny, on the porch of his house. They made a perfect picture against the crisp dawn and the glorious snowcapped mountains.

Thank you, Chester, Reed thought, patting the files that Murdon had given him. They were vibrating on the passenger seat. Reed was speeding into Wisdom, intending to get to the FBI in Glacier without wasting a second. Thanks to Murdon, he had a new angle. Tomorrow the man who murdered Emily Baker's sister twenty-two years ago in Glacier National Park would be executed while searchers try to locate Baker's daughter, Paige, in the same region. It was an incredible story. A haunting tale. He had surpassed everyone; even the Montana press had missed Emily's connection to Hood. And if the police knew, they certainly were mute on it. Maybe there was more to it?

It was coming up on the hour. Reed switched on the radio news, bracing for any break in the search. He'd have to alert the desk and Molly, he thought as the dramatic radio jingle led into the news from an AM station in Bozeman.

". . . our top stories this morning . . . Isaiah Hood will be executed tomorrow as scheduled, Montana's attorney general says. The U.S. Supreme Court rejected Hood's latest appeal and the governor will not delay the sentence. The Montana Board of Pardons and Paroles convened an emergency meeting last night and did not recommend the governor intervene in the case. And, it's day four of the massive search up in Glacier National Park for Paige Baker. The ten-year-old San Francisco girl reportedly wandered from her mother and father while camping in the remote and rugged Grizzly Tooth Trail region of the park. Across the nation, a deadly heat wave in Dallas claimed three lives as temperatures soared—"

Reed's cell phone trilled. He killed the radio and took the call.

"Tom Reed, *San Francisco Star.*"

"This is David Cohen."

Cohen? Cohen? Hood's lawyer.

"Yes, Mr. Cohen. I just heard the latest on your case. Sorry."

"No you're not."

Reed was just exercising professional courtesy.

"I'll come to the point. How fast can you get to Deer Lodge?"

"Why, what's happening there?"

"I'm offering you an interview with Isaiah, right now today in the prison."

"Exclusive?"

"Exclusive."

The ABS brakes on the rental engaged, bringing Reed to a halt.

CHAPTER FORTY-THREE

Maleena Crow arrived early at her law office on South Main in downtown Kalispell to await an expected referral call from Philadelphia. She went over a file while sipping herbal tea, stopping to consult "the partners," the exotic fish gliding in the aquarium that bubbled and hummed in the corner of her redbrick storefront office.

At twenty-nine, the University of San Diego grad was living her dream as a criminal attorney, operating her one-lawyer practice in what she told her law school friends were "the mystical Rockies." She recently won back-to-back acquittals for clients in two separate assault cases: a stabbing that was self-defense; a shooting ruled accidental. Crow smiled at her aquarium. The partners seemed pleased. She was pondering booking a vacation on the luxury train that traveled through the Canadian Rockies between Vancouver and Banff when her call came.

"Maleena? I'm so glad you're there. It's Legal Services. We just took a call from the county attorney's office—"

"Can this wait? I'm expecting a call."

"I'm just passing this to you. You're to call a Ms. Nora Lam from the U.S. Justice Department. It's urgent."

"Justice? What is this about?"

"Someone in Glacier National Park needs a lawyer right away and I guess you've been designated for the area."

Glacier? Crow was up on the news. She called Lam, connecting with the first ring on her cell phone.

"Nora Lam." Very professional. Authoritative.

"Maleena Crow. Criminal defense attorney in Kalispell."

Lam was to the point, underscoring the severity and confidentiality of Doug Baker's circumstances. Crow agreed to represent him.

She changed to jeans, T-shirt and a blazer, grabbed her Penal Code, briefcase, sunglasses. Within a half hour, a Montana Highway Patrol officer was waving her new silver VW Jetta to park behind the virtual army of TV satellite trucks, scores of news crews and the growing press contingent.

"Press over there, please."

"Uh-uh. I was summoned." Crow held out her card.

"Certainly, ma'am." The officer reached for his radio. "Follow me."

He trotted, leading Crow to a parking spot among the park, forestry and FBI vehicles at the community center. She was whisked inside to the small paneled room where she met Nora Lam, Frank Zander and Lloyd Turner.

"Doug's been Mirandized. He's agreed to be polygraphed to be cleared as a possible suspect in his daughter's disappearance," Zander said.

Crow produced a legal pad, noting everyone's name, their positions and the time.

"Is he a suspect? You got a case? You going to charge him?"

Zander listed the domestic call, the school complaint, the

argument in the mountains witnessed by a vacationing NYPD detective.

"Circumstantial and hearsay," Crow said. "Continue."

The bloodied T-shirt, the bloodied ax, his wounded hand, the opportunity when Doug and Emily were separated.

Crow absorbed it. "You find the little girl, or any part of her?"

"Not yet."

"This is what you want to polygraph him on?"

Zander nodded. "Right away."

"What about the mother?"

"She's not your client," Zander said. "This is all you get."

"Where is Mr. Baker? I'd like to speak with him."

Zander took Crow to the paneled storage room where Doug Baker was standing at the small window, watching a helicopter disappear.

"Doug Baker?" He turned.

"Maleena Crow. I've been appointed to be your attorney."

"Yes, sit down."

Crow put her briefcase on the small table and sat in one of the chairs.

"You were given your rights and understand them?"

"Yes."

"Why did you ask for a lawyer?"

"I figured it was best, under the circumstances."

"You agreed to be polygraphed?"

"Yes, whatever it takes."

"Doug, you understand that whatever they tell you, the fact is they are trying to build a case against you. They want to charge you."

"I've known from the start. I would do the same thing ... because I am guilty."

"No. You do not determine that. A court determines that."

"You don't understand."

"Doug, they are working to build a murder case against you,

probably against your wife, too. In this state, the penalty is death. You are not guilty of anything at this time.''

"No, Maleena. It's not like that,'' Doug said. "I did not harm Paige. God, no. I am guilty of making it look like I did in every way, through my own action, my own selfish stupidity."

He slammed his back against the wall and slid to the floor, placing his elbows on his knees, and over the next hour, he recounted everything while Crow took notes.

"I am the reason Paige fled. Sure, it was easy for me to blame Emily. We were arguing over her refusal to tell me about the problems of her childhood growing up here.''

"Which are . . . ?''

"She never got over the death of her parents. It destroyed her family. The whole time I've known her she refused to talk about it. We came here so she could deal with her ghosts. The night before Paige vanished, Emily told me she has a sister. I never knew this. If we live through this, I'm hoping we can rebuild the remnants of her family.''

"Doug, you do not need to take a polygraph—''

"After we realized Paige had disappeared, we searched into the night, just Emily and me. Nothing. Emily withdraws and I decide to hike out for help at daybreak. During my hike, all I can think of is how I caused this, how ashamed I am. Her T-shirt on my hurt hand reminds me. So I toss it. Then my ax banging from my pack reminds me, so I toss it.''

"But, Doug, how will taking a polygraph help? If Paige is lost, the searchers will find her.''

He shook his head.

"I pray for that to happen. But if she doesn't come back. If they don't find her. If she's already dead out there, then I killed her. I am guilty because I forced her out there. And I will have to live with it for the rest of my life. Can you understand? I want to take that polygraph to let them know I have nothing to hide. To let them know I am ashamed, to let them know exactly what I am guilty of. Because if my daughter is dead, then I might as well be dead, too. And there is nothing the FBI can do to hurt me any more than I am already hurting.''

Crow swallowed hard, finishing her notes, touching the back of her hand to her nose and nodding.

"Okay, Doug."

"Will you help me?"

"Yes."

CHAPTER FORTY-FOUR

About an hour after his call from David Cohen, Tom Reed arrived in Deer Lodge, pulling into the lot of the Four Bs Restaurant, parking among the pickups, Macks, Peterbilts and Freightliners. Inside he spotted a man in his thirties, alone at a booth with an open briefcase that had erupted with files and papers. He was wearing jeans and a navy shirt. An intelligent-looking man; neat, dark hair; serious face behind rimless glasses.

"David Cohen?"

Cohen lifted his attention from his work, nodding.

"You must be Tom Reed." They shook hands. "Thanks for coming."

A waitress freshened Cohen's coffee and poured a cup for Reed. She took his order of a toasted BLT on white. Cohen came to the point.

"Your interview is in one hour. I talked to the prison. Your background check has been cleared. I'll be present."

"What's the deal here, David?"

"You're obviously familiar with the case of Emily Baker, the mother of the little girl missing in Glacier?"

"Of course."

"Emily is the sister of the girl my client, Isaiah Hood, is accused of killing twenty-two years ago."

"Yes. I just discovered this myself. A friend, expert on state criminal history, pointed out the similarity with the old news photos."

"Why didn't you report it?"

"I intend to. I just learned about Isaiah's connection to Emily Baker—literally—a few hours ago. It's a compelling story."

"How much of it do you know?"

"That he killed her sister, Rachel Ross. And now, twenty-two years later on the eve of his execution, Emily's daughter is missing in the same remote area. It's an epic tragedy." Reed sipped his coffee.

"It's a miscarriage of justice." Cohen looked out the window. "You have just scratched the surface."

"I know Emily's name was Natalie Ross. Since then it's been changed. Likely the reason nobody else has reported the link yet."

"And why do you think her name was changed?"

Reed shrugged.

"You're a reporter. You should be digging into this."

"Don't have to."

"Why's that?"

"Because you're going to tell me."

Cohen liked Reed for being right.

"Her name was changed because *she* killed her sister. Isaiah is innocent of murder, and this state is going to execute him."

Dawning. It suddenly made more sense to Reed. Sydowski's presence. Emily's aunt telling Molly Wilson that Emily was undergoing counseling for the death of a child years ago.

"You can prove she killed her sister?"

Cohen slid legal-size pages of court transcripts across the table.

"Look at this."

It was an excerpt of her testimony on what had happened that day. The girls were on a camping trip with other girls. They had wandered from the campsite collecting butterflies when they had come upon Isaiah Hood.

Q: Did you feel threatened?
A: Yes.
Q: How?
A: He was bigger. Creepy.
Q: Why didn't you run away?
A: I tried. I said we better go back, but—
WITNESS: (sobbing)
COURT: Would you like a short recess?
WITNESS: (shakes head)
Q: You have to speak.
A: No.
Q: What prevented you from running away?
A: She let go of my hand and went to him, and then—
Q: Take your time.
A: And then he picked her up and held her over the edge. I begged him and fought with him to stop. "Please stop." I grabbed at his arms. He was bigger and so strong. He wouldn't stop. He said, "Guess what I'm going to do. I am going to see if she can fly." And then—
WITNESS: (sobbing)
Q: Go ahead.
WITNESS: (sobbing)
A: He let her drop.
WITNESS: (sobbing)

Reed saw a handwritten notation on the photocopied transcript. The distance of the fall was measured at 540 feet. Cause of death was cranial trauma, massive internal injuries. Her neck was broken. She was five years old. Reed thought of his son, Zach, then chased it from his mind. The transcript was a straight-forward accounting of how Hood murdered her, consistent with the old material Chester Murdon dug up for him. He slid the papers back to Cohen.

"This proves nothing, David. There's nothing new there." Reed sipped some coffee.

"Bear with me. This testimony essentially convicted him on her say-so. She was not cross-examined effectively."

"So? That's the loser's mantra in every capital case."

"She later recanted her testimony."

"What?"

"Her father died about a year after the trial. Her mother sold their ranch and they moved away. When I took on the case a few years ago to work on Isaiah's appeals, we hired a PI to find her. No luck. He did learn Emily's mother had changed their names frequently. At one point, we believed they moved to Canada, even sought citizenship there."

"You said she recanted."

"After the trial, Emily confided to a little girlfriend in Buck-horn that she felt confused, sad and guilty over her sister's death."

"Seems only natural, if she witnessed it." Reed nodded at the court transcript.

"Yes, but after her father died and her mother took her away, Emily resumed her confidential revelations in a series of letters from Kansas City to the friend in Montana. She discusses her guilt in her letters."

"You got the letters?"

Cohen shook his head.

"How about the friend?"

"Killed five years ago. Car accident in France."

Reed's food arrived. "No proof then?"

"I have proof. When the little girl first told her father about the conversations, he was unconcerned. Later, when he saw Emily's letter to his daughter, he had a change of heart and quietly informed the county attorney, who kept copies, producing a summarized report of their contents. At the time, the county attorney did not regard the letters as enough to warrant reopening the case. He categorized them the manifestation of young Emily's shock, trauma and grief at having witnessed her sister's death, which was followed by her father's death. He considered questioning her, but the state could not locate her. So it faded."

"Have you talked to the county attorney?" Reed bit into his sandwich.

"Deceased. Last winter. Cancer."

"No letters. No one alive to confirm them. Where's your proof?"

"Last week, I made another request to the state for a departmental-wide records search. A piece of the case had fallen through the cracks. This came this morning."

Cohen slid several pages to Reed. A fax with a cover page, dated that day, from the state's legal library research branch in Helena. The attached documents were some twenty years old with the letterhead GOLIATH COUNTY ATTORNEY. Reed flipped through the pages, reading snatches of Emily's words quoted in the report:

"I am guilty of her death. She begged me to save her. I don't know what happened. She pleaded and screamed. I had her hand but I don't know what happened that day. I will never forget her eyes staring into mine as she fell. God, please forgive me."

Reed swallowed and stared at Cohen, who was returning from the counter after paying the tab.

"Let's go, Tom. Isaiah will tell you the truth about what happened that day."

CHAPTER
FORTY-FIVE

Special Agent Reese Larson was a small bookish man. Soft-spoken, bespectacled, pale with short blondish hair that resembled an infant's, Larson looked more like a bank manager or choirmaster in a small Midwest town than one of the FBI's top polygraphers.

At fifty-one, Larson was a low-key behind-the-scenes wizard. Over a number of decades, he had pointed agents in the right direction in some of the FBI's biggest investigations. He was also a grand master at chess. He had flown in from the Manhattan Division the previous night.

Larson left his Kalispell motel room, dressed in a summer business suit, and arrived at the command center.

He spent several hours with Zander, Sydowski and then Bowman, who choppered in from the command post. The investigators revealed every aspect of the case to him in preparation for "examining the subject," as Larson insisted on putting it.

Then he worked with Doug Baker and his lawyer, Maleena

Crow, explaining the process of preparing Doug for "a polygraph examination."

"As you likely know, in most jurisdictions the results of the examination are inadmissible in court." Larson brushed a fly from his face while familiarizing Doug with his machine.

It used instruments that would connect near Doug's heart and fingertips to measure electronically respiratory activity, galvanic skin reflex, blood, pulse rate, breathing and perspiration. It would record the responses on a moving chart as he answered questions.

"I'll be the one asking the questions and analyzing the results," Larson said. "Upon completion, I will give the investigators one of three possible answers: 'The subject is truthful, untruthful, or the results are inconclusive.' "

Larson had given this prep-talk a thousand times.

"I know you will be very nervous. I am fully aware of that and expect you to be." Larson smiled, showing baby-size teeth. Larson made notes with an elegant fountain pen as he conducted a pretest interview, then discussed pretest questions with Doug.

About an hour later, Larson very expertly seated Doug in the most comfortable chair available, then connected Doug to the instrumentation of his machine. He made a point of sharing how he personally enjoyed the *Factfinder* model of polygraph.

The examination began casually with routine establishing questions. Zander, Sydowski, Thornton, Crow and Bowman were present but sat behind Doug. Larson repeatedly went over various areas as the ink needles scratched the graph paper.

"Why have you agreed to the examination, sir?"

"So you will know what I am guilty of."

"What are you guilty of?"

"Forcing my daughter to run away, to become lost."

"Did you harm her directly in any way during this trip?"

What is happening? This examination seems to be eternal. Doug tried concentrating but was slipping into a surreal world. Only a few days ago his family was singing along to rock songs on the CD of their rented SUV as they drove to Glacier National Park. This was going to be the healing trip. The one that brought them together, closer than they had ever been. Emily was going to bury the past and they were going to help her. What happened? *Sweet Jesus Fucking Christ. Help me. How did I come to be sitting here, wired to a lie detector, with the FBI thinking I killed my own child? My only child?* Something was forming in his throat. Someone was repeating his name.

"Doug?"

"Did you harm her directly in any way during this trip?"

"No."

"Are you an ex-marine?"

"Yes."

"Did you have to be tough?"

"Yes."

Larson's eyes were fixed on the graph paper.

"Are you a high school English teacher?"

"Yes."

"Do you know Cammi Walton?"

"Yes."

"Did you ever touch her in any way?"

"Yes."

"Was it appropriate?"

"Yes."

Larson made tiny indecipherable notations on the graph paper with his fountain pen.

"Did you strike her?"

"What?"

The chart needles tremored.

Maleena Crow glared at Frank Zander.

"Doug, did you strike her?"

"No."

Tears were stinging his eyes.

"Are you a high school football coach?"

"Yes."

God, he was going round and round with the same questions.

"Do you yell?"

"Yes."

"You ever lose your temper?"

"Yes."

"Did you ever threaten physical violence at home to your wife or daughter?"

"No."

"Were police ever summoned to your home?"

"Yes."

"Was it because of a report of violence?"

"I don't know."

"Were you violent physically before police arrived at your home?"

"No."

"Did you yell at your daughter during this trip?"

"Yes."

"Have you been violent?"

"I've yelled."

"Have you been physically violent?"

"No."

"Have you ever struck anyone in anger?"

"No."

A notation.

"Did you hurt your hand chopping wood?"

"Yes."

"Did you bleed?"

"Yes."

"Are you right-handed?"

"Yes."

"Was your daughter present when you injured your hand chopping wood?"

"Yes."

"Did you harm her with the ax?"

"No."

"Was you wife present?"

"No."

More notations and a pause.

"Who harmed your daughter?"

"I don't know that she is harmed."

"Do you believe your wife could have harmed your daughter?"

Doug did not answer. Paige, running to where Emily was—the last image.

"I sent her to you."

Five seconds passed. The needles scratched. Ten seconds. Larson watched the graph, repeating.

"Do you believe your wife could have harmed your daughter?"

"No, she loves her."

"Do you know who Isaiah Hood is?"

What? Doug was puzzled. "Yes, the guy who is going to be executed."

The needles swiped the page.

"Does your wife have a sister?"

"Yes."

"Did you know her sister was dead?"

What? What did he say? Jesus. What?

The needles swayed wildly.

"Did you know her sister was dead?"

"No."

"Did you know your wife was present with Isaiah Hood when her sister was killed?"

What? The needles lurched wildly.

Doug was turning white with fear and rage. Standing, he ripped the polygraph instrumentation from his body. Larson was urging, *"please sit down!"* Doug turned and confronted

Zander. The other investigators rose defensively. Doug eyed their sidearms.

He did nothing. Stood there. Felt the earth shifting under his feet. Heartbroken. Defeated. Unshaven. His hair wild. He looked every bit the man suspected of hacking his daughter to death with an ax.

CHAPTER FORTY-SIX

Respect and revulsion were internal twin forces Tom Reed battled whenever he conducted death row interviews.

From San Quentin near San Francisco, to St. Catherine District Prison, a seventeenth-century nightmare near Kingston, Jamaica, to Ellis One, a criminal warehouse rising from the snake-infested swamps northeast of Huntsville, Texas, he had wrestled both emotions when he talked with killers.

Respect—because he was looking into the eyes of a person who knew the date of his own death, sometimes within days of their conversation. One guy, a cop killer from Lufkin, Texas, had sent him a letter postmarked the day of his execution. Reed got it a few days later. It was like a voice from the grave: "Thanks for your interest in my sorry life, Tom." Reed had tacked it up at his newsroom cubicle, not as a trophy but as a personal reminder of something he struggled to understand. He actually liked a few of the killers he interviewed.

But in most cases, he could switch off any lingering fondness with a good riddance or hallelujah because of his revulsion.

Because the others were evil, motherfucking, stone-cold, remorseless, degenerate, defective, dangerous attempts at human beings who needed to be dispatched back to the factory.

Reed never lost sight of the pain, the sorrow, the soul-destroying result of their presence on earth. They added nothing of value to this world. Nothing but cemetery headstones.

Isaiah Hood had fallen into that category, a psychotic cold-blooded bottom-feeder who threw a little girl off a mountain in front of her sister. He deserved death.

Or so Reed thought up until a few minutes ago.

Now his guilt no longer seemed so absolute.

Driving to Montana State Prison, Reed supported Cohen's strong case for reasonable doubt over the circumstances of Rachel Ross's death. The elements swirled. Only two witnesses to the murder of the five-year-old daughter of a respected churchgoing, ranch family. Her thirteen-year-old sister and Hood, the mentally disturbed child of an abusive hermit monster.

In her letters, Emily acknowledges "feeling guilty." Her mother takes her on the run, changing their names. Her aunt tells Molly, "She's undergoing counseling for the death of a child."

Why?

Because she's guilty and knows an innocent man will die? Why do Emily and Doug Baker come to the mountains at the time of Hood's execution? Why do they hike to the region of Emily's sister's death? Reed felt a shiver vibrate up his spine.

Better call the desk. En route to the prison, he grabbed his cell phone and punched the direct line of Zeke Canter, metro editor of the *San Francisco Star,* who picked up on the first ring.

"Canter."

"It's Reed."

"Nice of you to check in, Tom. AP moved a story this morning, quoting sources saying that the FBI is finding evidence and looking hard at Dad. Enlighten me on what you know. Hold on. Violet's here; you're going on speaker.''

Reed pulled over. Within a few intense minutes, he informed his editors of what he had. They agreed. No matter how you looked at it, Cohen had presented a compelling case of reasonable doubt. Anticipating a huge story, they had dispatched Molly Wilson and a *Star* photographer to Montana. Reed resumed driving. He was nearing the turnoff for the prison.

"You wanted me to tell you a story about Isaiah Hood, Violet. Looks like you're getting one.''

As the prison loomed before the mountains, Canter came on.

"Tom, we've got some time. I want you to back this up with Cohen's stuff from the county attorney. Fax us a copy, maybe graphics can do something with it. And confront the FBI in Glacier for reaction. Grab Molly in Glacier to help out with anything, like calls to the governor.''

Reed pulled into the prison parking lot, where David Cohen was waiting.

Isaiah Hood sat on his bed, staring at his poster of the Rocky Mountains. He had spoken with his lawyer on the phone earlier that morning. He knew about the governor's refusal to intervene, about the old records from the county attorney's office Cohen had just obtained. About the interview with the reporter.

Hood was tired. Tired of paying for sins that were not his. Hell, he was a sin—a living, breathing mistake. And he had paid for that all of his life. Now, that had to count for something. He had paid his debt. *Now I'm owed.* It was time to put him back, return him to the place where he was free.

The mountains.

Whatever it took, he would return.

It would happen.

God owed him.

Because one way or another, he was leaving this place tomorrow.

Hood almost smiled.

At the central desk with the console, where the guards on death row watch the security video cameras, one of the guards nudged a colleague.

"Look. Hood's going into one of his trances."

Both men stared at Camera 8, the one trained on the interior of Hood's cell. He was sitting on his cot, arms outstretched toward his poster of the Rockies. Fists clenched as if gripping something unseen. Eyes closed. Frozen.

"Creepy, huh?" said the younger of the two.

The older one nodded, blinking.

"After his interview, we move him into the death cell and he goes on deathwatch. Then that will be the end of it."

"What do you make of him saying he didn't kill that girl?"

"I don't. And you shouldn't, either."

The intercom buzzed.

"The lawyer and reporter are here. Move Hood to the visitor's room."

Waiting in the small visitor's room on death row, Cohen and Reed did not speak. They watched the muted TV news. There appeared to be nothing significant in Paige Baker's case, Reed thought, playing absentmindedly with his small tape recorder. They heard the approach of Hood's chains. The door opened to Hood, in his orange jumpsuit, prison sandals and shackles.

"You got twenty minutes," said one of the guards.

"I was told we had an hour," Cohen protested.

"Twenty minutes because he's got to be processed."

Reed shook Hood's hand, flipped on his tape recorder.

Hood sat down, his chains knocking on the veneer tabletop, looking coldly at Reed, who met his gaze.

"Isaiah, are you innocent of the murder of Rachel Ross?"

Hood looked into Reed's eyes.

"Yes, I am."

"Who killed her?"

"No one."

"What do you mean?"

"It was an accident."

"An accident?"

Hood looked at Cohen, then back at Reed.

"I was out there that day, minding my own business, when they came to me. The little girls were playing some game. Chasing birds or butterflies with some little girl camp. They run from the forest and I said, 'Be careful.' But they laughed at me, saying they're playing some game. Called me names."

"What sort of names."

"Like I'm trash, and they're not supposed to play with me. I mean, all over town, me and my family was the joke of the county. They were the proper little girls of ranchers, bankers, merchants. I told them to be careful near that ledge. They never stopped playing and the little one slipped to the lower ledge there. Got herself dazed and I jumped down to get her, and her sister's screaming at me to stay away, she's going to help her sister up. But I see the little one's stunned, crawling in the wrong direction toward the ledge. This ain't no part of the game. She goes over the ledge; the big sister's got her by the hand and I reach over to help, but it's too late. She's gone over. She's dangling for a bit. The big sister's got her hand but not good. She falls, almost taking the big sister with her. I pulled her up and she runs off screaming I did it. Whole thing happened in less than a minute."

"Why would she accuse you if it was an accident?"

"Because they hated me. The whole town hated the Hoods. Never, ever thought I would be capable of trying to help. Regarded me as trash."

"Why didn't you explain this to police and the county attorney?"

"I did. They didn't believe me. They kept me awake for nearly two days until I confessed. That's what they wanted. Later, my lawyer says the judge will believe me and toss the confession, but it didn't work out that way."

Reed said nothing.

"Why?" Hood's eyes were shining, pleading.

Reed searched them.

"I'd like to know why she put me here." Hood stared at the walls. "The shrinks tested me. They should test her. She's the one with mental problems."

"I don't understand why you didn't reveal this twenty-two years ago?"

"You deaf? I did tell them. They wouldn't believe me. They made me confess. Said it was no accident. Started asking how my mother had died years ago. Would not let me sleep. Had me bawling to the point I didn't know the truth. Where *you* woulda confessed to anything. Now look at what's happened! And they want to execute me!"

In the time they had left, Reed went over Hood's version with him. Cohen did not interfere. Hood seemed to have an answer or explanation for every aspect.

A guard appeared.

"Sorry, time is up. Mr. Cohen, you can stay a bit with your client."

"Tom," Cohen said, extending his hand. "We'll talk in about an hour?"

"Sure." Then to Hood. "Thank you, Isaiah."

Hood said nothing but nodded. Then the guard led Reed from death row through the prison's inner yard toward the main gate. It was one of the older guards, a friendly-faced, silver-haired veteran who probably knew as much about inmates as there was to know. During the short walk between death row and the prison's main gate, the guard and Reed looked to the mountains.

"Mr. Reed, it's not my place, but I'm going to say this anyway."

"Say what?"

"At this stage of the game, that fella you just talked to is liable to tell you just about anything and hope you'll believe it."

Reed knew that. He also knew that folded in his rear pocket was a copy of the report on Emily's confessional letters from the county attorney's office. So it didn't matter if what Hood said was true or not.

Reed had a helluva story.

CHAPTER FORTY-SEVEN

After his polygraph test, the FBI placed Doug under guard in the maple-paneled storage room where he had slept on a cot the night before. They were so subtle it went unnoticed by the rangers and officials involved in search operations of the command center. An FBI agent sat in a chair outside the door to Doug's room.

His cell.

This wasn't happening. It couldn't be happening. Sooner or later, he was going to wake up from this, right?

But Maleena Crow, his appointed lawyer, was real. The words she was speaking were real, even though Doug was hearing them as if they were coming from a great distance, through the storm pulsating in his eardrums.

"Clearly, it does not look good, Doug, but ..." As Crow went on, the final part of the polygraph exam pounded over and over in Doug's brain.

Emily's sister was dead.

His world, his senses, were reeling. Confused. Exhausted.

If they did not suspect him, did they suspect Emily?

Emily was present with Isaiah Hood when her sister was killed. *"Do you believe your wife could have harmed your daughter?"* What? Oh, Jesus, help me. What was Crow saying? What?

"They cannot hold you for more than seventy-two hours without laying a charge. They cannot charge you without solid evidence. They have none." Then something about awaiting the results of Larson's examination before their next step. "Unless there is something you're not telling me, Doug? Is there?"

What? She was asking him something.

"Is there something you're not telling me?"

"No. . . ."

Doug is asking Emily . . . hadn't he asked her it so many times? And for so many years? Hadn't it enraged him that she refused to tell him about her past? The night before Paige vanished, Emily's tears are shining in the firelight. She raises her face, her beautiful pain-filled face, to the stars, searching for the words. "My—my sister . . ." She stops, leaving her words in the air.

"Sister?" *he says.* "You never told me you have a sister?"

Oh Christ.

"Do you believe your wife could have harmed your daughter?"

No. No. No. It can't be.

Find something real—when we were happy. The honeymoon. Mexico. The little seaside town. The sun setting. Kissing the Pacific. Palm fronds hissing. Breezes. Paradise. A perfect time. She is his dream come true. Together, on the warm private beach, she kisses his cheek.

"Will you love me always no matter what, Doug?"

"No matter what."

"Forever?"

"Forever."

"For better or worse?"

"For better or worse."

"No matter what the worst may be?" She smiled, so beautiful.

"I will love the worst you can give me."

She laughs, slipping off her swimsuit, mounting him there on the beach; afterward, leading him into the warm surf. He would love her no matter what the worst could be. . . .

Even if she killed Paige?

Did he really know everything about Emily? Why ask the question? He knew the answer. That's what this trip to the mountains was all about. That's what the last few years of hell had been all about.

It was all beginning to fit.

Her behavior.

Their first night in Great Falls at the Holiday Inn. He saw her slip out of bed, the room's digital clock displaying 3:04 A.M. Saw her switch on the TV, mute it, and surf, stopping at a local-community cable channel that showed the teletype-style text of local and state news briefs. Saw her absorb the item about the execution of Isaiah Hood. Watched her shroud herself in an extra blanket from the closet, pull her chair to the window, stare at the twinkling lights of the city and weep.

Doug had paid scant attention to Isaiah Hood. Now he remembered how Emily reacted in the Holiday Inn restaurant, seeing him reading the article in the *Tribune* on their way to Glacier.

"Do not read that. We're on vacation!"

Rachel Ross was Emily's sister. She was Natalie Ross, the witness who testified against Hood. Emily's aunt knew. Damn. Willa knew. She had invited them to join them on the RV trip, to get away *during the time the execution was carried out.* It all fit now—Willa wanting to get them far away, cutting off his attempts to learn more of Emily's past.

"Whatever it is she's sorting out, Doug, she has to tell you. Only she can tell you."

A dark realization was dawning on him. His heart was racing.

In the last article about Hood, he was claiming innocence. Paige was practically the same age as Emily's sister. It was Emily who had insisted they hike to the same region. In his anger, Doug sent Paige running to Emily. Was Emily the last person to see Paige?

Why had the searchers failed to find any trace of Paige?

Of Kobee?

Nothing.

Hood was claiming innocence.

"Will you love me no matter what the worst may be?"

Doug's heart was pounding in time with an approaching helicopter.

He buried his face in his hands.

"Doug," Crow said, "is there something you're not telling me?"

He looked at her. Lost.

". . . and the student of yours, Cammi Walton? Why would they ask you if you struck her? Does that line of questioning make sense to you? Is there something you're not telling me?"

He'd forgotten all about the accusation from Cammi.

CHAPTER
FORTY-EIGHT

From the edge of the command post, Brady Brook scanned the ridges and ledges through his high-powered binoculars.

Against the mountains, the on-site commander of the search embodied the calm, consummate professional, confidently sorting out strategies to locate Paige Baker.

But in Brook's gut, fear and fury churned.

He pulled his face from the binoculars, rubbed his tired eyes, then replaced his frameless glasses. Never in all his experience as Incident Commander had he faced a case like this.

Paige was well into her fourth day of being lost in the wilderness, well over seventy-two hours. In that time, there had been rain, fog and near-freezing temperatures. The overnight forecast called for snow. The region had some of the most dangerous terrain, the most dramatic climbs. Taking all factors into consideration, she was in the death zone now.

Had they lost her?

As far as he knew, nothing had surfaced. Nothing. Not a candy wrapper, an item of clothing, equipment, trace of feces, a scent or trail. Nothing of her dog, either. Brook had always held that his people could find something. If she was mobile, she was defeating the searchers. Was she lost to a river, lake, fall, bear? What?

The chief factor now was the FBI.

One of the rangers, who handled the computer work for the search, had used a sat phone to get onto the Internet this morning. They captured the news reports that the FBI suspected criminal intent and had not ruled out Doug and Emily Baker as suspects. Whenever Brook tried to find out anything, no one would confirm a syllable to him.

Keep searching. That's the priority. That's the order.

But it was also getting around that the FBI was finding some sort of evidence within the search perimeter and struggling to keep a lid on the nature of their discoveries, threatening anyone who leaked with "obstruction of justice" charges.

The FBI would simply take control of a sector, turn search crews away with no explanation, making a lot of people unhappy. Brook understood emotions were taut but urged his people to maintain a professional attitude and perform their duty. Yet in his gut, it really pissed him off when the guys like Holloway and Taylor were simply pulled from his roster.

Given that the official search had so far found nothing, Brook was growing angry his people were being left in the dark. Were they a futile diversion for what was ostensibly a homicide investigation? The news report fit with Doug Baker's absence. And the way the FBI watched Emily.

Damn it. Shouldn't they give him some sort of indication how to deploy his people? Searchers sometimes died or got hurt during operations. Tell him to call it off, if that was the case.

Brook pulled his binoculars to his eyes again, trying to determine what was happening near that ridge. It was out of sight, but there seemed to be some FBI activity there. A steady flow of helicopter traffic to the region. It was a heavily fissured, treacherous area.

Nobody told him anything.

Shaking his head, Brook glanced at Emily Baker.

Will we ever know what the hell happened to your daughter?

Brook then looked across the campsite toward the paramedics, playing checkers as they waited. Folded precisely among their gear, and kept respectfully out of sight, was a body bag.

CHAPTER FORTY-NINE

It was late afternoon and overcast when Tom Reed returned to the news media camp at Glacier National Park.

The area was congested. Motor homes, SUVs, news trucks. Reed was stuck behind a FOX affiliate from Minneapolis. A Montana Highway Patrol officer flagged him over at one of the checkpoints.

"You've got to park down there, sir." He pointed to an area a hundred yards from where Reed had parked before, almost out of sight.

"Way down there?"

"Sorry, the press people just keep coming."

"Why, what's going on? Something break in the case?"

"I wouldn't know, sir." The officer touched his brim and tapped Reed's car. "Move it along, please."

After parking, Reed worked his way through the chaos. He had to get to the FBI for reaction to his information on Emily Baker. He still had a few hours before he had to start writing. It was a wild scene. Helicopters droned overhead; networks and big-city TV crews had set up colorful canopies flying their logos and station letters. Reed overheard a reporter speaking Japanese into a phone. Next to him, another reporter, on her cell phone, trying to get information from Doug Baker's high school, had identified herself as a reporter with the *Toronto Star*. Then Reed passed two TV technicians speaking German while a nearby woman with a British accent gripped a microphone. Holding an earplug in her ear, she talked to a camera. It was an electronic village of satellite dishes, laptops, cell phones and scores of conversations.

A podium had been erected, suggesting news conferences. That was new. What was going on? Had he been scooped? No way. Nobody could have his angle on Emily, Reed assured himself, catching a glimpse of her file photo as he passed a network TV monitor. The case was going to explode when the *San Francisco Star* rolled out his story. He needed to find the FBI agent heading the investigation. He was nearing the tape that restricted press access to the command center when he heard a familiar clinking sound, then: "Tom!"

It was Molly Wilson.

Hurrying to him. A brilliant smile under her Oakleys. Auburn hair pulled into a tight, feathery tail. Navy T-shirt. Cargo pants. Bracelets. Looking very fine.

Next to her, his tanned face showing a fashionable three days' growth, was Levi Kayle. Eyes hidden behind his Romeos, he towered over six feet in his hiking boots, faded torn jeans, a Springsteen T-shirt from an LA concert and a news photographer's vest. A $30,000 state-of-the-art Nikon digital camera hung from his neck. Kayle rested his forearms on it. He was one of the best shooters in the country.

Wilson took Reed's arm, pulling him aside urgently.

"We have to talk. Zeke called me and told me what you've got. It sounds like dynamite, Tom." Wilson looked in all directions, finding some measure of privacy for them between two parked Cherokees. "Let me see it."

Wilson began reading the county attorney's old report on the letters Emily had written as a child shortly after her sister's murder.

"I am guilty of her death. . . ."

Wilson put a hand to her mouth. "This is good. Kayle, Kayle. Copy these. Can you shoot them and send them to San Francisco?"

"Hey, ask nice, Wilson. I don't work for you."

"Please, Levi. Pretty please, you big sweet lug."

"Sure." Kayle grinned as he took the pages, stepped into better light, adjusted his lenses, then set pebbles on the page corners to hold them down as Wilson checked her watch and began updating Reed.

"This is compelling. Do you think they'll go ahead and execute Hood after we come out with this?"

"Impossible to know. It's cutting things close. I just know it's a fantastic story. What did the desk say?"

"They want one big take ASAP putting our stuff together. They're going to publish your document as part of a package. You know, big exclusive, execution cliff-hanger, missing child, murder mystery."

Reed nodded. Sounded like a novel. But it was true.

"A newser starts"—Wilson checked her watch—"in a few minutes. We figure it's reaction to the AP story that they're questioning the dad."

"Pick up anything else?"

"Yes. When we got here this morning, we got lucky. I bumped into a guy one of my girlfriends used to date, Vince Delona with the *New York Daily News*. We're talking and this strange-looking little man in a suit walks by us and says, 'Hi, Vince.'"

"Who was he?"

"Reese Larson, the FBI's top polygraph examiner. He's based in New York. Vince profiled him a few years back after the World Trade Center bombing. Kayle got pictures. Nobody but Vince and I know he went in to conduct polygraph tests.''

"That means they're building a case against the dad and likely the mother. Or possibly clearing the dad to focus on the mother."

Wilson nodded. "And I talked to some guys with the search. They're pissed because the FBI is telling them squat. There's supposedly no trace of the kid, and if she were out there, she's either dead or will be by morning. It's going to snow out there tonight."

Kayle was finished with Reed's documents. "Pretty damning stuff there, Reed. You going to the news conference?"

"I am," Wilson said. "After it's over, we'll meet here, sort out how we'll put our story together. Okay, Tom?"

While the press pack went to the conference, Reed went down the road to the police tape near the command center. He needed the FBI agent in charge of the investigation to react to what he had.

A young agent, his ID hanging on a chain around his neck, came to life to meet Reed, eyeing his plastic press credentials clipped to his waist. His face was not friendly.

"Press conference is that way."

"I know that." Reed smiled. *Agent Evan Crossfield.* That's all he needed. "Tom Reed with the *San Francisco Star.* I am making a formal request to speak with the agent heading the investigation. The *Star* is going to publish some critical information we've obtained. The FBI might want to know about it before we publish."

The agent was unfazed, scowling at Reed.

"Our press people are over there at the conference. Run along."

Run along?

"Listen, your press people are not investigating the case. If you could please alert the agent in charge that I have very critical information."

"Sorry, just go over there with the rest of them."

"Don't be sorry"—Reed handed the agent his card—
"because when our story comes out tomorrow, it will contain
the line that 'the FBI refused to comment' on our information.
The people above you will search for the agent who took it
upon himself to make the decision not to alert the investigators.
This information could seriously embarrass the Bureau. When
they call me, and they will, asking who the heck was it 'that
refused,' I'll have to tell them it was you, Agent Evan Crossfield, who never even bothered to look at what I had to show
the FBI. So I would not be sorry now, if I were you, Agent
Evan Crossfield. Save it for tomorrow when our story hits the
wires and certain people in the Hoover Building start speaking
your name. You'll be very sorry then."

Reed smiled, turned, walked off. Five yards. Ten yards. He
could hear Agent Evan Crossfield thinking. Fifteen—

"Hey, just a minute, wiseass!"

Within three minutes, Special Agent Frank Zander emerged
from the command center, looking very irritated, holding
Reed's card in his hand. Zander went to the tape, lifted it, took
Reed out of view to the shade of a tall spruce.

"You Reed?"

"That's me."

"Sydowski says you are an asshole who stumbles onto
things."

"Is that on my card?" Reed answered with a shrug. "Who
might you be?"

"Frank Zander, on the investigative side of the search for
Paige Baker."

"So you going to charge the parents?"

"Don't waste my time. What do you have that's so important?"

Reed gave Zander the old report. He read it. Reed could not
tell from his poker face if it was news to him. Zander passed
it back.

"That it, Reed?"

"Does this change the direction of your investigation?"

"No comment."

"Do you suspect anything beyond the report of a lost girl?"

"No comment."

"Do you deny polygraphing Doug Baker?"

"This is not twenty questions, Reed. You are wasting my time."

Zander escorted him outside the perimeter.

"Zander, that's Z-A-N-D-E-R?"

Zander walked off, leaving Reed at the tape.

"Happy now?" Agent Crossfield grinned. "Asshole."

Zander was good. Reed got nothing from him. Zip. Not even a "where did you get this?"

The press conference offered little new information to a nation gripped by the drama of ten-year-old Paige Baker facing her fourth night lost in the rugged Rocky Mountains near the Canadian border.

As night descended on the press village, the TV lights created intense halos. The temperature dropped and snow flakes swirled as TV reporters in hooded jackets talked solemnly about the ratio of survivability, quoting experts about "the death zone" and reports that the FBI had not ruled out anything. This included a possible criminal act, such as abduction, an Internet connection or accidental death.

Inside Reed's rented car, the only sound above the idling motor and the heater's humming fan was the clicking of laptop keyboards as Reed and Wilson worked against the *Star*'s early deadline. Their story was going to push the case to an unbearable level. Wilson glanced over Reed's shoulder at the article he was drafting:

THE SAN FRANCISCO STAR

WEST GLACIER, Mont.—Tonight the state of Montana will execute Isaiah Hood, who claims to be innocent of murdering the five-year-old sister of Emily Baker 22 years ago in Glacier National Park.

Hood's attorney revealed what he said is proof Baker played a role in her sister's death.

It comes amid a massive search by park rangers, FBI agents and volunteers for Baker's 10-year-old daughter, Paige, who vanished with her beagle, Kobee, five days ago in a remote region known as the Devil's Grasp.

It is the same elevated corner of the park where Emily Baker's little sister, Rachel Ross, was thrown to her death by Hood while on an outing with a local youth club two decades ago.

Baker witnessed the tragedy and revealed aspects of it in private letters to a childhood friend shortly after giving testimony that led to Hood's death sentence. . . .

The FBI conducted a polygraph test on the missing girl's father, Doug Baker, a popular San Francisco high school football coach and English teacher, and are expected to subject Emily Baker to one . . .

CHAPTER FIFTY

The sky darkened outside the command center.

The members of the task force had watched the national newscasts, jaws tightening as each report suggested the Rangers and FBI were not revealing everything they knew, citing "sources" who indicated Doug Baker was under suspicion.

"That kind of crap does not help. We've got to plug these leaks." Zander finally snapped off the room's large set.

Empty coffee cups, crumpled notepaper, creaking chairs, buffeting winds rattling a loose window, contributed to the tension in the cramped room.

"Frank, by our last count, there are three hundred newspeople out there. It's not an excuse, but rumors are going to fly," said a sergeant with the Montana Highway Patrol.

Zander conceded his point.

It was late. Everyone was irritable. On edge. Zander wanted to move things along.

The San Francisco ERT was en route with special gear to confirm Paige's corpse was somewhere deep in the crevasse.

The equipment could not be put to use until morning. Zander's gut told him the crevasse was the case clincher. Once that was solid, everything else would fall into place. Until then, they had plenty of loose ends.

"I'd like to know how the hell Tom Reed got the jump on Emily Baker's connection to Isaiah Hood. How could he obtain that old document from the county attorney he waved in my face?"

"I think I know." Bowman was going over the FBI's copy of the county attorney's record on Emily's letters. She explained how after she reported to Zander on what Emily had revealed to her about her sister's death and her connection to Hood, the FBI immediately ordered an urgent search of all Bureau and state files on Hood's case. The pertinent records that Helena managed to retrieve were faxed to the FBI at the command center, and the discovered pieces of the old file confirmed what Emily had revealed to Bowman: her mother had moved frequently, changing their names so that the state lost track of them. She had essentially disappeared. It explained why the FBI did not make the connection between Emily and Hood when Paige's case broke.

"So how did Reed get his copy so soon after we did? Who tipped him to the connection?"

"David Cohen, Isaiah Hood's lawyer," Bowman said. "I called the capital and they told me there was a simultaneous request for the file from Cohen's law firm."

"More vital," said Turner, "do you think Hood's claim of innocence is valid, Tracy, based on the records and your work on Emily Baker?"

"It's too difficult to be conclusive. It is accepted Emily was present at the time of her sister's death and that she tried to reach for her. It is crystalline in her mind, even in her emotional state, that Isaiah Hood is guilty."

"Could she be putting on a show to make sure we buy Hood's guilt, and that her daughter's vanishing is just a coincidence?"

Thornton asked. "This woman has had some strong emotional outbursts during this ordeal. Weigh that with her undergoing counseling in San Francisco."

"I agree, Pike." Bowman gazed at the county attorney's report. "Consider her old letters and the fact her daughter is now missing. Same location. Certainly raises a lot of questions." Bowman shook her head. "I just don't know."

"I don't buy it. Paige could have fallen in that crevasse," Sydowski said. "We know the dad has a temper. We know the mother's been hearing voices, that she has a troubled past. But I just can't see how this fits together. I really don't buy it. Not yet."

"That's your opinion, Walt." Zander was icy. "Any word from San Francisco on the schoolgirl complaint on Dad? Do we know who Emily's shrink is? Maybe she confessed the old murder, which would impact the disappearance."

"The counselor is traveling in Asia. I am expecting to be updated on the school allegation against Doug Baker."

Zander told everyone the preliminary lab reports showed the blood found on the pink T-shirt and ax were one type: O positive. Doug Baker's military records show he is O positive.

"If Paige has a different blood type, we should have a mix, but if they're the same, which I think they are, we may need DNA done to separate them."

"I recall Paige's school records show she's O positive," Sydowski said.

"Yes. They need more time for testing if they can determine a gender distinction in the blood."

"What is the blood at the crevasse?" Pike Thornton asked.

"O positive."

"The hair?"

"Matches with Paige's taken from her sleeping bag."

Someone knocked on the door. It was Reese Larson.

"Sorry to interrupt. I have concluded my analysis."

Reese opened an FBI file folder, unscrewed his fountain pen, went over notes that were so neat they resembled calligraphy.

Zander was impatient but polite. "Reese, first your opinion on Doug Baker's response to the questions, please."

"Inconclusive. I am sorry. The results of my examination are inconclusive."

Zander gritted his teeth, looked out the window into the night.

"On every single point, Reese?"

"No, not the mundane aspects. He was truthful there. But on the points salient to the investigation, I could not form an opinion as to whether he was truthful or not truthful. He was a difficult subject. I'd be willing to retest him, if you would like?"

Turner, a veteran of many battles, steepled his fingers.

"Reese, is there any area, any critical area, where you even came close to forming an opinion one way or the other?"

Reese flipped through his file folder, with the FBI seal, leafed very purposely through page after page of graph paper with their inky spikes, nearly touching them with his fountain pen as he reviewed his notations.

"Hmmm. Well, there was one area that was close, very close."

"Close to what, Reese?" Zander sighed.

"I'd say he was very close to being untruthful here on this important area, which we visited several times." A neatly manicured little finger touched the graph paper at an area marked "1473" with an asterisk. "See?"

"Reese, I don't understand. What was the area of questioning?"

Larson flipped though a separate note sheet. "Here it is: 'Do you believe your wife could have harmed your daughter?' He answered no. He answered the same way each time we came back to that one."

"Yes, Reese?"

"Well, in my opinion, he was very close to being untruthfu there; when you study these numbers, heart rate, skin . . ."

Zander looked at the others as Larson went on with technica details.

We're close. We're getting close, he thought.

After Larson finished, Zander used one of the FBI's satellite phones to call the agents at the command post. The ones assigned to watch Emily Baker. The darkness and the rough snowy weather made it too treacherous to fly out that night.

"This is Zander. Who's this?"

"Fenster."

"What's Emily doing, Fenster?"

"In her tent."

"Her demeanor?"

"Restless. Keeps asking if we know anything. Wants to know when Doug is coming back."

"I want someone watching her all night. Go in shifts. Do not let her out of your sight. We're coming out for her a daybreak. Understand?"

When Zander finished, he asked Sydowski if he knew if Emily had traveled as a freelance news photographer to any hot spots.

"I seem to remember something about East Timor, why?"

"Her blood type would be on file with the Pentagon. We'll get it," Zander said. "Look, there are a number of scenarios here. She could have done something and Doug's covering up. He could have helped her. We'll be keeping him in custody for a while."

"You going to charge him?" asked Nora Lam, punching a number in her cell phone.

"Not yet," Zander said. "And who are you calling, please?"

"County attorney. If you're bringing the mother in to go hard on her, you'll have to Mirandize her. She may request an attorney."

"All you tell them is to be prepared to send another lawyer here in the morning," Zander said. Lam nodded.

Pike Thornton was a study of concern.

"Frank, if this goes the way it is shaping up to go, what does that mean for Hood? We can't sit here and let the state execute an innocent guy."

"What time is he scheduled to go?" Turner said.

"Midnight our time, tomorrow night." Thornton studied his watch.

Zander nodded to Lam, who was speaking softly on her phone. "We'll get Nora to give the governor's office a heads up, depending on how things go. It's looking like it will all come down tomorrow."

Thornton said it would be seen as Washington interfering in the state's jurisdiction. "Governor has aspirations of running for national office."

Painfully familiar with the sleaze within the Beltway, Zander shook his head. "Executing an innocent man would not really enhance his chances, not that I give a rat's ass, mind you. Hood is his problem. It was his state that convicted him."

Afterward, everyone got into their vehicles, driving wearily through the night to their hotel rooms.

Looking out at the darkness, Zander was convinced Paige Baker's corpse was at the bottom of the crevasse deep in the mountains. Her mother's history, her father's wound, their argument, the bloodied ax. The shaky polygraph results.

But he noticed Sydowski was subdued, his body language telegraphing that he was holding something back. *Something we missed?*

Zander shook it off. It would be over tomorrow. Once they pulled that little girl's corpse from the crevasse and autopsied her, it would all be over.

CHAPTER
FIFTY-ONE

That night, Inspector Walt Sydowski was sitting up in the bed of his pine-scented room at the Sky Forest Vista Inn, wearing his bifocals, attempting to read an article on bird droppings. He wanted to take his mind from the case long enough to let him sleep.

It was a technical overview of what to look for in droppings. They were a warning of illness. Understanding could help prevent a bird's death. He set the article on the nightstand, removed his glasses and rubbed his tired eyes.

Paige Baker's face would not let Sydowski rest. He could not take his mind off the case. In all his years as a homicide cop, this was one of the most baffling files he had ever known. Zander was an excellent investigator, doing everything Sydowski would do. Were they missing something?

Sydowski was exhausted.

What was he doing here? The Rockies were not his streets. It was an FBI file. It was unusual for them to arrange a team this way on an unfolding case, working a homicide when it

had not been established you have a body. *Or even a crime.*
Was it conceivable that Doug and Emily Baker murdered their
daughter? They could not execute an innocent man if there was
reasonable doubt about his guilt. Too many times, Sydowski
had seen firsthand how evil manifests itself. His tired eyes
burned at the memory of one case of two sisters, aged two and
four. Their mother had bound them together with duct tape,
put them in a cage built for a large dog, and . . .

Sleep, he told himself.

But he couldn't. He was suddenly overwhelmed with loneli-
ness. He dialed the number for his father's unit at Sea Breeze
Villas in Pacifica. He imagined the old man spending the day
tending his seaside vegetable garden while snow swirled outside
Sydowski's Montana motel.

"Hahllow."

"Hey, Dad, so you're awake?" Sydowski said in Polish.

"Yeah, sure. Watching a movie."

Sydowski smiled. "So how are you doing?"

"No problems. You going to be in the mountains a long
time?"

"Hard to say, Dad."

"The TV says you think the father killed his little girl. The
bastard, why would he do something like that? It's crazy."

"We don't know anything for certain, Dad. You know how
it is."

"I know how it was for you with that last case with the baby
girl and the kidnapped kids. I think you want to retire, maybe
have something new in your life. But you're afraid."

"Who knows? Listen, Dad, I was thinking when I'm done
here, how about we drive down the coastal highway to Los
Angeles?"

"What for?"

"We could see the Dodgers. There's a doubleheader coming
up. We could have some fun, do something you always wanted
to do."

"Like what?"

"Go to Hollywood. Get a map of the stars' homes and check them out. See Brando's house?"

"He's a great actor. The best. Played a good Polack in that *Streetcar*. Kowalski. 'Stellllaaaa.' Heh-heh. He's put on weight, though. Hey, and maybe I can give you a haircut and shave like the last time?"

Sydowski winced at the memory.

"Listen, Pop, we'll think about everything. I got to go."

"You better call your girlfriend, Louise."

"She's not my girlfriend."

"She's worried about you."

"How do you know?"

"She called me asking how you were doing. So call her."

A warm feeling flowed through Sydowski. In the six years since his wife's death, when was the last time a woman cared about him? Maybe she was his girlfriend, he thought, brushing his teeth, inspecting his old face in the mirror. What did she see in him? She was so smart, so comfortable to be with. She made him feel so good. *You're like a lovesick pup, you dumb flatfoot.* He picked up the phone and put it down. Christ, he was acting like a teenager. *Go ahead. Call.* Before he knew it, her number in San Jose was ringing. He was suddenly guilty. Betraying Basha's memory. *Hang up. It's better to be alone—*

"Hello?"

"Louise? Uhm, I know it's late. I'm sorry if I woke you. It's Walt. Sydowski."

"You didn't wake me, Walter." Her voice was like medicine. He could hear her smile. He nestled the phone closer. "I just had an evening swim in the pool."

"Oh." He tried envisioning her figure in a swimsuit. "Look, I won't keep you. Uhm, it's just, well, my father said you called."

"I did. I was concerned about how you were doing. It is such a huge story. Tragic. On the radio, TV, the papers. Nonstop, so many twists and turns. It has got to be so stressful.''

"Yes, well, it has its complications.''

"Are you holding up okay, Walter?''

"I'm fine. How are your budgies doing?''

"They are singing up a storm. But now you didn't call just to ask about my birds?''

"Well, no. How are *you* doing?''

"Oh, for Pete's sake, Walter, are you going to ask me for a date or not?''

He was at a loss. Positively impressed and stunned.

"Uh, sure. How about dinner when I get back?''

"That would be lovely.''

"Okay. I'll call you.''

"Sounds wonderful. Now, good luck on your case.''

"Thanks, Louise. For everything.''

For several minutes afterward, Sydowski sat on his bed, in his boxers and T-shirt, listening to the wind howling outside, struggling to think of nothing. Then he switched off the room's lights and was overcome with a thousand thoughts and worries. His father, his new relationship, Tom Reed and his relentless pursuits, the real possibility that an innocent man was going to be executed in a few hours.

Sleep. He ordered himself. Sleep.

Drowsiness was coming for Sydowski, but it was coming with visions of ten-year-old Paige Baker's corpse, stiff and frozen in the mountain night at the bottom of a crevasse, so deep, so eternal that none of the flakes swirling amid the celestial peaks of the Rocky Mountains would ever reach her.

CHAPTER FIFTY-TWO

The Blueberry Hill Lodge was an independently owned first-rate motel located a few miles south of Glacier National Park's west gate, not far from Columbia Falls. Its spacious lobby had hardwood floors, oversize leather sofas, floor-to-ceiling windows framing mountain views, log walls and a massive stone fireplace, where a dying blaze crackled.

In the dimmed tranquility of the late hour, a solitary guest sat near the soft light of a lamp, her hands working on the needlepoint scene of a hummingbird hovering at a glacier lily. Embroidery was the only way Special Agent Tracy Bowman could keep her hands from trembling since coming away from the task force briefing an hour ago.

Well, you wanted field work, girl.

She could not stop thinking of Paige Baker, Emily, Doug. Isaiah Hood.

If Hood is innocent? Dear God.

Bowman had held Emily in her arms just a few hours ago. Was she comforting a murderer? Had she been manipulated by a calculating, cold-blooded woman who killed her little sister?

And now her own daughter?

Bowman thought of Mark, ached to hold him. She ached for Carl. Ached for him in every way. She should sleep. *Stop this. I've been an FBI special agent for over seven years now.* Respectable on the GS pay scale. She'd done well at Quantico and Hogan's Alley. She'd had a duty to carry out. *So much is riding on this case. For Mark. Just concentrate on the job.*

"Tracy?" A large warm hand touched her shoulder. "Are you okay?"

Frank Zander came from behind.

"Oh!" She smiled. "Sure. Just a little wound up and saddened, thinking of Paige Baker."

"I understand."

Zander had obviously showered, changed into fresh clothes, and had a clipboard and records with him. She detected some cologne. Looked good.

"That a hobby?" He nodded to the needlepoint.

"Helps me relax. This case has been tough."

"It's one of the most difficult files I've ever had."

"It's so intense. So much. So fast. I guess I didn't expect it to take so much out of me."

"They all take something from you."

"You got kids?"

"No. I'm not married. I'm sep—Well, I'm getting a divorce."

"I didn't mean to pry. It's just that I think of this case and Paige Baker, wondering if she's dead out there. Then I think of Mark. He's nine, and I think of Doug and Emily Baker. We look into their eyes. We talk to them. What's the truth here? I fully appreciate that it's our job to find out fast, but it just eats at you."

"I know." Zander glanced around to ensure they were alone,

keeping his voice low. "Perform our duty in silence. That is what you do."

"I'm sorry. I should get to bed and not lay this on you."

"Tracy, it's okay to talk about it. I don't mind."

"Really?"

"It eats at me, too. Always has. If it's any comfort, I think you're a good investigator."

She nodded appreciatively, staring at her needlepoint.

"You're incredibly intuitive and come at things from different angles. Tell me your story. You're in Missoula."

"Yes. Mostly computer work, government fraud. Pretty low key. I applied for extra course work at Quantico and rotation to a big-city division. I'm up for a job in Los Angeles . . . if I don't screw up here."

"You won't screw up, Tracy."

"You sound so sure."

"Trust me."

She actually liked being with him. It had been so long since she had talked, really talked to a man.

"So, Frank. What's your story?"

He told her. Everything. About the two wives, his loathing for the snake pit within the Beltway and his desire for a new start. His dedication to the job. His life-defining case in Georgia, which earned him his reputation as a prick and shaped his legendary status as an investigator.

When he finished, she said, "It's getting very late. We should turn in."

Zander walked Bowman to her room. She thanked him at her door and was about to say good night, when his eyes held hers.

"Tracy, I—"

She saw desperation in his face. In the short time they talked, they both realized they were two painfully lonely people at the crossroads of their lives. Each had something the other wanted, needed, yearned for. Yet each was so afraid. A strange feeling came over her.

Would he be good with Mark?

What was happening? It was like meeting someone wonderful at a funeral. *There is time,* Bowman thought. *If it is meant to be, there is time.*

"The morning is almost here, Frank," she said. "We've got to see this thing through to the end."

He nodded and walked off, checking his watch. He was going to his room to review the videotaped interviews of Doug and Emily Baker. In a few hours, he expected to be laying charges in the death of their ten-year-old daughter, Paige.

CHAPTER FIFTY-THREE

Emily was alone, listening to the night wind whipping her tent at the command post. Depriving her of sleep, of rational thought, fraying her soul.

She was slipping from sanity into a yawning abyss.

Paige's face. Rachel's eyes. Falling.

God. Please.

Darkness into darkness. The accusing wind.

"Where's Rachel? Where's your sister?"

Where's Doug? He's been gone so long. The FBI took him. Zander took him. Leaving her alone with strangers. The agents, who never smiled, were watching her, and it was so cold. *Lord, help me. I am begging you. End this, please. If Paige is not alive, I cannot bear to face it again.*

My Sun Ray. Her eyes. Her hand brushing mine, slipping from mine.

The wind would not stop.

Remembering her obsession after it happened. After Rachel died, her need to comprehend, to understand, *to know* . . . what a human being experiences in the seconds they are falling to their death.

She *had* to know.

Emily actually studied it.

Terminal velocity. Vestibular sensory input. *Horror in her eyes.* The overload of messages through the neurological system. The automatic impulse to defy reality by "grabbing at air" in order to save one's self. *Fear in her face. Hands reaching.* Suspended in space as the earth rushes to hammer your life into heaven. *Knowing death was upon her.* The "agonal phase," the instant before death when all that is physical in a being ends. *Did she suffer?* Emily had spent her life searching to know if her sister could have been comforted by some spiritual phenomenon.

Rachel was only five years old.

Did she suffer? She had to know.

The wind would not tell her.

Where's your daughter, Emily? Where's your husband? Doug had been alone with Paige. Had been the last to see her.

"Emily, I sent her to be with you. I thought she was with you. She followed you with Kobee, I swear, not more than five minutes after you left. I thought all this time she was with you."

His hurt hand. Her T-shirt was wrapped around it. Chopping wood. They had argued so intensely. He was incensed with her for not talking to him about her family history.

No.

Stop thinking like that. She was drunk with exhaustion. Struggling.

She was slipping. Falling.

Paige, come back, please.

CHAPTER FIFTY-FOUR

Is Paige still alive?

She has to be.

Doug had to hope beyond hope. Not give in to doubt, the traitor. Paige had to know he had not abandoned her.

Bitter winds shook the command center, clattering the window of his room. He lay on a soft, dry cot, under the warmth of a woolen blanket. A huge bowl of vegetable soup and butter biscuits sat cold, untouched a few feet from him, tempting him, mocking him. He broke down and wept.

If Paige was alive, she was fighting for her life.

He had no appetite.

Oh, Paige, can you ever forgive me?

If you're dead . . .

Doug stared at his wounded hand.

She had only wanted to talk and I chased her away with an ax in my hand. "Get the hell away from me and go find your damned mother!"

Emily.

Emily had a sister. Her sister was dead. Emily was present with Isaiah Hood when her sister was killed. Do I actually believe my own wife could have harmed my daughter?

The night they arrived in Montana.

He recalled again watching Emily slip out of bed at the Holiday Inn and watch the TV item about Hood's execution. He remembered glimpsing her as she rummaged through her purse, retrieving something. She sat by the window, staring at the retrieved item, then into the night, weeping softly.

In the morning when Emily showered, he scoured her bag and found it. Old snapshots. She had sat up studying old pictures. Girls. A group of girls playing in the mountains. Smiling, laughing. Childhood friends, he thought.

One of the girls looked familiar.

It became clear to him now.

The face in the newspaper. The little girl Isaiah Hood had murdered. Emily's sister.

Rachel.

Oh Christ. It's true. The FBI is not lying. He had not wanted to think about it. It was starting to fit together. This was the ghost of her past.

What did the police know that he didn't?

His skin prickled.

They were digging hard into their lives. Revealing nothing.

"Do you know Cammi Walton?"

Yes. Most teachers knew Cammi was having terrible problems with her parents' divorce.

"Did you strike her?"

Had she made a wild accusation about him? It was possible. Her life was in turmoil. She'd had outbursts. He had done nothing wrong.

His lawyer telling him, "The fact is they are trying to build a case against you. They want to charge you."

Doug had to find out the truth about his family.

About his wife.

They know. The FBI knows something.

The wind swirled.

"Will you love me always no matter what, Doug?"

Paige.

Not a trace of her. Not a trace.

Doug searched the darkness for answers.

CHAPTER FIFTY-FIVE

Tom Reed called his wife, in Chicago, on the chance she would be up so he could say good night to her and their son, Zach.

"He's sleeping like a log. Went to a Cubs game tonight with his uncle. Do you want me to wake him?"

Ann had just returned from her sister's bridal shower.

It was late. Reed was alone in his darkened room at the Sunshine Motel. Missing his family as the night winds blew down from the Rockies near Kalispell. His TV muted on *All the President's Men.*

"No. Let him sleep. Say, he's been doing pretty good, hasn't he?"

"Yes, he's doing quite well, since . . . the thing."

"The thing."

That was Ann's name for Zach's abduction and near murder in the case of a madman who held three San Francisco children hostage several months ago. Reed had been reporting on it when "the thing" reached into their lives and nearly destroyed his family.

"Tom, you never answered my question. What do you think happened to that little girl in the mountains?"

He had told her about obtaining Emily Baker's confessionlike letters, interviewing Hood, the looming execution, the FBI polygraphing Doug Baker, how everything was mounting with increasing intensity.

"It's difficult to know what happened. Isaiah Hood could be innocent. The Bakers—Emily Baker, because of her troubled past—could be guilty of something. You and I know firsthand *that* scenario is realistic. But she could be the victim of circumstance. Who knows?"

"Hmmm." Ann digested what her husband said. "Well, the entire search story is playing big here. Front of the *Tribune* and the *Sun-Times*. Local TV have people on the scene."

"It's the story of the moment."

"I'd love it if you were here right now, Tom."

"Would you?"

"Mmmm. To help me undress and rub my back."

"Well, I'd love it if you were here in the Sunshine Motel with me."

"Hey, are you sure you're going to make it to Chicago for the wedding?"

"Yes. Molly Wilson's here. I've checked flight times and—"

"*Molly's there?* Why?"

"The *Star* wanted more bodies on the story; it's building. Besides, I can throw to her when it's time for me to go."

"Well, you just better make it for the wedding in Chicago, or you're fired."

"Fired. From what?"

"Your job as my personal masseur."

"Don't rub me the wrong way, lady."

He loved the way she giggled.

"Good night, idiot. I love you," she said.

Reed switched off the TV and fell into a fitful sleep, wondering if Isaiah Hood, a man he had met a few hours ago, was innocent of the crime he was going to be executed for a few hours from now.

In the darkness, Reed saw Hood's eyes. Pleading.

"I'd like to know why she put me here?"

Emily Baker sobbing before the cameras for her lost daughter.

"She is all we have in this world."

Her letters to her friend over her little sister's murder twenty-two years ago.

"I am guilty of her death. I will never forget her eyes staring into mine as she fell. God, please forgive me."

CHAPTER FIFTY-SIX

Four guards, bearing chains and somber faces, came to Isaiah Hood's cell, standing before him like his pallbearers.

The most senior guard, the one with the kind eyes, touched his shoulder and said softly, "It's time, Isaiah. We have to move you now."

Move you closer to your death.

The other men averted Hood's gaze, allowing him a final, private look at the eight-by-ten-foot space that had served as his tomb for twenty-two years of his life. All of his personal effects had been dispatched, given to other inmates—his books, his chess game. Hood swallowed hard, absorbing his cherished poster of Montana's Rocky Mountains. That was going to David Cohen for his Chicago law office. Hood was transfixed by it. His gateway to paradise.

That is where I live. That is my home.

Although it was a practiced security ritual, the guards were more solemn than usual while slipping the chain around the waist of Hood's orange prison jumpsuit, locking a link to the handcuffs that secured his wrists.

Hood closed his eyes, clasping his hands.

Tense seconds ticked down with all four corrections officers hoping Hood's sessions with his spiritual adviser and the Warden, who gently stressed the virtues of "being a man and facing his consequence with dignity," would make the process a smooth one for them.

Hood opened his eyes to his poster. A last drink of paradise.

Then he faced the senior guard. His knees weakened. He overcame it, nodding.

"Let's go, boss."

The machine was in motion.

A certified copy of Hood's death warrant had long ago been delivered to the Helena office of the state's director of the Department of Corrections. In accordance with Montana's Corrections Act, Montana's Execution Procedural Manual requires that at least twenty-four hours before execution, a condemned offender is moved from his cell to an isolated holding cell.

The Death House.

The ringing of Hood's shackles echoed as he was escorted down death row's corridors, past the cells of other condemned men, who offered farewells.

"God's speed, Isaiah."

"Meet you on the outside, my friend."

"Freedom, brother. Freedom."

Hood looked straight ahead. Unblinking. His body numb. He was taken to a seldom used area of death row. Out of range of the noise and clamor of prison activity, the place where his death sentence would be carried out in the manner prescribed by law.

Electric current hummed. Keys jingled. Steel doors clanked, rolled and thudded. Hood entered his new reality.

The Death House.

He felt the temperature drop. His heart skipped a beat. He

exhaled slowly. They had incarcerated him in the holding cell with floor-to-ceiling bars so they could easily keep a suicide watch.

The senior guard, his eyes mixed with duty and compassion, looked hard into Hood's face after they had removed his restraints.

"You take it easy now, Isaiah," he said softly.

Hood nodded.

Then the barred door closed on his cell.

It was the same size as other cells, only its walls were cream colored. Supposedly, psychologically soothing. There was a bunk, a pull-down shelf table, a pad of lined yellow prison-issue paper and envelopes for letters, and a form for last meal request. Nearby, outside the bars, there was a TV stand supporting a small color TV controlled by the prison. Near it stood a small table draped in white linen with a telephone and a Bible resting upon it. A short distance down the corridor was a private shower. As the Warden had already explained to Hood days earlier, "You can shower beforehand if you choose, Isaiah." Several feet from Hood's cell sat a guard at a desk with a computer and telephone. He gave a gentle wave. According to the procedural manual, guards would take shifts performing the preexecution duty of keeping a vigil over the condemned offender.

Upon Hood's arrival, the guard's computer keyboard began clicking as he created a new file and typed:

AO# A041469
ISAIAH HOOD
DEATH WATCH

The guard noted the time and Hood's activity.

"Sitting on bunk."

An hour later, the guard typed: "Talking with spiritual adviser."

Reverend Phillip Wellsley was from a small church near Anaconda. In his late seventies, with a hunched back, he had white hair and a pale wrinkled face. He smelled of vinegar and sat in the chair on the other side of the bars of Hood's cell, reaching in to pat his shoulder as he talked.

"Soon you will stand before the Creator debt-free, my son. To begin life anew in eternity."

Hood was motionless. His eyes glistening. His whole life was a mistake.

The first of the cars and vans of death penalty opponents began arriving in Deer Lodge. They had come at their own expense from all over the United States and Canada. College students, doctors, mothers, clergy, retired soldiers, schoolteachers, compelled to act on their beliefs. They assembled that night at a local church to make placards and begin a prayer vigil. At dawn on the day of Hood's execution, they would travel to the edge of state property where they would stand in serene protest before prison security vehicles within sight of the penitentiary and the majestic Rocky Mountains. Among prison staff in death penalty states across America, they were known as "the candle people."

Inside the prison, as Reverend Phillip Wellsley said good night to Hood, preparations for Hood's death were being made.

Outside, just beyond Hood's cell, within a few final paces, was the double-wide trailer that has been fashioned into Montana's execution chamber.

Hood knew the procedure. Every detail of it. Tomorrow night, at the stroke of midnight, the warden would come to his cell and read his death warrant; then he would be handcuffed, removed from the cell, escorted outside a few short steps to the small death chamber and the waiting gurney. Hood would be requested to hop up onto it, whereupon his body would be secured at five points by thick caramel-colored leather belts. His arms would be extended and secured onto the armrests, which were encased in white medical tape, filling the chamber with the antiseptic smell of a health clinic.

As a medical official would affix an IV to Hood's arms and a monitor cable to his heart, Hood would gaze around the intimate plain room, at the bright light above, hearing the witnesses shuffle into place at the nearby viewing area, feeling their steps vibrate on the trailer's floor. He would look at the two dedicated phone lines on the wall of the room. One to the governor's office, the other to the attorney general's office. The lines would remain open during the process in the event of a last-minute stay.

The warden would ask him for any final words, then offer him best wishes, as the prison chaplain would pray and the process would commence. Beyond the prison walls, the candle people would begin singing "Amazing Grace." The IV tubes from Hood's arm would run through a small port into the executioner's room where an anonymous medical official would begin the lethal injection as the chaplain would pray.

"Naked and alone, we enter this world. Naked and alone, we leave it."

First, a flow of Sodium Thiopentol would put Hood into a deep sleep.

"Look to the light, son."

Followed by a large measure of Pancuronium Bromide to relax his muscles. Then the lethal dose of Potassium Chloride, which stops the heart. The price of death? About $75 for a process that would take less than ten minutes. Hood would be declared dead and his death certificate would be signed. A hearse waiting at a secured area within the prison walls would take his body to a local Deer Lodge funeral home where his remains would be cremated and, in keeping with his wish, his ashes taken by his lawyer, David Cohen, to be dispersed in Glacier National Park among the Rocky Mountains.

"It is not over yet, Isaiah."

Odd, he heard David's voice comforting him. Then Hood saw him, on the other side of the bars of his cell, as he came back from his thoughts to listen to his lawyer.

"The interview with Tom Reed will help. His story will have an impact, take us closer to our goal."

Hood just stared at him. He could see David was ashen, scared to death himself. "I've got something planned for tomorrow morning, Isaiah."

So do I, Hood thought.

Hood heard the clicking of the guard's computer keyboard. "Visiting with lawyer."

"I am not guilty of her death anymore, David."

"Yes, I believe you. I am doing something in the morning."

"What is there left to do?"

Cohen did not answer because the guard apologized and said their "time was up."

Cohen patted Hood's hand. He bowed his head and left. "I'll be back to see you tomorrow."

That night, after the lights dimmed in Hood's cell, he lay on his bunk. For a time, he watched the computer screen glow on the face of his guard, then closed his eyes.

He felt her little wrists in his hands.

Smelled the sweet forest-scented breezes sweeping up to the cliff as she gasped, sobbed, pleaded for her life. She was so light in his large hands.

It was just a game.

He'd played it before with the dog, then the rabbit.

Now the butterfly girl with bright eyes.

She said she wanted to play.

She weighed nothing at all. Surely, she would float in th
air. He had to know if she could fly.

All of them thought they were better than him.

"We're not supposed to play with you."

Like they walked on air.

How could they say he murdered her? It was just a game.

The keyboard was clicking.

"Sleeping."

But Hood was not sleeping.

He was awakening his plan.

He would not die here.

DAY 5

DAY 5

CHAPTER FIFTY-SEVEN

The chief pressman of the *San Francisco Star* and his crew were hard at work in the massive basement of the *Star* building in downtown San Francisco.

They were testing ink, aligning newsprint, readying the *Star*'s twenty-five-ton Metroliner presses to roll the paper's second edition, which would consist of some 310,000 copies destined for subscribers in the city and in the Greater Bay Area.

The story by Tom Reed and Molly Wilson was a front-page wallop, lined under the paper's flag, above the fold, across six columns. A copyrighted exclusive. Even before ink stained newsprint of the first paper, it set off a chain of events that would cause the nation to question their outpouring of sympathy for Emily and Doug Baker.

Just after 1:00 A.M. Pacific Standard Time, the *San Francisco Star* released its final summary list of forthcoming front-page stories to the Associated Press wire service. At the AP's world headquarters in Manhattan, the national night editor read the short sentence summarizing the Reed-Wilson article: ''Condemned killer's lawyer claims proof missing girl's mother is child killer.'' The editor was picking up her phone to make a call when an incoming line rang. The *New York Times* Internet night editor demanded the *Star*'s story; that call was followed immediately by the *Washington Post,* then CNN and CNBC. Others were coming in. The AP editor implored the *Star*'s night desk to move the entire story on the AP wire. The *Star* was reluctant but agreed to release a 250-word summary of the article on its Internet site by 3:00 A.M. PST and a full version by 4:00 A.M. PST.

"The demand is intense," said the AP editor, mindful of the paper's right to protect exclusive enterprise work. She reasoned that AP could quickly grab a damp copy from the *Star*'s San Francisco loading docks.

The paper gave the wire its full story with the understanding that it would not release it until well beyond the deadline of the *Star*'s California newspaper competitors.

The AP then issued a wire service alert that went to virtually every subscribing newsroom in the United States and on most of the planet. Thirty-six minutes later, it moved the article. Just before 5:00 A.M. Eastern Standard Time, large news radio networks were rewriting the AP item and reading it on the air, crediting the *San Francisco Star.* The same was happening with Internet news groups and 24-hour TV news operations around the world, which aired footage of "the drama in the Rocky Mountains," the Bakers' news conference, still photographs of Isaiah Hood, Montana State Prison, the execution chamber gurney. By 5:00 A.M. in New York, the staff at network news breakfast shows were flipping through rolodexes, waking professors, lawyers, authors, victims' right advocates, experts on the topics of "mothers/fathers who kill"; "wrongful convictions"; "fragile justice system"; "anti–death penalty"; "halting executions"; "political fallout of wrong decisions"; "compensating the innocent"; "media distortion"; "reopening and prosecuting old cases.''

By the time most Americans awoke, they not only knew what the Bakers were accused of, but *if guilty,* why they likely did it; how they likely did it; what led the FBI to think they likely did it; why poor Isaiah Hood was likely innocent; why people should consider, sadly, that ten-year-old Paige Baker was likely dead; how this case illustrates "precisely what is wrong with our flawed justice system"; the "American media machine"; "the stresses on urban families"; and the "state of California." Throughout the morning, every network news producer was screaming at their staff, "Why can't we get Hood's goddamn lawyer on the goddamn air?"

By 7:00 A.M. California time, the first "flowers of remembrance" for Paige Baker were delivered anonymously to the doorstep of her family home in the Richmond District.

CHAPTER
FIFTY-EIGHT

FBI Special Agent Frank Zander took another swallow of his black coffee. He needed to concentrate on what Agent Rob Clovis was telling the task force members gathered at the command center office in the predawn.

Clovis was a gravel-voiced technical wizard from the FBI's Evidence Response Team in San Francisco, which had responded to the call-out for Glacier. He'd flown in last night with remote video camera equipment to assist Bill Horn's team in the search for Paige Baker's corpse deep in the crevasses among the cliffs of Sector 23. Clovis was completely bald and had the sober intensity of an engineering professor who realized he was talking over the heads of his students.

"It's one of the most advanced remote fiber-optic camera systems in the world," Clovis said. "It's still under development by a company in Silicon Valley. They worked nonstop adapting this system for us to probe the crevasse. That's why it took a little time to get it here. We wanted to set up last night but the snow and high winds grounded us. It's clear this morning.''

The air was a mingling of cologne, mouthwash, perfumed hotel shampoo and coffee as Clovis directed his technical team to set up what looked liked laptop computers and high-tech electrical equipment on the tables of the cramped room.

"How does it all work, Rob? Run that by me again. In English," Lloyd Turner asked.

Clovis set his coffee down.

"We've got just over two thousand feet of hybrid cable not much bigger in diameter than, say, a yo-yo string." He held his thumb and forefinger nearly touching. "We have a miniature remote video camera and high-intensity light attached to the end of the cable. The cable is connected to a control panel so we can direct the camera. The images it captures are carried by the cable to a color monitor, like a TV screen."

Turner was nodding.

"Think of it as the same principle used in microsurgery. Or what cities use to inspect sewer systems for damage to avert expensive exploratory excavation. But we're going to do something a little different."

Clovis nodded to the room's large TV monitor.

"We're going to transmit our probing of the crevasse to you live, in real time. The company boosted the signal strength for the cable and customized the satellite transmitter and receiver."

"You're going to bounce the images off a series of satellites from the crevasse to our monitor here in the command center?" Zander said.

"Correct. Following some of the principles NASA uses for sending signals for its missions. You will see what the camera sees after a two- or three-second delay. We'll transmit narration from the crevasses about depth and conditions."

Zander looked at the other members. All seemed impressed. He had one concern. "Isn't there a risk of TV people with their satellite gear intercepting the images?"

338   *Rick Mofina*

Bowman shuddered at the thought.

Clovis shook his head. "Our signal is encrypted."

The radio clipped to Clovis's waist came to life.

"Chopper's loaded and ready, Rob."

"Roger." Clovis nodded to the others and grabbed a small case of equipment. "That's our ride."

On his way out of the task force room, Clovis had to shuffle past Nora Lam, who was on her way in. Her face was grave as she studied the agents, slamming her files and clipboard on one of the tables.

"Did anybody have any warning this story by the *San Francisco Star* was coming? My phone has not stopped ringing."

"Tom Reed was here," Zander began, halted by Lam's hand as she interrupted to answer her trilling cell phone for a short, terse call.

"That was the Office of the Attorney General in Washington," Lam said. "They want to know if you intend to charge somebody soon. This appears to them to be a slam dunk. And I've got Maleena Crow demanding you release Doug Baker."

"Well, we need to wait for—" Zander was cut off again.

"And the governor's office in Helena has been calling since the story broke this morning demanding to know what the hell is going on. Isaiah Hood's execution is set for midnight tonight."

Zander sat down, steepling his fingers in front of his face.

Lam sat next to him.

"Frank, this case has suddenly become the top file in the nation and these are the facts: the clock is ticking down on an execution directly related to your investigation; nobody wants to confront the fact that Hood may be innocent; Washington is demanding a resolution fast. We've also got a governor who's frantic over Hood, over this whole thing. You have to assure people the FBI is in control of this file and not the other way around."

"I heard enough, Ms. Lam," Zander snapped. "I am aware

of the stakes here. Our priority is our investigation, not politics *and* not public opinion. It is also not my concern to clean up any wrongful convictions rendered by the state of Montana. If the governor has doubts, they are his to deal with." Zander's heart rate was increasing in time with the distant thumping of an approaching chopper. "If we laid charges now, it could all crumble to dust in our faces."

Lam's face flushed as she nodded.

"The crevasse should do it," Zander said. "We're close, very close."

The helicopter was nearing. Zander stood. It was time for him to leave with Bowman to get Emily Baker at the command post.

"One way or another, we'll be resolving this case," he said. "But we'll need a few hours."

Zander and Bowman left, just as Lam's cell phone trilled again.

CHAPTER FIFTY-NINE

Emily Baker awoke. Or maybe she didn't. She was not sure she had even slept.

The wet snow had long since vanished. Warmer breezes were caressing her tent. Dawn was breaking. Her body ached as the horror of her daughter's disappearance came sharply into focus, engulfing her.

She heard low radio transmissions of searchers getting their assignments from rangers at the command post search table. How many hours had Paige been lost in the wilderness? Emily's thoughts veered to images of her little sister's casket.

No. Please. She had to be strong for Paige. Today could be the day something good would happen. Something to awaken her from the nightmare.

Emily stepped slowly from her tent into the morning light under the watchful eyes of FBI agents and rangers. A young FBI agent from Salt Lake City approached her with a steaming tin cup of coffee.

"Did you get some sleep, Emily?"

"I'm not sure," she said, accepting the warm cup into both hands. "Is Doug coming back?"

"They haven't told us."

"Is Tracy Bowman at the command post? I don't see her."

"No. I think—uhm . . ." The agent glanced back to the others at the equipment tables. "They're searching the northern sectors today."

"Sure, like they did yesterday. And the day before." Emily followed the agent's attention to the other agents and rangers. "What's going on?" she asked and started moving toward the tables.

"I wouldn't—" the agent said.

"Excuse me." Emily ignored her.

This morning, it seemed a larger number of agents and rangers were huddled around the table. Brady Brook was busy studying a map and talking on his radio to a searcher in a far-off sector. Emily picked up how the others were stealing glimpses at her, over the brims of their coffee cups, from whispered conversations, diverted ever so subtly from laptop computers or the small color TV monitors that were flown in—*Was it yesterday?*—as the search gathered national news attention.

Their cool glances became stares of icy accusation as she stood before the table.

"Jesus Christ," somebody whispered at the realization Emily was standing before them.

"Has something happened? Did you find Paige? Did you find something? Please? Anything?"

No one answered.

Their attention had been fastened to the small TVs that had been tuned to the twenty-four-hour news networks and their reports stemming from the *San Francisco Star* story.

"What's going on? Somebody, please, tell me!"

One of the rangers had secured an Internet link through a phone and had found the *Star*'s Internet site—and the full story by Tom Reed and Molly Wilson.

"What is it?" Emily's voice was breaking; she was inching around the tables in order to see what the others were seeing, reading. "What's happened? Did you find her?"

Thunder filled the sky as a helicopter flew by their ridge, en route to Sector 23. The air was quiet again as Emily began catching the images on one of the TV screens.

"Will someone tell me, please?"

No one wanted to inform her. Another helicopter was approaching, hovering near the command post. Emily heard snatches of the TV news reports: "As preparations are made for tonight's execution of Isaiah Hood, disturbing evidence has surfaced challenging his guilt; evidence that may explain the mystery behind the disappearance of ten-year-old Paige Baker. . . ." That was all she could hear. The noise of the landing helicopter overwhelmed the TV news report, leaving Emily to stare at the images of her dead sister's face, Isaiah Hood, Paige, Doug, the execution chamber at Montana State Prison and herself at the earlier news conference, in anguish over Paige. The chopper kicked up the wind; it thumped on Emily's back as she raised a hand to cover her mouth.

What was happening?

The others stared at her. She saw the laptop computer, its large screen displaying the *Star* story on the Internet under the headline: CONDEMNED MAN CLAIMS PROOF MISSING GIRL'S MOTHER IS A KILLER.

The young ranger, realizing Emily was reading the story, reached to fold the screen closed. Emily shot out a hand to stop her and continued to read.

TOM REED and MOLLY WILSON
THE SAN FRANCISCO STAR

WEST GLACIER, Mont.—Tonight, the state of Montana will execute Isaiah Hood, who claims to be innocent of murdering the five-year-old sister of Emily Baker 22 years ago in Glacier National Park.

Hood's attorney offered what he said was proof Baker played a role in her sister's death. It comes as rangers and FBI agents search for Baker's 10-year-old daughter, Paige, who vanished with her beagle, Kobee. . . .

Emily groaned.

"I don't think you should see any more." The ranger raised her voice over the helicopter's whirling blades and tried in vain to close her computer as Emily held the screen up and read . . . the haunting words from letters she'd written as a child coming to life, leaping into her soul.

". . . I am guilty of her death. She begged me to save her. I don't know what happened. She pleaded and screamed. I had her hand, but I don't know what happened that day. I will never forget her eyes staring into mine as she fell. God, please forgive me. . . ."

Rachel's eyes. Falling.

Emily dropped her coffee cup. *Oh God.* Eyes blurring, heart pounding in time with the helicopter, a roaring in her ears.

Oh God, please.

She moved from the table.

Someone shouted her name. Inching from the table. Numbed. Her face in her hands. Dust, pebbles, swirling about her, blocking the sun, calling her name. She was falling; she was lost until someone, something . . . a firm hand on her shoulder. Her name above the fury.

"Emily."

A woman. A voice she knew.

"Emily, it's time."

Bowman. Tracy Bowman.

"It's time for you to come with us to the command center. We need to talk."

Special Agent Frank Zander was standing behind Bowman.

CHAPTER SIXTY

Isaiah Hood's execution would take place in sixteen hours.

The press was searching for his lawyer, David Cohen, but he had switched off his cell phone; even his concerned Chicago law firm could not reach him.

Newspaper, radio and wire service reporters, as well as TV network news bureaus from across the nation, were calling every hotel and motel near West Glacier, Montana, frantically trying to find him. Magazine and tabloid reporters, and three Hollywood scouts wanting to discuss buying Hood's rights, joined the hunt.

Cohen did not want to be found.

Not yet, he thought after finishing his breakfast and checking out of his tiny motel near Flathead Lake, a few miles south of Glacier National Park.

Watching the TV behind the manager, he saw another report of the case. It showed a three-year-old still photo of himself that one of the Chicago stations had fed the network. Fortunately, Cohen was traveling to Glacier wearing sunglasses and a baseball cap.

Nearing the park, he knew Hood was sitting in the death cell under a death watch as the clock ticked down. The way things stood, there were no tomorrows for him. Only hours.

Cohen passed a news satellite truck lumbering northbound. He picked up his cell phone and switched it on to retrieve messages. Listening only for the caller, then skipping through the message. "Francis Lord with the *LA Times.*" Next. "Chuck Ryker, ABC News, New York." Next. "Nancy Womack, *Great Falls Tribune.*" Next. "Mr. Cohen, this is Phil Braddock with the *Washington Post.*" Next. "Hi, David, it's Dianna Strauss at the *New York Times.*" Next. "Anna Barrow, *Newsweek.*" Next. "This is Larry Dow, *USA Today.*" Next. "David, it's Lane. Please call me. Please!" Next. "Abe Gold at the firm. We've seen the news reports. What the hell do you think you're doing? Don't you make another move without informing us. Is that understood? Call me on my personal cell phone number. . . ."

The old man himself. Pissed off. The senior partner. Cohen glanced at the stack of photocopies on the passenger seat next to him. Copies of the county attorney's old summary of Emily's confessional letters.

He switched off his phone. No, he was not calling back.

Tom Reed's news story was effective beyond his expectations, accomplishing exactly what Hood needed: attention to the questions that needed to be raised, to the injustice that was about to be committed at midnight. Cohen would embark on the next stage of his struggle, one that may cost him everything. He had to halt the execution.

He reflected on his days at Harvard, brooding along the Charles River, or hopping a train downtown to Fenway while grappling with philosophy or ethics problems. *If a good man does nothing when confronted with a moral wrong, what is lost?* It was just theory. Academic posturing. He had expected the only time he would face such a question was during a law exam.

Not in reality.

In his heart, he knew Hood should not be executed. Lane knew that, too. The principle that had guided Cohen was now a legal certainty that compelled him. If he was a moral man, he must take action. Or he could never face himself again.

A Montana Highway Patrol officer was now directing Cohen to turn away from the main gate to Glacier National Park.

"We're limiting traffic at this entrance, sir. What is your business here?"

Cohen identified himself. The officer sent him to park with the press vehicles. Precisely where he wanted to go. The press camp was in full force.

Cohen grabbed his stack of photocopies and searched for the podium that had become familiar to the nation and the world following the story of Paige Baker. She was still missing, according to the latest update from the rangers. While weaving his way to the microphones, Cohen handed out his sheets to every newsperson he saw. Word spread at the speed of sound. Network field producers, reporters, photographers, encircled Cohen, advising him to hold off starting his news conference for fifteen minutes for technical reasons, peppering him with prep questions, talking at once. Cohen did not see who was asking what.

"You Hood's lawyer?"

"Yes."

"Spell your first and last name."

"You're giving a press conference?"

"Why did you come?"

"Well, I—"

"Hold it—" Someone was shouting on his cell phone to New York. "Well, get them out of the meeting. We found him! He's right here—"

"What are you going to say, David?"

"I think that's clear by what's already come out. We're talking life and death here."

"Good, OK," a bearded man with a southern accent shouted "Everyone, we're going with the lawyer in ten."

Radios and cell phones became intense with staccato conversations as more people gathered around Cohen. A helicopter passed overhead.

Soon dozens of TV news and newspaper cameras were trained on Cohen as he stood at the microphones, licking his dried lips, realizing he had no choice. *This has to be done. There's no turning back.*

"Go ahead," someone said.

"No, wait!" Someone was on a radio phone. "OK."

Cohen nodded, hands on hips. He was wearing a faded denim shirt and khakis; his tanned face was stubbled with a day's growth; his hair, just the right amount out of place, made him look like the idealistic, anguished attorney he was. Eyes staring honestly into the cameras. The networks loved it. Cohen cleared his throat and explained who he was, answering rapid-fire questions.

"I am calling on the governor to reconsider his position on the fate of my client, Isaiah Hood, whose execution is set to go ahead at midnight tonight."

The questions started at once. Still cameras clicked.

"Why?"

"On what basis, Mr. Cohen?"

"What's your reason for . . ."

"In light of evidence that has surfaced showing the connection of Emily Baker to my client, showing the documents that never surfaced at trial or in subsequent appeals—"

"You're referring to her so-called confessional letters?"

"Yes, and given the circumstance we're seeing played out before us—"

"Sir, are you implying that Emily Baker murdered her sister?"

"No. What I am saying is look at this profoundly disturbing evidence. We have always maintained reasonable doubt permeated this case, that his conviction was based on circumstantial evidence. Now we have only hours before my client is executed. I am pleading for relief here so we can sort things . . ."

Some seventy floors above downtown Chicago, Abe Gold and other senior partners of Cohen's law firm were watching with apprehension the boardroom's large television.

"What the hell is he doing?" said one of the partners. "Did we know this was coming, Abe? Did we know any of this crap was coming?"

Gold shook his head. The intercom on the boardroom phone buzzed.

"Mr. Gold, a Mr. Jackson from the Montana attorney general's office."

"Yes," Gold said, eyes fastened to the news conference.

"Abe, what is this shit?" Jackson said from Helena. "Call in your kid now. Phone him right now! We're contemplating filing a complaint with Washington, charging him with obstruction."

Gold said nothing, weighing the situation. While he was upset that David had not advised the firm, he admired Cohen's spine, recalling his own days of youthful fire.

"Mr. Jackson, am I to understand Governor Nye will grant our client relief until these serious issues raised by Mr. Cohen are addressed?"

Jackson hung up.

Gold almost smiled.

"I think the other guy blinked," he said.

The boardroom phone rang again.

"The U.S. attorney general's office in Washington, Mr. Gold."

* * *

In Montana, Maleena Crow slammed her palms on the steering wheel of her Jetta. Traffic had halted her progress near Glacier National Park's main gate. En route to see the FBI, Crow had tuned in her VW's radio and to her surprise caught the start of David Cohen's news conference. Immediately, she was outraged.

"How dare he do this!"

The previous night, Nora Lam had advised her that Emily Baker would be Mirandized before being questioned this morning. No other attorneys were available. Lam alerted Crow to return in case something developed with Emily. Did they know this Cohen character was going to pull this stunt? she asked herself as she abandoned her car on the side of a road and stormed toward Cohen's press conference.

A patrol officer chased her. "Miss, you can't leave your car . . ."

Crow hurried to the conference, elbowing her way through the throng of reporters, until she was standing next to Cohen, startling the newspeople. No one knew the striking woman in jeans, T-shirt and pastel blazer, holding a briefcase. She had the intelligent air of an official. Cohen was answering a question.

"I think there is more than sufficient evidence and reason to reopen—"

"Excuse me," Crow said. "I think you've all been duped by some legal sleight of hand here."

"Identify yourself, please, miss!"

"I am Maleena Crow, attorney for Doug Baker. It is unethical and immoral for Mr. Cohen to direct this accusation at the Baker family at this time and in this manner."

"I disagree—"

"Just let me finish, please, sir. You've had *your* say." Tension and the cameras tightened on her pretty face. The networks were eating up the drama. "Your accusations, innuendo and implications are all hypothetical and circumstantial, and it is unconscionable for an attorney, even one of your caliber, to do this—''

"There is disturbing and overwhelming evidence."

"Mr. Cohen, it is circumstantial at best and you are not privy to all the facts concerning the search for Paige Baker."

"Nor are you, apparently, Ms. Crow."

"I think you've crossed a line. There is a missing child and your accusations do not warrant a trial, not in court and not in the press—''

A chopper was approaching, drowning out the news conference.

As was the ritual with each approaching landing helicopter, the news cameras zoomed in to see who was aboard.

This time, they were rewarded.

All the crews kept the audio rolling as Cohen and Crow argued.

As if cued, FBI agents Tracy Bowman and Frank Zander stepped from the chopper, crouching as they each took an arm, escorting Emily Baker to the command center.

The pictures told the story.

Emily Baker was a suspect in her daughter's disappearance and now her sister's murder twenty-two years ago; meanwhile, the clock ticked down on the life of a man who claimed to be innocent.

CHAPTER SIXTY-ONE

On her previous trip to the center, Emily regarded the news media as an ally. Now they had swollen into a ravenous force. She closed her eyes, gripping her knees as the chopper touched down.

Oh, Paige. Please come back to me.

Agents Zander and Bowman escorted her to the center as dozens of cameras and press questions were aimed at her; the wind from the rotating blades thumped a sobering score. Above it all, Emily swore she heard someone shouting, "Did you kill your sister and daughter?"

Inside the center, conversations stopped, and heads turned as Emily and the agents, their steps echoing on the maple floor, swept by the search operations people. Everyone knew. Bowman signaled to another female agent and they entered the washroom with Emily. She was asked to leave the stall door open; later, they scrutinized her in silence as she washed her face.

Zander entered the task force room, where the others were waiting. Mugs of fresh black coffee, thick closed file folders and clear notepads sat before them at a large table. The tension was suffocating. He paced, stopping to stare at the large TV, taking in the soft sounds of the latest on the case from CNN. He tapped the corner of the monitor, then switched it to 00, the special channel Agent Clovis had set up. The screen was still black. He switched the set off as Maleena Crow arrived.

"Have a seat." Zander's tone was neutral.

Her chair scraped the floor. No one spoke. A search helicopter flew overhead. No one spoke of the surreal twists of the case. Even having Crow present before they went at Emily was unusual.

The young lawyer reasoned that the FBI was striving to see that every aspect of their investigation, no matter how wrongheaded it was, went by the book and then some.

Emily arrived with Bowman, who helped her to the same position she had taken before.

"Would you like coffee or anything?" Bowman asked.

"Just some water, please." Emily cleared her throat.

Bowman set a small plastic cup before her. Zander folded his arms and began.

"Emily Baker, you have the right to remain silent. Anything you say can and will be used against you in a court of law. . . ."

She bowed her head and wept softly.

This is not real. What is happening? Is Paige dead? Where is Doug? Oh God.

"You have the right to consult an attorney and have them present with you while you are being questioned. If you cannot afford to hire a lawyer, one will be appointed to represent you before any questioning. Do you understand these rights as I have explained them to you?"

Emily nodded slowly. Tears streamed down her face.

"Please answer."

"Yes, I understand my rights."

"Knowing your rights, are you willing to answer our questions without an attorney present?"

Emily stared at her juice cup, blinking through her tears, looking toward the window, the mountains, rubbing her nose and nodding.

"Yes."

"Emily, no!" Crow was startled. "Emily, no! I advise you—"

Emily was puzzled.

"That's enough, Ms. Crow, please leave us," Zander said.

"Who are you?" Emily asked. "Who is she?"

Standing, Crow scowled at Zander. "I am Doug's lawyer."

"What!" Emily glared at Bowman. *This is a betrayal.* "You never . . . no one told me Doug has a lawyer. Has he been charged?"

"Emily, do you want an attorney present?" Zander thundered.

"No."

"No?" Crow was incredulous. "Emily, I advise you—"

"Get out now, Ms. Crow. You are interfering."

Emily slammed her palms on the table; her cup jumped without spilling.

"Please. I just want to find Paige. I do not need a lawyer for that. I don't care what they think or suspect. I do not care." Eyes wide, she looked into her empty hands. "All I want to know is if I will ever hold my daughter in my arms again. I'll answer any questions for that. Oh, please, I—" Emily covered her face with her hands. "Why does Doug have a . . . oh God . . . let me talk to my husband. Can I please talk to Doug?"

No one answered her.

"Emily, this is a mistake," Crow called as she was escorted from the room. Zander closed the door behind her.

Bowman passed Emily a tissue.

The only sound to be heard in the room was Emily's sobbing.

Zander let several long tension-filled moments pass before he asked his first question.

"Emily, it's been five days since Paige disappeared. The rangers know that region. They have been scouring it relentlessly, even risking injury. The Royal Canadian Mounted Police and Canadian officials are doing the same on the Canadian side of the park. Now, why do you suppose we have not found any trace of Paige or her dog? Why is that?"

"I don't know."

"Now, why is it we did not find out about your connection to your sister's death in the same region of the park, twenty-two years ago, and your connection to Isaiah Hood?"

"It was a very painful part of my life. Very painful."

"So you admit keeping that from us when we asked you to tell us everything about your history, anything that might help us understand what happened to Paige?"

"I did not even tell my husband. It was very painful. Doug will tell you. Has he told you?"

"He has told us things."

"What things? Where is he? There's something you're not telling me."

"What is the real reason you came to Montana with your family, Emily?"

"To deal with my sister's death, the deaths of my parents. My counselor told me if I was here when Isaiah Hood was executed, I could use his ending as a turning point, as a way to put it all behind me."

"Or try to get away with it again."

"What?" Emily began weeping. "I cannot understand . . . why—"

Suddenly, a radio crackled.

"This is Clovis to Zander. Over."

Zander reached for his radio, quietly acknowledging Clovis's call from the crevasse.

Clovis then reported: "All set to broadcast here. Over."

Zander moved closer to Emily.

"You and Doug have been evasive and deceptive from the beginning. But here are the facts." Zander was leaning on the table, his face inches from Emily's. "We found Paige's T-shirt. Bloodstained." Zander thumped the table with his forefinger, causing Emily to flinch. "We found Doug's ax. Bloodstained." Zander thumped the table again. Emily raised her hands to her ears. "You and Doug tell us either one of you could have been alone with Paige for hours, unseen by anyone. What you've done is given each other convenient alibis that are difficult to challenge. Then we find disturbing questions have been raised about your involvement in your sister's death in the *very same area* and in the *very same fashion* as Paige's case."

"No."

"Only a few days before you came here, the San Francisco Police Department was called to your house. A neighbor reported Doug was violent."

"No, that was a misunderstanding."

"We also learned that a student at Doug's school has accused him of a violent outburst, of striking her, in the days before you came here."

"No. I didn't know that—"

Striking a student? Doug. No.

"Twenty-four hours before Paige vanishes, your family is witnessed having a heated argument on the trail."

"That was about me. It had nothing to do with—"

"And we found some blood, tiny drops of blood, and some of Paige's hair near the mouth of a remote crevasse, just under two miles from your campsite. Soon we'll put it all together and you can tell us what went wrong and how."

"Oh God." Emily began shrieking. "She's not d-d—"

Zander switched on the room's large TV, turning to 00, nodding to Bowman, who raised her radio to her mouth. "Go ahead, Clovis."

A blurring image began swimming on the screen, filled with static.

"Can you hear us, task force? Over." Clovis's voice was tinny but clear.

"We hear you fine. Go ahead, Rob. Over."

"OK, we've just set up and we'll start lowering the camera. It's going to take time. Over."

"Can you tell us anything at this point? Over," Zander said.

"Roger. We dropped a vapor probe. Early indications are there is definitely a body mass down there. Confirmed."

Zander's eyes burned into Emily's.

Her face went white.

CHAPTER SIXTY-TWO

High atop the treacherous fissured cliffside of Sector 23, the ultrasoft hum of a lightweight gas-powered generator traveled throughout the glacial valley and alpine forests.

Members of the FBI's ERT worked quietly at the mouth of the crevasse where traces of Paige Baker's blood and hair had been discovered.

Special Agent Rob Clovis knew it was a critical procedure. The probe would determine the outcome of the investigation. He felt the weight of it on his shoulders. In twenty years of duty, he had been called out to work on some difficult FBI operations, but he had never attempted anything quite like this. He looked at his watch again. It seemed he was looking at it every five minutes, well aware Frank Zander and the other investigators were counting on ERT.

No one beyond the people atop the cliff and the task force knew about the probe. The massive search operation for Paige Baker in all other sectors was ongoing and would not be officially terminated until Clovis and the evidence team concluded their work here.

Clovis surveyed the area, again grappling between his professional expectations and private emotions. It was an ideal location to dispose of a body. A small body. The mouth opened wide to swallow it into an eternal abyss. He tried to block out the images of her slipping and scraping down into the darkness. He had two granddaughters about the same age as Paige Baker.

Imagine the condition her corpse will be in. What kind of monster would ...

Clovis shifted his thoughts, to inventory the equipment, anxious about its reliability. Much of it had been put together urgently for this emergency by the high-tech company in Mountain View. The stuff was not field-tested. There had been no time.

The generator was a new model with a microprocessor that controlled its sine-wave inverter, greatly reducing voltage fluctuations and wave distortion. It had an output of 3000 watts to power the highly sensitive remote-controlled fiber-optic probe and video transmission system that was linked to a network of satellites. The two thousand feet of flexible hybrid cable was coiled on a spool straddled over the crevasse. Controls for it and the tiny camera at the end of it were linked to a powerful computer and monitors.

Clovis watched as the technician, wearing a headset microphone to narrate, used the keyboard to command the drop rate of the camera, pivot and focus, retrieving images and displaying them on the computer screen and monitors at the worktable, which were connected in tandem. At the same time, with a two- to three-second delay factor, the images and his narration were transmitted to the large TV in the task force room at the command center.

"We're ready," the technician advised Clovis, who nodded.

This better work, Clovis told himself, hoping he could trust the untried system.

He heard a dog's yelp. It was Lola, the shepherd who found the site. Her handler, the kid from Colorado, soothed her. He sat off to the side with the rangers, SAR people and paramedics. All were somber.

Clovis knew the work from this point on would be meticulous. The process would be agonizingly slow, moving at a rate of a few inches or feet every few minutes.

The screen showed nothing but sweating black rock as the tiny camera slowly descended.

Clovis and the task force at the command center were riveted to their monitors.

Yes, this was a perfect place to dispose of a body.

Perfect.

CHAPTER SIXTY-THREE

Isaiah Hood stood in his death cell and rubbed his stomach tenderly, taking comfort in feeling the small lump of hardness near his navel.

Soon. Very soon.

"Feeling all right, Isaiah?" his deathwatch guard asked.

Hood nodded, careful to display the precise measure of discomfort on his face.

Biting his lip, studying the closed-circuit TV, the guard was wary. Determined to have no incidents of any sort on his watch, he reviewed his options. He knew Hood's medical history and risk of seizures. Most officers in the death row housing unit did. He heeded DOC policies and procedures.

"Want the nurse or Medical Services, Isaiah?"

Because the law requires we keep you healthy for your execution.

Hood shook his head.

The keyboard clicked as the guard entered the small development into the death watch activity log. Then his phone rang.

"Really?" he said. "Fine, I'll ask him." He replaced the hand
set. "Isaiah, seems your lawyer is live on CNN discussing you
case. Would you like to watch it?"

Hood nodded.

Then David Cohen was there before him, telling Americ
about his case.

". . . the governor to reconsider his position on the fate c
my client, Isaiah Hood, whose execution is set to go ahead ;
midnight tonight."

"Why?"

"On what basis, Mr. Cohen?"

"What's your reason for . . ."

"You're referring to her so-called confessional letters?"

"Sir, are you implying that Emily Baker murdered he
sister?"

Yes, that's right, David. Hood smiled to himself.

The cameras captured Emily Baker escorted by the FBI fror
a helicopter; then they once again showed Hood's picture, Paig
Baker's picture, the prison, the gurney, and an old photograp
of the dead girl from over twenty years ago.

The only girl who ever agreed to be Hood's friend.

He stared at her eyes, feeling everything around him dissolv
ing into a bright light.

The guard's jaw dropped.

Isaiah's eyes rolled back. Just the whites were visible. Hi
arms rose from his sides, extending before him.

Jesus Christ, he's going into one of the friggin' trances.

"Isaiah!"

*He feels her little wrists in his hands. Smells the sweet forest
scented breezes sweeping up to the cliff as she gasps, sobs an•
pleads for her life. She is so light in his large hands. Her littl•
feet dangle, kick.*

It is just a game. One where he can strike fear in the heart of a weaker thing. He has learned that from his father.

The hooks.

Those rounded, steel, hard hooks hammering his forearms, his shoulders, his neck, his head. One day a direct blow connected like lightning, exploding in his brain. His eyes blinded with a painful white flash.

He ran from the house and spent the next few days alone in the mountains. So painfully alone. All of his life he had no one but the mountains. His head hurt so god-awful bad he thought his skull had split and his life and thoughts were leaking out. He had a hard time concentrating. Forming a thought. The whole time he ached to be with someone. Anyone to play his game.

Just a game.

He'd played it before with the dog, then the rabbit.

But it didn't feel right.

They did not walk on air.

Then he came upon the butterfly girls with bright eyes.

The big one did not want to play. But the little one did.

She comes to him right away.

Eager.

But the big one pushes him. Snotty. Stuck up.

"We're not supposed to play with you."

Like they walk on air. Go to church every Sunday and treat people the way they do. It was their doing. All of them in town.

"We're not supposed to play with you."

Well, he was going to play with them. He'd show them.

The little one weighs nothing at all. Surely, she does not walk on air, like the rest of them. That was the game. She plays it well. How she kicks and screams. But the big one tries to stop him. She is trying to ruin it, trying to ruin everything. Like she is now. It was just a game. Just the game of a lonely boy in the mountains.

Now they want his life for it.

They could not have it.

No. He is tired of paying. He has given them twenty-two years. That is enough. Maybe Emily, the big one, should pay something for what she took from him. She knew it was a game but she never told them that. He knew why she came back.

To watch him die.

Well, that is not going to happen.

It is time for her to learn.

"Isaiah!"

Someone was calling him. Far off and far away.

It was time.

Hood's heart began throbbing, slamming against his rib cage. His brain began pulsating. Bringing this one on could kill him. That was one secret he kept from the doctors. He could bring on his seizures and almost control them depending on the magnitude. They were dangerous to control. This time, he needed to bring on the largest fit he had ever summoned. It was time. It was coming. He felt it rising from within his brain waves, popping like malfunctioning electrical circuits. His heart stalling, galloping . . .

"Isaiah!" the guard yelled.

Hood's body was quaking and flopping on the floor like a fish jerked from a lake to a dock. His head was banging against his cot, his chair, he was growling and howling, his head twitching spasmodically.

"Open the cell! Open the cell!" one of the male nurses shouted. The guard had summoned medical help. Two nurses and two guards arrived, one pushing a defibrillator. They worked on him swiftly. Checked vital signs. One nurse opened the medical bag, placing a rubberized tongue guard in Hood's mouth. "He's going into cardiac arrest!"

They prepared an injection.

"Call the warden! He better alert the director," said one of the nurses.

"His heart has stopped! I'm getting nothing!" said the nurse with the stethoscope.

"Get him out of the cell. Set the machine! Pass me the paddles! Clear!"

They worked on Hood on the floor outside his death cell.

After two attempts, Hood's heart resumed beating. One of the guards quickly cuffed Hood's hands and put restraints on his ankles.

"He's in bad shape. He's got to be airlifted to Missoula."

Everyone stared at each other, then down at Hood.

The guard on the phone passed it to the senior nurse.

"The warden needs to talk to you."

CHAPTER SIXTY-FOUR

Emily Baker's world turned black.

Voices. Yes, she heard voices.

The FBI agent was talking to her. The technicians at the mountain on their radios. Everyone distant, distorted, like people talking underwater, drowned out by the beating of her heart ringing in her ears.

". . . we're at one hundred feet now . . ."

Every iota of Emily's being was focused on the TV monitor and the tiny camera searching the crevasse for her daughter. The horror was clawing at her; the camera was dropping deeper and deeper, its intense light reflecting the slick, sweating rock walls, like the throat of some overwhelming evil entity.

". . . one hundred twenty . . ."

Did she fall here?

Was Emily's only child devoured by the very same mountains that haunted her for much of her life?

The camera was descending.

Darkness into darkness.

"Every family has secrets, Emily." Zander's attention, like that of the others in the small task force room, was on the monitor. "Tell us what you think happened."

Doug?

Where is Doug? What did they do to him? He has that cut on his hand. He has a lawyer. He was the last to be with her. Emily sobbed. Her body convulsing.

". . . one hundred ninety . . ."

This time, no one comforted Emily as she wept.

"Oh, Paige," she whispered through her tears.

Inspector Walt Sydowski glanced at her briefly. He was troubled. Zander was the lead and he was very good, but Sydowski did not like this approach. Something about the pieces just didn't fit. It was close but it wasn't there. Hood's case was forcing them to accelerate. Lives and careers were on the line. The entire file was a national, political time bomb ticking in their hands. But what they had so far didn't feel right to Sydowski. It gnawed at him; yet he couldn't put his finger on it.

"Maybe we should consider removing Emily from the room for the time being, Frank, since we don't know what's coming."

Zander's attention remained on the monitor.

". . . two hundred ten feet . . ."

Zander did not respond.

"Frank?"

"You can step out if you like, Walt." Zander didn't turn from the TV. "Emily, are you prepared to tell us what happened? It might help you."

"I don't know what happened."

". . . two hundred twenty—wait, we've got something. . . ."

Everyone in the task force room froze as the three-second delay passed. The FBI agent operating the probe narrated as a white fabric-looking object came into view. "It looks like a . . .

wait—" The camera turned and moved in, then pulled back. The object was hung up on a small, sharp edge.

Emily groaned. "It's her sock." She thrust her face into her hands.

"Should I bring this pair, Mom?" White cotton with pink frilled ankles. *"Will these work in the mountains?"* Purchased one night a few weeks ago during a mother-daughter shopping expedition to Stonestown. *Oh, my baby.*

The camera resumed its descent.

Emily trembled; someone said something.

"It would be in your interest to tell us what happened, Emily." Zander continued to work on her. "To tell us *what you think* happened?"

". . . two hundred forty . . ."

"Doug told us things."

Emily sniffed.

Tracy Bowman passed her a tissue. She didn't know what to think, couldn't believe what was happening. Was Zander a genius or a monster?

Was Emily the monster?

". . . three hundred feet . . . three hundred ten . . . hold it! Got something—"

The images floated on the TV screen. It was impossible to determine what it was. Then, yes, it was a backpack. A small backpack. The task force members knew it from the photos of the Baker family.

It was Paige Baker's backpack.

"Everybody got that? A backpack?" The camera operator's voice crackled over the radio.

Emily moaned, raising her palms slowly from the table, replacing them silently as if in unbearable pain, as if begging for an end to it.

"Please," she whispered. "Oh, please."

The camera descended.

"Emily, how do you think Doug hurt his hand?"

She did not answer Zander.

"We understand he can be a violent man sometimes."

". . . three hundred seventy . . ."

"What happened twenty-two years ago with your sister? What really happened?"

Her monster, Isaiah Hood, was laughing.

"Why did your mother change your name? It seemed like you were running from something. Show her the old report from the attorney general, Tracy."

Bowman slid an FBI file folder to Emily, opening it for her. But Emily did not need to read it. She knew about the letters she had written all those years ago.

". . . four hundred feet . . ."

Paige. Rachel. Oh, why?

". . . four hundred twenty—wait. Christ! You see that! Jesus—"

The task force room tensed. The three-second delay passed and something shining fluttered on the monitor.

A pair of eyes.

Dead. Soulless. Reflecting the light. Not quite in focus. Strange-looking.

"Dear God," Bowman said.

And a row of white teeth near the eyes. Slammed tight against the rock. But the transmission was unclear. A blizzard of static hissed. The image vanished.

"What the hell happened?" Zander said.

"Stand by. We've got satellite trouble."

Emily's breathing quaked. Her skin and scalp prickled with horror.

Please, God. Not again.

Her soul was screaming.

CHAPTER SIXTY-FIVE

In his newly restored office in the neoclassical capitol building, which dominated Helena's skyline, Montana's Governor Nye was grappling with a crisis.

His stomach tensed as he witnessed the early-morning news reports of Isaiah Hood's eleventh-hour claim for clemency.

He watched Hood's Chicago lawyer, David Cohen, tell the country live on every network that Montana was going to murder his client.

That cocksure SOB had pushed him into a corner and he didn't like it.

Every news organization in the nation wanted the governor to state his reaction and intentions.

He sat at his desk, studying the framed photograph of his wife and their daughter.

Two quick knocks on his door were followed by his attorney general and John Jackson, his chief counsel. The governor had been talking and meeting with them since 6:00 A.M. when the *Washington Post* called him on his personal cell phone. How the *Post* reporter got the number was a mystery to him. He had declined to comment until he had reviewed the latest events.

The AG and Jackson seated themselves. The governor gritted his teeth, then exhaled. "I am not backing down here."

The two men exchanged quick glances. The governor had given the wrong answer.

"Sir, there are many considerations," the attorney general began.

"Cohen went public with his claims; as I see it, that's it."

"You have to take into account the Glacier situation," the attorney general said. "At least what we know of it. Not a trace of the little girl has surfaced. Investigators have mounting evidence of criminal intent."

"My feeling at this point is that we cannot link the two cases," the governor said. "What if Doug Baker killed his daughter? Or someone else? That has nothing to do with Hood's case. Tragic for Emily Baker. But Montana convicted Hood fairly. The letters after the fact were in the possession of the county attorney, who felt no compunction to reopen the case."

"Of course he didn't. It would have been political suicide. An admission of failure, to point at the big sister and free the person whose blood the community wanted for the death of this child. It is understandable the county attorney would have downplayed or diminished the role of the letters. Would you like to follow that course, in light of what is now happening in Glacier?"

The governor sighed, sitting back in his chair, looking at his daughter's face.

"You seem to be singing a different tune from the other day," the governor observed.

"I just think this is a dreadful case and we should not push too fast in any direction that is not reversible."

"Be indecisive? Soft on crime?"

"Be responsible, respectful and responsive to facts at hand."

The governor turned to Jackson. "What is going on in Glacier, John? The last we had was the ax, the T-shirt, Dad on the polygraph.''

"I'm awaiting word from our people on the task force. Indications are some new evidence has surfaced."

"Something indicating she is alive?"

"Not sure. I expect to hear soon."

"What was the reaction from David Cohen's boss in Chicago? They going to rein him in? Not that it matters now—the damage is already done."

"No is the short answer. They're proud of him."

"I don't like this. Not one damn bit."

The intercom buzzed.

"The U.S. Attorney General's Office in Washington, Governor."

It began as a short conversation to politely but forcefully let the attorney general know how "Montana is going to do the right thing here. After we examine all the facts, separating reality from rhetoric. I am sorry—what was that? Right. No, we did not know that. We are awaiting word from Glacier. An update? Yes. They are certain it's her? I see—"

As the call ended, John Jackson's cell phone rang. It was word from Glacier that they were 99 percent certain they had found the corpse of Paige Baker at the bottom of a crevasse nearly two miles from her parents' campsite.

The governor was nodding, his finger caressing the frame of his daughter's picture. He ran his hand over his face, stood, walked to his window, looked out to the mountains.

"They suspect the parents," the governor said. "The case is virtually sealed against them."

He had asked the attorney general if he could still invoke executive clemency for Hood after first refusing it.

"Yes, the statutes allow for it when new evidence surfaces," the attorney general had answered. "You can intervene and grant thirty days of relief for Hood's case to be investigated in light of events. If he has a case, he can make a new appeal to the Board, or he can go right to court with it.''

The governor nodded at his advisers.

''I'll do it. I'll call the director of DOC. I suppose I have to sign something, then fax it to Deer Lodge. Better alert Pardons and Parole, too.''

''I can arrange all that, Governor,'' Jackson said.

''Thanks. And call Cohen. He's probably going to be on with Larry King tonight. We better schedule a news conference, say in three or four hours here. Let the pack at Glacier get here.''

The attorney general checked his watch.

''Wait, Governor. You've got well over fourteen hours yet.''

''Yes?''

''Why not wait a few more hours? See what happens. We can keep everything in this room for the time being. See if someone plays a card. If charges are formally laid and the FBI announces it, then you're not seen as too eager but reacting accordingly. A few hours one way or the other are not going to matter much?''

Governor Nye considered the suggestion and agreed.

''We'll give it a few hours.''

CHAPTER SIXTY-SIX

"Yes, it's one of his seizures. A massive one. His vital signs are deteriorating." The anxious senior nurse was talking to the warden from the death watch guard's phone as he stared at Isaiah Hood.

"Can he be treated on-site?" the warden asked.

"Not a chance."

"Give me odds."

"Ninety-five percent likelihood he'll be dead within two hours if he's not airlifted now to Montana General Mercy."

"Is he secured?"

"Yes, but he's convulsing again. I have to go."

The warden immediately called the DOC director. Hood was high profile and it was imperative he alert the director so they could weigh the ramifications of transporting him.

"I'm sorry, sir. The director's in a meeting."

"Interrupt it now—"

"But—"

"Now!"

The director came on the line, annoyed until he caught the urgency of the situation.

"Are you going to give this one to the governor?" the warden said, aware of the director's legendary contempt for the man. The dislike was mutual, stemming from embarrassing grillings the director endured during corrections review committees chaired by the future governor.

"The governor does not run the prison. I do."

The director analyzed the situation. Hood's case, its entanglement with the Baker drama, was tainting the governor's administration and his aspirations for national office. If Hood died now, the crisis facing the governor would vanish. Or worsen if Hood was proven innocent or was wrongly convicted. The director considered the ramifications. He was bound to follow the laws of the state. That is what he would do.

"We can't execute Hood unless he's healthy. That's our law. I urge you to give him immediate medical attention, as is the policy under the Corrections Act," he told the warden.

The chain-of-command decision took just under two minutes.

An air ambulance in Missoula was dispatched. ETA was twenty minutes.

Under the warden's order, security escort procedures would be followed to the letter. Two uniformed officers would accompany Hood, who would be restrained. They would have radios and a cell phone. One would have a prison-issued firearm. The county sheriff's office was advised and confirmed two deputies would be standing by to assist at General Mercy in Missoula.

"I want a news media blackout, understand?" the warden told the security supervisor.

Johnson-Bell Field was situated on an expanse of flat terrain at the edge of Hellgate Canyon at Missoula's northwest edge. The air ambulance service for Montana General Mercy was known as Mercy Force. All flights were dispatched from its hangar where a crew stood by twenty-four hours a day, seven days a week. They could be airborne in eight minutes.

Park rangers had an air ambulance chopper out of Kalispell on-site for transport. The Mercy Force was on standby as backup. Shane Ballard, the pilot of Mercy Force, had just come on duty. The tanned, thirty-one-year-old, former U.S. Air Force pilot knew the terrain. He had flown Mercy's twin-engined chopper to scores of scene calls for hiking accidents within the park.

Like most Americans, Ballard was consumed by the live televised news reports on the case of Paige Baker and now Isaiah Hood, trying to decide what to make of it all.

"What do you think happened out there, Mya?" Ballard called to the on-duty paramedic, Mya Wordell, who was pouring coffee for the crew in the lounge. She was engaged to be married in two weeks to an emergency surgeon at Mercy.

"I just think it's so tragic." She passed coffee to Ballard. He was going to be one of the ushers at her wedding. Earlier, he showed her pictures of himself being fitted for his tux.

Wordell then passed a cup to Jane McCarry, the emergency nurse, who was her best friend in college and now her maid of honor.

"It's just a horrible thing to watch." McCarry sipped from her cup as Mercy's hot line rang. Ballard grabbed it, jotting notes.

"On our way!" Ballard slipped the note into a zippered pocket of his blue flight suit, then clapped his hands. "Let's go, ladies. Traumatic incident at Deer Lodge."

Isaiah Hood's medical records were pulled from Montana State Prison files by the nursing supervisor and clipped to the stretcher as they wheeled Hood through the penitentiary.

En route to the front gate, they were met by several officers and the grim-faced security chief, who was wearing a suit. He had canceled a departmental meeting and was gripping his own clipboard of checklists, hastily authorized offender-transfer sheets. He was relieved to visually confirm that Hood was restrained by straps, cuffs and shackles. *No SNAFU's on my watch. No sir.*

"I want him scanned on his way out," the security boss said as they rolled Hood along the exterior walkway from death row toward the main gate. Hood's head bobbed. An oxygen mask covered his mouth and nose. He appeared unconscious. Inside the main gate, they wheeled him near the prison's high-tech security equipment.

A state-of-the-art X-ray system, able to detect metal or drugs hidden anywhere, was connected to a camera wand with a high-definition screen. An officer slowly passed it over Hood's body as half a dozen pairs of eyes watched the monitor. Anything contraband would stand out on the screen and trigger a warning bell, which began pinging and displaying a metal object in Hood's lower abdomen, in the vicinity of his navel. The sound mixed with the beating of the approaching air ambulance. The security boss frowned.

"What the hell is that?" He pointed to the object on the screen.

"Bullet fragment," the nursing supervisor said. "Hood was shot as a teen. Hunting accident." The medical official was flipping pages of Hood's records. "Here, see? It's in his file."

The security chief studied the record, then the screen, slipping on his glasses. "It looks fairly large."

"Read his file."

Sure enough, a bullet fragment was duly noted, twenty-two years ago when Hood was first processed. He took drugs for it to prevent blood poisoning. Doctors recommended against it being removed. The discomfort was minimal but the surgery was risky.

The helicopter was nearing.

"Fine," the security boss said. "Let's move him. We've got an LZ in the parking lot."

Ballard brought the blue-and-white Mercy Force helicopter to a soft landing, keeping the rotors idling as Wordell and McCarry lowered the aircraft's rear clamshell doors. Prison staff helped load their patient into the compact interior, which was crammed with advanced life-support equipment.

Ballard flinched when he saw the two corrections officers squeezing in. *No way! The weight will kill us. It's too risky.* All Ballard could do over the noise was wave them away.

The security chief hurried inside to argue with Ballard in the cockpit, his face a scowl of authority.

"No damn way can they come," Ballard shouted. "We can only carry the patient. It is a weight issue and not one for debate."

"This is a security issue."

"Is he restrained?"

"Yes."

"We've taken prisoners before. You have police at the other end?"

"Yes."

"Then we're wasting time. You want him to die right here?"

The security chief thought it over. It was in contravention of policy.

"I'll send one officer."

Ballard considered it. "Just one, unarmed. Your lightest guy. Make it quick, I'm burning up fuel here."

"How long is the flight?"

"Twenty minutes."

McCarry was talking to Ballard on the intercom.

"Shane, we're losing him and we've got to remove one of his arms to fix an IV."

Ballard nodded, informed the supervisor of the urgency of leaving now and freeing one of Hood's wrists.

The supervisor summoned a young uniformed officer in his early twenties with a slight build. No more than 150 pounds.

"Sign here," the supervisor shouted in the officer's ear. "You're the escort. You will not be armed. Just take the radio and the cuff key. County deputies will pick him up at the hospital. We'll send the van after you."

The young officer nodded, watching his chief personally free one of Hood's wrists, then secure the other to the stretcher. The supervisor double-checked to ensure Hood's ankles were shackled together, then patted his officer's shoulder and exited.

The helicopter ascended over the prison.

As it banked, Hood's head turned; his eyes flickered open, glimpsing the prison shrinking below while they soared alongside his beloved mountains.

Hood rubbed the hardened lump near his navel.

He would never return.

CHAPTER
SIXTY-SEVEN

Two lifeless eyes stared from the TV monitor.

Zander had replayed the video recording of the crevasse probe to the task force members.

The blurry eyes frozen on the tape locked onto Emily Baker. She stared back, motionless, feeling nothing but the awful crushing weight of pain.

Her heart had been pierced.

Paige.

At the bottom of that dark, cold crevasse. Alone. Dead.

Rachel. Her falling eyes.

Oh, Paige. Falling. *Did she think of me? Did she cry out to me? When was the last time I held her, told her I loved her?*

God, why? Why are you punishing me?

Zander took a seat across the table from Emily, his blue eyes searching hers for answers.

"Are you ready to tell us what happened to Paige?"

How can you ask me that now?

She looked into his face.

How can you?

"Emily, make it easier on yourself. Unburden your conscience. It is clear you and Doug are involved. Maybe things got out of hand. Maybe it was not meant to end this way but it is clear something went wrong."

Words would not come to her.

Her life had ended at the bottom of the crevasse.

Inspector Walt Sydowski was astounded.

As much as he struggled with the case, deep in his gut he could not get the pieces to come together. Zander was masterful. It appeared to be over. Sydowski regarded Emily, then the eyes on the screen. He thought about a little girl from San Francisco who had set off only days ago to see the Rocky Mountains with her mom and dad. Going home in a body bag. Sydowski blinked, gazing through the window, through the trees to the peaks.

Bowman thought of her son, Mark.

Zander reflected on two little graves in Georgia, knowing he could never make up for the one he lost.

Pike Thornton shook his head slowly, knowing he was right to trust his gut on Doug Baker's hand wound. But why, he wondered, hadn't they found any trace of her little dog, Kobee?

Emily's mouth started to move and a mournful sound followed.

"What's that, Emily?" Zander said.

"I did not harm my daughter."

The temperature of Zander's gaze dropped. His eyes narrowed.

"Was it Doug?"

"No. No, he would never harm her."

"He has a temper."

"No. He yells because of coaching."

"The San Francisco Police were summoned to your house because of his temper."

"I told you, that was a misunderstanding. We were arguing. People argue."

"A student complained of an assault before you came here. Doug was on edge."

Emily shook her head, her face contorting with anguish.

"People witnessed you and Doug in a full-blown argument the day before Paige vanished."

"Oh God, please, my baby's dead! Why are you doing this?"

"I want you to tell me what happened?"

"I don't know. She must have fallen. It—it's—I'"

" 'She must have fallen?' Do you know that is the most common thing a parent says in child abuse cases? 'They must have fallen.' "

Zander slammed his hands on the table. Emily flinched.

"What happened!"

"It's not what you think, please."

"You tell me what to think, Emily. Your sister died here and you were there."

"No, please."

"The only other person there at the time says you're responsible."

"He's lying!"

"He's going to be executed for something he says he didn't do!"

"Please, I did not harm my sister. I was trying to save her. He passed her to me. She was slipping. . . . He knew what he was doing. . . . I see her eyes . . ."

"You wrote letters admitting your guilt! Your daughter disappears while you and your husband, Doug, the man with the violent temper, are out of sight with her."

"Please, no."

"He has a wound on his left hand. He's right-handed. The wound is consistent with someone swinging an object that slipped. We find the bloodied ax; we find your daughter's bloodstained T-shirt."

"God, nooooo," Emily sobbed.

"At the crevasse, we find traces of her blood and hair."

"Stop."

"Deep inside we find her sock!"

"No."

"Her backpack!"

"Pleeasse."

"Her corpse!"

"Paige . . . I'm sorry . . ."

"You saw it with your own eyes, Emily!"

"No, I can't. Please, please—"

"Now, Emily, you tell me what to think!"

Emily dropped her head onto her arms and sobbed. Bowman resisted patting her shoulders and looked away. The entire room was silent except for Emily's weeping. Zander turned to the windows, running a hand over his face, gazing off toward the mountains. He had won. He was indifferent to Emily's weeping. He had her in a vise. He would keep tightening it, forcing the truth out of her.

The radio from atop the crevasse came to life, a welcome intrusion.

"Clovis to Zander, come in. Over—"

Zander picked up his radio. "Go ahead."

"We're up again. Is your monitor on?"

"No, we're reviewing the previous search."

"Better turn it on."

The camera was now moving, resuming its transmission of more images from the grisly discovery of the eyes. Thornton was the first to utter a sound, half gasping, clicking his tongue.

The camera probed the eyes, the area near them, sharply

bringing the context into focus; something white, her face was
way too white, wrong, in fact, furry-looking; the eyes too wide
apart and the teeth too pointed with blackened lips; not human
at all, elongated jaw with a . . .

"Mountain goat," the probe's operator said. "And we're at
the bottom. Absolutely nothing else here. It's a mystery."

Emily lifted her head, dizzy with emotion, struggling to
comprehend.

"It's not Paige?"

Zander was stunned.

"No, it's not," Sydowski said, feeling as if someone had
just collapsed a house of cards.

CHAPTER SIXTY-EIGHT

Sergeant Greg Garner of the RCMP poured clear, cool water from his canteen into a tin bowl he'd set on the ground for his partner, whose lapping appreciation made him smile.

"We're really pushing you today, buddy." Garner knelt down, kneading the shoulders of Sultan, his purebred German shepherd.

"They want to call us in. Want to relieve us. But let's give it another couple hours. Then we'll go home, pack up everybody, head off on vacation."

Sultan yelped. He was a very affectionate, hardworking two-year-old who lived with the Garner family on their ranch in the foothills west of Red Deer, Alberta. Garner's wife and their children adored him.

"Sound good. You miss the kids?"

Sultan panted.

"Me too."

Garner took in the panoramic view of the Rocky Mountains

from just a few hundred yards north of the Canadian border in Waterton Lakes National Park. It met Glacier National Park, forming the International Peace Park system. He was reluctant to leave this case unfinished, but the order had come in from K-Division. Garner and Sultan would be relieved by a fresh K-9 team from Calgary subdivision.

Waves of sadness rolled over the thirty-five-year-old Mountie as he sat on a rock, surveying the glacier-carved valleys, the alpine forests and lakes.

Garner always got this way whenever he was pulled from a search before it was concluded. He and Sultan had been working this one since they got the call to assist four days ago. They had gridded the entire border area, where Grizzly Tooth Trail wound into Canada, so many times he'd lost count. Goat ledges, cliffs, dense forests, rivers, valleys, off-trail, searching some of the most dangerous, rugged, remote terrain on the continent. The fact no one had found anything, not even a sign of her beagle, Kobee, frustrated him.

Garner felt he had earned the right to at least know what had happened to that little girl, especially now that the story was taking some nasty turns. The FBI suspected the parents; his orders were to keep searching. Now what were they supposed to be searching for? A corpse? Had the massive search for a lost child suddenly become a homicide? Was he standing amid an enormous crime scene? Garner did not want to walk away from this without seeing it through to the end.

"You awake, Greg?" his radio said to him.

It was Corporal Denise Mayo of the RCMP. He heard a bark in the background from her Malinois, Prince. A real show-off pup.

"No, I am dreaming this conversation."

"They're going to chopper us to you now. Stay put. We're just getting the tank topped off. Shouldn't be long."

Garner wanted to try something before he left. He studied his laminated map and his notes. He was a veteran of some three hundred searches. Canadian high courts had recognized him as an expert witness when he gave testimony in major criminal prosecutions. His record was exemplary.

But that meant nothing to tourists, he laughed to himself.

Before he had been flown into his search zone, he had encountered the RCMP mystique while sitting with Sultan, resting at his feet, at an outdoor cafe in Waterton. Garner was dressed in jeans, T-shirt and sunglasses, knapsack and sidearm at his side.

"My, are you a police officer?" asked a woman in her seventies after stepping from a bus with Arizona plates.

"Yes, ma'am. I'm an RCMP officer."

"A Mountie?" She smiled. "You're not dressed like one."

Garner chuckled and showed her his badge with the bison head.

"We don't wear the red serge and Stetson everywhere."

" 'But you always get your man,' that's your motto, right?"

"I'm afraid not, ma'am. Actually, it's 'Maintain the Right.' "

He agreed to let her take his picture, happy to set the record straight, but not telling her that for him pride and tradition meant you never, ever gave up on a case. That was not only his motto, it was an emotion that burned inside, flaring as he studied his map, ready to make his last sweep the best one.

The Baker family campsite was a few miles south. It was remote but conceivable that the girl, if she was mobile, could have traveled into the Canadian side. Expect the unexpected. Everything is a factor: weather, state of mind, potential injury, confrontation with animals.

Garner reasoned that if she was moving, he would go back

to the sector he had not searched for the longest time, in case she had since moved into it. If she was still alive, that is.

"Let's go, pal. We're not pulling out of here yet."

Garner and Sultan paralleled Boundary Creek in the shadow of Campbell Mountain. Garner was happy Waterton officials had closed off the sectors he was searching. It was a little lonely but more effective. Since it was bear country, Garner commenced making noise, singing Del Shannon's "Runaway." It was a favorite of his while growing up as a farm kid near Lethbridge. He tried not to think of the tragic cases he had worked on, not now on the eve of his three-week vacation. He was renting a camper and driving across Canada to Niagara Falls. He was grateful he and his wife had time to take the kids to the Calgary Stampede this year.

Sultan led him toward a rugged boggy area.

With the snow moistening the ground, it might yield something. There was shelter under some ledges. Nothing but nothing.

Sultan froze.

"What is it?"

Sultan barked, hackles rising.

One of the ledges actually hid an opening, the mouth of a cave. Garner sang louder as they inched forward. It was large enough to be a bear den or wolf lair. It stank the way grizzlies stink.

"Hello in there?"

No response.

He unsnapped the strap for his holstered Smith & Wesson. Sultan's growling echoed into the cave as they neared its opening. Garner scanned their immediate area to ensure an escape route. He gently rolled a grapefruit-size rock into the hole, hearing it knocking around inside. He rolled in another, while singing. Nothing.

"You want to check it out, buddy?"

Sultan panted and barked, dutifully bounding into the darkness, his panting and whimpering echoing. Within seconds, he emerged with something in his mouth.

Garner's heart raced.

"What the heck is that?"

It was a plastic container for bottled water.

Sultan held it carefully in his jaws by the threaded lip, allowing Garner to take it. The cap was missing.

Garner moved quickly, putting it in a clear plastic evidence bag, making a quick note of the time and location, putting it in his knapsack, then producing his flashlight, crawling into the cave. His eyes adjusted to the light as his beam swept the cave several times and he called. Other than the horrible smell, nothing there.

Garner moved from the area to a spot less vulnerable and studied the bottle. The label said it was bottled in Northern California. There was some sort of small merchant's sticker, kind of damaged. It took Garner a moment to determine he was reading SAN FRANCISCO INTERNATIONAL AIRPORT.

"Geez." He rushed back to Sultan, whose snout was to the ground. They scoured the softer, muddied sections, until Sultan barked.

"Bingo!" Garner dropped to his knees at the beautiful sight.

A sneaker print, fresh. Very fresh.

"Steady. Good work."

He estimated it was a child's size. He found another footprint, a partial, then another. He checked his location with his compass, his map and landmarks. From the direction the person was traveling into the United States, the border was less than one hundred yards away.

Garner reached for his radio.

What concerned him was the condition of the plastic bottle. A jagged gash ran across its middle, as if it had been savagely mauled. Garner knew Sultan did not do that. He'd call in; then they'd try tracking.

"Go ahead, Greg, what have you got?"

"Alert everybody. She's been here. Recently."

"Give us your location."

CHAPTER SIXTY-NINE

Paige's hunger was unbearable. Her empty stomach constantly contracted, cramped, ached for food. Waves of dizziness passed over her.

Can't go on much longer.

She had eaten her granola bars long ago.

How many days has it been?

Don't know. Just lie down and die.

Her throbbing, swollen feet, pillows of pain. Cuts, blisters, scrapes, raw and stinging. She longed to bathe. Her filthy hair itching; her skin chafing; her parched throat burning.

Could she drink her tears?

She still had her water bottle, which had been punctured during her near-death encounter with the bear at the crevasse.

Oh God.

Paige quaked at the memory.

Kobee had saved her. *Brave little puppy.*

The bear had swatted her as if she were a stuffed toy, sending her tumbling to the mouth of the crevasse. As she struggled to keep from plunging into the fissure's narrow black opening, a claw tore into her backpack, entangling the bear long enough for her to slip from the straps while Kobee snapped at the bear.

It happened so fast.

The angry monster, snarling and growling at Kobee, contended with the backpack affixed to its paw, allowing Paige to clamber down a cliff ledge too narrow for the bear to follow, hiding there out of reach, praying Kobee could flee to safety.

Paige clung to the cold rock in the night until she believed the bear had left the area.

After more than two hours, she climbed out.

In the darkness, she found a small rock enclosure and squeezed into it. She tried not to cry out, not to scream, not to think of Kobee, but only to stop shivering long enough to sleep on the cold, hard limestone. She concentrated on dreaming of her mother, her father, her warm, soft bed, her San Francisco home, her friends.

Dawn came with sunshine and Kobee nuzzling next to her.

"You're safe! I love you, puppy. My hero," Paige whispered, pulling his smelly little body tight to hers, luxuriating in its warmth, fighting off thoughts of bananas, oranges, restaurants, a trip to the supermarket.

She wept with her face pressed into her beagle.

Got to keep moving. Get out to the open. Find water, food, help. Something.

Carefully, Paige eased out of her tight shelter, gripping her water bottle at the proper angle to ensure the few remaining ounces did not leak out of holes made by the bear.

She went to the crevasse that had almost claimed her.

My death spot.

Her backpack was lost.

She wrapped Kobee's leash around her hand, the way she did when they went to Golden Gate Park, then found a branch for a walking stick.

No sign of the bear. Thank you, God.

They headed for the low country.

In a few hours, they came to a small river. Maybe she could find berries or something. Paige set her bottle aside, knelt at the bank, washed her face and hands, feeling a little energized by the ice-cold mountain-fed water. She cupped her hands, letting Kobee drink from them. Then she drank a little herself, feeling the cold liquid fill her stomach. She gasped with pleasure, wiping the back of her wet hands across her lips.

Maybe she could find a shelter here.

She scouted around when she heard splashing.

A fish was caught in a small, shallow pool. Kobee barked. Paige went to it, not knowing what kind it was, but her stomach quivered.

Food.

It was about as long as a large submarine sandwich.

Its tail swished water as if objecting to being stared at.

Unconsciously, Paige began licking her lips.

Her stomach was roaring.

What do I do?

Stab it with a stick, like those island fisherman did on the education channel. Paige swallowed and looked around. She found a pointy, hand-size stick. She stood over the vulnerable creature.

Kobee yelped impatiently.

"It's not going to be like the fillets and fries at Skipper of the Sea."

Paige stood there, staring at the fish.

She could not cook it. She did not know how to clean it. What was she going to do?

Paige licked her lips.

She had eaten sushi with teriyaki sauce, rice and cold shrimp. Mom and Dad liked it. She aimed the stick; saw the fish, its little mouth opening and closing, its fins waving in the pool, awaiting death.

Kobee suddenly lunged at it, gripping it in his jaws as it

writhed and slipped free. Flopping on a stone, it wriggled back into the river, escaping.

Paige stood there, still gripping her spear, feeling more hungry than she ever felt in her life.

She sat by the river and wept.

Through the blur of her tears, she saw the grizzly approaching. She was mesmerized by its majestic blond-chocolate fur, its powerful menacing hump, its upturned snout that released a snarl.

This time, she was too tired to fight.

She sat there frozen, sobbing; her arms hurt as Kobee tugged at the leash to flee.

"Oh God, somebody save me, please."

CHAPTER SEVENTY

Pilot Shane Ballard knew how the air could get rough whenever Mercy Force flew near the Bitterroot Mountains.

Today was no exception.

The twin-engine air ambulance began shuddering.

Deer Lodge vanished in a shaky blur behind them; soon the ride was smoother.

"That's better," Ballard's tinlike, pressurized voice sighed as an alert came from Missoula Tower, requesting their ETA.

"Eighteen minutes," Ballard said. *Funny, procedure is for me to call in. I already did that upon liftoff. Why are they calling me?*

"Stand by for a patch-through from Montana General Mercy."

Now they really had Ballard curious. He searched for an answer atop the mountains, painted with gorgeous, big blue sky between the peaks. Breathtaking but no answer.

"Montana General to Mercy Force?"

"Mercy Force copy."

"You are on alert for a possible trauma transfer from Glacier Can you copy coordinates?"

"Mercy Force copy."

Ballard took down the location. It was a northernmost region of Grizzly Tooth Trail, which could mean something was up in the Baker case. Ballard had to ask.

"They find her?"

"May have, that's why we're alerted."

"What about the on-site unit?"

"Called to a horseback riding accident."

"Mercy Force copy and out."

Ballard switched on the intercom, informing McCarry, Wordell and the officer. "They think maybe Paige Baker's alive at the northern edge. They just gave me the coordinates. We've been activated to stand by to bring her in."

Hood's eye's flickered.

He could hear Ballard's loud, enthusiastic report leaking through McCarry's helmet headset as she removed his oxygen mask to adjust it.

"Oh my word!" McCarry did not believe her eyes. "You'll never guess who our customer is."

Ballard tried to look over his shoulder. No use, he could not see.

"It's Isaiah Hood." Wordell was looking over her friend's shoulder.

"No way!" Ballard was incredulous.

McCarry glanced at the young guard, who nodded. Suddenly, she wished the second larger guard was also aboard. She swallowed, replacing Hood's oxygen, ensuring his flow was satisfactory and his signs were stable, blinking with a modicum of relief at the shiny metal cuff linking his wrist to the stretcher. The young guard had never seen the Rockies from a chopper before. Fascinated, he gazed out the window as McCarry checked Hood.

"Well, he's stable and he's out cold."

McCarry was wrong.

Hood slowly worked his free hand under the sheet and
serted his pinkie finger forcefully into his navel, drilling and
visting it toward the hardened lump.

Some years ago, during one of the appeals of his conviction,
ood was jailed in the cells at the Goliath County Courthouse.
ecurity was laughable there. As usual, Hood's senses were
eightened for opportunity.

On that day, as it turned out, one of the guards was retiring.
ear the end of the guard's shift, in the moments before Hood
as to be returned to his death row cell at Deer Lodge, the
d-timer's utility belt gave way, falling just outside Hood's
olding cell. Everything spilled from it.

"Don't you move, son!" the old fart wheezed, quickly col-
cting everything. Making it worse, the guard's glasses slipped
om his head, too.

"Damn fine way to retire," the guard bitched.

"You missed this, sir."

Hood showed his brown-toothed smile, handing the guard
s notebook.

"Well, thank you now."

The old coot never figured that a more important item also
ll into Hood's cell.

His handcuff key.

It felt like a ticket to heaven, for it matched the key issued
y the Montana Department of Corrections to its officers. Since
was in the days before high-tech scanners, Hood swallowed
, retrieving it later in his cell, washing it thoroughly. He
oncealed it within a small chip in the steel hinge mechanism
the door to his cell for several years.

Two nights before he was to be moved to the death cell,
ood fetched the key. After lights out, he endured the painful
rocess of working it through his navel into the bullet track of
s old wound until it brushed up against the bullet fragment.
o its loop, he had affixed reinforced thread taken from a pair

of dark socks, letting it mingle with his body hair surrounding his navel.

Now, as Mercy Force thundered toward Missoula, Hood worked swiftly, looping the thread around his thumb, easing the key out with his pinkie, feeling the flow of warm blood and pus come with it. Success was painful. He gritted his teeth, feeling as if he had just extracted a truck from his stomach.

The young officer was staring out the window, which pleased Hood, who eyed his cuffed wrist and visualized his motions. Then in an instant when McCarry turned away, he unlocked the cuff. She did not hear the gentle click over the aircraft noise. He left the cuff open, but with his hand in place, and began to convulse. In one herculean effort, he rolled the stretcher to its side onto the floor.

"Oh my God!" McCarry's first thought was that Hood was having a seizure. She and the young guard watched in horror as he stood, holding the cuff, the stretcher strapped to his back, knocking over equipment as he began ripping open the straps with his free hands.

"Shane! Take us down!"

Ballard's eyes widened; the chopper shifted.

"Jesus, hang on!" He began descending. Nothing but mountains beneath them. He heard the thud of Hood swinging a small fire extinguisher against the side of the young guard's head, sending him to the back, unconscious.

Wordell screamed.

"Shane, get us down, get us down!"

Hood shoved McCarry violently to the back, forcing her to fall over equipment. His hand ripped open every strap and unshackled the cuffs from his ankles. He came at Wordell.

"Please, no! Oh, please!"

Ballard anticipated his move and banked the helicopter. Hood lost his footing and smashed his head against the steel frame.

is hands shot up to steady himself, reaching for the rapid-
en latch of the rear clamshell doors.

"Jesus, no!" Wordell screamed. "Shane!"

Sweat was burning into Ballard's eyes, blurring his vision.
e kept rocking the Mercy Force chopper to keep Hood off
alance. It was futile. Hood locked onto Wordell's throat with
s large hand and dragged her to the rear, gurgling, choking,
vatting in vain at his arms.

Hood snapped one of the cuffs on her wrist, then locked its
ate into a steel ceiling loop. With relative ease, he then lifted
e young guard, stretching his wrist, opening Wordell's free
uff, slamming it through the steel loop, slamming it tight
ound the guard's wrist.

Ballard, rocking the helicopter, was losing. Hood was too
st and too strong, lifting McCarry's right ankle, snapped a
uackle around it, then locked its mate to the same loop holding
Vordell and the guard. Then he was in the cockpit with a pair
f medical scissors pressed into Ballard's throat.

"I am going to die!" Hood shouted. "I'll take you with me
you don't do as I say. Understand?"

Ballard nodded. "Did you kill my friends?"

"I will. Depends on you, asshole!"

The young pilot struggled to keep calm, leveling the aircraft
s a show of good faith.

"What do you want?"

"Fly directly to the girl. I know you have the location in
lacier!"

"Why?"

Hood pushed the scissors a quarter inch into Ballard's neck,
uncturing his skin and surface veins; blood began cascading.

"Tell me what you're going to do, or I go back there and
tch you an eyeball. Asshole."

"OK, but I have to radio ahead."

Hood immediately moved for Wordell, triggering her
creaming.

"Shane! Oh God, Shane!"

Eyes ablaze with rage that had twenty-two years to fester locked onto her pierced ears and the small golden loops. He yanked on one, stretching the lobe. Wordell screamed. He let go, leaving the ear intact.

"OK!" Ballard shouted. "Don't hurt them. We're on our way!"

Ballard checked his position and banked, making a dead reckoning for the U.S.-Canadian border. Why not go there with this monster? It had to be crawling with FBI, park rangers and locals.

Hood was rifling through the chopper, filling a bag with supplies, happy to find a small backpack and extra flight suit. He changed out of his orange Montana State Prison overalls into the suit. He would need boots. He eyed the guard's feet. Looked too small. He liked Ballard's. They looked to be about the same size.

"Hey!" Ballard shouted at Hood. "I'm being called. Put on the radio headset and listen!"

"Missoula Tower to Mercy Force. Mercy Force, come in. You are way off course."

"Well, Mr. Isaiah Hood, what do I tell them? Do I tell them, Mr. Hood, that you're hijacking us to Glacier?"

Realizing Ballard had just transmitted that exact message, Hood reached over and ripped Ballard's helmet and radio set from his head, tossing it to the back as Mercy Force screamed at top speed over Glacier National Park, roaring over Lake McDonald, coming up on Flattop, making straight for Grizzly Tooth and the Boundary Creek area. Pilots of aircraft involved in search operations were dumbstruck, scrambling to avert Mercy Force, figuring the air ambulance was on a top-priority medi-vac mission. It was a clear, fast trip to the upper reaches of the park. Looking down at the rolling forests, the valleys, glaciers, Hood could feel his life returning and the helicopter descending.

"Take me down away from anybody," Hood ordered.

Ballard found a flat, grassy slope, offering a clearing within its lodgepole pine, and began his landing approach. Concentrating on putting down, he had about two seconds to wonder why Hood was tossing his little pack out the window. Less than fifteen feet from earth, Hood seized the controls.

"Hey, Christ" was all Ballard managed as Hood forced the chopper to crash down hard on its side, its rotors whipping wildly, clipping treetops, slicing earth, sparking against rock patches. The aircraft bucked like an angry mechanical animal amid the crash and squeal of metal, the screams, the pungent odor of hydraulic fluid and fuel as everyone was slammed and smashed.

Ballard and McCarry were unconscious. Wordell's moan would turn into screams when the small fire ignited. Hood had a gash in his leg but was determined to escape, working at removing Ballard's boots and socks. He searched his pockets for anything useful and was pleased to find a Swiss Army knife.

He took the young guard's high-band radio. He would try to monitor emergency frequencies. He emerged from the wreckage, found his pack, then disappeared into the mountains. He was home.

CHAPTER SEVENTY-ONE

"Going to pour on the magic now." That's what Frank Zander's old man used to say to him.

On rainy summer nights when Zander was just a little boy growing up in Shaker Heights, his old man would play the shell game with him. He'd place a pea under one of three walnut shells on the kitchen table.

"Keep your eye on the one with the pea, Frankie."

He would slide the shells in meshing circles, stopping to quickly reveal the pea, then resume. "Are you watching, Frankie? Where's the pea?"

Even at a tender age, Zander was acutely perceptive. He never missed finding the pea, until one night his dad had a cool glint in his eye.

"Going to pour on the magic now, Frankie."

After his tabletop juggle of the shells, his father lifted Zander's choice, then began laughing. No pea. Nothing. Zander was stunned. That was the shell. It had to be. He lifted the others. Nothing. He lifted his original to find the pea wedged inside. His old man, a Cleveland robbery detective, beamed.

"You're a natural investigator, Frankie." His dad winked and tussled his hair, then finished his Old Milwaukee. "You never know the truth until you hold the facts in your hand. Never forget that, son."

Zander now clung to his old man's advice as the task force began debating its next move.

Tracy Bowman had taken Emily Baker outside the command center for air while Zander and the others analyzed the circumstances.

"I think we have to really consider that the Bakers have told us the truth, Frank." Walt Sydowski flipped through his file.

"And what is that?"

"That she ran off."

"What if they took her out there to perish?"

"That's a theory. Where's the hard evidence?"

"The region is littered with it. Blood, articles from her. And the whole business with Emily's sister and Isaiah Hood. Come on, Walt. It's too early to cave on anything. Until we know the truth about Paige Baker's disappearance, her parents are suspects."

"I just don't know, Frank." Sydowski twisted a rubber band. "It just doesn't fit for me. I can't put my finger on it. It's just my read on the parents. I think they were a family in crisis hit with horrible misfortune."

"How did her pack and sock get down a crevasse?"

"She could have been taken by an animal." Pike Thornton had seen it before. "The goat carcass is a strong indicator, plus the fact that whole region is bear country."

"What about the ax, her T-shirt, Doug Baker's wound?"

"Frank," Sydowski said, twisting his pen cap, "it could have happened just like they said."

Zander flipped through his clipboard: updates from the park's

SAR people, the county attorney's old report on Emily's letters, Isaiah Hood's claim of innocence, the complaints with SFPD concerning Doug Baker's temper, the New York cop's account of an outburst the day before Paige vanished.

"There are too many red flags." Zander shook his head, remembering how the deranged young mother in Georgia fooled detectives, including him. He recalled the face of the little boy he talked with, played with, while on the case. Killed by his mother on their watch because everyone let their guard down. *Oh yeah, that psycho poured on the magic.* Zander made a vow that he would never be fooled again.

"You never know the truth until you hold the facts in your hand."

Zander ran his hands over his face. "We'll go back to Doug Baker for an explanation of Paige's sock and backpack in the crevasse."

Someone rapped on the door. An FBI agent stuck his head in.

"Inspector Sydowski? An urgent call for you from San Francisco. It's Inspector Turgeon. Can I put it through here?"

Emily Baker and Tracy Bowman walked in the shade of lodgepole pines behind the cabin dorms for the park's trail and fire crews. Half a dozen FBI agents formed a security circle around them, watching from a distance.

Emily reached under her sunglasses, dabbing her eyes with a tissue. "You know, I used to put her hair in pigtails when she was just learning to walk."

Bowman nodded.

"She was so adorable, the way they bounced when she toddled all over the place. I must've shot a thousand pictures. The way her eyes just radiated joy and then that camera in the crevasse and those dead eyes—oh God."

"Emily, it was not her."

"Why did he do that to me? Did he know?"

Careful, Agent Bowman, she cautioned herself.

"We're just trying to understand what happened."

"Uh, do you think there is any chance, um—" Emily stopped and removed her glasses. "Tracy, tell me what your heart feels as a mother. Please tell me if you think there is any hope Paige is still alive out there."

Bowman met her eyes. "I would never give up hope. No mother could until—" Bowman looked up as a blue-and-white helicopter pounded overhead.

"Until what, Tracy?"

"Until you knew the truth. The absolute truth."

Emily was motionless with her thoughts.

"I want to talk to Doug," she said. "Will you help me?"

Nora Lam of the U.S. Justice Department entered the task force room without knocking, her face taut.

"Not now, Ms. Lam, please!" Zander said. Sydowski was on the phone.

"Maleena Crow wants Doug Baker released. You can't hold him much longer."

"Not now!"

"And Washington called demanding an update."

Washington. Zander felt his stomach lurch, thinking of his soon-to-be ex and the egocentric, bureaucratic dunghill. . . .

"Damn it! We're in the middle of something."

"The Hood case is critically linked—"

"Hood's case was investigated twenty-two years ago!"

Sydowski placed his hand over his ear, struggling to hear Inspector Turgeon, who was on a cell phone driving on a San Francisco freeway.

"What do you have, Linda?"

"The complaint against Doug Baker by Cammi Walton is bogus."

"You have that confirmed?"

"The kid admitted to making it up after we pressed her. I'll be faxing my report to Golden Gate and they'll forward it to your team there. You're getting it hot off the press."

"What happened?"

"I talked to the history teacher whose classroom is across the hallway from Baker's. He said teachers, especially male, have a policy to never, ever be alone with a student, especially female teens in a classroom."

"Good policy."

"Well, the history teacher and two students all gave me statements that they witnessed Baker talking to Ms. Walton at the doorway of his class during the time she claimed he flipped out. It never happened."

"All right."

"There's more. We ran Ms. Walton's name through Juvenile and it turns out she had a shoplifting beef a week or so before her alleged incident with Baker. The store manager was late reporting it."

"Why?"

"Cammi tried to keep it quiet, and almost succeeded, by threatening to say a manager 'made advances toward her' and she would be believed because her mother is a police commissioner. The store staff backed off but filed the report later. We just got it."

"The little—"

"We took this to Cammi, who fessed up and gave us a statement."

"Did you take it to Mother Walton?"

"Yes. I feel for the lady. She's a class act."

"What about the domestic call to the Baker house?"

"I talked to the responding officers and reviewed the call."

"Right."

"Talked to the neighbor who called in the complaint. Pushed him hard. He couldn't swear about a bat or any real threats.

The best we get, it was just a little shouting. That part is on your plate.''

"Thanks, Linda.'' Sydowski turned to inform Zander.

Lloyd Turner had just entered the room with Park Superintendent Elsie Temple, clutching a sheet of notepaper.

"This is less than two minutes old from our communications center,'' Temple began. "The Royal Canadian Mounted Police report finding a footprint, very fresh, fitting the shoes worn by Paige Baker, and a plastic bottled-water container purchased at San Francisco International Airport. It's a significant indication that she's alive in the northern reach of the park.''

Temple immediately ordered all search operations concentrated in the border area.

"The Mounties indicate she was moving back into Montana.''

CHAPTER SEVENTY-TWO

Tory Sky, the sunset blond photographer from Santa Monica with the Malibu tan, was bewitching Levi Kayle, news shooter from the *San Francisco Star*.

"Well, I simply tired of celeb-stalking in LA, so I freelance news images. I sell everywhere through my service on the Internet. I'm here for a German magazine." Brushing her hair from her sunglasses, she touched her ear, pressing her earphone tighter.

"Something's up!"

Tory's new, ultracompact, $3,000 digital radio scanner enabled her to listen in on the emergency frequencies used by some of the agencies searching for Paige Baker. Kayle's unit was not as good. Tory's green eyes were intense as she listened to the urgent transmissions to the rangers on the RCMP's discovery. She grabbed her cell phone.

"They may have found her!"

Tory's thumb expertly pushed her cell's speed-dial button.

"At the northern edge. I might be able to get you in. Come on," she said into her phone. "Be there, be there."

Kayle was intrigued. With the exception of ranger-controlled chopper flights for pool shots of the search, the press was barred from any part of the search region. It was virtually inaccessible. Tory had a connection.

"Rawley? Tory. Yes, I heard it. Can you?—You can!—How many? West Glacier ASAP? Five spots, right. Five hundred. On our way. Do not dare leave without us! Yes, I will be there."

"What's up?"

"Get your friends, Kayle, we're airborne. Dieter! Where is that guy?"

The search for Paige Baker had swollen into a major air operation largely dependent upon helicopters. More than a dozen federal, state, national guard and private contractors were involved in searching, moving people and equipment, or ferrying supplies. One of the contractors was Rawley Nash, a burned-out 1970s relic who listened to Creedence Clearwater Revival through his supercharged eight-track tape system. Nash had it amplified so he could hear his speakers inside his bird, the *Widowmaker*. Nash was an out-of-state mercenary, a gypsy cab with rotors, who flew by his own rules, operating a big old reconditioned Huey.

He had just been assigned to deliver a K-9 team from Idaho to join the refocused search near Boundary Creek at Grizzly's northern edge. The rendezvous was at West Glacier, where he had met Tory Sky earlier. They worked out a standing deal. If the critical moment came, Nash would duck the rules and fly her in to get her pictures for $1,000—with the understanding that depending on the heat he drew, it might be a one-way trip. The bonus was that if Tory could find at least three other press types to pay five hundred each for their ride, hers was free. "Could she dig it?"

At least that was the version Kayle was explaining to Molly Wilson and Tom Reed. Kayle was at the wheel of his rented Sunbird, racing behind Tory Sky's Taurus. She was ahead of them with Dieter, the quiet man from Hamburg, stringing out of LA for *Der Speigel*, the big German magazine.

"We have to go," Kayle said to Reed. "Nothing is going to happen at the command center. It's a press internment camp."

"Kayle, what if we get dropped and don't get out? How are you going to get us back? Have you looked at the map—we'll be as good as in Canada."

"We'll just talk this guy into picking us up. We've got our sat phone and computers. We can file from there. Just chill, Reed."

"Didn't Tory say her pilot was flying in a K-9 guy?" Wilson said.

"That's right," Kayle said. "We'll follow the tracker. Chances are he'll lead us to the kid, or at least the action in there. Besides, he'll have a radio to call for our ride. Reed, everyone is likely attempting to get in now. If she's alive, we have to get the picture and story!"

Reed calculated the time. The *Star*'s desk in San Francisco had not yet decided if he or Wilson was covering Hood's execution tonight. Either way, they would want Kayle there for whatever art they could grab.

"We have to get to Deer Lodge tonight for Hood," Reed said.

"We'll have time," Kayle said.

Reed remembered being dispatched to Montana with Kayle for the Unabomber arrest and how Kayle loved pushing things to deadline. Like most newspeople, he thrived under pressure.

At West Glacier, Rawley Nash, carrying a tattered leather briefcase, came to them, swiftly laying down his rules as his machine was being fueled amid helicopters lifting off and landing at the helispots. Reed pegged him as being in his early fifties. A good-looking man with two days' growth, a shark's smile and eyebrows arching over his aviators that told you not to tangle with him because his charm alone would defeat you.

Nash removed his sunglasses. "Five hundred each." His winkle suggested Tory would show her appreciation later. And the way his eyes walked all over Molly Wilson. "Well, well, now . . ." Glancing backward over his shoulder, he produced an old credit-card imprint machine on the hood of Kayle's Sunbird. "All major cards accepted. Let's go, kiddies. Flash that company plastic."

Transactions done, Nash instructed them to walk one hundred yards or so to a clearing behind a stand of pine. "That's 'Gate Nine,' " he chuckled. "Going to leapfrog over there and pick you up. Now."

Within minutes, the group was boarding Nash's *Widowmaker*. He instructed them to put on intercom headsets, close and lock the doors, and buckle up. He came on the air.

A woman in her twenties, with a leashed German shepherd, was in the rear, her face a question mark. "What's going on here?" Her dog barked at Dieter.

"Nice dog." Dieter's accent was heavy. "Don't bite, nice dog."

"Kids, meet Hilda Sim and her pup, Lux, with Idaho SAR. Sim, these are some people critical to the operation. Ask no questions. No beverages will be served on this mission. Please check your belts and get ready to rock and roll." Nash gave the old Huey some throttle and slammed in an eight-track, which began blaring "Up Around the Bend."

Wilson felt her stomach flutter as the airship climbed rapidly, then roared. All the while, Creedence Clearwater Revival blared through Nash's sound system. Nash grinned as if he were king of the Rocky Mountains.

Reed thought they were making good time, but then a faster, sleeker chopper shot past in the same direction at two o'clock. A blue-and-white blur that disappeared. *Jesus. They must have found something.* Reed felt his adrenaline stirring, glad Kayle and Wilson talked him into the trip. The story was definitely out here.

After several minutes, Nash eased up, slowing down.

"We're a few miles from the coordinates. I want to check on the activity down there, uh, for a safe drop." Reed knew right off that Nash didn't want anyone official to know he was operating black-market press tours.

Kayle and Tory were checking their cameras.

Kayle was first to spot a threadlike pole of black smoke ahead. Instinctively, he began shooting.

Can't be a signal fire, Nash thought. *Nothing on the radio. What the hell?* As they neared the scene, it came over him full force.

Chopper crash!

"Goddamn! We're landing!" Nash reached for his radio and called in the incident and location. "We're going to check for survivors!"

As they descended, Tory and Kayle, faces locked in professional concentration, took news photos without saying a word. Nash continued calling for help until he was acknowledged. He made out the downed craft's call numbers, relaying them. It was Mercy Force, the Missoula air ambulance that had rocketed by them earlier.

Missoula Tower acknowledged Mercy Force was off course and indicated trouble, relaying to Nash that it should have five souls aboard. He put down a safe distance from the wreckage. Grabbing an ax, fire extinguisher and medical kit, he led his group to the rescue. Kayle and Tory took pictures along the way.

Nash and Dieter hauled the pilot out quickly. He was alive,

oaning, bleeding. "Why does he have bare feet?" Kayle ondered.

Sim leashed Lux, who was barking wildly. No one could elieve the scene inside—two women and a Montana State rison officer, shackled in the back, unconscious, bleeding from e head and hands.

"What the hell happened here?" Kayle shot pictures.

"We're going to help you. You're alive. Help *is* coming," ash told the victims. "Dieter, douse the fire," he ordered. I've got bolt cutters in my machine." Nash returned. His utters did their work on the cuffs, freeing the guard and women. ll four victims were pulled to safety. Sim worked on their uts.

"They're going to make it," she said.

Lux was still barking.

"Quiet down, boy!" Sim ordered.

"I don't like this," Nash said. "Supposed to be five people. Ve've got four. Three of them were in chains. Christ." He ad heard earlier radio chatter about a medical standby and a ight to Deer Lodge. *Montana State Prison is in Deer Lodge. hains. Medical. Five people, only four.* It was becoming clear. ash hurried into the wreckage, knowing he had glimpsed omething a second ago. He tossed debris. *Yes. Here. Orange!* prison-issue pair of coveralls. He held them up.

Kayle and Tory took pictures.

"The fifth passenger is a convict who escaped," Nash said, canning the area.

Dieter followed Nash's gaze through his rimless glasses.

"This is the area where the Mountie thinks the little Califor-ia girl is alive, and this prison escaper is now here, after the elicopter crashes."

Wilson swallowed at the realization, watching Nash head to is helicopter to report and update.

Kayle studied Sim and Lux. "Bet your dog could pick up is trail."

"Yes, he could."

Everyone exchanged glances, passing around the question no one wanted to raise.

Who was willing to chase after an escaped convict?

CHAPTER
SEVENTY-THREE

The governor's intercom buzzed in his Capitol Building
ffice in Helena.

"The Department of Corrections director, sir. Says it's urgent
 the Hood case."

"Put him on hold, please." The governor's cell phone was
lling as the attorney general and John Jackson swept into the
oom.

"Gentlemen? Do we have more from the Mounties? Did we
d her?"

Faces grim, they ignored him, switching on the large TV. A
ve network news channel.

BREAKING NEWS was the caption under a map of Glacier
ational Park, Montana. A graphic showing a lightning bolt
ar the Canadian border and the banner HELICOPTER CRASH
 the newsreader described details.

"*Crash?* Just a minute," the governor said to his cell phone
ll. "Turn it up."

"We think Isaiah Hood was on that chopper." The attorney general was pressing numbers on his cell phone.

"What?"

". . . if you're just joining us, we have a confirmed report that an air ambulance, a Mercy Force flight from Missoula General Mercy Hospital, has crashed in the Rocky Mountains in the northern extremity of Glacier National Park. Five people were aboard. Four are believed to have survived and are in stable condition. The fifth person is missing. . . ."

"Missing?"

"It's Isaiah Hood, sir," the attorney general said. "He's escaped."

The governor's intercom buzzed again.

"The director of DOC calling back, sir."

The governor punched the line: "Tell me what happened."

"It was a traumatic medical emergency. We were bound by the regs to transfer him to Missoula."

"But you had security aboard?"

"One rookie officer. He was the lightest. It was a last-minute situation because of weight restrictions."

"But how . . . tell me just how the hell did this—"

"Missoula Tower picked up a transmission from the pilot that Hood had hijacked the flight. Directing it northbound through the Park—"

"But how? What was this medical injury? He's high profile. I should have been told. Why wasn't—"

"One of his seizures. We think he feigned illness."

"Oh, *you think* that, do you?"

The governor hung up. "John, how bad are the survivors? Update me."

"A pilot, a guard and two emergency nurses. Preliminary reports indicate all are alive. In process of being transported to Mercy General. Families alerted."

"Get me on the line to them."

"U.S. Marshals, State Police, FBI, Transportation are first in line."

"Relatives, then." Governor Nye ran his hands over his face, thinking. "Where the hell is Hood? Have they started looking? Do they need the National Guard? We've got to pick him up before he finds Paige. . . . Jesus, right in the same region . . . why was he directing them? John, turn that up again, please."

"All right," the newswoman at her desk said to the camera, "stand by. We're going live to Van Heston, our reporter covering the story in Glacier National Park. . . ."

". . . Tawni, let me preface—hold it—" Static. A man in his early thirties was talking to the camera. His voice urgent, dramatic. "OK, Tawni, let me preface by saying this is unconfirmed. I repeat unconfirmed, but what we're hearing are two astounding developments. First, the Mercy Force helicopter that crashed is, according to sources, or was, transferring a patient from Montana State Prison to a local hospital. The patient—this is unconfirmed—was Isaiah Hood, the inmate scheduled for execution at midnight tonight. Also unconfirmed is that he hijacked the flight, directed it toward Canada before it crashed within a few short miles of the Canadian border. . . ."

The governor's stomach was lurching.

". . . again, Tawni, it is all unconfirmed. There is speculation he was bound for Canada, which has no death penalty and a somewhat involved extradition process . . ."

"Van, you said there were two developments?"

"Yes, coming to the second. Prior to the crash, the FBI was said to be 'aggressively' questioning the parents of Paige Baker. They have fallen under suspicion because of doubts about Hood's guilt in the murder of Emily Baker's five-year-old sister, in the park twenty-two years ago. Sources tell us that the FBI was taking a hard line with her parents to answer for their daughter's whereabouts. We know that Doug Baker, Emily's father, has an attorney. The Bakers, we are told, were undergoing further questioning by the FBI when word came that the Royal Canadian Mounted Police found a recent footprint, consistent with the footwear worn by Paige Baker, a few yards inside the Canadian side of the park.''

The governor's intercom buzzed again.

''It's CNN, sir.''

''Not now. Tell them we'll make a statement later.''

The intercom buzzed once more.

''No press, please,'' the governor said.

''It's the White House, sir.''

The attorney general was on his cell phone. Jackson turned the TV volume down.

''Put it through.''

''Governor?'' A man's voice.

''Yes.''

''It's the Oval Office. Please stand by for the president.''

The governor pursed his lips, knowing full well what this was all about.

''Governor.'' The famous voice was deeper over the phone. ''Our hearts go out to everyone involved in the events in Montana.''

''Thank you, Mr. President.''

The governor rubbed his eyes, knowing the chief's ironclad stance on the death penalty was legendary when he was governor of his state. Never blinked. Even under extreme political and international pressure.

''How are Cynthia and Ellen, Grayson?''

The president had the names right. Probably had executive staff pull up his Montana bio, he thought, touching the pictures of his wife and daughter.

''Fine. Thank you. We're appreciative no lives were lost and for your call, sir. Thank you.''

''Now listen, if you need any *more* federal help to see this thing through—I mean this is a federal park and federal jurisdiction, except for the prison. But if I can provide you with any resources, do not hesitate to call me.''

The governor swallowed. He knew the subtext of the call.

"Thank you, sir."

"Our thoughts and prayers are with you for a peaceful resolution."

"Yes, I really should be—"

The president cut him off, dropping his tone to a gut-tightening degree.

"You really should be reconsidering your national aspirations, Governor. You were supposed to be strapping this guy to a gurney, not giving him goddamned helicopter rides over the Rockies."

The line went dead in the governor's ear.

CHAPTER SEVENTY-FOUR

Doug Baker's tears stained the printout pages as he read the Internet copy of the *San Francisco Star* article his lawyer gave him that morning.

"It's important you see what the rest of the country sees, Doug." She left him in the small room of the command center where the FBI was holding him.

He read the story over and over:

"Baker was responsible for her sister's death. It comes as the FBI searches in vain for Baker's 10-year-old daughter, Paige."

Then from the county attorney's report, "She begged me to save her. . . . I will never forget her eyes staring into mine as she fell. God, please forgive me."

The horror hammered at Doug's heart, but he refused to succumb to it, composing himself, seeking strength from the mountains where Paige was. He ached to be out there searching for her.

He tossed the pages aside.

Concentrate. Concentrate on what you know.

Emily was psychologically chained to her tortured childhood. If she was present when her little sister was murdered by Isaiah Hood, naturally she would feel guilty. That is how he saw it.

But could you ever truly know what is in a person's heart?

Did he know Emily? Really know her? She kept so much hidden from him. What if she was sick? What if she was guilty?

Doug scanned the mountains, rubbing his eyes. What should he believe? Believe this. He did not kill his daughter. He was guilty of some terrible behavior, but he did not kill his daughter. And he did not believe Emily killed her.

"You sure about that?"

"Do you believe your wife could have harmed your daughter?"

Emily would give her life for Paige.

No.

They were guilty of being victims of horrible circumstances. Look at the awful wound on his hand. Tossing his ax as if hiding it. Arguing in front of that family. A New York detective, Crow had told him. Losing it in front of a New York cop the day before his daughter disappears and then he shows up with an ax-murderer's gash on his hand. Doug did not blame the FBI for their suspicions.

But everyone's thinking on this was dead wrong.

He heard more helicopters outside, the activity intensifying. He yearned to take part in the search. What was happening now? No one told him anything. No one updated him.

What if Paige is dead?

A gentle knock. The door opened. Tracy Bowman and Maleena Crow with Emily. His eyes brightened.

"You'll have just a few moments with your wife," Bowman said.

"Then what? What is happening?"

"Just a few minutes. I'm sorry that's all I can tell you."

Crow touched his shoulder. "Doug, I am working on getting you released." Nodding to the Bakers, leaving with Bowman, closing the door.

Emily stood before him, looking broken; her hands were clenched in fists touching her lips, eyes brimming with tears.

"Doug, they think I—you—we, oh God . . ."

He took her into his arms. Doug drew strength from holding her. "I know everything. Maleena gave me the article."

"I did not hurt anyone, Doug."

"I believe you. I did not harm her, Em."

She nodded and swallowed. "I know."

"You listen to me. We are going to get through this. She is not dead. We have to believe that."

"Doug, the police, they said so many horrible things. They take the truth and mix it up and then they showed me part of the search when we thought it was her b-b-body—"

"What was it? Did they find her?"

Emily shook her head. "An animal in a crevasse. So awful. It has been horrible. Then they said a student has accused you of some sort of violent act with her. They said your wound, your ax, her T-shirt—Oh God—"

"I know, Emily. I know about that stuff. The student business is not true. A kid with problems at home. The ax, the blood and T-shirt. We know all of it. But I never hurt anyone. I can't blame the FBI. That is why I took the polygraph, to prove I have nothing to hide. We have to believe Paige is alive. Whatever we are going through, it is far worse for her out there. If we give up hope, it's over. She has to feel we are pulling for her against all the odds."

Emily nodded.

"Em, she has Kobee. She's a smart girl. I've been going over it. I think she had food and water in her pack—"

"She doesn't have her pack anymore, Doug."

"What?"

"They found it. In the crevasse where there are bears. But they did not find her—Oh—I—God—"

A knock sounded.

It was Maleena Crow, breathless. "There's been a break."

"Oh Lord, what?"

"Just inside the Canadian border, the Mounties found a footprint matching her sneaker. It is very fresh. They also found an empty water bottle from San Francisco Airport."

"I bought her bottled water there before we boarded!" Emily said.

Doug looked hard at Maleena. "You're sure of this?"

"Elsie Temple, the park's superintendent, just told me."

Doug felt as if a mountain of pain had shifted.

"It's a sign that she's alive," he said.

"It's something for sure." Crow nodded. "I'm working on them to return you to the mountain command post. That's where the focus will be now."

CHAPTER SEVENTY-FIVE

Cool breezes glided up the sloping forests, carrying the fragrance of western red cedar, larch and hemlock to Isaiah Hood, who surveyed the Rockies from his God's-eye view.

Like a reawakening mountain spirit, Hood inhaled deeply, drawing power from an ancient force, activating his acute senses of hearing, vision, smell and animallike intuition.

He spotted a white-tail deer amid a stand of spruce, some seventy-five yards off; heard the rustling of a bald eagle's wings skirting the treetops of a valley below; detected the sweetness of glacier lilies; sensed mountain butterflies zigzagging among them.

Hood was home. Free. A king in his kingdom. He pushed on swiftly.

He had cheated his executioners. Cheated his scheduled death, as he knew he would. For it was only right. He had given them twenty-two years for a game. Time for him to take control.

Hood had plans—intricate designs—drafted, polished, taken

apart and reassembled in a million dreams dreamed while living in a concrete casket. His poster of the Rockies was his portal to his paradise. His trances, visions and "apprehension of the mind," the vehicles that got him here.

A network of ancient Indian, trapper and miners' trails existed among the ranges that traversed the U.S.-Canadian border. They were not on maps but burned into Hood's heart. He knew them all. Knew them better than any other human being. He had traveled them as a boy, disappearing for weeks after a savage thrashing with the hooks. All part of his education. It took him years to learn who he was and how the world loathed the thing he had become.

The Mark of Cain, some called it. Living with the sin of the father.

"Don't you understand?" his sister whispers to him the night she packs and runs away for the last time. "Dad murdered Mom! Dropped her from a mountain. I'm messed up because of it. Get away from him! Why are you so loyal? He beats you like a dog. Get away, Isaiah, before he kills you, too!"

In his heart, Hood knew his sister was right but could not accept it. He was fourteen at the time. She ran away to Seattle; he escaped to the Rockies, where he would spend days and weeks alone in the alpine trails. Perhaps in some way he was hoping to prove his sister wrong by somehow finding their mother. But more likely, it was because he realized that, like his father, he was afflicted with the malevolent need to have those under his control plead for mercy, giving currency to his power.

But for Hood, it was a consuming game.

"A psychopath with a destructive psychological neurological disorder most likely brought on by his father's beatings."

That is how the doctors defined it.

It was a game, one he was compelled to play. That is how Hood lived it.

It started with the dog, the rabbit, the cat. Then the butterfly girl. No one understood that, to him, it was a game.

He pushed on fast, relishing the gift he had left behind. The warden, the DOC boss and the governor, the guards on death row. Hood could picture them, finger-pointing, ass-covering. He feasted on that one.

Hood was startled, sensing a helicopter in the distance.

Stepping under a thick stand of cedars, he rummaged through the pack, produced the guard's radio, flipped the channels. It was fully charged, coming to life with emergency transmissions from rangers, SAR and others in the region. He secured it in the holster clipped to the belt around his waist, inserted an earpiece.

Hood's nostrils flared. Tracking dogs were in the area far off, searching.

Quickly, he rooted through the bag: a hatchet, fruit, water, first-aid kit, pilot's wallet with cash and credit cards, sunglasses, several other items. Then he found the lunch kit belonging to one of the nurses. Had some sliced vegetables, crackers, cheese and cookies. He tore off a patch of towel in the bag, rubbing it under his armpits, his sweating groin, his stomach, still oozing blood and pus. He headed into an area dense with trees for nearly fifty yards, then backtracked carefully. He placed the towel down.

Ought to tie up the first dog behind me, he thought before pushing north.

Dressed in the blue flight suit, wearing the pilot's boots, sunglasses, a cap, a utility belt with the radio, a small knapsack, using a walking stick, Hood resembled someone with search operations. His plan was to slip into Canada using the most treacherous trail, a long-forgotten ancient Indian path on the western slopes.

But a message was coming.

There was a critical twist to his plan. The special reason he came here.

A headache, one of his mega-pounders, seized him.

He knew he possessed the power to find her.

No, I shouldn't.

Yes. Find her. It is key to the plan.

The message was building. Triggering rage pent-up for twenty-two years.

Why not find her and play?

One more time.

Anger and adrenaline coursed through him, bubbling into a dangerous mixture. His head quaked with pain. Twenty-two years. He made one critical mistake with the butterfly girl. He let her big sister live.

Look what she cost him.

The message was clear now.

The lost one is very near.

CHAPTER SEVENTY-SIX

Frank Zander was shouting into a telephone.

"Yes, we know Isaiah Hood was on that helicopter! He walked away! No, I do not know why he was . . . Hello? You there?"

Zander lost his connection to the marshals. He swore while following a park ranger's finger pinpointing the crash site on the wall-size map of Glacier National Park.

Radios sizzled with chatter, and cell phones, including Zander's, trilled constantly in the command center. Its five TVs blared, each tuned to a different network's live report.

". . . an incredible series of events unfolding in the case of . . ."

". . . Montana death row inmate Isaiah Hood, whose execution was . . ."

". . . has confirmed Hood is a fugitive at large in the same area . . ."

At the Ops table, an EMS supervisor spoke above the bedlam into his radio.

"No, no, no! They are transporting them to the LZ at the command center now! That's right! Then ground from here to Kalispell. Three ships. Yes. Stable. Kalispell's alerted. Get one of them to stand by at the command post now until we get our air ambulance back . . . Yes, the largest one. Just a standby . . . at the post—talk to Brady Brook out there—"

Phones were ringing.

The National Transportation Safety Board, the U.S. Marshals Service, news organizations, urgently demanding information.

"Frank! A quick meeting." Lloyd Turner was calling Zander to an urgent, intense conversation with Maleena Crow. Nora Lam and the other detectives were there.

"All we're requesting is that you release them back to the command post, back to their campsite," Crow said.

"What do you think, Frank?"

"This is not a good time for this discussion."

"You cannot hold Doug without charging him. Let them go back to the command post. Consider what they're going through."

Zander was wary. The case had taken a dramatic turn, but he refused to let his guard down.

"They know about the RCMP's report," Crow said.

"I told them, Frank." Elsie Temple answered the question in his face. "They have a right to hope."

Zander inventoried the group for allies. Bowman was absent, searching for David Cohen. Walt Sydowski's subtle shrug suggested it would make little difference if the Bakers were under watch at the command post.

"I do not have a problem returning them *for the time being,*" Turner said. "No one has been charged. No one is under arrest or in custody. It's an open investigation. No one is suggesting it is concluded, Frank."

But Zander sensed that Turner and the others thought so; they believed events had miraculously cleared the Bakers.

"This is exactly what happened in Georgia. He would not

be fooled again. *"You never know the truth until you hold the facts in your hand."*

Zander felt the decision to return the Bakers had already been made. "We still have agents at the command post?" he asked Turner.

Turner nodded.

"Frank, let's see what transpires with these other events. Let's just see."

Zander swallowed. "It's your call."

"We'll send them back with an escort," Turner said. "But it will be some time before a helicopter is available. Until then, they are free to wait in this room."

Stepping from the storage room, Doug and Emily were hurled into the maelstrom. Before Crow could alert them to Hood's escape, they confronted his face displayed next to their daughter's on one of the large TVs.

". . . death row inmate Isaiah Hood escaped within the last hour when the air ambulance crashed in the same region the . . ."

Emily covered her mouth.

Doug was horrified. "Maleena, what is going on? *Hood escaped!* But how? Paige. Any sign?"

Crow worked quickly to explain, sitting them down.

Emily searched the chaos for Zander. Was this a blatant psychological trick? She saw him, looking angry on a phone call, carving notes. *No. It's real!* She looked at the TV. Saw Doug and Paige, with Kobee, smiling back from it. Then an old photograph of Rachel. Her eyes. Rachel.

Crow could not put it any other way. Hood had escaped in the very same area where the Mounties found fresh signs of Paige.

Emily groaned, began trembling.

"Doug! It's happening again. Please not again!" Emily raised her face to the ceiling. "God, why!"

Doug's heart nearly broke from his chest; his mind, a whirlwind of rage, fear, desperation. He pulled Emily tight, as much to hang on to his sanity as to comfort her.

Paige is alive! At least it appears they have signs she is alive. God! They have to find her! They have to do something. Anything. Think, Baker. Time is running out. Damn it. Think. You are not going to sit here doing nothing. Not anymore.

There had to be a way out of this. Amid the confusion, Doug was half-listening to Crow telling him about waiting for a helicopter to deliver them to their campsite, the point from where all the rescue efforts would be directed. Doug's military training, his coaching skills, were kicking in, using the pressure to fuel his thoughts. Holding Emily. He took careful stock of the crowded room, watching as rangers, FBI agents, searchers, came and went.

He *had* to get them out of here. Fast.

Isaiah Hood's eyes met his.

No other options existed.

CHAPTER SEVENTY-SEVEN

Instinct compelled Paige to flee for the goat ledges of the high country.

She could smell the grizzly coming for her. She had become accustomed to its horrible odor. In her ten-year-old heart, she reasoned it to be the stench of death.

My death.

Again, she heard it huffing; its jaw clicked, gaining on her. In what had become a slow, dark ballet, she climbed as swiftly as her depleted, aching body would permit; the huge carnivore lumbered steadily after her.

Paige sobbed, scrambling for her life, stopping for a brief moment, certain she heard a helicopter nearby. Then a distant thud. Then nothing.

Keep moving. Keep moving.

Kobee had learned now not to bark.

But it didn't matter.

Paige's tormentor was an eight-foot one-thousand-pound mother sow. Pale cream, measuring nearly four feet at its humped shoulders, she ruled much of the Devil's Grasp, having fiercely killed deer, goats, wolves. She was the manifestation of forces as ancient as the mountains. As the victim of circumstance, Paige continually trespassed in the most intimate regions of her territory, becoming enemy prey to be hunted, killed, buried in a shallow grave, then eaten by her cubs.

Reaching a higher elevation, Paige quickly scoured the area, finding a small shelter enclosed in rock that was naturally barricaded by two large, fallen trees. Paige squeezed her way inside with Kobee. The trunks were huge, but the bear was of nightmare proportions.

Hugging Kobee, Paige waited, realizing she was losing against a beast determined to kill her.

She began weeping softly. Closing her eyes. Waiting.

Waiting to die.

Paige peeked through the bright cracks between the trees, seeing only daylight and the snowy summits of the Rocky Mountains. She began praying.

Please, God. Don't let it hurt. Just don't let it hurt. God, please.

Paige searched her cold dark shelter for something—anything—with which she could write her parents a final note. A stick or stone to scratch something in the mud, or scratch on a rock.

I'm so sorry I got lost. I love you, P.

She found nothing, and continued weeping until her world went dark.

The grizzly arrived in silence, blocking the sun, fouling the air, weaving and bobbing, deciding how it would open the container to its food source.

Paige squeezed Kobee.

The grizzly reached in with one of its huge paws.

Feeling it brush her, Paige screamed.

The bear groaned, thrusting its paw deeper, under an inch from Paige's face.

It climbed up on the trees, making them creak from its weight.

"Oh, please, no! Oh, please, please, no!"

The bear growled at the sky, enraged, clawing, pounding at the trunks, carving into them with its terrifying claws. Paige screamed; Kobee yelped.

Suddenly, one of the trees shifted as the bear rolled it away, reaching inside, touching Paige.

The grizzly slammed at the second trunk, nudging, pushing, shoving it aside. Paige screamed, clutching Kobee, sobbing, pushing back, deeper into the hole with nothing to defend herself.

No escape.

Paige saw its huge yellow fangs barred, white foam collecting around its mouth; she smelled its horrid breath, and braced for its attack.

Suddenly, the bear vanished. Daylight filled the shelter.

Paige remained frozen, heart beating wildly, holding her breath.

The grizzly was gone.

I can get out? Run?

She was trembling.

Without sound or warning, everything went black. Faster than Paige could scream, the monster reached into the cave, its claws locking into her. It dragged her out, standing victorious over her.

God, please, oh, please don't let it hurt.

She hugged Kobee.

The grizzly grunted and dragged her out farther. She was totally at its mercy. Paige did not move as it growled, lifting its head to the sky, its saliva glistening. It shook its head savagely, nearly standing on its hindquarters, driving its opening jaws toward Paige.

Mommy, Daddy, please . . . please don't let it hurt. . . .

Paige looked to the blue sky. . . . Suddenly, a glint-flash of metal blurred into the grizzly's skull, forcing the beast to suspend itself as the object was instantly removed, then pounded again swiftly into its head. A second, third, fourth and final time by someone, *something,* forcing the animal to drop its huge head and neck, landing on Paige's lower abdomen, its snout nearly touching her face. An ax was embedded between its ears some four inches deep into its brain; warm blood erupted from the wound onto her stomach, its stinking death gasp blowing up her nostrils.

Paige was too stunned to scream.

Someone, a man, lifted the head from her. Paige rolled clear. The man stood in the sun, a silhouette in a blue jumpsuit.

Her savior.

"You're safe now," Isaiah Hood said.

CHAPTER SEVENTY-EIGHT

The debate at the crash site between photographer Levi Kayle and Hilda Sim from Idaho SAR ended when Rawley Nash took charge.

"No one is going anywhere right now. Not until we make sure these injured people are safely on their way to the hospital."

"I agree," Tom Reed said, along with Molly Wilson and Sim, who were comforting the victims.

Nash said two choppers would be arriving shortly to transport patients to the command center, where ground ambulances would take them to Kalispell. "I need you guys to help us load. After that, form a posse, do your thing."

The first helicopter, dispatched from the command post, approached.

"If anyone asks, you press people were already here when Sim and I spotted the wreck, got it?" Nash said.

He directed the aircraft to a makeshift landing zone, then supervised the quick loading of the pilot and the small guard.

who looked to be in the worst shape. Both were now conscious and moaning.

The second helicopter took Nurse McCarry. No one asked questions. Attention was focused on airlifting the victims. Nash was last to depart. He had Wordell. Lifting off, he flashed a thumbs-up to the others, seeing Lux enthusiastically tugging Sim north into the forest, commencing pursuit.

Glancing over his shoulder at Wordell laid out across his rear seats, he noticed her diamond engagement ring.

Don't worry, baby. Nash will get you to the church on time.
He could not shake off the images of the scene.
Handcuffs and shackles.

He had pushed them to the back of his mind, but they leaped forward as he tried to comprehend what the Mercy Force crew had endured. Who was the con? What happened in the air? *Christ, it looked bad.*

Nash had ditched a number of times. Struck by lightning flying traffic reports over Atlanta. Not fun. In New York, some fuselage gave way flying a TV news crew over Manhattan. Nearly died from fear at the controls when he veered into the World Trade Center, averting disaster at the last second. Those two were dicey. Nash gazed down at the mountains. *But handcuffs and shackles.* He could not imagine what kind of hell the Mercy Force people survived. Who was their passenger?

On the subject of passengers, Nash considered the quick two grand he just made. He apologized for his actions, but he had bills to pay. Should he call that San Francisco TV guy at the park's press camp, offering him a deal on a ride in for the return trip? Depended on his next assignment.

Putting down at the command center, everything went like clockwork. Enough paramedics were standing by to transport the victims.

Nash's instructions were radioed to his call numbers.

"Kill your rotor. Stay in your chair and on the air. Next

assignment's coming up. Stand by. An FBI call. Four bodies to the command post.''

''Roger. Standing by.''

Sitting back in his seat to catch his breath, Nash removed one earcup from his radio headset and began fiddling with his emergency radio for any updates. Mostly marshalling from the ranger's command post. Next channel. Paramedic hospital talk—vital signs and stuff. Next channel. Weather conditions. Next Channel. Static. Next. *Wait!* Nash snapped back to the weak static. It was breaking up badly.

''... Ser—*hiss*—Garner *hiss pop pop*—CMP—have *pop pop* in *pop* sight—*hiss hiss* visual—see—girl—*pop* alive *pop*—kilometer from me *pop pop hiss hiss*—coordinates— *pop*—*hiss* she is walking—dog—''

''What was that?''

Nash sat upright. Adjusted his headset.

''What was that?'' Fiddling with the radio. Was he the only one who heard that? ''Come back! Come back!'' He slammed his radio. ''Please, baby.''

CHAPTER
SEVENTY-NINE

Doug Baker watched the command center fill with rangers, FBI agents, Montana officials and SAR people.

"We are going to get out of here," he whispered to Emily. Eyes vacant, she nodded.

Some of the agencies were changing shifts, reassigning bodies, redirecting resources.

"Listen up, people." An unseen voice was issuing instructions. "Search and rescue efforts are to be concentrated in the following sectors. . . ."

The teams who headed the camera probe of the crevasse had returned. Exhausted, they headed for the table with food and coffee. Removing their caps and utility belts, they listened to updates.

". . .because of the danger, each team will have one armed park law enforcement officer, or FBI agent, or patrol officer, or sheriff's deputy. The region is high elevation, one of the most remote and treacherous—"

Doug squeezed Emily's hand. They seemed to have been forgotten.

"Ground teams have already been dispatched or directed from the command post and are in the region. We are moving fast. . . ."

Doug overheard FBI officials demanding two helicopters be readied for sniper teams. Another conversation spilled over something about investigating the crash site and U.S. Marshals then someone moving dog teams.

Doug's thoughts raced. *Now.* It was their only chance. *Now.*

"Emily," he whispered. "Come with me."

The Bakers shouldered their way through the forest of bodies brushing against them toward the food table near the door; no one in the cramped room paid attention to them. Doug listened to every snippet of conversation.

A deep, tired voice: "I'm going to sleep for a spell in my truck."

Inching closer to the food table.

"Do you believe they flew Hood to the hospital on execution day?"

The heap of caps, sunglasses, utility belts.

". . . a Mountie spotted her footprint. . . ."

"I gotta take a leak. . . ."

"Listen up, the following are to stand by, Hinkle, Prue Framington, Barrow . . ."

Most backs were turned from the food table to the speaker issuing instructions. Doug casually picked up two caps and two belts, reached down for two small packs under it, smoothly pulled Emily toward the exit door. They quickly slipped on sunglasses and adjusted the caps, which read FBI.

Nodding to the officers milling outside, carrying the packs and radio belts, they walked toward the landing zone where one helicopter was lifting off. Another was approaching, and two were idle.

"Just keep walking, Emily. Don't look back."

Doug sized the two parked helicopters. A Bell and an old Huey. The Huey pilot was alone in the cockpit, listening to his radio. Ready. He noticed Doug, who pointed a finger in the air, swiveling it as a signal to go up now, as he and Emily approached.

The pilot nodded. Relief washed over Doug, hearing the ignition start and blades commencing rotation.

"I'm supposed to take four. Where are the other two?" Rawley Nash shouted.

"Change of plan because of the circumstances." Buckling up in the seat beside Nash, Doug expertly slipped on the headset, adjusted his mouthpiece. "We've got to move now."

"Roger that," Nash said. "All right back there?"

"All set." Emily knew her way inside a chopper. She was buckled and connected. Her eyes drawn to the bloodstained seats. "You've got blood all over back here," she shouted.

The rotors gathering momentum. Nash activated the intercom.

"Transported one of the nurses from the Mercy Force crash. Didn't have time to clean up. Sorry."

"You were at the site?" Doug said. "How bad was it?"

"Everyone will make it, but it was chilling inside. You probably heard that the con had cuffed them before he escaped. Hey, I just heard on the radio that it was the death row guy. That true?"

Doug swallowed, nodding behind his dark glasses and cap.

"Christ," said Nash, radioing his call letters, hesitating. "You've got the coordinates? It was all broken up on my radio."

"Which coordinates?" Doug said.

"Where the Mountie sighted the girl?"

"You mean the footprint?"

"*I mean the girl.* The lost Baker girl. Just a few minutes ago, it came across all broken up. The Mountie spotted her alive. That's where we're headed, right?"

Doug and Emily were speechless.

"Right." Doug thought quickly. "You're supposed to take us to the general area. We'll get the coordinates on the way."

"OK. If you say so. I think it's near the crash site. Where Hood is running around. I know they got people after him." Nash called in his flight path and increased the throttle. "Here we go."

The Huey rattled; the ground began dropping beneath them.

Emily's knuckles whitened as she clasped her hands tightly, tears rushing down her cheeks from under her dark glasses.

Mommy and Daddy are coming, sweetheart.

Doug reached back, his hand finding Emily's, squeezing it as they gained speed.

Strange, Nash thought. Never saw FBI agents holding hands on duty.

"Hey, you guys like CCR?"

CHAPTER EIGHTY

It was her.

Paige Baker. Yes. And her dog. A beagle. A glimpse through his binoculars. One, maybe two kilometers off before they vanished into a thick spruce forest. He had to locate her again.

RCMP Sergeant Greg Garner continued radioing reports but knew his signal was weak from the valley. No response. If there was, he did not receive it.

"Let's go, pal."

Garner and Sultan were about half a mile south of the Montana-Alberta border. He put an eighteen-foot-long line on the German shepherd, which had locked onto the girl's scent. Garner knew it was a good, strong track. Sultan was panting, excited, pulling hard, moving so fast he had to slow it down after slipping in a few places.

"Hold on there, big guy. I'm no good to you with a twisted ankle."

Garner's exhaustion melted. Having spotted the Baker girl energized him.

Against all odds, she was alive. He saw her.

If he could just get to her, or get a chopper to her.

So close but so far.

Good. They were climbing now. Good.

It was clear to Garner the girl went this way, but ascending the rocky slope made things difficult. At the top of the next significant rise, he would stop to use his powerful field scope. The radio should transmit better, too. They attacked the climb, practically clawing up at double time.

"Oh, boy." Garner huffed at the top several minutes later, perching himself near a rock, upon which he could steady his telescope. He drank some water to help his breathing normalize so he could look calmly through the eyepiece.

Sultan yelped impatiently.

"I know. Me too."

A moment passed. Garner squinted through his scope, sweeping the slopes across the vast alpine valley to the area where he expected the girl to be.

Sultan sat, ears pricked, panting.

"Relax, relax. We'll find her." Garner sounded like a surgeon probing slowly, confidently. A minute passed. Nothing but forest, rock, forest, rock. A deer. Forest, rock, forest, rock— what, a flash of color!

"Hold it!"

Blue? Large. A man?

"What the—"

A blue jumpsuit. A man. Cap. Sunglasses. Looked like a SAR guy. A ranger maybe. Then a small dog, the beagle. *Come on. There!* She was with him, walking slowly. It was her! Walking. Alive. *Thank God.* But who was that with her? No chopper nearby. Nothing. SAR ground people must have her. *We're done then.* Relieved.

"Looks like she's safe, buddy."

But wait. Better confirm. They should get a chopper out here.

Actually, he'd like to hear the status. Garner pulled out his map, detailing his coordinates, then reached for his radio.

"Garner to base."

"That's better, Greg," his radio said. "Must be on high ground now because you are loud and clear. What do you have for us?"

"I'm going to tell you exactly where Paige Baker is."

CHAPTER EIGHTY-ONE

Saved.

Paige watched the man in blue. Her savior.

She was not dreaming. The bear was real. Its blood still warm on her shirt. The stench lingering.

It was real. But she was alive. Saved.

Paige wept with joy, fear, exhaustion.

"Drink this." The man passed her a canteen. They were under the shade of lodgepole pine, resting on an oasis of soft grass. He had given her water, some pieces of vegetables and fruit. Paige had never known such thirst or hunger. She shared some with Kobee and sobbed quietly while chewing. She could not stop shivering from the cold. The man searched his pack, pulling out a large clean T-shirt, fixing it on her, tying its waist. It warmed her. The blood bled through, but she didn't care. She was saved.

His radio was bleating. As Hood expected, it didn't take long.

"Sounds like a helicopter is on its way," he said. "There's

a place it can land just over the ridge. A flat patch near a ledge.''

She nodded. She just wanted to see her parents, to go home to San Francisco, to her room, her bed. Never be scared again.

Paige looked at him.

"Everyone's been looking for you," he said.

She sniffed, pulling Kobee to her. She was so sorry she had run off. Sorry that her parents argued. She could not stop trembling.

"You are safe now," he said. "Nothing will harm you now."

"How—" Her voice was weak. "How did you know where to find me?"

The sunglasses stared at her.

"I just knew, Paige. I just knew."

Like I know this part of the world, its secrets and promises.

"Ready to go wait for the helicopter? Think you can make it a little farther?"

She nodded. It was a short, easy walk to the small, flat table that reached to a cliffside. Hood heard the helicopters first. Far off, approaching fast.

If I time it just right, they will all learn what I am capable of.

"Can you hear that?" he said.

Paige heard nothing.

"Helicopters. They're coming. They'll be here soon."

They stood there waiting.

Butterflies darted by, stirring his memories. He walked to the cliff's edge. Standing there, gazing down the rock face to the bottom, some four hundred feet below, he turned at the cliff and extended his arms.

"This is where I live."

Paige was exhausted. Puzzled. Not certain she understood him.

"But I have no friends," he said. "Will you be my friend?"

Paige blinked. Thinking. Trying to comprehend, she nodded slowly.

"Come closer. I'd like to show you something."

She heard the helicopters. Kobee barked.

"I like it over here. The cliffs make me a little nervous."

Kobee continued barking a warning.

"Please." Hood raised his voice. "You'll never guess what I'm going to do."

"Look, the helicopters are getting closer!" Paige began waving. "Over here! Over here! Over here!"

"Please, Paige, you said you were my friend. Come over here."

She saw no harm. He had saved her. Cautiously, she neared him.

"Want to play a game?"

She stretched to gaze down, shaking her head.

"Let's play a game."

A game? Paige tried to understand. *This is weird.*

"I don't think so."

"Just a quick game?"

She was backing away, shaking her head.

"You are just like your goddamn mother," Hood shouted. Smiling, he revealed his jagged brown teeth. "Guess what I'm going to do."

Hood snatched Kobee, who yelped as he was tossed from the cliff.

Paige screamed.

Hood came for her.

CHAPTER EIGHTY-TWO

The two FBI agents crouching under the whirling blades of the helicopter looked familiar to Bowman.

Glimpsing them trotting to the old Huey distracted her as she waded into the press camp to retrieve David Cohen.

Curiosity kept her shooting glances in their direction.

Something is up.

Bowman caught a partial view of Cohen's head through a wall of TV cameras. And kept looking at the agents.

Their body composition. Posture. It was gnawing at her.

Cohen was giving impromptu interviews when Bowman got to him.

"Please come now, Mr. Cohen. We need you at the command center."

Seeing the Justice Department seal on Bowman's shirt, Cohen agreed.

"If it is about Isaiah's alleged escape, I am as dumbstruck as anyone. I—"

Bowman was not listening. Working their way to the command center, it dawned on her watching the old Huey lift off *Doug and Emily Baker. Wearing FBI caps. Dark glasses.* Gripped with concern, Bowman was hurrying now.

What is going on? It doesn't look right. The chopper climbed. Bowman eyed it while rushing into the Ops room. She sought out Frank Zander, leaving Cohen in the middle of the activity perplexed.

Zander was studying a report near one of the rangers. "Frank, what's going on with the Bakers?"

"What do you mean? They're over there." He nodded to a corner with a large TV. "They're waiting to be taken back—"

"Superintendent Temple!" a ranger shouted. "Urgent call for you from Communications!"

Zander stepped closer to Bowman.

"Say that again, Tracy?"

"I saw them seconds ago, getting on a helicopter."

"What?" Zander walked to the TV where the Bakers had been. "Tracy, were they escorted?"

"Attention, everyone!" Temple shouted. "The RCMP have a visual on the girl. She's alive!"

Cheers and high fives rippled through the operations room.

Bowman and Zander heard the report, accepting backslaps while grappling with the new Baker situation.

"No, Frank, they were wearing FBI caps and sunglasses. Boarding an old Huey. One of the charter contractors, I think."

"The ancient Huey is Rawley Nash." A SAR pilot overheard them while jotting down the coordinates of the hot Mountie sighting. "He's a character."

"What do you mean?" Zander said.

"A rebel. Likes to bend the rules."

Zander's mind rocketed through a million scenarios. "Are you good to go now?" he said to the pilot.

"Sure, I got the fastest bird out there, but I've been told to wait for an assignment—"

"This is your assignment," Zander said. "You take us to where this Nash guy is taking the Bakers." Zander took the pilot's upper arm. "Now. No discussion. FBI emergency. Come on, Tracy!"

Within minutes, the command center was shrinking beneath them as the new Bell thundered over the lake, then past Howe Ridge, then Heavens Peak.

Zander brushed the handle of his holstered gun, battling the fear eating at him as forests blurred below.

Let me be wrong. Let me be wrong.

Their pilot had reached Nash by radio, confirming the Huey was a few miles ahead. They were gaining on it, bound for the same coordinates. At Zander's insistence, Nash was not questioned on his passengers.

The Bell's radio crackled again. The pilot adjusted it for Zander.

"It's for you."

"Turner to Agent Zander, come in?"

"Zander here."

"We just learned of our subjects' unauthorized departure."

Zander looked at the mountains, leaving the air dead, forcing Turner to continue.

"No one could have foreseen these events, Frank."

That's what they said about the Georgia file.

"Frank?"

"Have you got the right people moving on this, Lloyd?"

"Two sniper teams coming behind you in National Guard rescue aircraft."

Zander and Bowman's Bell roared alongside Flattop Mountain. "Well, sir," Zander said, using the senior agent's words, "let's see what transpires. Over."

Let me be wrong.

How did the Bakers know where to go and when? How? And Isaiah Hood's escape. At this moment? As if calculated?

Why did Emily Baker return to Montana? To the same spot where her sister died? Why?

It was horribly tragic. Or horribly obvious.

Right under their noses.

Let me be wrong.

The chopper banked hard. Gravity pulled on Zander's stomach.

Let me be wrong about the Bakers.

Zander was unsure if he could handle cases like this anymore.

When this one was over, he was unsure where to go with his life.

He looked at Bowman, suddenly glad she was here.

He needed her here.

CHAPTER EIGHTY-THREE

Hilda Sim carefully rolled the knurled focus wheel of her binoculars.

Levi Kayle gently turned the focus of the telephoto lens on his digital Nikon camera.

Sim's radio received nonstop alerts to the sector, confirming Isaiah Hood as the fugitive convict who escaped the crash.

"It's them." Kayle's face creased behind his viewfinder. "Hood has the girl!"

"Oh my God!" Wilson squinted, her hand shielding her eyes. "Can't we get to them?"

Tory Sky was adjusting her video camera lens. "We're too far away."

The group was a thousand yards off, with a lethal four-hundred-foot gorge between them. Sim grabbed her radio.

Helicopters were approaching.

Through his small binoculars, Tom Reed could distinguish a large figure in blue and a smaller figure. They were near the lip of the gorge. The group's perspective only permitted them to see the upper segment, the edge.

Kayle's camera began clicking.

"Christ, Hood's throwing something over the cliff!" Kayle clicked. "Those choppers better hurry, man!"

Rawley Nash's Huey was first to the cliff area. Emily Baker was striving to see what was happening through the binoculars vibrating against her skull.

"Doug! It's Paige!" Emily pulled the eyepieces tight to see. "It's Hood! He's throwing—God, Doug, he's—he's—nooo!"

Doug?

Instantly, Nash knew. His passengers were the parents.

"Hey, what is—"

Doug Baker saw the horrible scene unfolding. Hood in his blue jumpsuit struggling with his daughter. He shouted at Rawley.

"Put us down now!"

Nash was descending from some two hundred feet when the FBI radioed, ordering him to evacuate immediately so agents could commence a rescue.

"Damn! I can't! I've been ordered out!" Rawley started pulling up.

Emily began screaming at the sight below. Hood was dragging Paige to the cliff edge.

"He's going to kill her!"

"For the love of God, put us down!" Doug thundered.

Emily was screaming. Doug was yelling. The FBI was demanding Nash to clear so agents could land. It was surreal. Nash hovered. Emily screamed, banging, kicking at the chopper's interior.

"Paige! No. God! Drop us! Drop us! Drop us! He's going to kill our daughter!"

Nash witnessed the horror below. Suddenly, he dropped the Huey. The FBI raged over the radio. Hood was struggling with Paige. Airwaves were pulsating. The Huey descended some thirty yards from the cliffside to the small flattop. Emily leaped from her seat before it hit the ground, numb with shock, forcing her legs to pump as Doug rushed behind her.

Emily felt everything was in slow motion, like a horrible dream.

Nash's Huey ascended, clearing for the FBI. The rotors blew Hood's cap and glasses over the edge.

Paige's face was blistered and scraped. Her eyes found her mother. Horrified. Hands reaching to her in vain. *Rachel's eyes. Her hand slipping.* Hood locked his powerful arms around Paige's waist. Turned, dropped.

"No!"

Doug was shouting.

Hood with Paige. Vanishing. Over the edge.

No. Please.

The National Guard helicopters arrived, the first taking a point just over the gorge some sixty yards out. An FBI sniper worked quickly to sight Hood through his scope.

"Not yet," his commander said. "He's all over her."

The second helicopter took a one o'clock point one hundred yards above Hood; another sniper was prepared to lock him in his crosshairs.

The aircraft were keeping enough distance so the drafts from the rotors would not create a risk. "Stand by," the FBI commander said.

*   *   *

Eyeballing Hood from one hundred feet up. Calm. Cool. His jaw muscles pulsating. Zander forced himself to let his training kick in.

"Down. Down. Down," he urged the pilot.

Bowman was stunned by the scene below.

Hurry. Hurry. Hurry.

The Bell swooped, landing behind the Huey. Bowman and Zander exploded from their helicopter behind Doug and Emily.

It was as if Emily were underwater. Coming to the cliff, she saw Hood's head. He had jumped to a large lower ledge.

Her eyes filled with terror. She froze at the nightmare before her.

Oh God. No.

Hood stood at the lip of the gorge. Arms extended, big hands locked on Paige's wrists, swinging her like a pendulum out beyond the edge, over nothing but four hundred feet of dizzying dead drop.

"Oh, please! Oh, please!" Paige pleaded. Sobbing, toes kicking, reaching for the rock in a vain attempt to save herself. Looking down the abyss at death, sobbing, gasping. Her arms aching.

"Mommeeeee!"

The helicopters were deafening.

Hood moved with animal speed, lowering Paige down the side of the rock face, barely allowing her to catch her toes solidly on a two-inch rock ledge. Only her fingers were visible now, clinging precariously above her on the cliff. Slipping. Slipping. Clinging for her life. Gasping. Pleading. Hood lowered himself beneath Paige to a second lower ledge, looking up in time to see Emily dropping to her stomach, reaching for Paige.

"Mommy, please!"

"I've got you, baby!"

Emily seized her daughter's wrists and began sliding backward, pulling her up while suddenly feeling the horrible weight.

Hood is gripping Paige's ankles!

"Mommeee!"

Paige's eyes pleading. *Rachel's eyes.* Save me. Help me.

Emily shouting: "Isaiah, let her go! You can't have her! Let her go!"

Two rock chips flew from the rock wall near Hood's head. His eyes burned into Emily's.

"I just wanted one friend in my life!" he shouted.

Emily pulled. Paige screamed as Hood stepped from the ledge, his full weight locked on her ankles, nearly pulling her and Emily down as Doug caught her.

"God," Doug grunted. "Hang on."

Paige shrieked, feeling her body stretching. Three rock chips flew near Hood. The snipers were inches from his back.

Zander and Bowman arrived, flinging themselves down. Bowman reached for Paige's upper right arm; Zander worked his fingers toward his pistol. Paige was screaming, nearly fainting from the excruciating agony.

Emily shouted above the choppers, "Isaiah, if you let her go, I'll be your friend forever! Let her go, please!"

He smiled his brown-tooth smile.

"It was just a game, Natalie Ross. Just a game."

Hood surrendered, releasing his hold on Paige. His arms shot out, his eyes met Emily's.

Face lifting to heaven, smiling, falling; sweet air rushing, embracing him. No more hooks, no more prison, no more pain—only blue sky, mountain peaks, sunlight, serenity, peace. Free in his home, forever with a friend.

*   *   *

Paige sobbed hysterically.

Pulled to safety.

Emily hugged her.

"It's over. It's over." She wept.

Doug crushed them both in his arms.

Zander peered over the edge at Hood's body smashed against the rocks below. Bowman tried catching her breath on the flattop near the Bakers.

No one spoke. Nothing but the helicopters as Emily soothed Paige, sobbing.

Then Bowman heard it. A faint cry. "What was that?"

A yelp.

Zander investigated. A dozen yards away, he located Kobee.

"Hey there!"

Secured by his harness, the terrified beagle was dangling from his leash that had looped on a jagged ledge when Hood tossed him over the cliff.

Zander stepped down and retrieved the dog, reuniting him with Paige.

"Kobee!"

The Bakers were frozen in their embrace, staring at Zander and Bowman.

Helicopters thundered.

Radios crackled.

The Bakers smiled at Zander, warming his weary heart.

It was over.

EPILOGUE

After Paige Baker downed a pizza and a large root beer, she slept.

Doctors at Montana General Mercy in Missoula told reporters she had suffered exposure, dehydration, sunburn, some shoulder separation, strain of tendons, ligaments and post-traumatic stress from her ordeal.

"She is in remarkable shape considering her exposure to such extremes for five days and nights. Her dog was a factor. His warmth helped her endure the cold. His presence was a psychological boost; another being to care for and keep her company," Dr. Oliver Veras, Mercy's chief of staff, told the press in a news conference that was broadcast live across the nation.

"When can America see her, Doctor?" one network TV reporter asked.

"That's up to her family. But when she wakes tomorrow, we expect she'll be in good condition."

* * *

That evening, Tom Reed, Molly Wilson and Levi Kayle filed their pictures and account of the Baker story. The *San Francisco Star* moved quickly to lock up worldwide syndication rights, and the story-picture package was purchased by newspapers from Columbus to Cairo, from Buffalo to Bucharest. It ignited speculation about a Pulitzer.

"Violet's ecstatic," Wilson said, passing her cell phone to Reed after they filed. "Cripes, Reed. Send you to fish for a story, you bring back Moby Dick. Good stuff."

Later that night, Reed called Ann in Chicago.

"Didn't forget about the wedding, dear. I'll be on a plane tomorrow night after the news conference."

Paige slept for twenty hours. Kobee was allowed in her hospital bed and never left her side.

For this moment in history, Paige Baker was the most famous ten-year-old girl on earth. Her story was known around the world.

Montana Highway Patrol Officers guarded her hospital room, which filled with balloons, teddy bears, flowers, toys and cards from well-wishers.

The flow would not stop.

It spilled across the hall to the room where Doug and Emily Baker slept.

At one point in the night, Emily awoke and went to Paige's door. Two FBI agents posted there allowed her a glimpse of her daughter sleeping soundly with her arm around Kobee.

Emily strolled down the tranquil hall, finding Bowman in the lounge, awake in a chair. She sat beside her.

Neither woman spoke for the longest time. Then Bowman took Emily's hand and their eyes met in the night.

"Emily, I—"

"We both know what it's like to lose someone, Tracy."

Bowman nodded. "Uhm. You know, Frank and I must talk to her first. It's not officially closed yet."

Emily nodded. "Yes," she whispered, with a half-smile, before returning to bed.

Tracy stared into the night, remembering Carl, then thinking of Mark.

The doctors summoned the FBI when Paige awoke. Zander and Bowman entered her room. Her bed was blanketed with stuffed toys. She was drinking orange juice, an IV connected to her arm. Hair in a ponytail, face dotted with some scrapes but radiating the bright aura of a happy little girl. The agents introduced themselves and chatted for several minutes with Paige, joking about all the presents she received.

Eventually, Bowman asked, "So what happened?"

Paige knitted her brow. "What do you mean?"

"Tell us how you got separated from your mom and dad," Zander said.

"Kobee chased a chipmunk. I went to find him and got us lost."

"That it?" Zander smiled. "Was your dad mad or anything?"

Paige chewed her straw, nodding. "Cut his hand chopping wood."

"Then what happened?"

"I went to find my mom and got lost. It was Kobee's fault."

"The man who found you," Bowman asked, "other than at the cliff, did he harm you in any way?"

Paige shook her head. "He killed a bear that was trying to get me. He saved me."

Bowman and Zander exchanged glances.

"Can I see my mom and dad now?"

Zander patted Paige's shoulder. "Absolutely."

In the hall, Zander informed the doctor they were done. Bowman's cell phone began to ring. Zander walked to the empty lounge at the end of the hall, searching for something in the Rockies that crowned the horizon.

"You made all the right calls, Frank." Walt Sydowski had followed him.

"Ah, well, I'm not so sure about that."

"Look what you were confronted with, the time frame, the circumstances, the politics. You're a helluva cop. I'd be honored to work with you again."

Zander looked down and accepted Sydowski's hand. They shook.

"Heading back to San Francisco?"

"Got a flight tonight." Sydowski smiled. "There's a date I got to keep and some money I have to win back in a card game from a wily old fox who claims to be my father. How about you? Any plans after this?"

"Maybe take some time off to think things over."

"Listen to me. We never know how a case will twist. Believe me, I know. I also know you are a good investigator, Frank."

Sydowski gripped Zander's shoulder, then left him alone with the mountains.

Zander sat staring at the sky for some time when he heard someone say his name. It was Emily Baker, standing in the doorway of the lounge. Doug was next to her. Zander stood, searching his heart for the right words. Emily spoke first.

"We understand."

"It was very complicated," Zander began.

"Frank," Doug said. "I know it looked very bad because it *was* very bad. For everybody. Inspector Sydowski told us everything, including the Georgia case."

Emily had tears in her eyes. Her face was a portrait of kindness. She embraced Zander. "In your way, you were fighting for Paige, too."

"Yes, I was," Zander whispered. "I'm happy for you."

"Paige turns eleven in two months. We would like it if you and Tracy would consider coming to her birthday party."

Zander blinked. "You bet."

Emily told him that before returning to California, they were going to go to Buckhorn Creek. "Going to put things to rest," she said.

Zander nodded. "Sounds like the right thing to do."

Doctor Veras entered, pushing Paige in a wheelchair. Kobee was in her lap. "I think they're ready downstairs," Veras said.

Emily dabbed her eyes. Smiling, they left for Paige's press conference.

Zander decided to watch it alone on the TV in the lounge.

The hospital had turned its cafeteria into a press room. Nearly three hundred newspeople had crammed into it for an event broadcast live on virtually every channel in the United States.

It began with Emily and Doug Baker thanking the rangers of Glacier National Park, the search and rescue people, everyone involved.

"In particular," Emily Baker said, "we want to thank Agents Frank Zander and Tracy Bowman of the FBI, who performed a difficult duty with the utmost respect, courtesy and professionalism under the most challenging circumstances."

Exhausted and watching alone, Zander put his hand over his eyes.

Where do they find the grace?

Reporters began asking Paige to recount her ordeal.

In Helena, Montana's governor and his staff watched with relief.

The injured prison guard and crew of the Mercy Force helicopter watched from their hospital rooms in Kalispell.

David Cohen watched from his lonely Deer Lodge motel

room, where he would wait until a local funeral director provided him with Hood's ashes. Cohen would return to Glacier National Park and disperse them there. Maybe he would take Maleena Crow up on her offer of lunch in Kalispell. Cohen planned a long, soul-searching drive across the western United States back to Chicago. It would give him time to decide what to say in his letters to the Baker family, the governor, Lane Porter, and to his firm. He wanted a year's sabbatical.

The news conference was ending when Bowman entered the lounge.

"There you are, Frank!" Her smile lit up the room. "We've been looking all over for you."

"We?"

"That's right. Got someone here I'd like you to meet."

A boy, about the same age as Paige Baker, entered.

"This is my son, Mark. My friend drove him over this morning. Missed his mom. Marshal, say hello to Frank Zander." She looked straight into Zander's eyes. "One of the best there is."

"Hello, sir." Mark extended his hand.

Young eyes met his.

"Well, hello yourself, Mark."

"Whatcha doin' here all glumlike, Frank? Mark and I are going downtown later. We know a place that makes the best cheeseburgers east of the Rockies. We're going to celebrate. Join us."

"What are you celebrating?"

"A happy ending and the fact my Los Angeles job came through."

"We're moving to California," Mark said.

"Sunshine, surf and movie stars."

"Will you come with us?" Mark said.

"Sure," Zander said. "Guess I could use a burger."

Later, as they ate, Zander felt unbelievably comfortable with Tracy and Mark. It was as if he had found something he had lost long ago. Something that he needed. Over apple pie and ice cream, he told her he had an offer from the SAC in LA to join the Division.

"Do you think it would be a good thing if I accepted, Tracy?" She licked her ice cream spoon and considered his eyes.

"I think that would be a very good thing, Frank."

ACKNOWLEDGMENTS

Experts familiar with the realities in this story may debate areas where I have taken liberty. But for those who enjoyed the journey through regions of precedent and plausibility, I direct credit and my special thanks to: Fred Vanhorn, Assistant Chief Ranger, Glacier National Park; Ronald Nolan, Supervisory Special Agent, and Ms. Maureen Schutz, Federal Bureau of Investigation, Washington, DC; Tom Laceky, the Associated Press, Helena, Montana; Staff Sergeant Daniel Rahn, Crime Scene Bloodstain Pattern Analyst; and Sergeant Warren Ganes, Police Dog Service Section, Royal Canadian Mounted Police.

I also extend gratitude to John Rosenberg, Samantha Banton, Susan Bowness, Lynn Reid, Wendy Dudley, Mildred Marmur, Ann LaFarge, Jeff Aghassi, Mary Jane Maffini and Linda Wiken at Prime Crime, and members of "The Club." I am deeply grateful to the many friends, more than is possible for me to list here, who provided their support.

I am especially indebted to booksellers everywhere who have so graciously enlightened me while introducing my work to readers.

ABOUT THE AUTHOR

Rick Mofina is a reporter with a national newswire service. His work has appeared in such publications as the *New York Times* and *Reader's Digest*. He is married with two children and is at work on his next book.

For an advance look at
Rick Mofina's next novel,
coming next year from Pinnacle Books,
just turn the page. . . .

Iris Wood had feared this would happen, driving home after her first night course at San Francisco State University.

She rarely traveled this far south in the city. Her world was limited to the boundaries of her apartment in the Western Addition and her researcher's job in a downtown office building on Montgomery. Her decision to attend an introductory astronomy class at SFSU was a brave, new personal step. Not because she was interested in the stars, but because she needed to venture beyond her solitary universe, something she accepted weeks ago after the last office party where the resident busybody cornered her before she could escape.

"You never stay at our parties, Iris. You are so mousy in your cubicle. Most of the time, we don't even know you are here. Have some wine, dear."

"No, I really should be going. I have someone waiting at home."

"Like who? You live alone, don't you?"

"No. I don't. I'm living with somebody. My boyfriend."

"You have a boyfriend? Since when, Iris? You never told me." Miss Busybody's engagement ring sparkled as she sipped her wine.

"Well, I—"

"What does he do?"

"Works at home. He's the quiet type."

"What's his name?"

"Jack."

"Jack? We'd love to meet him, you should—"

"Really, I have to go."

In the elevator, Iris Wood's face reddened, stinging with the realization of how pathetic she was. That night at home, as she fought her tears while working on her computer, Jack, the four-legged male in her life, plopped himself in her lap, purring and nudging at Iris Wood to overcome her shyness and wade into the real world.

Now, here she was, lost in it. This is exactly what she had feared. She had left the map she had made back in the lecture hall. Her attempt to navigate from memory was futile after a dozen blocks or so. Iris Wood was terrible at finding her way around. The fog from the Pacific did not help.

This was silly. Getting back should be a no-brainer. If she could just get on 19th Avenue, it would take her right to Golden Gate Park; from there she knew she could find Fulton, then east on Fulton to her apartment near Alamo Square, in time to curl up and catch the last half of *Sleepless in Seattle*.

Where are you, 19th Avenue?

She could ask somebody for directions, but the streets seemed abandoned tonight. Besides, she did not really want to approach anybody. She pressed the automatic lock button, again, before seeing a flashing emergency light in her rearview mirror. It came out of the darkness. She pulled her car over and was bathed in pulsating red from the dash-mounted police light of the unmarked cruiser that stopped behind her.

Iris Wood had never encountered traffic police before. "Evening, ma'am," said the man's voice from behind the intense flashlight beam flooding the interior of her car, hitting her face.

"Did I do something wrong, Officer?" She squinted as she tried to look at him.

"Your license and registration, please."

Iris Wood switched on her dome light, producing the items from her wallet. The officer put them on his small clipboard, then directed his flashlight on them. "You drove through an intersection, missed the stop sign."

Stop sign? What stop sign? "I guess I didn't see it. Sorry."

"Happens all the time. Where are you coming from, tonight, ma'am?"

"A class at SFSU."

"You consume any alcohol tonight?" The flashlight was directed at her face.

"No. I don't drink."

"Drugs?"

"No."

"Would you please shut off your ignition and step out of the car?"

"Why?"

"Roadside sobriety check, ma'am."

Iris Wood saw a pale half-moon peeking through the clouds and she stood next to the tall officer. His face was darkened by the night and distorted by the strobing red light of his patrol car. From what she could see of the area, they were situated between a schoolyard and a heavily wooded park.

"Would you please count aloud backward from one hundred while walking heel to toe in a straight line for me, ma'am?"

Iris Wood accomplished it without difficulty.

"Thank you, ma'am. I am going to have to cite you for the stop sign. You can wait in your car, or in my cruiser. It won't take long, but I will require your signature after I run a check on your particulars."

The area seemed a little creepy so Iris chose to wait in the police car, then ask for directions home. The officer opened the rear right passenger door.

Iris thought it odd how the car did not seem to have a police radio crackling or any other police equipment. In fact, it had that new-car smell and a plastic recycle bag from a car rental agency. The red emergency dash light was almost blinding.

She still could not see the officer's face as he wrote up her ticket from behind the wheel.

"Ma'am, can I ask you a personal question?"

"I guess so."

"What exactly do you look for in a man?"

She had heard this question before. Where? "I'm not sure I understand."

"Yes, you do. Tell me something, Iris. How's Jack?"

"Excuse me?" Iris froze.

"Jack, the guy you're living with. Or should I say, cat."

She was dumbstruck. Paralyzed. How could he possibly know . . .

"I think I'll wait in my car."

"The back doors have child-safety locks. Won't open from inside."

Iris Wood swallowed. She could not speak; her blood was pounding in her ears. The stranger grunted, turning in his seat. He gripped a device that looked like an electric razor and pressed it against her. Instantly, it overwhelmed her neuromuscular system, disorienting her until she collapsed.

He switched off the red light, then drove away, vanishing into the fog with Iris in his backseat.

BOOK YOUR PLACE ON OUR WEBSITE AND MAKE THE READING CONNECTION!

We've created a customized website just for our very special readers, where you can get the inside scoop on everything that's going on with Zebra, Pinnacle and Kensington books.

When you come online, you'll have the exciting opportunity to:

- View covers of upcoming books

- Read sample chapters

- Learn about our future publishing schedule (listed by publication month *and author*)

- Find out when your favorite authors will be visiting a city near you

- Search for and order backlist books from our online catalog

- Check out author bios and background information

- Send e-mail to your favorite authors

- Meet the Kensington staff online

- Join us in weekly chats with authors, readers and other guests

- Get writing guidelines

- AND MUCH MORE!

**Visit our website at
http://www.pinnaclebooks.com**

A World of Eerie Suspense
Awaits in Novels by Noel Hynd

"Book 'em!"
Legal Thrillers from Kensington